*He'll make her his bride – to
settle the score!*

HIS WIFE, HIS
Revenge

Three timeless novels from
bestselling authors

Also available:

HIS *Mistress*
HIS RULES

Three passionate stories,
three powerful heroes

Lynne Graham was born in Northern Ireland and has been a keen Mills & Boon® reader since her teens. She is very happily married with an understanding husband, who has learned to cook since she started to write! Her five children keep her on her toes. She has a very large dog, which knocks everything over, a very small terrier which barks a lot, and two cats. When time allows, Lynne is a keen gardener.

Lucy Monroe started reading at age four. After she'd gone through the children's books at home, her mother caught her reading adult novels pilfered from the higher shelves on the book case…alas, it was nine years before she got her hands on a Mills & Boon® romance her older sister had brought home. She loves to create the strong alpha males and independent women that people Mills & Boon® books. When she's not immersed in a romance novel (whether reading or writing it) she enjoys travel with her family, having tea with the neighbours, gardening and visits from her numerous nieces and nephews. Lucy loves to hear from readers: e-mail Lucymonroe@Lucymonroe.com or visit www.LucyMonroe.com

Sara Craven was born in South Devon, and grew up surrounded by books, in a house by the sea. After leaving grammar school she worked as a local journalist, covering everything from flower shows to murders. She started writing for Mills & Boon in 1975. Apart from writing, her passions include films, music, cooking and eating in good restaurants. She now lives in Somerset. Sara Craven has appeared as a contestant on the Channel Four game show *Fifteen to One* and is also the latest (and last ever) winner of the 1997 *Mastermind of Great Britain* championship.

HIS WIFE, HIS
Revenge

Lynne Graham
Lucy Monroe
Sara Craven

M&B™ and M&B™ with the Rose Device
are trademarks of the publisher.
Harlequin Mills & Boon Limited, Eton House,
18-24 Paradise Road, Richmond, Surrey TW9 1SR

HIS WIFE, HIS REVENGE © by Harlequin Books S.A. 2009

The Vengeful Husband © Lynne Graham 1998
The Greek Tycoon's Ultimatum © Lucy Monroe 2003
The Forced Marriage © Sara Craven 2002

ISBN: 978 0 263 86901 9

024-0109

Printed and bound in Spain
by Litografia Rosés S.A., Barcelona

The Vengeful Husband

Lynne Graham

CHAPTER ONE

A SLENDER fragile beauty in a silvery green gown.
Translucent skin, a mane of vibrant Titian hair and
spellbinding eyes as green as peridots behind her flirtatious little mask. A hoarse, sexy little voice, sharp
enough to strip paint and then sweet enough to make
honey taste bitter...

'No names...no pack drill,' she had said.

'I don't want to know,' she had said, when he had
tried to identify himself. 'After tonight, I'll never see
you again. What would be the point?'

No woman had ever said that to Gianluca Raffacani
before. No woman had ever looked on him as a one-
night stand. The shock of such treatment had been pro-
found. But her eagerness in his bed had seemed to dis-
prove the dismissive words on her lips...until he'd
wakened in the early hours and found his mystery lover
gone and the Adorata ring gone with her. And then Luca
had simply not been able to credit that some unscru-
pulous little tart had contrived to rip him off with such
insulting ease.

His memory of that disastrous night in Venice almost
three years earlier still biting like salt in an open wound,
Luca surveyed the closed file labelled 'Darcy Fielding'
on his library desk, his chiselled features chillingly cast.
With the cool of a self-discipline renowned in the world
of international finance, he resisted the temptation to rip
open the file like an impatient boy. He had waited·a

long time for this moment. He could wait a little longer. 'It is *her* this time…you're sure?' he prompted softly.

Even swollen with pride as Benito was at finally succeeding in his search, even convinced by the facts that he had to have the right woman, Benito still found himself stiffening with uncertainty. Although the woman he had identified matched every slender clue he had started out with, by no stretch of his imagination could he see his famously fastidious and highly sophisticated employer choosing to spend a wild night of passion with the female in that photograph…

'I will only be sure when you have recognised her, sir,' Benito admitted tautly.

'You're backtracking, Benito.' With a rueful sigh that signified no great hope of satisfaction, Luca Raffacani reached out a deceptively indolent brown hand and flipped open the file to study the picture of the woman on the title page.

As Luca tensed and a frown grew on his strong dark face, setting his pure bone structure to the cold consistency of granite, Benito paled, suddenly convinced that he had made a complete ass of himself. That bedraggled female image sported worn jeans, wellington boots, a battered rainhat and a muddy jacket with a long rip in one sleeve. More bag lady than gorgeous seductress. 'I've been too hasty—'

'She's cut off her hair…' his employer interrupted in a low-pitched growl.

After a convulsive swallow, Benito breathed tautly, 'Are you saying that…it *is* the same woman?'

'Was she got up like this for a fancy dress party?'

'Signorina Fielding was feeding hens when that was taken,' Benito supplied apologetically. 'It was the best the photographer could manage. She doesn't go out much.'

'Hens...?' Bemusement pleating his aristocratic ebony brows, Luca continued to scan the photo with hard, dark deepset eyes. 'Yet it is her. Without a doubt, it is her...the devious little thief who turned me over like a professional!'

Darcy Fielding had stolen a medieval ring, a museum piece, an irreplaceable heirloom. The Raffacani family had been princes since the Middle Ages. To mark the occasion of the birth of his son, the very first *principe* had given his wife, Adorata, the magnificent ruby ring. Yet in spite of that rich family heritage, and the considerable value of the jewel, the police had not been informed of the theft. Initially stunned by such an omission, Benito had since become less surprised...

According to popular report within the Raffacani empire, some very strange things had happened the night of the annual masked ball at the Palazzo d'Oro. The host had vanished, for one thing. And if it was actually true that Gianluca Raffacani had vanished in order to romance the thief with something as deeply uncool for a native Venetian as a moonlit gondola tour of the city, Benito could perfectly understand why the police had been excluded from the distinctly embarrassing repercussions of that evening. No male would wish to confess to such a cardinal error of judgement.

In spite of the substantial reward which had been dangled like bait in the relevant quarters, the ring had not been seen since. Most probably it had been disposed of in England—secretly acquired by some rich collector content not to question its provenance. Benito had been extremely disappointed when the investigator failed to turn up the slightest evidence of Darcy Fielding having a previous criminal record.

'Tell me about her…' his employer invited without warning, shutting the file with a decisive snap and thrusting it aside.

Surprised by the instruction, Benito breathed in deep. 'Darcy Fielding lives in a huge old house which has been in her family for many generations. Her financial situation is dire. The house is heavily mortgaged and she is currently behind with the repayments—'

'Who holds the mortgage?' Luca incised softly.

Benito informed him that the mortgage had been taken out a decade earlier with an insurance firm.

'Buy it,' Luca told him equally quietly. 'Continue…'

'Locally, the lady is well-respected. However, when the investigator went further afield, he found her late godmother's housekeeper more than willing to dish the dirt.'

Luca's brilliant eyes narrowed, his sensual mouth twisting with distaste. In an abrupt movement, he re-opened the file at the photograph again. He surveyed it with renewed fascination. What he could see of her hair suggested a brutal shearing rather than the attentions of a salon. She looked a mess, a total mess, but the glow of that perfect skin and the bewitching clarity of those eyes were unmistakable.

Emerging from his uncharacteristic loss of attention, Luca discovered that he had also lost the thread of Benito's report…

'And if the lady pulls it off, she stands to inherit something in the region of one million pounds sterling,' Benito concluded impressively.

Luca studied his most trusted aide. 'Pull what off?'

'The late Signora Leeward had three god-

daughters…possibly the god-daughters from hell.'
Benito labelled them with rueful amusement. 'When it
came to the disposing of her worldly goods, what was
there to choose between the three? One living with a
married man, one an unmarried mother and the other
going the same way—and not a wedding ring or even
the prospect of one between the lot of them!'

'You've lost me,' Luca admitted with controlled impatience.

'Darcy Fielding's rich godmother left everything to
her three godchildren on condition that each of them
find a husband within the year.'

'And Darcy is one of those women you described.'
Luca finally grasped it, bronzed features freezing into
charged stillness. *'Which?'*

'She's the unmarried mother,' Benito volunteered.

Luca froze. 'When was the child born?'

'Seven months after her trip to Venice. The kid's just
over two.'

Luca stared into space, rigidly schooling his dark face
to impassivity, but it was a challenge to suppress his
sheer outrage at the news. *Cristo*…she had even been
pregnant with another man's child when she slept with
him! Well, that was just one more nail in her coffin.
Luca swore in disgust. Whatever was most important to
her, he would take from her in punishment. He would
teach her what it was like to be deceived and cheated
and humiliated. As *she,* most unforgettably, had taught
him…

'As to the identity of the kid's father…' Benito continued wryly. 'The jury's still out on that one.
Apparently the locals believe that the child was fathered
by the fiancé, who ditched the lady at the altar. He fig-
ures as a rat of the lowest order in their eyes. But the

godmother's housekeeper had a very different version of events. *She* contends that the fiancé was abroad at the time the kid was conceived, and that he took to his heels because he realised that the baby on the way couldn't possibly be his!'

Luca absorbed that further information in even stonier silence.

'I shouldn't think the lady will remain a single parent for long,' Benito advanced with conviction. 'Not with a million pounds up for grabs. And on page six of the file you will see what I believe she is doing to acquire that money…'

Luca leafed through the file. 'What is this?' he demanded, studying the tiny print of the enclosed newspaper advertisement and its accompanying box number.

'I suspect that Darcy Fielding is discreetly advertising for a husband to fulfil the terms of that will.'

'Advertising?' Luca echoed in raw disbelief.

> *Country woman seeks quiet, well-behaved and domesticated single male without close ties, 25-50, for short-term live-in employment. Absolute confidentiality guaranteed. No time-wasters, please.*

'That's not an advertisement for a husband…it's an ad for an emasculated household pet!' Luca launched with incredulous bite.

'I'm going to have to advertise again,' Darcy divulged grimly to Karen as she mucked out the stall of the single elderly occupant in the vast and otherwise horse-free stable yard. She wielded the shovel like an aggressive weapon. Back to square one. She could hardly believe it—and that wretched advertisement had cost an arm and a leg!

Standing by and willing to help, but knowing better than to offer, Karen looked in surprise at her friend. 'But what happened to your shortlist of two possibilities? The gardener and the home handyman?'

Darcy slung the attractive thirty-year-old brunette a weary grimace. 'Yesterday I phoned one and then the other in an attempt to set up an interview—'

'In which you planned to finally spill the confidential beans that matrimony was the *real* employment on offer.' Karen sighed. 'Boy, would I like to have been a fly on the wall when you broke that news!'

'Yes, well…as it turns out, I shan't need to embarrass myself just yet. One had already found a job elsewhere and the other has moved on without leaving a forwarding address. I shouldn't have wasted so much time agonising over my choice.'

'*What* choice? You only got five replies. Two were obscene and one was weird! The ad was too vague in one way and far too specific in the other. What on earth possessed you to put in ''well-behaved and domesticated'? I mean, talk about picky, why don't you? Still, I can't really say I'm sorry that you've drawn a blank,' Karen admitted, with the bluntness that made the two women such firm friends.

'Karen…' Darcy groaned.

'Look, the thought of you being alone in this house with some stranger gives me the shivers!' the brunette confided anxiously. 'In any case, since you didn't want to risk admitting in the ad that you were actually looking for a temporary husband, what are the chances that either of those men would have been agreeable to the arrangement you were about to offer?'

Darcy straightened in frustration. 'If I'd offered enough money, I bet one of them would have agreed. I *need* my inheritance, Karen. I don't care what I have to do to get it. I don't care if I have to marry the Hunchback of Notre Dame to meet the conditions of Nancy's will!' Darcy admitted with driven honesty. 'This house has been in my family for four *hundred* years—'

'But it's crumbling round your ears and eating you up alive, Darcy. Your father had no right to lay such a burden on you. If he hadn't let Fielding's Folly get in such a state while *he* was responsible for it, you wouldn't be facing the half of what you're facing right now!'

Darcy tilted her chin, green eyes alight with stubborn determination. 'Karen...as long as I have breath in my body and two hands to work with, the Folly will survive so that I can pass it on to Zia.'

Pausing to catch her breath from her arduous labour, Darcy glanced at her two-year-old daughter. Seated in a grassy sunlit corner, Zia was grooming one of her dolls with immense care. Her watching mother's gaze was awash with wondering pride and pleasure.

Zia had been blessed at birth, Darcy conceded gratefully. Mercifully, she hadn't inherited her mother's carroty hair, myopic eyesight *or* her nose. Zia had lustrous black curls and dainty, even features. There was nothing undersized or over-thin about her either. She was a strikingly pretty and feminine little girl. In short, she was already showing all the promise of becoming everything her mother had once so painfully and pointlessly longed to be...

Zia wouldn't be a wallflower at parties, too blunt-spoken to be flirtatious or appealing, too physically plain to attract attention any other way. Nor would Zia ever be so full of self-pity that she threw herself into the bed of a complete stranger just to prove that she *could* attract a man. Pierced to the heart by that painful memory, Darcy paled and guiltily looked away from her child, wondering how the heck she would eventually explain that shameful reality in terms that wouldn't hurt and alienate her daughter.

Some day Zia would ask her father's name, quite reasonably, perfectly understandably. And what did Darcy have to tell her? Oh, I never got his name because I told him I didn't want it. Even worse, I could well walk past him on the street without recognising him, because I wasn't wearing my contacts and I'm a little vague as to his actual features. But he had dark eyes, even darker hair, and a wonderful, wonderful voice…

Beneath Karen's frowning gaze, Darcy had turned a beetroot colour and had begun studiously studying her booted feet. 'What's up?'

'Indigestion,' Darcy muttered flatly, and it wasn't a lie. Memories of that nature made her feel queasy and crushed her self-respect flat. She had been a push-over for the first sweet-talking playboy she had ever met.

'So it's back to the drawing board as far as the search for a temporary hubby goes, I gather…' Releasing her breath in a rueful hiss, Karen studied the younger woman and reluctantly dug an envelope from the pocket of her jeans and extended it. 'Here, take it. A late applicant, I assume. It came this morning. The postmark's a London one.'

To protect Darcy's anonymity, Karen had agreed to put her own name behind the advertisement's box number. All the replies had been sent to the gate lodge which Karen had recently bought from the estate. Darcy was well aware that she was running a risk in advertising to find a husband, but no other prospect had offered. If she was found out, she could be accused of trying to circumvent the conditions of her godmother's will and excluded from inheriting. But what else was she supposed to do? Darcy asked herself in guilty desperation.

It was *her* duty and *her* responsibility alone to secure Fielding's Folly for future generations. She could not fail the trust her father had imposed on her at the last. She had faithfully promised that no matter what the cost she would hold on to the Folly. How could she allow four hundred years of family history to slip through her careless fingers?

And, even more importantly, only when she contrived to marry would she be in a position to re-employ the estate staff forced to seek work elsewhere after her father's death. In the months since, few had found new jobs. The knowledge that such loyal and committed people were still suffering from her father's financial incompetence weighed even more heavily on her conscience.

Tearing the envelope open, Darcy eagerly scanned the brief letter and her bowed shoulders lifted even as she read. 'He's not of British birth...and he has experience as a financial advisor—'

'Probably once worked as a bank clerk,' Karen slotted in, cynically unimpressed by the claim. A childless divorcee, Karen was comfortably off but had little faith in the reliability of the male sex.

'He's offering references upfront, which is more than anyone else did.' Darcy's state of desperation was betrayed by the optimistic look already blossoming in her expressive eyes. '*And* he's only thirty-one.'

'What nationality?'

In the act of frowning down at the totally illegible signature, Darcy raised her head again. 'He doesn't say. He just states that he is healthy and single and that a temporary position with accommodation included would suit him right now—'

'So he's unemployed and broke.'

'If he wasn't unemployed and willing to move in, he wouldn't be applying, Karen,' Darcy pointed out gently. 'It's a reasonable letter. Since he didn't know what the job was, he's sensibly confined himself to giving basic information only.'

As she paced the confines of Karen's tiny front room in the gate lodge five days later, Darcy pushed her thick-lensed spectacles up the bridge of her nose, smoothed her hands down over her pleated skirt and twitched at the roll collar of her cotton sweater as if it was choking her.

He would be here in five minutes. And she hadn't even managed to speak to the guy yet! Since he hadn't given her a phone number to contact him, she had had to write back to his London address and, nervous of giving out her own phone number at this stage, she had simply set up an interview and asked him to let her know if the date didn't suit. He had sent a brief note of confirmation, from which she had finally divined that his christian name appeared to be a surprisingly English-sounding Lucas, but as for his surname, she would defy a handwriting expert to read that swirling scrawl!

Hearing the roar of a motorbike out on the road, Darcy suppressed her impatience. Lucas was late. Maybe he wasn't going to show. But a minute later the door burst open. Karen poked her head in, her face filled with excitement. 'A monster motorbike just drew up…and this absolutely edible hunk of male perfection took off his helmet! It has to be Lucas…and Darcy, he is *gorgeous*—'

'He's come on a motorbike?' Darcy interrupted with a look of astonishment.

'You are *so* stuffy sometimes,' Karen censured. 'And I bet you a fiver you can't work up the nerve to ask this particular bloke if he'd be prepared to marry you for a fee!'

Darcy was already painfully aware that she had no choice whatsoever on that count. She *had* to ask. She was praying that Lucas, whoever he was and whatever he was like, would agree. She didn't have the time to readvertise. Her back was up against the wall. Yesterday she had received a letter from the company that held the mortgage on Fielding's Folly. They were threatening to repossess the house and, since she already had a big overdraft, the bank would not help without a guarantee that she would in the near future have the funds to settle her obligations.

Darcy winced as the doorbell shrilled. Karen bolted to answer it. Bolted—yes, that was the only possible word for her friend's indecent eagerness to reach the front door. Face wooden and set, Darcy positioned herself by the fireplace. So he was attractive. Attractive men had huge egos. She grimaced. All she wanted was someone ordinary and unobtrusive, but what she wanted she wouldn't necessarily get.

'Signorina Darcy?' she heard an accented drawl question in a tone of what sounded like polite surprise.

'No…she's, er, through here…er, waiting for you,' Karen stammered with a dismayingly girlish giggle, and the lounge door was thrust wide.

Blinking rapidly, Darcy was already glued to the spot, a deep frown-line bisecting her brow. That beautiful voice had struck such an eerie chord of familiarity she was transfixed, heart beating so fast she was convinced it might burst. And then mercifully she understood the source of that strange familiarity and shivered, thoroughly spooked. Dear heaven, he was Italian! It was that lyrical accent she had recognised, *not* the voice.

A very tall, dark male, sporting sunglasses and sheathed in motorbike leathers, strode into the small room. Involuntarily Darcy simply gaped at him, her every expectation shattered. Black leather accentuated impossibly wide shoulders, narrow hips and long, lean powerful thighs. Indeed the fidelity of fit left little of that overpoweringly masculine physique to the imagination. And the sunglasses lent his dark features an intimidating lack of expression. And yet…and *yet* as Darcy surveyed him with startled eyes she realised that he shared more than an accent with Zia's father. He had also been very tall and well-built.

So what? an irritated voice screeched through her blitzed brain. So you're meeting *another* tall, dark Italian…big deal! The silver-tongued sophisticate who had got her pregnant wouldn't have been caught dead in such clothing. And if she hadn't had such a guilt complex about her wanton behaviour in Venice, she wouldn't be feeling this incredibly foolish sense of threatening familiarity, she told herself in complete exasperation.

'Please excuse me for continuing to wear my sunglasses. I have been suffering from eye strain…the light, it hurts my eyes,' he informed her in a deep, dark drawl that was both well-modulated and unexpectedly quiet.

'Won't you sit down?' Darcy invited, with an un-characteristically weak motion of one hand as she forced herself almost clumsily down into a seat.

But then Darcy was in shock. She had hoped he would be either sensible and serious or weak and bid-dable. Instead she had been presented with a rampantly macho male who roared up on a motorbike and wore trousers so tight she marvelled that he could stand in them, never mind sit down. With what she believed was termed designer stubble on his aggressive jawline, he looked about as domesticated and well-behaved as a sabre-toothed tiger.

'If you will forgive me for saying so…you look at me rather strangely,' he remarked, further disconcerting her as he lowered himself down with indolent grace onto the small sofa opposite her. 'Do I remind you of someone, *signorina?*'

Darcy stiffened even more with nervous tension, and she was already sitting rigid-backed in the seat. 'Not at all,' she asserted with deflating conviction. 'Now, since I'm afraid I couldn't read your signature…what is your full name?'

'Let us leave it at Luca for now. The wording of your ad suggested that the employment on offer could be of a somewhat unusual nature,' he drawled softly. 'I would like some details before we go any further.'

Darcy bristled like a cat stroked the wrong way. She was supposed to be interviewing him, not the other way round!

'After all, you have not given me your real name either,' he pointed out in offensively smooth continu-ance.

Darcy's eyes opened to their fullest extent. 'I beg your pardon?'

'Before I came down here, I checked you out. Your surname is Fielding, *not* Darcy, and you do *not* live here in this cottage; you live in the huge mansion at the top of the driveway,' he enumerated with unabashed cool. 'You have gone to some trouble to conceal your own identity. Naturally that is a source of concern to me.'

Stunned by that little speech, Darcy sprang upright and stared down at him in shaken disbelief, her angry bewilderment unconcealed. '*You* checked *me* out?'

He lifted a casual brown hand and slowly removed the sunglasses. 'The light is dim enough in here…'

He studied her with a curiously expectant quality of intensity.

And without warning Darcy found herself staring down into lustrous dark eyes fringed by glossy, spiky black lashes. He had the sort of eyes that packed a powerful punch. Gorgeous, she thought in helpless reaction, brilliant and dark as night, impenetrably deep and unreadable. With the sunglasses on he had looked as if he might be pretty good-looking, without them he zoomed up the scale to stunningly handsome, in spite of the fact that he badly needed a shave. And she now quite understood that hint of expectancy he betrayed. This was a guy accustomed to basking in female double takes, appreciative stares and inviting smiles.

But Darcy tensed and took an instantaneous step back, her retreat only halted by the armchair she had vacated. Yet the tiny twisting sensation of sudden excitement she had experienced still curled up deep in the pit of her taut stomach, and then pierced her like a knife with sudden shame. Her colour heightening, Darcy plotted her path out of the way of the armchair behind her, controlled solely by a need to put as much distance as possible between them.

Throughout that unchoreographed backing away process of hers, she was tracked by narrowed unflinchingly steady dark eyes. 'Signorina Fielding—'

'Look, you had no right to check me out...' Darcy folded her arms in a defensive movement. 'I guaranteed your privacy. Couldn't you have respected mine?'

'Not without some idea of what I might be getting into. It's standard business practice to make enquiries in advance of an interview.'

Darcy tore her frustrated gaze from his. Antipathy darted through her in a blinding wave. With difficulty, she held onto her ready temper. Possibly the reminder had been a timely one. It was, after all, a business proposition she intended to make. And this Luca might think he was clever, but she already knew he had to be as thick as two short planks, didn't she? Only a complete idiot would turn up for an interview with a woman unshaven and dressed like a Hell's Angel. A financial advisor? In his dreams! Conservative apparel went with such employment.

Bolstered by the belief that he could be no Einstein, and rebuking herself for having been intimidated by something as superficial and unimportant as his physical appearance, Darcy sat down again and linked her small hands tightly together on her lap. 'Right, let's get down to business, then...'

The waiting silence lay thick and heavy like a blanket. Settling back into the sofa in a relaxed sprawl of long, seemingly endless limbs, Luca surveyed her with unutterable tranquillity.

Her teeth gritted. Wondering just how long that laidback attitude would last, Darcy lifted her chin to a challenging angle. 'There *was* a good reason behind the offbeat ad I placed. But before I explain what that rea-

son is, I should mention certain facts in advance. Should
you agree to take the position on offer, you would be
well paid even though there is no work involved—'

'*No* work involved?'

Darcy was soothed at receiving the exact response
she had anticipated in that interruption. 'No work whatsoever,' she confirmed. 'While you were living in my
home, your time would be your own, and at the end of
your employment—assuming that you fulfil the terms
to my satisfaction—I would also give you a generous
bonus.'

'So what's the catch?' Luca prompted very softly. 'In
return you ask me to do something illegal?'

A mortified flush stained Darcy's perfect skin. 'Of
course not,' she rebutted tautly. 'The ''catch'', if you
choose to call it that, is that you would have to agree
to marry me for six months!'

'To…*marry* you?' Luca stressed the word with a
frown of wondering incredulity as he sat forward on the
sofa. 'The employment you offer is…*marriage?*'

'Yes. It's really quite simple. I need a man to go
through a wedding ceremony with me and behave like
a husband for a minimum of six months,' Darcy extended, with the frozen aspect of a woman forcing herself to refer to an indecent act.

'Why?'

'Why? That's my business. I don't think you require
that information to make a decision,' Darcy responded
uncomfortably.

Lush black lashes semi-screened his dark eyes. 'I
don't understand… Could you explain it again, *signorina,*' he urged, in a rather dazed undertone.

You certainly couldn't call him mentally agile, Darcy
thought ruefully. Having got over the worst, however,

she felt stronger, and all embarrassment had left her. He was still sitting there, and why shouldn't he be? If he was as single as he had said he was, he stood to earn a great deal for doing nothing. She repeated what she had already said and, convinced that the financial aspect would be the greatest persuader of all, she mentioned the monthly salary she was prepared to offer and then the sizeable bonus she would advance in return for his continuing discretion about their arrangement after they had parted.

He nodded, and then nodded again more slowly, still focusing with a slight frown on the worn carpet at his feet. Maybe the light was annoying his eyes, Darcy decided, struggling to hold onto her irritation at his torpid reactions. Maybe he was just gobsmacked by the concept of being paid to be bone idle. Or maybe he was so shattered by what she had suggested that he hadn't yet worked out how to respond.

'I would, of course, require references,' Darcy continued.

'I could not supply references as a husband...'

Darcy drew in a deep breath of restraint. 'I'm referring to character references,' she said drily.

'If you wanted a husband, why didn't you place an ad in the personal column?'

'I would have received replies from men interested in a genuine and lasting marriage.' Darcy sighed. 'It was wiser just to advertise my requirements as a form of employment—'

'Quiet...domesticated...well-behaved.'

'I don't want someone who's going to get under my feet or expect me to wait on him hand and foot. Would you say you were self-sufficient?'

'Si...'

'Well, then, what do you think?' Darcy demanded impulsively.

'I don't yet know what I think. I wasn't expecting this kind of proposal,' he returned gently. 'No woman has ever asked me to marry her before.'

'I'm not talking about a proper marriage. Obviously we'd separate after the six months was up and get a divorce. By the way, you would also have to sign a pre-nuptial contract,' Darcy added, because she needed to safeguard the estate from any claim an estranged husband might legitimately attempt to make. 'That isn't negotiable.'

Luca rose gracefully upright. 'I believe I would need a greater cash inducement to give up my freedom—'

'That's not a problem,' Darcy broke in, her tone one of eager reassurance on that point. If he was prepared to consider her proposition, she was keen to accommodate him. 'I'm prepared to negotiate. If you agree, I'll double the original bonus I offered.'

Disconcertingly, he didn't react to that impulsive offer. Darcy flushed then, feeling more than a little foolish.

Veiled dark eyes surveyed her. 'I'll think it over. I'll be in touch.'

'The references?'

'I will present them if I decide to accept the...the position.' As Luca framed the last two words a flash of shimmering gold illuminated his dark eyes. Amusement at the sheer desperation she had revealed in her desire to reach agreement with him? Darcy squirmed at the suspicion.

'I need an answer very soon. I have no time to waste.'

'I'll give you an answer tomorrow...' He strode to the door and then he hesitated, throwing her a questioning look over one broad masculine shoulder. 'It surprises me that you could not persuade a friend to agree to so temporary an arrangement.'

Darcy stiffened and coloured. 'In these particular circumstances, I prefer a stranger.'

'A stranger...I can understand that,' Luca completed in a honey-soft and smooth drawl.

CHAPTER TWO

'So what sort of impression did Lucas make on you?' Karen demanded, minutes later.

'It's not Lucas, it's Luca... My impression?' Darcy studied her friend with a frowning air of abstraction. 'That's the odd thing. I didn't really get a proper impression—at least not one I could hang onto for longer than five seconds,' she found herself admitting in belated recognition of the fact. 'One minute I thought he was all brawn and no brain, and then the next he would come out with something razor-sharp. And towards the end he was as informative as a brick wall.'

'He didn't accuse you of dragging him down here on false pretences? He didn't laugh like a drain? Or even ask if you were pulling his leg?' It was Karen's turn to look confused.

Darcy shook her head reflectively. 'He was very low-key in his reactions, businesslike in spite of the way he was dressed. That made it easier for me. I didn't get half as embarrassed as I thought I would.'

'Only you could conduct such a weird and loaded interview with a male that gorgeous and not respond on any more personal a level.'

'That kind of man leaves me cold.' But Darcy's cheeks warmed as she recalled that humiliating moment when she had reacted all too personally to the sheer male magnetism of those dark good looks.

Karen's keen gaze gleamed. 'He *didn't* leave you stone-cold...did he?'

Cursing her betrayingly fair skin, Darcy strove to continue meeting her friend's eyes levelly. 'Karen—'

'Forget it... I can tell a mile off when you're about to lie through your teeth!'

Darcy winced. 'OK...I noticed that Luca was reasonably fanciable—'

'Reasonably fanciable?' her friend carolled with extravagant incredulity.

'All right.' Darcy sighed in rueful surrender. 'He was spectacular...are you satisfied now?'

'Yes. Your indifference to men seriously worries me. Now at least I know that you're still in the land of the living.'

Darcy pulled a wry face. 'With my level of looks and appeal, indifference is by far the safest bet, believe me.'

Karen compressed her lips and thought with real loathing of all the people responsible for ensuring Darcy had such a low opinion of her own attractions. Her cold and critical father, her vain and sarcastic stepmother, not to mention the rejections her unlucky friend had suffered from the opposite sex during her awkward and vulnerable teen years. Being jilted at the altar and left to raise her child alone had completed the damage.

And these days Darcy dressed like a scarecrow and made little effort to socialise. Slowly and surely she was turning into a recluse, although the hours she slaved over that wretched house meant that she didn't know what free time was, Karen conceded grimly. Anyone else confronted with such an immense and thankless challenge would've given up and at least sold the furniture by now, but not Darcy. Darcy would starve sooner than see any more of the Folly's treasures go to auction.

'I get really annoyed with you when you talk like

that,' Karen said truthfully. 'If you would only buy some decent clothes and take a little more interest in—'

'Why bother when I'm quite happy as I am?' Visibly agitated by the turn the conversation had taken, Darcy glanced hurriedly at her watch and added with a relief she couldn't hide, 'It's time I picked up Zia from the playgroup.'

As Darcy left the gate lodge, however, that final dialogue travelled with her. Demeaning memories had been roused to fill her thoughts and unsettle her stomach. All over again she saw her one-time fiancé, Richard, gawping at her chief bridesmaid like a moonsick calf and finally admitting at the eleventh hour that he couldn't go through with the wedding because he had fallen in love with Maxie. And the ultimate insult had to be that her former friend, Maxie, who was so beautiful she could stop traffic, hadn't even *wanted* Richard!

That devastatingly public rejection had been followed by the Venetian episode, Darcy recalled wretchedly. That, too, had ended in severe humiliation. She had got to play Cinderella for a night. And then she had got to stand on the Ponte della Guerra and be stood up like a dumb teenager the following day. She had waited for ages too, and had hit complete rock-bottom when she finally appreciated that Prince Charming was not going to turn up.

Of course another woman, a more experienced and less credulous woman, would have known that that so casually voiced yet so romantic suggestion had been the equivalent of a guy saying he would phone you when he hadn't the slightest intention of doing so, only *she* hadn't recognised the reality. No, Darcy reflected with a stark shudder of remembrance, she had been much happier since she had given up on all that ghastly embarrassing and confusing man-woman stuff.

And if Luca, whoever he was, decided to go ahead and accept her proposition, she would soon be able to tune him and his macho motorbike leathers out entirely…

Perspiration beading her brow, Darcy wielded the heavy power-saw with the driven energy of necessity. The ancient kitchen range had an insatiable appetite for wood. Breathing heavily, she stopped to take a break. Even after switching off the saw, her ears still rang with the shattering roar of the petrol-driven motor. With a weary sigh, she bent and began laboriously stacking the logs into the waiting wheelbarrow.

'Darcy…?'

At the sound of that purring, accented drawl, Darcy almost leapt out of her skin, and she jerked round with a muttered exclamation. Luca stood several feet away. Her startled green eyes clung to his tall, outrageously masculine physique. Wide shoulders, sleek hips, long, long legs. *And* he had shaved.

One look at the to-die-for features now revealed in all their glory struck Darcy dumb. She wasn't even capable of controlling that reaction. In full daylight, he was so staggeringly handsome. High, chiselled cheekbones, sharp as blades, were dissected by an arrogant but classic nose and embellished by a wide, perfect mouth. Even his skin had that wonderful golden glowing vibrancy of warmer climes…

'Is there something wrong?' An equally shapely ebony brow had now quirked enquiringly.

'You startled me…' Heated colour drenching her skin as she realised that she had been staring, Darcy

dragged her attention from him with considerable difficulty. As her dazed eyes dropped down, she blinked
in disbelief at the sight of her cocker spaniels seated
silently at his feet like the well trained dogs they unfortunately weren't. Strangers usually provoked Humpf
and Bert into a positive frenzy of uncontrolled barking.
Instead, her lovable but noisy animals were welded to
the spot and throwing Luca upward pleading doggy
glances as if he had cast some weird sort of hypnotic
spell over them.

'I wasn't expecting you,' Darcy said abruptly.

'I did try the front entrance first…' His deep-pitched
sexy drawl petered out as he studied the sizeable stack
of wood. 'Surely you haven't cut all that on your own?'

Threading an even more self-conscious hand through
the damp and wildly curling tendrils of hair clinging to
her forehead, she nodded, aware of the incredulity in
those piercing dark eyes.

'Are there no men around here?'

'No, I'm the next best thing…but then that's nothing
new,' Darcy muttered half under her breath, writhing at
her own undeniable awkwardness around men and hating him for surprising her when she wasn't psyched up
to deal with him.

Forgivably thrown by that odd response, Luca
frowned.

Darcy leapt straight back into speech. 'I assumed you
would phone—'

'Nobody ever answers your phone.'

'I'm outdoors a lot of the time.' Stripping off her
heavy gloves, Darcy flexed small and painfully stiff fingers and averted her scrutiny from him, her unease in
his presence pronounced. What on earth was the matter

with her? She was behaving like a silly teenager with a crush. 'You'd better come inside.'

Hurriedly grabbing up an armful of logs, Darcy led the way. The long, cobbled passageway that provided a far from convenient rear entrance to her home was dark and gloomy and flanked by a multitude of closed doors. Innumerable rooms which had once enjoyed specific functions as part of the kitchen quarters now lay unused. But not for much longer, she reminded herself. When she achieved her dream of opening up the house to the public all those rooms full of their ancient labour inten- sive equipment would fascinate children.

And she *was* going to achieve her dream, she told herself feverishly. Surely Luca wouldn't take the trouble to make a second personal appearance if he intended to say no?

She trod into the vast echoing kitchen and knelt down by the big range at the far end. Opening the door, she thrust a sizeable log into the fuel bed. 'Did you come all the way from London again?'

'No, I stayed in Penzance last night.'

Darcy was so rigid with nervous tension, she couldn't bring herself to look at him as she breathed tautly, 'So what's your answer?'

'Yes. My answer is *yes*,' he murmured with quiet emphasis.

Her strained eyes prickled with sudden tears and she blinked rapidly before slamming shut the door on the range. The relief was so immense she felt quite dizzy for a few seconds. Feeling as if a huge weight had dropped from her shoulders, Darcy scrambled upright and turned, a grateful smile on her now softened face. 'That's great...that's really great. Would you like some coffee?'

Lounging back against the edge of the giant scrubbed pine table, Luca stared back at her, not a muscle moving in his strong dark face. It was a rather daunting reaction and she swallowed hard, unaware that that shy and spontaneous air of sudden friendliness had disconcerted him.

'OK…why not?' he agreed, without any expression at all.

Darcy put on the kettle and stole an uneasy glance at him in the taut silence. She didn't know where the tension was coming from, and then she wondered if his brooding silence was a kind of male ego thing. 'I suppose this isn't quite the sort of work you were hoping to get,' she conceded awkwardly. 'But I promise you that you won't regret it. How long have you been unemployed?'

'Unemployed?' he echoed, strong features stiffening.

'Sorry, I just assumed—'

'I have never been employed in the UK.'

'*Oh…*' Darcy nodded slowly. 'So how long have you been over here?'

'Long enough…'

Darcy scrutinised that slightly downbent dark glossy head, taking in the faint darkening of colour over his sculpted cheekbones. He was embarrassed at his lack of success in the job market, she gathered, and she wished she had been a little less blunt in her questioning. But then tact had never been her strong point. And when she had interviewed him she had been so wrapped up in her own problems that it hadn't occurred to her that Luca must have been desperate to find a job to come so far out of London in answer to one small ad. Furthermore, now that she took a closer look at those leathers of his, she couldn't help but notice that they were pretty worn.

Sudden sympathy swept Darcy. She knew all about being broke and trying to keep up appearances. She had looked down on him for wearing motorbike gear to an interview, but maybe the poor guy didn't have much else to wear. If he hadn't worked since he had arrived in the UK, he certainly couldn't have financed much of a wardrobe. Smart suits cost money.

'I'll give you half your first month's salary in advance,' Darcy heard herself say. 'As a sort of retainer…'

This time he looked frankly startled.

'You probably think that's very trusting of me, but I tend to take people as I find them. In any case, I don't have a lot of choice *but* to trust you. If you were to get the chance of another job and decide to back out on me, I'd be in trouble,' she said honestly. 'How do you like your coffee?'

'Black…two sugars.'

Darcy put a pile of biscuits on a rather chipped plate. Setting the two beakers of coffee down on the table, she sat down and reached for the jotter and pencil lying there. 'I'd better get some details from you, hadn't I? What *is* your surname?'

There was a pause, a distinct pause as he sank lithely down opposite her.

'Raffacani…' he breathed.

'You'll need to spell that for me.'

He obliged.

Darcy bent industriously over the jotter. 'And Luca— is that your first and only other name? You see, I have to get this right for the vicar.'

'Gianluca…Gianluca Fabrizio.'

'I think you'd better spell all of it.' She took down his birthdate. Raffacani, she was thinking. Why did she have the curious sense that she had come across that name somewhere before? She shook her head. For all she knew Raffacani was as common a name in Italy as Smith was in England.

'Right,' she said then. 'I'll contact my solicitor, Mr Stevens. He's based in Penzance, so you can sign the pre-nuptial contract as soon as you like. Those references you offered...?'

From the inside of his jacket he withdrew a somewhat creased envelope. Struggling to keep up a businesslike attitude when she really just wanted to sing and dance round the kitchen with relief, Darcy withdrew the documents. There were two, one with a very impressive letterhead, but both were written in Italian. 'I'll hang onto these and study them,' she told him, thinking of the old set of foreign language dictionaries in the library. 'But I'm sure they'll be fine.'

'How soon do you envisage the marriage ceremony taking place?' Luca Raffacani enquired.

'Hopefully in about three weeks. It'll be a very quiet wedding,' Darcy explained rather stiffly, fixing her attention to the scarred surface of the table, her face turning pale and set. 'But as my father died this year that won't surprise anyone. It wouldn't be quite the thing to have a big splash.'

'You're not inviting many guests?'

'Actually...' Darcy breathed in deep, plunged into dismal recall of the huge misfired wedding which her father had insisted on staging three years earlier. 'Well, actually, I wasn't planning on inviting anybody,' she admitted tightly as she rose restively to her feet again.

'I'll show you where you'll be staying when you move in, shall I?'

At an infinitely more graceful and leisurely pace, Luca slid upright and straightened. Darcy watched in helpless fascination. His every movement had such...such *style,* an unhurried cool that caught the eye. He was so self-possessed, so contained. He was also very reserved. He gave nothing away. Well, would she have preferred a garrulous extrovert who asked a lot of awkward questions? Irritated by her own growing curiosity, Darcy left him to follow her out of the kitchen and tried to concentrate on more important things.

'What did you mean when you said you were the next best thing to a man around here?' Luca enquired on the way up the grand oak staircase.

'My father wanted a son, not a daughter—at least...not the kind of daughter I turned out to be.' As she spoke, Darcy was comparing herself to her stepsister. Morton Fielding had been utterly charmed by his second wife's beautiful daughter, Nina. Darcy had looked on in amazement as Nina twisted her cold and censorious parent round her little finger with ease.

'Your mother?'

'She died when I was six. I hardly remember her,' Darcy confided ruefully. 'My father remarried a few years later. He was desperate to have a male heir but I'm afraid it didn't happen.'

She cast open the door of a big dark oak-panelled bedroom, dominated by a giant Elizabethan four-poster. 'This will be your room. The bathroom's through that door. I'm afraid we'll have to share it. There isn't another one on this side of the house.'

As he glanced round the sparsely furnished and decidedly dusty room, which might have figured in a

Tudor time warp, Darcy found herself studying him
again. That stunningly male profile, the hard, sleek lines
of his muscular length. A tiny frisson of sexual heat
tightened her stomach muscles. He strolled with the
grace of a leopard over to the high casement window
to look out. Sunlight gleamed over his luxuriant black
hair. Unexpectedly he turned, dark eyes with the dramatic impact of gold resting on her in cool enquiry.

Caught watching him again, Darcy blushed as hotly
as an embarrassed schoolgirl. She was appalled by her
own outrageous physical awareness of him, could not
comprehend what madness was dredging such re-
sponses from her. Whirling round, she walked swiftly
back into the corridor.

As he drew level with her she snatched in a deep,
sustaining breath and started towards the stairs again.
'I'm afraid there are very few modern comforts in the
Folly, and locally, well, there's even fewer social out-
lets…' She hesitated uneasily before continuing, 'What
I'm really trying to say is that if you feel the need to
take off for the odd day in search of amusement, I'll
understand—'

'Amusement?' Luca prompted grimly, as if such a
concept had never come his way before.

Darcy nodded, staring stonily ahead. 'I'm one of
these people who always says exactly what's on their
mind. I live very quietly but I can't reasonably expect
you to do the same thing for an entire six months. I'm
sure you'll maybe want to go up to London occasionally
and—'

'Amuse myself?' Luca slotted in very drily.

In spite of her discomfiture, Darcy uttered a strained
little laugh. 'You can hardly bring a girlfriend here—'

'I do not have a woman in my life,' he interrupted, with a strong suggestion of gritted teeth.

'Possibly not at present,' Darcy allowed, wondering what on earth was the matter with him. He was reacting as if she had grossly insulted him in some way. 'But I'm being realistic. You're bound to get bored down here. City slickers do...'

Brilliant eyes black as jet stabbed into her. A line of dark colour now lay over his taut cheekbones. 'There will not be a woman nor any need for such behaviour on my part, I assure you,' he imparted icily.

They were descending the stairs when a tiny figure clad in bright red leggings and a yellow T-shirt appeared in the Great Hall below. 'Mummy!' Zia carrolled with exuberance.

As her daughter flashed over to eagerly show off a much creased painting, Luca fell still. Interpreting his silence as astonishment, Darcy flung him an apologetic glance as she lifted her daughter up into her arms. 'My daughter, Zia...I hadn't got around to mentioning her yet,' she conceded rather defensively.

Luca slid up a broad shoulder in an infinitesimal shrug of innate elegance. The advent of a stray cat might have inspired as much interest. Not a male who had any time for children, Darcy gathered, resolving to ensure that her playful and chatty toddler was kept well out of his path.

'Is there anything else you wish to discuss?' Luca prompted with faint impatience.

Darcy stiffened. Minutes later, she had written and passed him the cheque she had promised. He folded the item and tucked it into his inside pocket with complete cool. 'I'll drop you a note as soon as I get the date of the ceremony organised. I won't need to see you again before that,' she told him.

Luca printed a phone number on the front of the jotter she had left lying. 'If you need to contact me for any other reason, leave a message on that line.'

A fortnight later, Darcy unbolted the huge front door of the Folly and dragged it open, only to freeze in dismay.

'About time too,' Margo Fielding complained sharply as she swept past, reeking of expensive perfume and irritation, closely followed by her daughter, Nina.

Aghast at the unforewarned descent of her stepmother and her stepsister, Darcy watched with a sinking heart as the tall, beautiful blonde duo stalked ahead of her into the drawing room.

She hadn't laid eyes on either woman since they had moved out after her father's funeral, eager to leave the privations of country life behind them and return to city life. The discovery that Darcy could not be forced to sell the Folly and share the proceeds with them had led to a strained parting of the ways. Although Morton Fielding had generously provided for his widow, and Margo was a wealthy woman in her own right, her stepmother had been far from satisfied.

Margo cast her an outraged look. 'Don't you think you should've told me that you were getting married?' she demanded as she took up a painfully familiar bullying stance at the fireplace. 'Can you imagine how I felt when a friend called me to ask *who* you were marrying and I had to confess my ignorance? How dare you embarrass me like that?'

Darcy was very tense, her tummy muscles knotting up while she wondered how on earth the older woman had discovered her plans. The vicar's wife could be a bit of a gossip, she conceded, and Margo still had friends locally. No doubt that was how word had travelled farther afield at such speed. 'I'm sorry…I would've informed you after the wedding—'

Nina's scornful blue eyes raked over the younger woman. 'But of course, *when* it's safely over. You're terrified that your bridegroom will bolt last minute, like Richard did!'

At that unpleasant and needless reminder, which was painfully apt, the embarrassed colour drained from Darcy's taut cheekbones. 'I—'

'Just when I thought you must finally be coming to your senses and accepting the need to sell this white elephant of a house, you suddenly decide to get married,' Margo condemned with stark resentment. 'Is *he* even presentable?'

'With all this heavy secrecy, it's my bet that the groom is totally *un*presentable…one of the estate workers?' Nina suggested, with a disdainful little shudder of snobbish distaste.

'You're not pregnant again, are you?' Margo treated Darcy to a withering and accusing appraisal. 'That's what people are going to think. And I *refuse* to have my acquaintances view me as some sort of wicked stepmother! So you'll have to pay for a proper wedding reception and I'll act as your hostess.'

'I'm afraid I haven't got the money for that,' Darcy admitted tightly.

'What about *him?*' Nina pressed instantaneously.

Darcy flushed and looked away.

'Penniless, I suppose.' Reaching that conclusion, Margo exchanged a covert look of relief and satisfaction with her daughter. 'I do hope he's aware that when you go bust here, we're entitled to a slice of whatever is left.'

'I'm not planning to go bust,' Darcy breathed, her taut fingers clenching in on themselves.

'I'm just dying to meet this character.' Nina giggled. 'Who is he?'

'His name's Luca—'

'What kind of a name is that?' her stepmother demanded.

'He's Italian,' Darcy confided grudgingly.

'An immigrant?' Nina squealed, as if that was the funniest thing she had ever heard. 'I do hope he's not marrying you just to get a British passport!'

'I'll throw a small engagement party for you this weekend in Truro,' Margo announced grandly with a glacial smile. 'I will not have people say that I didn't at least *try* to do my duty by my late husband's child.'

'That's very kind of you,' Darcy mumbled, after a staggered pause at the fact that Margo was prepared to make so much effort on her behalf. 'But—'

'No buts, Darcy. Everyone knows how eccentric you are, but I will not allow you to embarrass me in front of my friends. I will expect you and your fiancé at eight on Friday, *both* of you suitably dressed. And if he's as hopeless as you are in polite company, tell him to keep his mouth shut and just smile.'

Her expectations voiced, Margo was already sweeping out to the hall. Darcy unfroze and sped after her. 'But Luca...Luca's got other arrangements for that night!' she lied in a frantic rush.

'Saturday, then,' Margo decreed instead.

Darcy's tremulous lips sealed again. How could she refuse to produce her supposed fiancé without giving the impression that there was something most peculiar about their relationship? She should never have practised such secrecy, never have surrendered to her own shrinking reluctance to make any form of public appearance with a man in tow. In her position, she couldn't afford to arouse suspicion that there was anything strange about her forthcoming marriage.

'I'm so glad you've finally found yourself a man.' Nina dealt her a pitying look of superiority. 'What does he do for a living?'

Darcy hesitated. She just couldn't bring herself to admit that Luca was unemployed. 'He...he works in a bank.'

'A clerk...how *sweet*. Love blossomed over the counter, did it?'

Utterly drained, and annoyed that she had allowed her stepmother to reduce her yet again to a state of dumbstruck inadequacy, Darcy stood as the two women climbed into their sleek, expensive BMW and drove off without further ado.

'Luca, haven't you got *any* of my other messages? I realise that this is terribly short notice, but I do really *need* you to show up with me at this party in Truro...er...our engagement party,' Darcy stated apologetically to the answering machine which greeted her for the frustrating fourth time at the London number he had left with her. 'This is an emergency. Saturday night at eight. Could you get in touch, please?'

'The toad's done a bunk on you with that cheque!' Karen groaned in despair. 'I don't know why you agreed to this party anyway. Margo and Nina have to be up to something. They've never done you a favour in their lives. And if Luca fails to show up, those two witches will have a terrific laugh at your expense!'

'There's still twenty-four hours to go. I'm sure I'll hear from him soon,' Darcy muttered fiercely, refusing to give up hope as she hugged Zia, grateful for the comforting warmth of her sturdy little body next to her own.

'Darcy...you have written to him as well. He is obviously not at home and if he is home, he's ignoring you—'

'I don't think he's like that, Karen,' Darcy objected, suddenly feeling more than a little irritated with her friend for running Luca down and forecasting the worst. From what she had contrived to roughly translate of her future husband's references, one of which was persuasively written by a high court judge, she was dealing with a male of considerable integrity and sterling character.

Late that night the frustratingly silent phone finally rang and Darcy raced like a maniac to answer it. *'Yes?'* she gasped with breathless hope into the receiver.

'Luca... I got your messages this evening—all of them.'

'Oh, thank heaven...thank heaven!' Just hearing the intensely welcome sound of that deep, dark accented drawl, Darcy went weak at the knees. 'I was starting to think I was going to have to ring my stepmother and say you'd come down with some sudden illness! She would've been absolutely furious. We've never been close, and I certainly didn't want this wretched party, but it is pretty decent of her to offer, isn't it?'

'I'm afraid we have one slight problem to overcome,' Luca slotted softly into that flood of relieved explanation. 'I'm calling from Italy.'

'Italy...?' Darcy blinked rapidly, thoroughly thrown

by the announcement. *'It-Italy?'* she stammered in horror.

'But naturally I will do my utmost to get back in time for the party,' Luca assured her in a tone of cool assurance.

Darcy sighed heavily then, unsurprised by his coolness. What right did she have to muck up his arrangements? This whole mess wasn't his fault, it was hers. After all, she had told him she wouldn't need to see him again before the wedding. Obviously he had used the money she had given him to travel home and see his family. 'I'm really sorry about this,' she said tiredly, the stress of several sleepless nights edging her voice. 'Look, *can* you make it?'

'With the best will in the world, not to the party before nine in the evening...unless you want to meet me there?' he suggested.

Aghast at the idea of arriving alone, Darcy uttered an instant negative.

'Then offer my apologies to your stepmother. I'll come and pick you up.'

Darcy told herself that she was incredibly lucky that Luca was willing to come back from Italy to attend the party at such short notice. 'I really appreciate this...look, you can stay here on Saturday night,' she offered gratefully. 'I'll make up the bed for you.'

'That's extraordinarily kind of you, Darcy,' Luca drawled smoothly.

CHAPTER THREE

ZIA was spending the night with Karen in the gatehouse. Returning to the Folly to nervously await Luca's arrival, Darcy caught an unsought glimpse of her reflection in the giant mirror in the echoing hall...

And suddenly she was wishing she had spent money she could ill afford on a new outfit. The brown dress hung loose round her hips and flapped to an indeterminate length below her knees. The ruffled neckline, once chosen to conceal the embarrassing smallness of her breasts, looked fussy and old-fashioned. She was much more comfortable in trousers—never had had much luck in choosing clothes that flattered her slight and diminutive frame...

And in the back of her wardrobe the green designer evening dress which had been Maxie's wedding present three years earlier still hung, complete with shoes and delicate little beaded bag. Maxie, no longer a friend and always rather too reserved and too confident of her feminine attraction for Darcy to feel quite comfortable in her radius. As for the dress, Darcy hadn't looked near it once since her return from Venice. She needed no reminder of that night of explosive passion in a stranger's arms. Yet somehow she still hadn't been able to bring herself to dispose of that exquisite gown which had lent her the miraculous illusion of beauty for a few brief hours.

The Victorian bell-pull shrieked complaint in the piercing silence, springing Darcy out of a past that still felt all too recent and all too wounding. In haste, she yanked open the heavy door. There she stopped dead at the sight of Luca, her witch-green eyes widening to their fullest extent in unconcealed surprise.

He was wearing a supremely elegant black dinner jacket when she hadn't dared even to ask if he possessed such an article. And there he stood, proud black head high, strong dark face assured, one lean brown hand negligently thrust into the pocket of narrow black trousers to tighten them over his lean hips and long powerful thighs, his beautifully tailored jacket parted to reveal a pristine white pleated dress shirt. He looked so incredibly sophisticated and gorgeous he stole the breath from Darcy's convulsing throat.

'Gosh, you hired evening dress,' she mumbled, relocating her vocal cords with difficulty.

Luca ran brilliant dark eyes over her, a distinct frown-line drawing together his ebony brows. 'Possibly I'm slightly over-dressed for the occasion?'

'No...no...not at all.' Never more self-conscious than when her personal appearance was under scrutiny, Darcy flushed to the roots of her hair. Her attention abruptly fell on the glossy scarlet Porsche sitting parked beside the ancient Land Rover which was her only means of transport. 'Where on earth did you get that car?' she gasped helplessly.

'It's on loan.'

Slowly, Darcy shook her curly auburn head. It would be madness to turn up in an expensive car and give a false impression of Luca's standing in the world. Margo would ask five hundred questions and soon penetrate the truth. Then Luca, who could only have borrowed the car for her benefit—and she couldn't help but be touched by that realisation—would end up feeling cut off. 'I would really love to roar up in the Porsche, but it would be wiser to use the Land Rover,' she told him in some disappointment.

'*Dio mio*…you are joking, of course.' Luca surveyed the rusting and battered four-wheel drive with outright incredulity. 'It's a wreck.'

Darcy opened the door of the Land Rover. 'I do know what I'm talking about, Luca,' she warned. 'If we show up in the Porsche, my stepmother will get entirely the wrong idea and decide that you're loaded. If we're anything less than honest, we'll both be left sitting with egg on our faces. We want to blend in, not create comment, and that car must be worth about thirty thousand—'

'Seventy.'

'*Seventy* thousand pounds?' Darcy broke in, her disbelief writ large in her shaken face.

'And some change,' Luca completed drily.

'Wish I had a friend willing to trust me with a car like that! We'll park the Land Rover out on the road and run away from it fast,' Darcy promised, worriedly examining her watch and then climbing into the driver's seat to forestall further argument. 'I'd let you drive, but this old girl has a number of idiocyncrasies which might irritate you.'

'This is ridiculous,' Luca swung into the tatty passenger seat with pronounced reluctance, his classic profile hard as a granite cliff in winter.

As she stole a second glance at that hawkish masculine profile, Darcy found herself thinking that he had a kind of Heathcliffish rough edge when he was angry.

And he *was* definitely angry, and she didn't mind in the slightest. It made him seem far more human. Posh cars and men and their egos, she reflected with sudden good cheer. Even *she* understood that basic connection. 'Believe me, you're about to cause enough of a stir tonight. You're very good-looking…'

'Am I really?' Luca prompted rather flatly.

'Oh, come on, no false modesty. I bet you've been breaking hearts from the edge of the cradle!' Darcy riposted with a rueful sound of amusement.

'You're very frank.'

'In that garb you look like you just strolled in off a movie set,' Darcy reeled off, trying to work herself up to giving the little speech she had planned. 'Do you think you could contrive to act like you're keen on me tonight? No…no, don't say anything,' she urged with a distinctly embarrassed laugh. 'It's just that nobody can smell a rat faster than Margo or Nina, and you are not at all what they are primed to expect.'

'What are they expecting?'

'Some ordinary boring guy who works in a bank.'

'Where do you get the idea that bankers are boring?'

'My bank manager could bore for Britain. Every time I walk into his office, he acts like I'm there to steal from him. That man is just such a pessimist,' Darcy rattled on, grateful to have got over the hint about him acting keen without further discussion. It was so unbelievably embarrassing to have to ask a man to put on such a pretence. 'When he tells me the size of my overdraft, he even reads out the pence owing to make me squirm—'

'You have an overdraft?'

'It's not as bad as it sounds. The day we get married, I will have some really good news for my bank manager…at least I hope he thinks it's good news, and loosens the purse-strings a little.' She shot him an apprehensive glance, wishing she hadn't allowed nervous tension to tempt her into such dangerous candour. 'Don't worry, if the worst comes to the worst, I could always sell something to keep the bank quiet. I made a commitment to you and I won't let you down.'

'I'm impressed. Tell me, have you thought of a cover story for this evening?' Luca enquired with some satire.

'Cover story?'

'Where and how we met, et cetera, et cetera.'

'Of course,' she said in some surprise. 'We'll say we met in London. I haven't been there in over a year, but they're not likely to know that. I want to give the impression that we've plunged into one of those sudden whirlwind romances and then, when we split up, nobody will be the slightest bit surprised.'

'I see you're wearing a ring.'

'It's on loan, like your Porsche. We can't act engaged without a ring.' Darcy had borrowed the diamond dress ring from Karen for the evening, and her finger had been crooked ever since it went on because it was a size too big and she was totally terrified of losing it.

'Don't you think you ought to fill me in on a few background details on your family? My younger sister is the only close relative I have,' he revealed. 'She's a student.'

'Oh…right. My stepmother, Margo, was first married to a wealthy businessman with one foot in the grave. They had a daughter, Nina, who's a model,' she shared. 'Margo married my father for social position; he married her in the hope of having a son. Dad was always very tight with money, but Margo and Nina could squeeze juice out of a dehydrated lemon. He was extremely generous to them. That's one of the reasons the estate is in such a mess…I inherited the mess and a load of death duties.'

'Very succinct,' Luca responded with a slight catch in his voice.

'Margo and Nina are frantic snobs. They spend the summer in Truro and the rest of the year in their London apartment. Margo doesn't like me but she loves throwing parties, and she is very, very conscious of what other people think.'

'Are you?'

'Good heavens, no, as an unmarried mother, I can hardly afford to be!'

'I think I should at least know the name of the father of your child,' Luca remarked.

The silence in the car became electric. Darcy accelerated down the road, small hands clenching the steering wheel tightly. 'On that point, I'm afraid I've never gratified anyone's curiosity,' she said stiffly, and after that uncompromising snub the silence lasted all the way to Truro.

Some distance from her stepmother's large detached home, which was set within its own landscaped grounds on the outskirts of town, Darcy nudged her vehicle into a space. And only with difficulty. They walked up the sweeping drive and Darcy's heart sank as she took in the number of cars already parked. 'I think there's going to be a lot more people here than I was led to expect. If anyone asks too many probing questions, pretend your English is lousy,' she advised nervously.

'I believe I will cope.' Luca curved a confident hand over her tense spine. Her flesh tingled below the thin fabric of her dress and she shivered. He bent his glossy dark head down almost to her level, quite a feat with the difference in their heights. The faint scent of some citrus-based lotion flared Darcy's sensitive nostrils. Her breath tripping in her throat, she collided with deep, dark flashing eyes and her stomach turned a shaken somersault in reaction.

'*Per meraviglia…*' Luca breathed with deflating cool and impatience. 'Will you at least smile as if you're happy? And stop hunching your shoulders like that. Walk tall!'

Plunged back to harsh reality with a jolt, her colour considerably heightened, Darcy might have made a pithy retort had not Margo's housekeeper swept open the door for their entrance.

And entrance it certainly was. Margo and Nina were in the hall, chatting in a group. Their eyes flew to Darcy, and then straight past her to the tall, spectacularly noticeable male by her side. Her stepmother and her stepsister stilled in astonishment and simply stared. Suddenly Darcy was wickedly amused. Luca was undeniably presentable. How unexpectedly sweet it was to surprise the two women whose constant criticisms and cutting comments had made her teenage years such a misery.

Retaining that light hold on her, Luca carried her forward.

'Darcy…Luca,' Margo said rather stiltedly.

After waiting in vain for Darcy to make an introduction, Luca advanced a hand and murmured calmly, 'Luca Raffacani, Mrs Fielding…I'm delighted to meet you at last.'

'Margo, *please,*' her stepmother gushed.

Nina hovered in a revealing little slip dress, her beautiful face etched with a rigid smile while her pale blue eyes ran over Luca as if he was a large piece of her own lost property. 'I'm surprised…you don't look remotely like Richard,' she remarked. 'I was so sure you'd be horsy and hearty. Darcy always did go for the outdoor type.'

'Richard?' Luca queried.

'Oh, dear, I do hope I haven't been indiscreet,' Nina murmured with a little moue of fake dismay. 'Sorry, but I naturally assumed you would know that Darcy was engaged once before—'

'Left at the altar too. A ghastly business altogether. That's why it's so wonderful to see you happy now, Darcy!' Margo continued.

Darcy cringed as if her dress had fallen off in public, unable to look anywhere near Luca to see how he was reacting to this humiliating information. Her stepmother took advantage of her disconcertion to rest a welcoming hand on Luca's sleeve and neatly impose herself between them.

'Oh, do let us see the ring,' Nina trilled.

Darcy extended her hand. An insincere chorus of compliments followed.

They moved into a large reception room which was filled to the gills with chattering, elegantly dressed people. Margo turned to address Luca in a confidential aside. 'I'm really hoping that marriage will give Darcy something more to think about than that pile of bricks and mortar she's so obsessively attached to. What *do* you think of Fielding's Folly, Luca?'

'It's Darcy's home and of obvious historic interest—'

'But such a dreadful ceaseless drain on one's financial resources, and a simply *huge* responsibility. You'll soon find that out,' Margo warned him feelingly. 'Worry drove my poor husband to an early death. It's always the same with these old families. Land-rich, cash-poor. Morton was almost as stubborn as Darcy, but

I don't think he ever dreamt that she would go to such nonsensical lengths to try and hang on to the estate—'

'I don't think we need to discuss this right now,' Darcy broke in tautly.

'It has to be said, darling, and your fiancé *is* part of the family now,' her stepmother pointed out loftily. 'After all, I'm only thinking of your future, and Luca does have a right to know what he's getting into. No doubt you've given him a *very* rosy picture, and really that's not very fair—'

'Not at all. I have an excellent understanding of how matters stand on the estate,' Luca inserted with smiling calm as he eased away from the older woman and extended a hand to Darcy, closing long fingers over hers to tug her close again, as if he couldn't quite bear to be physically separated from her.

'That's right. You work in the financial field,' Nina commented with a look of amusement. 'I can hardly believe you're only a bank clerk…'

'Neither can I. Darcy…what *have* you been telling this family of yours?' Luca scolded with a husky laugh of amusement. 'Pressure of work persuaded me to take what you might call a sabbatical here in the UK. Meeting Darcy, a woman so very much after my own heart, was a quite unexpected bonus.'

'How on earth *did* you meet?'

'I'm not sure I should tell you…' Luca responded in a teasing undertone.

'Feel free,' Darcy encouraged, already staggered by the ease with which he was entertaining and dealing with Margo and Nina. Yet he had been so very, very quiet with her. But then why was she surprised at that? Her soft mouth tightened. Here he was with two lovely, admiring women hanging on his very word; quite naturally he was opening up and no longer either bored and impatient.

'OK. It happened in London. She reversed into my car and then got out and shouted at me. I really appreciate a woman with that much nerve!' Luca divulged playfully, and Darcy's bright head flew up in shock. 'You do everything behind the wheel at such frantic speed, don't you, *cara mia?* I wanted to strangle her, and then I wanted to kiss her...'

'Which did you do?' Darcy heard herself prompt, unnerved by his sheer inventiveness.

'I believe *some* things should remain private...' To accompany that low-pitched and sensually suggestive murmur, Luca ran a long brown forefinger along her delicate jawbone in a glancing caress. Darcy gazed up at him, all hot pink and overpowered, every muscle in her slender length tensing. Her tender flesh stung in the wake of that easy touch, leaving her maddeningly, insanely aware of his powerful masculinity.

'To think I used to believe my little stepsister was painfully shy,' Nina breathed, fascinated against her will by this show of intimacy.

'Hardly, when she's already the mother of a noisy toddler,' Margo put in cuttingly. 'Do you like children, Luca?'

'I *adore* them,' he drawled, with positive fervour.

'How wonderful,' Margo said rather weakly, having shot her last bitchy bolt and found him impregnable. 'Let me introduce you to our guests, Luca. Don't be so possessive, Darcy. Do let go of the poor man for a second.'

Darcy yanked her hand from Luca's sleeve. She hadn't even realised she had been hanging onto him. Feeling slightly disorientated, she watched as he deftly reached for the glasses of champagne offered by one of the catering staff.

She studied those lean brown hands, the beautifully shaped long fingers and polished nails. She recalled the smoothness of that fingertip dancing along her oversensitive jawbone, sending tiny little tremors down her rigid spine with an innate sensuality that mesmerised. And for the shocking space of one crashing heartbeat, as she met those astonishing dark golden eyes in concert, there had been nobody and nothing else in the room for her.

'You're not making much effort, are you?' Luca gritted in her ear.

'I never challenge Margo if I can help it,' she whispered back. 'She fights back with my most embarrassing moments. I learnt that lesson years ago.'

'Strange…you didn't strike me as a woman who lies down to get kicked.'

Darcy flinched at that damning retaliation. 'Excuse me,' she muttered, and hurried off into the cool of the less crowded hall.

'You won't hold onto that guy for ten seconds,' a sharp voice forecast nastily from the rear. 'I can't think what he imagines he sees in you, but he'll soon find out he's made a big mistake.'

Darcy swung round to face her stepsister. 'Time will no doubt tell.'

'Luca's not even your type,' Nina snapped resentfully. 'How long do you think you're likely to hold off the opposition? He doesn't look dirt-poor to me either. I know clothes, and what he's wearing did not come out of any charity shop.'

'Luca likes to dress well.' Darcy shrugged.

'A peacock with a dull little peahen fluttering in his

wake?' Nina sneered. 'He'll soon be out looking for more excitement. No, if there's one thing I'm convinced of now that I've seen him, it's that he's playing a double game. It *has* to be the British passport he's after...why else would he be marrying you?'

Why else? Darcy repeated inwardly as Nina stalked off again. What a huge laugh Margo and Nina would have were they ever to discover that Luca was no more than a somewhat unusual paid employee, prepared to act out a masquerade for six months. And every word her stepsister had spoken was painfully true. In the normal way of things a male of Luca's ilk would *not* have looked at her twice.

'Darcy...' Luca was poised several feet away, a slanting smile for show on his beautiful mouth and exasperation glittering in his deep-set dark eyes. 'I wondered where you had got to.'

He could act. Dear heaven, but he could act, Darcy found herself acknowledging over the next few hours. He kept her beside him, dragged her into the conversation and paid her every possible attention. Yet increasingly Darcy became more occupied in watching and listening to *him*.

In vain did she strive to recapture the image of the far from chatty male in motorbike leathers. For Luca Raffacani appeared to be a chameleon. With the donning of that dinner jacket, he appeared to have slid effortlessly into a new persona.

Now she saw a male possessed of a startling degree of sophistication and supremely at his ease in social company. He was adroit at sidestepping too personal enquiries. He was cool as ice, extremely witty and, she began to think, almost frighteningly clever. And other people were equally impressed. He gathered a crowd. Far from blending in, Luca commanded attention.

At one in the morning, he walked her into the conservatory, where several couples were dancing, and complained, 'You've been incredibly quiet.'

'And you're surprised?' Darcy stared up at him and stepped back. In the dim light, his lean, dark face had a saturnine quality. Brilliant eyes raked over her as keen and sharp as laser beams. 'You're like Jekyll and Hyde. I feel like I don't know you at all—'

'You don't,' Luca agreed.

'And yet you don't quite fit in here either,' she murmured uncertainly, speaking her thoughts out loud and yet unable to properly put them together. 'You stand out too much somehow.'

'That's your imagination talking,' Luca asserted with a smoky laugh as he encircled her with his arms.

He curved his palm to the base of her spine and drew her close. Her breasts rubbed against his shirt-front. A current of heat darted through her and she felt her nipples spring into murderously tight and prominent buds. She went rigid with discomfiture. 'Relax,' he urged from above her head. 'Margo is watching. We're supposed to be lovers, not strangers...'

The indefinable scent of him engulfed her. Clean and warm and very male. She quivered, struggling to loosen her taut muscles and shamefully aware of every slight movement of his big, powerful body. She wanted to sink in to the hard masculinity of him, but she held herself back, and in so doing missed a step. To compensate, he had to bring her even closer.

'I'm not a great dancer,' she muttered in a mortified apology.

'*Dio mio*…you move like air in my arms,' he countered.

And in his arms, amazingly, she did, absorbed as one into the animal grace and natural rhythm with which he whirled her round the floor. It was like flying, she thought dreamily, and the reflection could only rekindle a fairy tale memory of dancing on a balcony high above the Grand Canal in Venice. No wrong steps, no awkwardness, no need even for conversation—just the sheer joy of moving in perfect synchronisation with the music.

'You dance like a dream,' she whispered breathlessly in the split second after the music stopped, and she found herself as someone unwilling to awake from that dream, plastered as surely as melted cheese on toast to every abrasive angle of his lean, hard body.

Somehow her arms had crept up round his neck, and her fingers were flirting deliciously with his thick silky black hair. Unnaturally still now, she gazed up at him, green eyes huge pools of growing confusion. Dear heaven, those eyes of his. Even semi-screened with luxuriant black lashes, their impact was animal direct and splinteringly sensual.

As his arrogant dark head lowered, her breath feathered in her throat. But she was still stunned when he actually kissed her. He parted her lips with his and took her soft mouth with a driving, hungry assurance that blistered through every shocked atom of her being with the efficiency of a lightning bolt. In the very act of detaching her fingers from his hair she clung instead, clung to stay upright, vaguely attached to planet earth even though she was no longer aware of its existence.

Heat engulfed her sensation-starved body, swelling her breasts, pinching her nipples into distended prominence and sending a flash-flood of fire cascading down between her quivering thighs. As his tongue searched out the yielding tender sensitivity of her mouth, raw excitement scorched to such heights inside her she was convinced she was burning alive.

Luca lifted his hips from hers, surveyed her blitzed expression and dealt her a curiously hard but amused look. 'Time to leave,' he informed her lazily. 'I believe we've played our part well enough to satisfy.'

As Luca spun her under the shelter of one seemingly possessive arm and walked her off the floor, Darcy was in shock. Her legs no longer felt as if they belonged to the rest of her, and she was still struggling to breath at a normal rate. In the aftermath of that passionate kiss she was a prey to conflicting and powerful reactions, the craziest of which was the momentary insane conviction that Luca and Zia's father could only be one and the same man!

Oh, dear heaven, how could she have forgotten herself to that extent? And the answer came back. He kissed like Zia's father. Earthquake-force seduction. Smooth as glass. Going for the kill like a hitman, faster on his feet than a jump-jet. She was devastated by the completeness of her own surrender, and utterly dumbfounded by that weird sense of the familiar which afflicted her, that crazy paranoiac sense of *déjà vu...*

For her Venetian lover had known nothing about her and could never have discovered her identity. Her secrecy that night had been more than a game she'd played to tantalise. She had been honestly afraid that reality would destroy the magic. After all, he had been attracted by a woman who didn't really exist. And his uninterest in further contact had been more than adequately proven when he'd left her standing on the Ponte della Guerra the following day!

Yet only he and Luca had ever had such an effect on her, awakening a shameless brand of instant overpowering lust that sent every nerve-ending and hormone into overdrive and paid not the slightest heed to self-control or moral restraint. She breathed in deep to steady herself.

Maybe all Italian men learned to kiss like that in their teens, she told herself grimly. Maybe she was just a complete push-over for Italian men—at least those of the tall, dark, well-built and sensationally desirable variety. Maybe living like a nun and refusing to recognise that she might *have* physical needs had made her a degradingly easy mark for any male with the right sensual technique.

But what was technique without chemistry? she asked herself doggedly. It was pathetic for her to try and deny one minute longer that she was wildly, dangerously attracted to Luca Raffacani. For what pride had refused to face head-on, her own body had just proved with mortifying eagerness.

As Luca thanked her stepmother for the party, Margo gave Darcy's hot cheeks a frozen look while Nina surveyed her stepsister as if she had just witnessed a poor, defenceless man being brutally attacked by a sexually starved woman. Darcy's farewells were incoherent and brief.

The night air hit her like a rejuvenating bucket of cold water. 'We've played our part well enough to satisfy,' Luca had said, only minutes earlier. At that recollection Darcy now paled and stiffened, as if she had been slapped in the face.

Naturally that kiss had simply been part of the masquerade. He had been *acting*. Acting as if he was attracted to her, in love with her, on the very brink of marrying her. Oh, dear heaven, had he guessed? Did he for one moment suspect that *she* hadn't been acting? How much could a man tell from one kiss? As kisses went, her response had been downright encouraging. Her self-respect cowered at that acknowledgement.

'That went off OK,' Luca drawled with distinct satisfaction.

'Yes, you were marvellous,' Darcy agreed, struggling to sound breezy, approving and grateful, and instead sounding as if each individual word had been wrenched from her at gun-point. 'The kiss was a real bull's-eye clincher too. Strikes me you could make a fortune as a gigolo!'

With a forced laugh, she trod ahead of him, valiantly fighting to control her growing sense of writhing mortification.

'Say that again…'

Stalking rigid-backed down the pavement, Darcy slung another not very convincing laugh over her shoulder. 'Well, you've got everything going for you in that line,' she told him with determined humour. 'The look, the charm, the patter, the screen-kiss technique. If I was some fading lonely lady with nothing but my money to keep me warm, I would've been swept off my feet in there!'

Without warning, a shockingly powerful hand linked forcibly with hers and pulled her round to face him again. Startled, Darcy looked up and clashed with blazing golden eyes as enervating as a ten-ton truck bearing down on her shrinking length.

'*Porca miseria!*' Luca growled in outrage. 'You compare me to a gigolo?'

Genuinely taken aback by that reaction, Darcy gawped at him. And then the penny dropped. Considering the monetary aspect of their private arrangement, her lack of tact now left her stricken. 'Oh, no, I never thought... I mean, I really *didn't* mean—'

'That I am a man who would sell himself for money?' Luca incised in a raw tone that told her he took himself very seriously.

Darcy was so appalled by her own thoughtlessness that her hand fluttered up between them to pluck apologetically at his lapel and then smooth it down again. 'Luca...*honestly,* I was just trying to be funny—'

'Ha...ha,' Luca breathed crushingly. 'Give me the car keys.'

'The—?'

'You've had too much champagne.'

Darcy had had only a single glass. But out of guilt over her undiplomatic tongue, she handed over the keys. He swung into the driver's seat.

'You'll need directions.'

'I have total recall of our death-defying journey here.'

She let that comment on her driving ability go unchallenged. She did drive pretty fast. And in three days' time they needed to get married. There was now some source of relief in the awareness that the marriage would be a fake. He had no sense of humour and a filthy temper. Even worse, he brooded. She stole a covert glance at his hard, dark chiselled profile...but, gosh, he *still* looked spectacular!

In the moonlight, she averted her attention from him, torn with shame at that betraying response. Deep in the pit of her taut belly, she felt a surge of guilty heat, and was appalled by the immediacy of that reaction. He reminded her of Zia's father...was that the problem? She shook her head and studied her tightly linked hands, but although she tried to fight off those painful memories, they began flooding back...

When Richard had changed his mind about marrying her three years earlier, Darcy had ended up taking their honeymoon trip solo. Of course it had been dismal. Blind to the glorious sights, she had wandered round Venice as if she was homeless, while she struggled to cope with the pain of Richard's rejection. Then, one morning, she had witnessed a pair of youthful lovers having a stand-up row in the Piazza San Marco. The sultry brunette had flung something at her boyfriend. As the thick gilded card had fluttered to rest at Darcy's feet the fiery lovers had stalked off in opposite directions. And Darcy had found herself in unexpected possession of an invite to a masked ball at one of the wonderful palaces on the Grand Canal.

Two days later, she had finally rebelled against her boredom and her loneliness. She had purchased a mask and had donned that magical green evening dress. She had felt transformed, excitingly different and feminine. In those days she hadn't owned contact lenses, and since her spectacles combined with her long mane of hair had seemed to give her the dowdy look of an earnest swot she had taken them off, choosing to embrace myopia instead. She had had a cold too, so she had generously dosed herself up with a cold remedy. Unfortunately she hadn't read the warning on the packaging not to take any alcohol with the medication...

When she had seen the vast *palazzo* ablaze with golden light she had almost lost her nerve, but a crush of important guests had arrived at the same time, forcing her to move ahead of them and pass over her invitation. She had climbed the vast sweeping staircase of gilded brass and marble. By the time she'd entered the superb mirrored ballroom, filled with exquisitely dressed crowds of beautiful people awash with glittering jewels, her nerve had been failing fast. At any minute she had feared exposure as a gatecrasher, sneaking in where she had no right to be.

After hovering, trying desperately hard not to look conspicuous in her solitary state, she had slowly edged her path round to the fluttering curtains on the far side of the huge room and slid through them to find herself out on a big stone balcony. One secure step removed from the festivities, she had watched the glamorous guests mingle and dance—or at least she had watched them as closely as her shortsightedness allowed.

When an unmasked male figure in a white jacket had strolled out onto the balcony with a tray bearing a single glass, to address her in Italian, she'd quite naturally assumed he was a waiter.

'*Grazie,*' she said, striving to appear as if she was just taking the air after a dance or two, and draining the glass with appropriate thirsty fervour.

But he spoke again.

'I don't speak Italian—'

'That was Spanish,' he imparted gently in English. 'I thought you might be Spanish. That dress worn with such vibrant colouring as yours is dramatic.'

In the lingering silence of her disinterested shrug, he remarked, 'You appear to be alone.' Not easily disconcerted, he lounged lazily back against the stone balustrade, the tray abandoned.

'I *was,*' she pointed out thinly. 'And I like being alone.'

He inclined his dark head back, his features a complete blur at that distance, only his pale jacket clearly visible to her in the darkness as he stared at her. In a bolshy mood, she stared back, nose in the air, head imperiously high. All of a sudden she was sick to death of being pushed around by people and forced to fulfil *their* expectations. Her solo trip to Venice had been her first true rebellion, and so far she could not comfort herself with the belief that she had done much with the opportunity.

'You're prickly.'

'No, that was *rude,*' Darcy contradicted ruefully. 'Outright, bloody rudeness.'

'Is that an apology?' he enquired.

'No, I believe I was clarifying my point. And haven't you got any more drinks to ferry around?' she prompted hopefully.

He stilled, wide shoulders tautening, and then unexpectedly he laughed, a shiveringly sensual sound that sent a curious ripple down her taut spine. 'Not at present.'

His easy humour shamed her into a blush. 'I'm not in a very good mood.'

'I will change that.'

'Not could, but *will,*' she noted out loud. 'You're very sure of yourself.'

'Aren't you?'

In that instant, her own sheer lack of self-confidence flailed her with shamed bitterness, and she threw her head back with desperate pride and a tiny smile of wry amusement. 'Always,' she murmured steadily then. '*Always.*'

He moved forward, and as an arrow of light from the great chandeliers in the ballroom fell on him she saw an indistinct image of the hard, bitingly attractive angles of his strong bone structure, the gleam of his thick black hair, the brilliance of his dark eyes. And her heart skipped a startled beat.

'Dance with me,' he urged softly.

And Darcy laughed with undeniable appreciation. Only she could gatecrash a high society ball and end up being chatted up by one of the waiters. 'Aren't you scared that someone will see you and you'll lose your job?'

'Not if we remain out here…'

'Just one dance and then I'll leave.'

'The entertainment doesn't meet with your approval?' he probed as he slid her into his arms, his entire approach so subtle, so smooth that she was surprised to find herself there, and then flattered by the sensation of being held as if she were fashioned of the most fragile and delicate spun glass.

'It's suffocatingly formal, and tonight I feel like something different,' she mused with perfect truth. 'Indeed, tonight I feel just a little wild…'

'Please don't let me inhibit you,' he murmured.

And Darcy burst out laughing again.

'Who did you come here with tonight?' he queried.

'Nobody…I'm a gatecrasher,' she confided daringly.

'A *gatecrasher?*'

'You sound shocked…'

'Security is usually very tight at the Palazzo d'Oro.'

'Not if you enter just in front of a party who require a great deal of attentive bowing and scraping.'

'You must've had an invitation?'

'It landed at my feet in the Piazza San Marco. A beautiful brunette flung it at her boyfriend. I thought you asked me to dance,' she complained, since they had yet to move. 'Are you now planning to have me thrown out?'

'Not just at present,' he confided, folding her closer and staring down at her with narrowed eyes. 'You are a very unusual woman.'

'Very,' Darcy agreed, liking that tag, which hinted at a certain distinction.

'And your name?'

'No names, no pack drill,' she sighed. 'Ships that pass and all that—'

'I want to board…'

'No can do. I am not my name…my name wasn't even chosen with me in mind,' she admitted with repressed bitterness, for Darcy had always been a male name in her family. 'And I want to be someone else tonight.'

'Very unusual and *very* infuriating,' he breathed.

'I am a woman who is very, very sure of herself, and a woman of that stature is certain to infuriate,' she returned playfully, leaning in to his big powerful body and smiling up at him, set free by anonymity to be whatever she wanted to be.

And so they danced, high above the Grand Canal, all the lights glittering magically in her eyes until she closed them and just drifted in a wonderful dreamy haze…

CHAPTER FOUR

A BURST of forceful Italian dredged Darcy out of that sleepy, seductive flow of memory. Eyelids fluttering, she returned to the present and frowned to find the Land Rover at a standstill, headlights glaring on the high banks of a narrow lane.

'What...*where—?*' she began in complete confusion.

'We have a flat tyre,' Luca delivered in a murderous aside as he wrenched open the rattling driver's door.

Darcy scrambled out into the drizzling rain. 'But the spare's in for repair!' she exclaimed.

Across the bonnet, Luca surveyed her with what struck her as an overplay of all-male incredulity. 'You have *no* spare tyre?'

'No.' Darcy busied herself giving the offending flat tyre a kick. 'Pretty far gone, isn't it? That won't get us home.' She looked around herself. 'Where on earth *are* we?'

'It is possible that in the darkness I may have taken a wrong turn.'

Considering that they were in a lane that came to a dead end at a field twenty feet ahead, Darcy judged that a miracle of understatement. 'You got lost, didn't you?'

Luca dealt her a slaughtering, silencing glance.

Darcy sighed. 'We'd better start walking—'

'Walking?' He was aghast at the concept.

'What else? How long is it since you saw a main road?'

'Some time,' Luca gritted. 'But fortunately there is a farmhouse quite close.'

'Fat lot of use that's going to be,' Darcy muttered. 'At two in the morning, only an emergency would give us the excuse to knock people up out of their beds.'

'This *is* an emergency!'

Darcy drew herself up to her full five feet two inches. 'I am not rousing an entire family just so that we can ask to use their phone. In any case, who would you suggest I contact?'

'A motoring organisation,' Luca informed her with exaggerated patience.

'I don't belong to one.'

'A car breakdown recovery business?'

'Have you any idea what that would cost?' Darcy groaned in horror. 'It's not worth it for a flat tyre! The local garage can run out the spare in the morning. They'll only charge me for their time and petrol—'

'I am not spending the night in that filthy vehicle,' Luca asserted levelly.

'You figure cosying up to those cows would be more fun?' Darcy could not resist saying, surveying the curious beasts who, attracted by the light and the sound of their voices, had ambled up to gawk over the gate at them.

'I passed through a crossroads about a kilometre back. I saw an inn there.' With the decisive air of one taking command, Luca leant into the car. 'I presume you have a torch?'

''Fraid not,' Darcy admitted gruffly.

Not a male who took life's little slings and arrows with a stiff upper lip, Darcy registered by the stark exhalation of breath. Not remotely like the charming, tolerant male she had encountered in Venice three years ago. And how the heck she had contrived to imagine the faintest resemblance now quite escaped her. This was a male impatient of any mishap which injured his comfort—indeed, almost outraged by any set of circumstances which could strand him ignominiously on a horribly wet night in a muddy country lane.

So they walked.

'I should have paid some heed to where we were going,' Darcy remarked, proffering a generous olive branch.

'"If onlys" exasperate me,' Luca divulged.

Rain trickling down her bare arms, Darcy buttoned her lips. With a stifled imprecation, Luca removed his dinner jacket and held it out to her.

'Oh, don't be daft,' Darcy muttered in astonished embarrassment at such a gesture. 'I'm as tough as old boots.'

'I *insist*—'

'No...no, honestly.' Darcy started walking again in haste. 'You've just come from a hot climate...you're more at risk of a chill than I am.'

'*Per amor di Dio...*' Luca draped the jacket round her narrow shoulders, enfolding her in the smooth silk lining which still carried the pervasive heat and scent of his body. 'Just keep quiet and wear it!'

In the darkness, a spontaneous grin of appreciation lit Darcy's face. As she stumbled on the rough road surface Luca curved a steadying arm round her, and instead of withdrawing that support, kept it there. It was amazing how good that made her feel. He had tremendously good manners, she conceded. Not unnaturally, he was infuriated by the inefficiency that had led to the absence of a spare tyre, but at least he wasn't doggedly set on continually reminding her of her oversight.

The inn perched at the juncture of lanes was shrouded in darkness. Darcy hung back in the porch. 'Do we *have* to do this?'

Without a shade of hesitation, Luca strode forward to make use of the ornate door-knocker. 'I would knock up the dead for a brandy and a hot bath.'

An outside light went on. A bleary-eyed middle-aged man in a dressing gown eventually appeared. Darcy heard the rustle of money. The security chain was undone at speed. And suddenly mine host became positively convivial. Getting dragged out of his bed in the middle of the night might almost have been a pleasure to him. He showed them up a creaking, twisting staircase into a pleasant room and retreated to fetch the brandy.

'How much money did you give him, for heaven's sake?' Darcy demanded in fascination.

'Sufficient to cover the inconvenience.' Luca surveyed the room and the connecting bathroom with a frowning lack of appreciation.

'It's really quite cosy,' Darcy remarked, and it was when compared with her own rather barn-like and bare bedroom at the Folly. The floor had a carpet and the bed had a fat satin quilt.

The proprietor reappeared with an entire bottle of brandy and two glasses.

Darcy discarded the jacket, studying Luca, whose white shirt was plastered to an impressive torso which gleamed brown through the saturated fabric. Her attention fairly caught as she stood there, tousled hair dripping down her rainwashed face, she glimpsed the black whorls of hair hazing his muscular chest in a distinctive male triangle as he turned back to her. Her face burned.

'Give me a coin,' Darcy told him abruptly.

A curious brow quirking, Luca withdrew a coin from his pocket. 'What—?'

Darcy flipped it from his fingers. 'We'll toss for the bed.'

'I beg your pardon?'

But Darcy had already tossed. 'Heads or tails?' she proffered cheerfully.

'*Dio*—'

'Heads!' Darcy chose impatiently. She uncovered the coin and then sighed. 'You get the bed; I get the quilt. Do you mind if I have first shower? I'll be quick.'

Moving to the bathroom without awaiting a reply, Darcy closed the door with some satisfaction. The trick was to get over embarrassing ground fast. Had money not been in short supply, she would've asked for a second room, but why bother for the sake of a few hours? Luca was highly unlikely to succumb to an attack of overpowering lust and make a pass... I should be so lucky, she thought, and then squirmed with boiling guilt.

Stripping off, she stepped into the shower. In five minutes she was out again, smothering a yawn. After towel-drying her hair, she put her bra and pants back on, draped her sodden dress over one exact half of the shower curtain rail and opened the door a crack.

The room was empty. Darcy shot across the bedroom, snatched the quilt and a pillow off the divan, and in ten seconds flat had herself tucked in her makeshift bed on the carpet.

Ten minutes later, Luca reappeared. '*Accidenti*...this isn't a schoolgirl sleep-over!' he bit out, sounding as if he was climbing the walls with exasperation. 'We'll share the bed like grown-ups.'

'I'm perfectly happy where I am. I lost the toss.'

Luca growled something raw and impatient in Italian.

'I've slept in far less comfortable places than this. Do stop fussing,' she muttered, her voice muffled by the quilt. 'I'm a lot hardier than you are—'

'And what is *that* supposed to mean?'

Her wide, anxious gaze appeared over the edge of the satin quilt. She collided with heartstopping dark golden eyes glittering with suspicion below flaring ebony brows. Her stomach clenched, her breath shortening in her dry throat. 'Why don't you go and get your hot bath and your brandy?' she suggested tautly, and in so doing tactfully side-stepped the question.

Dear heaven, but he was gorgeous. She listened to him undress. She wanted to look. As the bathroom door closed on him she grimaced, feverishly hot and uneasy and thoroughly ashamed of herself. He was a decent guy and he had made a real effort on her behalf tonight. A Hollywood film star couldn't have been more impressive in his role. And here she was, acting all silly like the schoolgirl he had hinted she was, reacting to him as if he was a sex object and absolutely nothing else. Didn't she despise men who regarded women in that light?

Sure, Darcy, when was the last time a male treated *you* like a sex object? *Venice.* She shivered. Instantly she remembered that passionate kiss out on the balcony high above the Grand Canal, how that fierce sizzle of electric excitement in her veins had felt that very first time. Excitement as dangerously addictive as a narcotic drug. And tonight she had experienced that same wild hunger all over again...

A hot, liquid sensation assailing the very crux of her body, Darcy bit her lower lip and loathed her weak, wanton physical self. But no wonder she had been shaken up earlier. No wonder she had briefly imagined more than a superficial resemblance of looks and nationality between Luca and her daughter's father. But there *was* no mystery. Her own shatteringly powerful response to both men had been the sole source of similarity.

The bathroom door opened, heralding Luca's return.

'Darcy...get into the bed,' Luca instructed very drily.

Darcy ignored the invitation, terrified that he might sense her attraction to him if she got any closer. 'I never really thanked you properly for tonight,' she said instead, eager to change the subject. 'You were a class act.'

'*Grazie*...would you like a brandy?'

'No, thanks.'

After the chink of glass, she heard the blankets being trailed back, the creak as the divan gave under his weight. The light went out. 'You know, when I said you'd make a great gigolo, I was really trying to pay you a compliment,' she advanced warily.

'I'll bear that in mind.'

Emboldened by that apparent new tolerance, Darcy relaxed. 'I suppose I owe you an explanation about a few things...' In the darkness, she grimaced, but she felt that he had earned greater honesty. 'When I was a child, Fielding's Folly paid for itself. But Margo liked to live well and my father took out a mortgage rather than reduce their outgoings. I only found out about the mortgage a couple of years ago, when the Folly needed roof repairs and the estate couldn't afford to pay for them.'

'Wasn't your stepmother prepared to help?'

'No. In fact Margo tried to persuade my father to sell up. I was really scared she might wear him down,' she confided. 'That was when we had a bit of *good* luck for a change. I had a piece of antique jewellery valued and we ended up selling that instead—'

'A piece of jewellery?' Luca interposed with silken softness.

'A ring. My father had forgotten it even existed, but that ring fetched a really tidy sum,' Darcy shared with quiet pride.

'Fancy that,' Luca drawled, and the dark timbre of his deep-pitched accented voice slid down her spine in the most curiously enervating fashion. 'Did you sell it on the open market?'

In the darkness, Darcy turned over restively. 'No, it was a private sale. I assumed the estate was secure then. I didn't realise how serious things really were until my father died. He never confided in me. But you have to understand that there is nothing I wouldn't do to keep the Folly in the family.'

'I understand that perfectly.'

Darcy licked at her taut lower lip. 'So when my wealthy godmother died a few months ago, I was really hoping that she would leave me some money...'

'Nothing more natural,' Luca conceded encouragingly.

'There were three of us...three god-daughters. Myself, Maxie and Polly,' Darcy enumerated heavily. 'But when the will was read, we all got a shock. Nancy left us a share of her estate, but only on condition that we each marry within the year.'

'How extraordinary...'

'So that's why I needed you...to inherit.' The hardness of the floor was starting to make its presence felt through the layers of both carpet and quilt. Shifting from one slender unpadded hip to the other with increased discomfort, Darcy added uneasily, 'I suppose you think that's rather calculating and greedy of me…?'

'No, I think you are very brave to take me on trust,' Luca delivered gently.

Darcy smiled, relieved by the assurance and encouraged. 'This floor is kind of hard…' she admitted finally.

'And you're being such a jolly good sport about it,' Luca remarked slumberously from the comfort of the bed. 'I really admire that quality in a woman.'

'Do you?' Darcy whispered in surprise.

'But of course. You're so *delightfully* democratic! No feminine sulks or pleas for special treatment,' Luca pointed out approvingly. 'You lost the toss and you took it on the chin just like a man would.'

Darcy nodded slowly. 'I guess I did.'

It didn't seem quite the moment to suggest that he took the floor instead. But a helpless little kernel of inner warmth blossomed at his praise. He mightn't fancy her but he seemed to at least respect her.

'*Buona notte,* Darcy.'

'Goodnight, Luca.'

Darcy woke with a start to find Luca standing over her fully dressed. She blinked in confusion. He looked so impossibly tall, dark and handsome.

'The Land Rover's outside,' he imparted.

'Outside…*how?*' She sat up, hugging the quilt and striving not to wince as every aching muscle she possessed shrieked complaint.

'I called your local garage. They were keen to help. I'll see you downstairs for breakfast,' Luca concluded.

It was already after nine. Darcy hurried into the bathroom and looked in anguish at her reflection. Overnight her hair had exploded into dozens of babyish Titian curls. She ran her fingers through them and they all stood up on end. In despair, she tried to push them down again.

Ten minutes later, Darcy went downstairs, curls damped down, last night's dress crumpled, and the sensation of looking an absolute mess doing nothing for her confidence. She slunk over to the corner table where Luca was semi-concealed behind a newspaper, beautifully shaped dark imperious head bent, luxuriant black hair immaculate, not a single strand out of place.

Darcy sank down opposite, in no hurry to draw attention to herself. And then her attention fell on the photograph of the statuesque blonde adorning the front page of his newspaper. 'Give me that paper!' she gasped. *'Please!'*

Ebony brows knitting in incomprehension, Luca began lowering the paper, but Darcy reached over and snatched it from him without further ado, spreading the publication flat on the table to read the blurb that went with the picture.

'She's married already...*married!*' Darcy groaned in appalled disbelief. 'Page four...' she muttered, frantically leafing through the pages to reach the main story.

'Who has got married?'

'Maxie Kendall...one of Nancy's other goddaughters.'

'The lady has beaten you to the finishing line?' Luca enquired smoothly.

Darcy was too busy reading to reply. 'Angelos Petronides...oh, dear heaven would you look at that dirty great enormous mansion they're standing outside?' she demanded in stricken appeal. 'Not only has she got herself a husband, he looks *besotted,* and he *has* to be loaded—'

'Angelos Petronides…yes…loaded,' Luca confirmed very drily.

'I feel *ill!*' Darcy confessed truthfully, thrusting the offending newspaper away in disgust.

'Jealous…envious?'

Darcy turned shaken eyes of reproach on him. 'Oh, no…it's just…it's just everything always seems so *easy* for Maxie…she's incredibly beautiful! We were practically best friends until Richard fell in love with her. That's why we didn't get married,' she completed tightly.

After that dialogue, breakfast was a silent meal. Darcy was embarrassed by her outburst and insulted by his response. Jealous? Envious? She thought about that as she drove them back to the Folly. *No*…Luca had got her completely wrong.

As her chief bridesmaid, Maxie had stayed at the Folly the week running up to that misfired wedding three years earlier. The glamorous model had accepted the bridegroom's attention and admiration as her due, responding with flirtatious smiles and amusing repartee. Richard had been, quite simply, *dazzled*. And Darcy had been naively pleased that her friend and her fiancé appeared to be getting on so well.

But on their wedding day Richard had turned to look at Darcy at the altar, only to confess in despair, 'I *can't* go through with this…'

The wedding party had adjourned to the vestry.

'I've fallen in love with Maxie,' Richard had admitted baldly, his shame and distress at having to make that admission unconcealed.

'What the hell are you talking about?' Maxie had demanded furiously. 'I don't even *like* you!'

Fierce anger had filled Darcy then. She could have

borne that devastating change of heart better had Maxie returned Richard's feelings. Then, at least, there might have seemed some point to the whole ghastly mess. But Maxie's careless encouragement of male homage had done the damage. Both Darcy *and* Richard had been bitterly hurt and humiliated by the experience.

Darcy had long since forgiven Richard, indeed still regarded him as a dear friend. Yet she had not been half so generous to Maxie, she conceded now. She had awarded her former friend the lion's share of the blame. Only now did it occur to her that Maxie had been a thoughtless teenager at the time, she herself only a year older. Perhaps, she reflected grudgingly, she had been unjust...

Face still and strained over her troubling reflections, for Darcy never liked to think that she had been less than fair, she climbed out of the Land Rover outside the Folly.

'Do you realise that you have not spoken a single word since breakfast?' Luca enquired without any expression at all.

Darcy tautened defensively. 'I was thinking about Richard.'

Dark colour slowly rose to accentuate the hard angles of Luca's slashing cheekbones, his lean, strong face tightening. He surveyed her from beneath dense inky black lashes, eyes broodingly dark and icy cold. Colliding unexpectedly with that chilling scrutiny, Darcy felt her stomach clench as if she had hit black ice. 'What's wrong?'

'What could possibly be wrong?'

'I don't know, but...' Darcy continued with a frown of uncertainty. 'Gosh, I owe you some money for our overnight stay—'

'I will present you with a bill for all services rendered,' Luca asserted with sardonic cool.

'Thanks...a cheque might bounce if I wrote it today.' But Darcy's green eyes remained anxious. 'When are you planning to move in?' she asked abruptly.

'The day of our wedding,' Luca revealed.

'So what time will you be here, then?' she pressed.

'I'll be at the church in time for the ceremony.' An almost dangerous smile curved his wide, sensual mouth. 'You need cherish no fear that I might fail to show. After all, in this materialistic world, you get what you pay for.'

Disturbed at having her secret apprehensions so easily read, Darcy watched him stroll fluidly towards the Porsche. How did he do it? she wondered then in fierce frustration. How *did* he contrive to make her agonisingly aware of that dynamic masculinity and virile sexuality even as he walked away from her? The angle of his proud dark head, the strong set of his wide shoulders, the sleek twist of his lean hips and the indolent grace of those long, powerful legs as he moved all grabbed and held her attention.

As he opened the car door he glanced back at her.

Caught staring again, Darcy looked as guilty as she felt.

'By the way,' Luca murmured silkily, 'I forgot to mention how impressed I was by that pre-nuptial contract I signed. That we each leave the marriage with exactly what we brought into it is very fair.'

'Sexual equality,' Darcy muttered, unable to take her eyes off the way the sunlight glistened over black hair she already knew felt like luxurious silk beneath her fingertips. And she recalled with a little frisson of helpless pleasure how good it had felt in Margo and Nina's radius to have a man by her side she could trust.

'I'm *all* for it,' Luca informed her lazily, angling the most shatteringly sensual smile of approval at her.

Even at a distance that fascinating smile had the power to jolt and send a current of all too warm appreciation quivering through her. As he drove off, Darcy gave him a jerky, self-conscious wave.

'Do you realise how often you have mentioned Luca's name over the past two days?' Karen prompted tautly.

'Luca *is* rather central to my plans, and we are getting married tomorrow,' Darcy pointed out with some amusement as she straightened Zia's bed, Karen having arrived in the midst of the bedtime story ritual. 'Love you, sweetheart,' she whispered, dropping a kiss on her daughter's smooth brow.

The toddler mumbled a sleepy response and burrowed below the duvet until only a cluster of black curls showed. Darcy switched off the bedside light and walked out into the corridor, leaving the door ajar.

'I'm scared that you're developing a crush on the guy,' Karen delivered baldly, determined to send the message of her concern fully home.

'I think I'm a little too mature for a crush, Karen—'

'That's what's worrying me.' The brunette grimaced. 'You are *paying* Luca to put on a good act. He's hired help—whatever you want to call it... You can't afford to fall in love with him!'

Darcy looked pained. 'I'm not going to fall in love with him.'

'Then why do you keep on talking about how much he shone at Margo's party?'

'Because I give honour where it's due and he *did!*'

'Not to mention how wonderful his manners are and how many and varied are the subjects on which he can converse like Einstein!' Karen completed doggedly.

'So I was impressed...' Darcy shrugged, but her cheeks were flushed, her eyes evasive.

'Darcy...you've had a pretty rough time the last couple of years and you're vulnerable,' Karen spelt out uncomfortably. 'I'm sure Luca is a really terrific bloke, but you don't know him well enough to trust him yet. In fact, he could be thinking you'll be a darned good catch with this house behind you.'

'He knows I'm in debt up to my eyeballs,' Darcy contradicted.

Confronted with the full extent of her friend's unease, however, Darcy took some time to get to sleep that night. Was it so obvious that she was attracted to Luca? Was it obvious to *him?* She cringed at the suspicion. But, even so, Karen was mad to suggest that she was in danger of falling for Luca.

She had returned from Venice with a heart broken into so many pieces she had been torn apart by her own turmoil. Falling like a ton of bricks for a complete stranger in the space of one night had been a hard lesson indeed. Her battered pride, her pain and her despair had taken a very long time to fade. Darcy had not the slightest intention of allowing her undeniable attraction to Luca go one step further than appreciation from a safe distance.

In its day, it had been a costly designer dress. The ivory silk wedding gown hugged Darcy's shoulders, smoothly clung to her slender waist and hips and fanned out into beautifully embroidered panels between mid-thigh and ankle. It had belonged to her late mother, and, foolish and uneasy as she felt at using the dress for such a purpose, she thought it would look very odd if she didn't make some effort to put on a show of being a *real* bride.

And this afternoon Darcy also had an important appointment to keep with her bank manager. Hopefully a candid explanation of the terms of her godmother's will would persuade the older man that the Folly was a more secure investment than he had previously believed. With his agreement she would be able to re-employ the most vital estate workers, and very soon things would get back to normal around her home, she thought cheerfully.

'Pretty Mummy,' Zia enthused, liquid dark eyes huge as she took an excited twirl in the pink summer dress and frilly ankle socks which she loved. 'Pretty Zia?' she added.

'*Very* pretty,' Darcy agreed with a grin.

Karen drove them to the church in her car. Darcy was shaken to see quite a crowd waiting in the churchyard to see her arrive. She recognised every face. Former estate staff and tenants, people she had known all her life.

An older woman who had retired as the Folly's last housekeeper moved forward to press a beautiful bouquet into Darcy's empty hands. 'Everybody's so happy for you, Miss Fielding,' she said with embarrassing fervour. 'We all hope you have a *really* wonderful day!'

As other voices surged to offer the same sincere good wishes for her future happiness, Darcy's eyes stung and flooded with rare tears. She blinked rapidly, touched to the heart but also wrenched by guilt that her coming marriage would only be an empty pretence.

As she entered the small church, Luca turned his imperious head to stare down the aisle. His strong, dark face stilled in what might have been surprise at her appearance in the silk gown, dark golden eyes glittering. Darcy's tear-drenched gaze ran over him. Sheathed in an exquisitely tailored charcoal-grey suit, he exuded the most breathtaking aura of command and sophistication. He had such incredible impact that she forgot how to breathe and her knees wobbled. There was just *something* about him, she thought with dizzy discomfiture.

Unexpectedly, another, younger man stood beside Luca. Slim and dark, he looked tense, his eyes slewing away from Darcy as she gave him a friendly nod of acknowledgement.

The ceremony began. Only at the point where Luca took her hand to put on the ring did Darcy register that she had totally overlooked the necessity of supplying one. Relief filled her when Luca produced a narrow gold band and slid it onto her wedding finger. 'Thanks...' she muttered, only half under her breath, reddening at the vicar's look of surprise at that unusual bridal reaction.

When the brief marriage service was concluded, the register was signed. Karen and the other man, whom Luca addressed as Benito, performed their function as witnesses. All formalities dealt with, Darcy rubbed her still damp and stinging eyes, and accidentally dislodged one of her contact lenses. With an exclamation of dismay, she dropped to her knees. 'Don't move, anyone...I've lost one of my lenses!'

Luca reached down and flicked up the tiny item from where it glimmered on the stone floor. He slipped it into his pocket, evidently aware that without the aid of cleansing solution she could not immediately replace the lens. 'Relax, I have it...'

Amazed by the speed of his reactions, Darcy skimmed a glance up at him. At the same time he bent down to help her upright again. As she focused myopically on him through one eye, she closed the other in an involuntary attempt to see better. In that split second his features blurred, throwing his strong facial bones into a different kind of prominence that lent them a stark, haunting familiarity. Darcy froze in outright disbelief. Her Venetian lover!

In that instant of incredulous recognition shock seized her by the throat and almost strangled the life force from her. 'You...*y-you?*' she began, stammering wildly.

Darcy gaped at Luca in an uncomprehending stupor. Her head pounded sickly and he swam back out of focus again. As she blacked out, Luca caught her in his arms before she could fall.

CHAPTER FIVE

'TAKE a deep breath...' Luca's deep, dark drawl instructed with complete calm.

Whoosh. The air flooded back into Darcy's constricted lungs. Perspiration broke out on her clammy brow. Her eyes fluttered open again. She found herself seated on a hard wooden pew.

'*See...*' Karen was soothing Zia, several feet away. 'Mummy's all right.' And then, in a whispered aside to Luca, 'I bet Darcy fainted because she's exhausted—she works eighteen-hour days!'

As Darcy lifted her swimming head everything came hurtling back to her. She simply gawped at Luca, still doubting the stunning evidence provided by that one myopic glance. Shimmering dark eyes held her bemused gaze steadily, and all over again that frantically disorientating sense of frightening familiarity gripped her.

'You can't be...you *can't* be!' she gasped abruptly, impervious to the presence of the others.

'Take it easy, Darcy,' Karen advised, evidently unaware that anything was seriously wrong. 'You passed out and you're confused, that's all. Look, I'll keep Zia with me until you're feeling better. You should lie down for a while. I'll call over later and see how you are.'

Still in a world of her own, Darcy moved her muzzy head as if she was afraid it might fall off her neck. Luca Raffacani could not be the man with whom she had spent the night in Venice; he could not *possibly* be the same man! And yet, he *was!* It made no sense, it seemed beyond the bounds of even the wildest feat of imagination, but those strong promptings of familiarity which had troubled her apparently had their basis in solid fact.

'Can you stand?' Luca enquired.

'I'm fine…really,' Darcy whispered unconvincingly as she fought to focus her mind. She got up on legs that felt like cotton wool sticks. She shook hands with the vicar, who was anxiously hovering. Then she stared at Luca again with a kind of appalled fascination and knew she would never feel fine again, knew she felt, rather, as if she had lost her mind in that devastating moment of recognition.

'The car's outside, sir.' Benito spoke for the first time as he turned from the window.

Darcy's attention swivelled to the younger man. *Sir?* She encountered a fleeting look of pity in Benito's gaze. The sort of pity one experienced for someone sick when all hope had gone, Darcy labelled with a bemused shudder.

What on earth was going on? Who *was* Gianluca Fabrizio Raffacani? And whoever he was, whatever he was, she had just made him her husband!

'Calm yourself,' Luca urged before they walked back out of the church to face the crowd of well-wishers waiting to see them off.

'But I recognised you…' she told him shakily.

'You mean you *finally* shuffled the memory of one face out of the no doubt countless one-night stands you have enjoyed?' Luca murmured in a silken smooth stab, making her shrink in stricken disbelief at such a charge. 'Am I to feel honoured by that most belated distinction?'

His cool confirmation that he was who she believed

he was shook Darcy up even more. In the back of her mind she had still somehow expected and foolishly hoped that Luca would turn with a raised brow to tell her that he hadn't a clue what she was talking about.

'You don't understand,' she began, in an unsteady attempt to defend herself, so confused was she still. 'I could hardly see you that night, not in any detail…your face was a blur and out of focus—you looked different…'

'I guess one bird for the plucking looks much like another,' Luca responded with a sardonic bite that sizzled down her spine like a hurricane warning and made her turn even paler.

A bird for the plucking? She didn't understand that crack any more than she could understand anything else. As they left the churchyard her attention fell on the big silver limousine waiting by the kerb. Pressed into a vehicle which was the very last word in expensive luxury, she was even more bewildered. Benito swung into the front seat. The tinted glass barrier between the front and the back of the limo was partially open, denying them privacy.

Darcy snatched in a shuddering breath. Her brain ached, all at once throwing up a dozen even more confusing inconsistencies. In a daze, she struggled hopelessly to superimpose the image of the Luca she had thought she was getting to know over her memory of the male who had romanced her in Venice, the sleek, seductive rat who had torn her inside out with the pain of loss…

Involuntarily she focused on Luca again. There was a strikingly relaxed quality to the indolent sprawl of his strong, supple body. In the state Darcy was in, that supreme poise and cool was uniquely intimidating.

Within minutes the limo drew up outside the Folly. Darcy scrambled out in haste, her heartbeat banging in her eardrums. With damp, nerveless hands she unlocked and thrust open the heavy front door to walk into the echoing medieval hall with its aged flagstoned floor.

She spun round, then, to face Luca, where he had stilled by the giant smoke-blackened stone fireplace. Her oval face was stiff with strain as she attempted to match his aura of complete self-command.

'I can't believe that coincidence has anything to do with this...' Darcy admitted jaggedly.

'Very wise.' Luca surveyed her with a grim satisfaction that was chilling.

'How could you *possibly* have found out who I was...or where I lived?'

'With persistence, no problem is insuperable. It took time, but I had you traced.'

'You had me traced...dear heaven, *why?*' Darcy could not hide her incredulity. 'Why the heck would you even want to do such a thing?'

'Don't play dumb,' Luca advised with derision.

Darcy shook her head dizzily as she braced her hands on the back of a tapestry-covered chair to steady herself. 'You came to that interview in disguise...you have to be certifiably nuts to have gone to such outrageous lengths—'

'No...merely guilty of the inexpressibly vain assumption that I might be in some danger of being recognised.'

Darcy winced at that jibe and closed her eyes, but then she had to open them again, possessed as she was by a sick compulsion to keep on watching Luca. But his lean, hard features betrayed nothing. 'Why did you *do* this? What's in it for you? You can't be unemployed or b-broke.'

'No... What was that vulgar term you used about your fortunate friend, Maxie? I'm "loaded",' Luca conceded with a scornful twist of his lips. 'But you will not profit from that reality, I assure you.'

'I don't understand...' Her hand flew up to her pounding temples. 'I'm getting the most awful headache.'

'Retribution hurts,' Luca slotted in softly. 'And by the time I am finished with you, a headache will be the very least of your problems.'

'What's that supposed to mean? For heaven's sake... are you *threatening* me?' Darcy gasped, releasing her hold on the chair to take an angry step forward.

'No, I believe I am revelling in the extraordinary sense of power I'm experiencing. I've never felt like that around a woman before,' Luca mused thoughtfully. 'But then, where you are concerned, I have no pity.'

'You're trying to scare me...'

'How easily do you scare?' Luca enquired with appalling self-possession.

'You don't behave like the man I met in Venice!' Darcy condemned shakily.

'You're not the woman I met then either. But she'll emerge eventually... I have this wonderful conviction that over the next six months whatever I want, I will receive.' Brilliant dark eyes gleamed with cruel amusement below level black brows. 'My every wish will be your command. *Nothing* will be too much trouble. I will just snap my fingers and you will jump...'

Darcy tried and failed to swallow. The living nightmare of her own confusion was growing. While one small part of her stood back and believed that he was talking outrageous nonsense, all the rest of her was horribly impressed by the lethal edge of cool, collected threat in that rich, dark drawl and the deadly chill in his level gaze. 'What are you trying to say?'

'As a sobering taste of your near future, consider this…depending on my choice of timing, if I walk out on this marriage *you* will lose *everything* you possess.' Luca spelt out that reminder with an immovable cool that made what he was saying all the more shocking.

The silence, broken only by the steady tick of the grandfather clock, hung there between them as breakable as a thin sheet of glass.

'No…no…' Every scrap of remaining colour drained from Darcy's shaken face as she absorbed the full weight of that threat. 'You *can't* do that to me!'

'I think you'll find that I can do anything I want…' Strolling closer with fluid ease, Luca stretched out a seemingly idle hand and closed it over her clenched fingers. Slowly, relentlessly employing the pressure of his infinitely greater strength, he pulled her towards him.

'Stop it…let go of me!' Darcy cried, totally unprepared for this even more daunting development, heartbeat thundering in panic, breath snarling up in her convulsing throat.

'That is no way to talk to a new husband,' Luca censured indolently as he skimmed a confident hand down to the shallow indentation at the base of her spine and held her there, mere inches from him. He studied her with satisfaction. 'And particularly not one with such *high* expectations of your future behaviour. All that cutesy tossing of coins and sleeping on the floor like a naive little virgin…it's *wasted* on a male who has perfect recall of being pushed down on a bed and having his shirt ripped off within hours of meeting you!'

As that rich, dark-timbred voice flailed down her taut spine like a silken whip, Darcy's eyes grew huge and raw with stricken recollection of her own abandon that night in Venice. She trembled, her pallor now laced with hot ribbons of pink.

'You were *wild*,' Luca savoured huskily. 'It may be the most expensive one-night stand I ever had, but the sex was unforgettable.'

Expensive? But she still couldn't concentrate. She gazed up at him, as trapped as a butterfly speared by a cruel pin. Only in her case the pin was the stabbing thrust of intense humiliation piercing her to the heart. Raising one lean brown hand, he rubbed a blunt forefinger over the tremulous line of her full lower lip and she shivered, spooked by the blaze of those brilliant dark golden eyes so close, the shocking effect of that insolent caress on her tender mouth. With stunned disconcertion she felt a spark of heat flame into a smouldering tight little knot that scorched the pit of her tense stomach.

'You burned me alive,' Luca whispered mesmerically. 'And you're going to do that for me again…and again…and again until I don't want you any more…is that understood?'

No, nothing was understood. Too much had happened too fast, and at absolutely the wrong psychological moment. Darcy had stood at that altar, firmly and exultantly believing that she was in the very act of solving her every problem. Everything had fallen apart when she was least equipped to deal with it. Now she was simply reeling from moment to moment in the suffocating grip of deep, paralysing shock.

'Who *are* you…why are you doing this to me?' she demanded all over again, her incomprehension unconcealed as he released her.

'Isn't it strange how the passage of time operates?' Luca remarked with a philosophical air. 'What you once didn't want to know for your own protection, you are now desperate to discover—'

'You can't do this to me…you can't threaten me…I won't *let* you!' Darcy swore vehemently.

'Watch me,' Luca advised, consulting the rapier-thin gold watch on his wrist with tremendous poise. 'Now, I suggest you locate your passport and start packing.'

'Passport…*p-packing?*' Darcy parroted.

'My surprise, *cara.*' His mocking smile didn't add one iota of warmth to the cold brilliance of his dark eyes. 'In a couple of hours a helicopter will pick us up and take us to the airport. We're flying to Venice. I want to go home.'

Darcy backed away from him, green eyes burnished by angry bewilderment. 'Venice? Are you out of your mind? I'm not going to Italy with you!'

A fleeting smile of sardonic amusement curved his expressive mouth. 'Think that refusal through. If I leave this house without you, I will not return, and you will forfeit any hope of winning your inheritance in six months' time.'

'You bastard…' Darcy mumbled sickly as that message sank in. Evidently Luca knew far more than she had naively told him. He knew the *exact* conditions of her godmother's will. A marriage that lasted less than that six-month deadline would not count.

His stunning dark eyes narrowed to an icy splinter of gold. 'In the light of the circumstances of your child's birth, I'm astonished to hear you use that particular word.'

Slashed with guilty unease by that unwelcome reminder, Darcy's facial muscles locked tight. *Zia*... her mind screamed with equal suddenness, as she finally faced up to and acknowledged the connection between this particular male and her child. *Their* child. The furious colour in her cheeks receded to leave her pale as milk. Zia was Luca's daughter as well—not that he appeared to have even a suspicion of the fact, although he seemed to have a daunting grasp of every other confidential aspect of her life.

'And by the way,' Luca murmured *sotto voce,* 'when you collect your daughter from the lodge, try not to forget the confidentiality clause in the pre-nuptial contract we both signed. If you talk about this, I will talk to the executor of your godmother's will.'

Darcy closed her eyes tightly again. 'I can't believe this is happening to me...' she ground out unsteadily.

And it was true. She had played into his hands so completely that she had tied herself in knots. Her home, her security, both her future and her daughter's were entirely reliant on Luca maintaining his verbal agreement with her. If they parted company a day before that six months was up, she would indeed lose everything she had worked so hard to retain.

Luca lifted one of her hands and lazily uncurled her fingers to plant something into her palm. 'Your missing lens...perhaps if you replace it, your view of the world will be clarified.'

Her lashes flew up. 'You are one sarcastic—!'

'And when you have shed the equivalent of Miss Havisham's wedding gown, which strangely enough does more for you than anything I have recently seen

you in, is it possible that you could dig very deep into
your wardrobe and produce something even passably
presentable in which to travel?' Luca enquired gently.

'I'm not going to Italy…I'm not leaving to go *anywhere*…I have too many responsibilities here!' Darcy
shot at him in a rising crescendo of desperation. 'This
is my home…you cannot make me leave it!'

'I can't *make* you do anything,' Luca conceded
softly. 'The choice is yours.'

Outrage gripped Darcy at that quip. Both her hands
closed into fierce fists of frustration. 'You're blackmailing me…what choice do I have?'

Luca surveyed her with immovable cool and said
nothing.

Unnerved by that lack of reaction, Darcy twisted
away and raced upstairs to her bedroom.

Her mind was in a state of utter turmoil, stray
thoughts hitting her like thrown knives thudding into a
shrinking target. How would Luca feel if he found out
that she had conceived his child that night in Venice?
She was in no hurry to find out. Wouldn't that give him
even more power over her? And why the heck had she
had Zia christened Venezia? Or was that fanciful use of
the Italian name of that great city too remote a connection to occur to anyone but her own foolish and senti-
mental self?

What the heck was Luca trying to do to her? Most
of all, her brain screeched, *why* was he doing it? His
behaviour made not the smallest sense. In fact her sheer
inability to comprehend why Luca Raffacani should
have employed diabolical cunning and deception to
sneak into her life and threaten to blow it asunder was
the most terrifying aspect of all. He knew so much

about her, but as yet she knew next to nothing about him—and ignorance was not bliss!

Galvanised into action by that acknowledgement, Darcy reached for the phone by her bed and punched out the number of Richard's stud farm, praying he was in his office because he hated mobile phones and refused to carry one. 'Richard...it's Darcy—'

'How are you, old girl?' Richard cut in warmly. 'Odd you should ring. I was actually thinking of dropping down this—'

'Richard...do you remember telling me that it's possible to find almost any information you want on the Internet?' Darcy interrupted with scant ceremony. 'Could you do that for me as a favour and fax anything you get?'

'Sure. What kind of information are you after?'

'Anything you can get on an Italian called...Gianluca Raffacani.'

'There's something vaguely familiar about that surname,' Richard commented absently. 'I wonder if he's into horses...'

'I'll be grateful for anything you can send me, but don't tell anyone I've been enquiring,' she warned nervously.

'No problem. Anything wrong down there?' he enquired. 'You sound harassed. What's the connection? Who is this chap?'

'That's what I'm trying to find out. Talk to you soon...thanks, Richard.' Darcy replaced the receiver.

She studied the framed photo of Richard by her bed and gave his grinning cheerful image the thumbs-up sign. To fight Luca she had to find out who and what she was dealing with.

No way could she go to Italy! The Folly could not

be left empty. And who would feed the hens and Nero, her elderly horse, look after the dogs? Work that the wedding had so far prevented her from carrying out today, she recalled dully. Shedding her late mother's gown, she pulled on her work jeans and an old sweater. She could not *bear* the idea of leaving her home...

But if she didn't, she would lose the Folly for ever. *For ever.* Perspiration beaded her upper lip. Her shoulders dropped in defeat. In the short term, what choice did she have but to play along with Luca's demands? And that meant going to Italy with Zia. Before she could lose her nerve, she dug a couple of suitcases out of a box room further down the corridor. She packed them with a hastily chosen selection of her clothing and her daughter's, squeezing in toys until both cases bulged.

A quiet knock sounded on the bedroom door.

It was Benito. His face a study of careful solemnity, he passed her several sheets of neatly trimmed fax paper. 'This was on the machine in the library when I went to use it, *signora.*'

Her fair complexion awash with disconcerted pink as she glimpsed the topmost page, which bore a recognisable picture of Luca, she said stiffly, 'You work for Luca?'

'As his executive assistant, *signora.*'

Closing the door again, wondering in hot-cheeked chagrin if Luca had personally censored the information sent by Richard or if, indeed, he considered her efforts to learn about him a source of amusement rather then a worrying development, Darcy spread the results of her former fiancé's surf on the Internet across the bed.

Then she started reading. A piece entitled 'Billion Kill on Wall Street'. It was three months old. Luca was described as a finance magnate, brilliant at playing the world currency markets, born rich and getting even richer. His personal fortune was estimated in a string of noughts that needed counting and incredulous re-counting before she could suspend scepticism. And this is the guy who took a cheque from me when I was stony broke and he *knew* it...? Darcy thought in numbed disbelief.

He was a louse—lower than a louse, even. He was microscopic bacteria! He had no honour, no decency, no shame, no scruples. She read on. Reference was made to Luca's reputation as a commitment-shy wom-aniser, his ruthless business practices, his implacable nature, his complete lack of sentiment. Darcy was chilled by the perusal of such accolades, and soon decided that it was better not to read any more because it was in all likelihood ninety per cent rubbish and gossip.

No Fielding had ever been guilty of running away from a fight, she reminded herself fiercely. But her problems with the estate were all financial, and Luca had probably been the sort of child who'd started investing his pocket money and playing the stock market at the age of six. She was outmatched, and she felt quite sick at the memory of having confided in him about her overdraft.

Even allowing for exaggeration, Luca was evidently a strikingly effective financial strategist. He was rich, feared and envied, doubtless used to wielding enormous power and influence. A control freak? She glanced down at the grainy picture. So forbidding, so severe, so utterly and completely unlike the male she had fallen madly in love with in Venice. But so dauntingly, chillingly like the male she had married today...

Nothing she had read suggested that he was secretly

insane, or given to peculiar starts and fancies, but she was not one bit closer to solving the mystery of his motivation in seeking to punish her. What did he want to punish her *for?* What had she done? She had spent only one night with him, yet for some inexplicable reason he had gone to huge lengths to track her down and hog-tie her by deception into a marriage that had never been intended to be anything but a sham. In achieving that feat, Luca now had the ability to influence and ultimately control her every move over the next six months. The price of defiance would be the loss of everything she held dear.

And although she didn't want to do it, she made herself remember that night in Venice, when her explosive response to his first kiss had shocked her inside out. Within seconds, Darcy was plunging back into the past—indeed, suddenly stung into eagerly seeking out those memories, almost as if some part of her believed they might be a comfort...

'I said just one dance before I leave,' she reminded Luca stiffly, thoroughly unnerved by her own behaviour and pulling hurriedly back from him.

For Richard had never *once* made her feel like that. Only now did she understand why her relationship with the younger man had failed. Neither of them had made an effort to share a bed before their wedding. Richard had said he didn't mind waiting. Theirs had been a love without a spark of passion, an unsentimental fondness which they had both mistaken for something deeper.

'Why should you leave?' Luca demanded.

'I don't belong here—'

He vented a soft, amused laugh. 'Running scared all of a sudden?'

'I'm not scared. I—'

'Are you committed to someone else?'

Recalling Richard's betrayal, fiery pride made her eyes flash. 'I don't believe in commitment!'

'If only that was the truth,' Luca drawled, supremely unimpressed by that declaration. 'In my experience all women ultimately want and expect commitment, no matter what they say in the beginning.'

Darcy flashed him a look of supreme scorn. Having come within inches of the deepest commitment a man could make to a woman and lost out, she no longer had any faith in the worth and security of promises. 'But I don't follow the common herd...haven't you realised that yet?'

As she stepped back from him, he shot out a hand and linked his fingers firmly with hers to keep her close. 'Either you're bitter...or extremely clever.'

'No, frank...and easily bored.'

'Not when I kiss you—'

'You *stopped!*' she condemned.

An appreciative smile of intense amusement slashed his dark features. 'We were attracting attention. I'm not a fan of public displays.'

In the mood to fight with her own shadow, Darcy shrugged. 'Then you're too sedate, too cautious, too conventional for me...'

And, like Neanderthal man reacting with reckless spontaneity to a challenge, Luca hauled her back into his arms and crushed her mouth with fierce, hungry passion under his again. When she had emerged, her lips tingling, every sense leaping with vibrant excitement and delighted pride at this proof of her feminine powers to provoke, she had giggled. 'I liked that...I liked that very much. But I'm still going to leave.'

'You can't—'

'Watch me...' Sashaying her slim but curvaceous hips, she had spun in her low-heeled pumps and moved towards the doors that stood open on the ballroom, willing him to follow her with every fibre of her being.

'If you walk out of here, you will never see me again...'

'Cuts both ways,' she murmured playfully over one slight shoulder, and then she recalled that he was a waiter...or *was* he? Somehow that didn't seem quite as likely as it had earlier.

'*Are* you a waiter?' she paused to ask uncertainly. 'Because if you are, I'm not playing fair.'

'What would you like me to be?'

'Don't be facetious—'

'So that treatment *doesn't* cut both ways! Of course I am not a waiter,' he countered in impatient dismissal.

She smiled then. So he had lifted a tray and brought her a drink specifically to approach *her*. She was impressed, incredibly flattered as well. 'Then you're a guest, a legitimate one, yet you're not masked.'

'I'm—'

'You really are dying to introduce yourself, aren't you? I don't want to know... After tonight, I'll never see you again. What would be the point?'

'You might be surprised—'

'I don't think so...are you going to follow me out of here?'

'*No,*' he delivered with level cool.

'OK...fine. I felt like company, but I'm sure I can find that elsewhere...but then I sort of like you—the way you kiss anyway,' she admitted baldly.

'One moment you behave like a grown woman, the next you talk like a schoolgirl.'

Darcy's face burned with chagrin. As she attempted to stalk off he tugged her back to him and spoke in a lazy tone of indulgence. 'Tell me, what *would* you like to do tonight that you cannot do here?'

She put her head to one side and answered on impulse. 'Sail in a gondola in the moonlight...'

Luca flinched with almost comical immediacy. 'Not my style. Tourist territory.'

Darcy pulled her fingers free of his. 'I am a tourist. I *dare* you.'

'I'll arrange a trip for you tomorrow—'

'Too late.'

'Then sadly, we are at an impasse.'

'It's your loss.' With a careless jerk of one shapely shoulder, Darcy strolled back into the ballroom. She took her time strolling, but he didn't catch up with her as she had hoped. She wondered why she was playing such dangerous games. She wondered if, her whole life through, she would ever again meet a man who could turn her bones to water and her brain to mush with a single kiss...

On that thought, her stroll slowed to a complete crawl. She glanced back in the direction she had come and froze, suddenly horrified by the discovery that she couldn't pick him out from all the other guests milling about on the edge of the dance floor. Already he was lost.

'Blackmail leaves me cold,' a familiar and undeniably welcome drawl husked in her ear from behind, making her jump a split second before a huge surge of relief washed over her, leaving her weak. 'But that look of pure panic soothes my ego!'

Whirling round, she laughed a little uneasily. 'I wasn't—'

'It is rather frightening to feel like this, isn't it, *cara?*'

'I don't know what you mean—'

'Oh, yes, you do…stay frank, I prefer it.'

'How do you feel about one-night stands?' she asked daringly.

He stilled. A silence thick as fog sprang up.

'I don't do them,' he said drily. 'I was rather hoping you didn't either.'

'How do you feel about virgins?'

'Deeply unexcited.'

'OK, you don't ask me any questions, I won't tell you any lies…how's that for a ground rule?'

'You'll soon get bored with those limitations,' he stated with supreme confidence.

But she *knew* she would not. Honest answers would expose the reality she longed to escape. The young woman who had disappointed from birth by being a girl, who had been denied the opportunity even to continue her education, and who had finally crowned her inadequacies by being jilted at the altar, subjecting her family, to whom appearances were everything, to severe embarrassment and herself to bitter recriminations. She had no desire to pose as an object of pity.

Within minutes he led her down that grand staircase. Realising only then that she had won and that they were leaving the ball together, she stretched up on her toes to kiss him in the crowded hall, generous in victory. Hearing what sounded like a startled buzz of comment erupt around them, she drew back, stunned by her own audacity. She blushed, but he just laughed.

'You're so natural with me,' he breathed appreciatively. 'As if you've known me all your life…'

A magnificent beribboned gondola was moored outside, awaiting their command. A gondola with a cabin swathed in richly embroidered fabric and soft velvet cushions within. And what followed *was* magical. Luca didn't just point out the sights, he entertained her with stories that entranced her. The Palazzo Mocenigo, where Lord Byron had stayed and where one of his many distraught mistresses threw herself from a balcony. The debtor's prison cell from which Casanova contrived a daring escape. The Rialto where Shakespeare's Shylock walked.

His beautiful voice slowly turned husky with hoarseness, and captured in that haze of romantic imagery she smiled dreamily, sensing his deep love and pride in the city of his birth, reaching up to him to kiss him and meet those dark deep-set eyes with a bubbling assurance she had never experienced in male company before. At one point they glided to a halt in a quiet side canal to be served champagne and strawberries by a sleepy-eyed but smiling waiter.

'You're a fake, *cara mia,*' Luca breathed mockingly then. 'You say you don't want romance, but you revel in every slushy embellishment I can provide.'

'I'm not a fake. Why can't we have *one* perfect night? No strings, no ties, no regrets?'

'I'll make you a bet—a sure-fire certainty,' Luca murmured with silken assurance. 'Whatever happens tonight, I'll meet you tomorrow at three on the Ponte della Guerra. You *will* be there.'

'Tomorrow doesn't exist for us,' she returned dismissively, not even grasping at that point that he might understand her better than she understood herself, that almost the minute she was away from him she would want to be back with him, no matter what the risk. 'Take me home,' she told him then, impatient of the deeply inhibiting need to keep her hands off him in public.

'Where are you staying?'

'*Your* home...'

'We'll have breakfast together—'

'I'm not hungry.'

He had stared steadily down at her. 'You know nothing about me.'

'I know I want to be with you...I know you want to be with me...what *more* do I need to know?'

A spasm of stark pain infiltrated Darcy as she recalled that foolish question. It shot her right back to the present, where fearful uncertainty and frustration ruled. At that moment she could not bear to relive the final hours she had spent with Luca in Venice. And she was tormented by the awareness that her own behaviour that night had been far more reckless, provocative and capricious than she had ever been prepared to admit in the years since.

The door opened without warning. Taken by surprise, Darcy scrambled awkwardly off the bed. Thrusting the door closed again, Luca surveyed her, sensual mouth curling as he scanned the shabby shrunken jeans. 'I always used to believe that a woman without vanity would be an incredible find. Then fate served me with you,' he imparted grimly. 'Now I know better.'

'What's that supposed to mean?' Darcy snapped defensively.

'You'll find out. Sloth in the vanity department won't be a profitable proposition.'

His frowning attention falling on the large framed photo, Luca strode across the room to lift it from the cabinet. There was a stark little silence. He was very still, his chiselled profile clenched taut. 'You sleep with a picture of Richard Carlton by your bed?' he breathed a tinge unevenly, a slightly forced edge to the enquiry that thickened his accent.

'Why not...? We're still very close.' Darcy saw nothing strange in that admission, particularly when her mind was preoccupied with more pressing problems. She drew in a sharp breath. 'Luca...I don't know what's going on here. This whole situation is so crazy, I feel...I feel like Alice in Wonderland after she went through the looking glass!'

'You astonish me. In every depiction I have ever seen Alice sported fabulous long curly hair and a pretty dress. The resemblance is in *your* mind alone.'

Darcy groaned. 'Now you're being flippant. From my point of view you are acting like a man who has escaped from an asylum—'

'That is because you have an extremely prosaic outlook,' Luca delivered softly. 'You cannot grasp the concept of revenge because you yourself would consider revenge a waste of time and effort. I too am practical, but I warn you, I also have great imagination and a constitutional inability to live with being bested by anyone. Setting the police on your trail wouldn't have given me the slightest satisfaction—'

'The...the *police?*' Darcy stressed with a look of blank astonishment.

Luca flicked her a shrewd, narrow-eyed glance, eyes black and cold as a wintry night. 'You play the innocent so well. I can ever understand why. You were far from home. You felt secure in the belief that you would never be identified, never be traced, never be punished for your dishonesty—'

'I don't know what the blazes you're talking about!' Darcy spluttered. 'My...*dishonesty?*'

'But you miscalculated...the role of victim is not for me,' Luca declared. 'And now it's your turn to savour the same experience. A flare for the prosaic will be of no benefit whatsoever in the weeks to come.'

'I've got a lot more staying power than you think!' Darcy fired back, determined to stand up to him. 'So why don't you tell me why you're making crazy references to the police and my supposed dishonesty?'

Luca sent her a winging glance of derision. 'Why waste my breath? I prefer to wait until you get tired of pretending and decide to make a pathetic little confession about how temptation got the better of you!'

'I can hardly confess to something I haven't done!' Darcy objected in vehement frustration.

Ignoring that fierce protest, Luca lifted up a sheet of the fax paper, directing his attention to the business address of the stud farm at the top. 'Carlton's place,' he registered grimly. 'So it was Carlton you got in touch with.'

'I didn't tell Richard anything...I just wanted to know who you really were—*not* an unreasonable wish when I find myself married to a man who hasn't told me one single word of truth!' Darcy shot at him in ringing condemnation.

'But you couldn't wait to get married to me,' Luca reminded her with gentle irony. 'And, I, who have never felt the tiniest urge to give up my freedom, was equally eager in this instance to see the legal bond put in place.'

'Because now you think you've got me where you want me.'

Luca regarded her with hard intensity. His arrogant

dark head tipped back. Eyes hard as diamonds raked her defiant face. 'Carlton's still your lover, isn't he?'

'That's none of your business...in fact if I had a lover for every different day of the week, it would be none of your business!' Darcy slung back.

'No?' Luca said softly.

'No!' As her temper rode higher, Darcy was indifferent to the menace of that velvet-soft intonation.

Luca shifted a lean dark hand with fluid grace and eloquence. 'Even the suspicion that you could be contemplating infidelity will be grounds for separation. You see, although I have laid it all before you in very simple terms, you still fail to appreciate that I hold every card. You cannot afford to antagonise a husband you need to retain.'

Darcy shivered with anger, outraged by that, 'very simple terms', which suggested she was of less than average intelligence. 'The price could well be too high—'

'But it *has* to be high, and more than you want to pay...how could I enjoy this otherwise?' Luca countered, the dark planes of his strikingly handsome features bearing a look of calm enquiry.

As her green eyes flashed with sheer fury, Luca shot her a provocative smile.

In that instant, Darcy lost her head. Temper blazing, she stalked forward and lifted a hand with which to slap that hateful smile into eternity. With a throaty sound of infuriating amusement, Luca sidestepped her. Closing two strong hands round her narrow ribcage, he lifted her clean off her feet and tumbled her down onto the bed behind her.

CHAPTER SIX

BREATHLESS and stunned as Luca captured her furiously flailing hands in one of his, Darcy whispered in outrage, 'What do you think you're doing?'

'I'm not thinking right now,' Luca confided, luxuriant lashes low on liquid golden eyes of sensual appraisal as he scanned the riot of bright curls on her small head. 'I'm wondering how long your hair will get in six months... You'll grow it for me, just as you will do so many other things *just* for me—'

'*Dream on!*'

Confident eyes gleamed down into scorching green.

As Luca slowly lowered his lean, well-built body down onto hers, a jolt of sexual awareness as keen and sharp as an electric shock currented through Darcy. The sensation made her even more determined to break free.

Luca banded both arms more fully round her violently struggling figure. 'Calm down...you'll hurt yourself!' he urged impatiently.

'You are in the wrong position to tell me to do that!' Darcy warned breathlessly.

'Assault would be grounds for separation too,' Luca informed her indolently.

Darcy's knee tingled. She, who had never in her entire life hurt another human being, now longed to deliver a crippling blow. Luca contemplated her with almost scientific interest, making no attempt to protect himself. 'I want to hurt you!' she suddenly screeched at him in driven fury.

'But this crumbling pile of bricks and mortar stands between you and that desire,' Luca guessed with galling accuracy. 'It will be interesting to see how much you will tolerate before you snap and surrender.'

Darcy's blood ran cold at that unfeeling response.

'You'll play the whore in my bed for the sake of this house...but then what you've already done once should come even more easily a second time,' Luca surmised icily.

'You're talking rubbish, because I'll never sleep with you...I will *never* sleep with you again!' In a wild movement of repudiation, Darcy garnered the strength to tear herself free. But Luca had frighteningly fast reflexes. With a rueful sigh over her obstinacy, he snapped long fingers round her shoulder before she could move out of reach, and simply tipped her back into his arms.

'Of course you will,' he countered levelly then, brilliant dark eyes locked to her furiously flushed face.

'I *won't!*' Darcy swore.

As Luca slowly anchored her back to the mattress with his superior body weight, the all pervasive heat of his big, powerful frame engulfed her limbs in a drugging paralysis. Momentarily Darcy forgot to struggle. She also forgot to breathe.

Luca angled down his arrogant dark head and tasted her soft mouth with a devastatingly direct hunger that shot right down to her toes. Her lips burned; her thighs trembled. She looked up at him in complete shock, her mind wiped clean of thought. But her heart pounded as if she was fighting for her life, her pupils dilated, her breath coming in tiny frantic pants. She collided with the blaze of sexual challenge in his gaze and it was as if he had thrown the switch on her self-control. Dear heaven, she loved it when he looked at her like *that*...

Deep down inside, she melted with terrifying anticipation of the excitement to come. Her breasts stirred inside her cotton bra, nipples peaking with painful suddenness into taut, straining buds. Luca shifted and she felt the hard, masculine thrust of his erection against her pelvis. She quivered, her spine arching as her yielding body flooded with liquid heat and surrender. Neither one of them heard the soft rap on the bedroom door.

His dark eyes burned gold with fierce satisfaction. He rimmed her parted lips with the tip of his tongue, teasing, taunting, the warmth of his breath fanning her, locking her into breathless intimacy. Every atom of her being was desperate for his next move, the moist, sensitive interior of her mouth aching for his penetration.

'Fight me...' Luca instructed huskily. 'After all the fun of the chase, an easy victory would be a real disappointment.'

Almost simultaneously, a loud knock thudded on the sturdy door. Darcy flinched and jerked up her knee in fright, accidentally connecting with Luca's anatomy in an unfortunate place. As he wrenched back from her in stunned pain and incredulity Darcy cried, 'Oh, no...*gosh,* I'm sorry!' and she reeled off the bed like a drunk, frantically smoothing down her rumpled sweater and striving to walk in a straight line to the door.

'Is Luca with you, *signora?*' Benito enquired levelly. 'The helicopter has arrived early.'

Hearing a muffled groan from somewhere behind her, Darcy coughed noisily to conceal the sound, and with crimson cheeks she muttered defensively, 'I don't know where he is...and we can't leave yet anyway. I have hens to feed.'

'Hens…' Benito echoed, and nodded very slowly at that information.

Closing the door again, and tactfully not looking in Luca's direction, Darcy whispered in considerable embarrassment, 'Are you all right, Luca?'

Luca gritted something that didn't sound terribly reassuring in his own language.

'I'll get you a glass of water,' Darcy proffered, full of genuine remorse. 'It was an accident…honestly, it was—'

'Bitch…' Luca ground out with agonised effort.

Darcy withdrew a step. The silence thundered.

'I'll see you later,' she muttered curtly. 'Right now, I've got work to do.'

'We're flying to Venice!' Luca shot at her rawly.

Only then did Darcy also recall the appointment she had made at the bank. Checking her watch, she emitted a strangled groan and took flight.

Half an hour later, having mucked out Nero's stable, Darcy mustered the courage to enter the poultry coop. Henrietta the hen, who regarded every human invasion as a hostile act, gave her a mean look of anticipation.

'Please, Henrietta, *not* today,' Darcy pleaded as she hurriedly filled a bowl with eggs, her thoughts straying helplessly back to Luca and the excruciating awareness that he could still rip away her defences and make her agonisingly vulnerable.

She was so desperately confused by the emotions flailing her. She knew now that prior to the revelation of Luca's real identity she had grown to trust him, *like* him, even. She had revelled in his sophisticated cool at Margo's party, his seeming protectiveness, even the envious looks of other women. Dear God, how pathetic she had been, and now she felt gutted, absolutely gutted by the most savage sense of loss and bewilderment, and quite incapable of comprehending what was going on inside her own head.

And as for her wretched body...? Recalling that kiss on the bed, reliving the shameless and eager anticipation which had flamed through her, Darcy hated herself. Luca had been taunting her, humiliating her with her own weakness. The tables had been turned with a vengeance, she acknowledged painfully. For hadn't she foolishly believed for the space of one night three years ago that she, too, could treat sex as a casual experience for which pleasure would be the only price?

Hadn't she been bitterly conscious that night in Venice that she was still a virgin? Hadn't she been rebelling against her own image? Hadn't she longed to taste the power of being a sexually aware and sexually appealing woman? And hadn't the idea of throwing off her inhibitions far from home been tempting? And hadn't she known the same moment Luca melted her bones with one passionate kiss that she wanted to go to bed with him and forever banish the demeaning memory of her sterile, sexless relationship with Richard?

And, worse, hadn't she thrown herself at Luca at every opportunity, stubbornly evading his every attempt to slow the pace of their intimacy? All that champagne on top of her medication had left her bereft of every inhibition. For so long she had used the alcohol in her veins as an excuse. But the imagery that now assailed Darcy in split-second shattering Technicolor frames, the undeniably shocking memories of how she had treated Luca that night, now filled her with choking shame.

She had never once allowed herself to remember exactly what she had done to Luca in that bedroom. She had been in the grip of a wanton hunger, a hunger fanned to white-hot heat by the knowledge that this beautiful, gorgeous, sophisticated guy was weak with lust for *her*. She hadn't wanted him to suspect that he was her first lover...and she had gone to indecent lengths not to give him the smallest grounds for that suspicion.

As a pained moan of mortification escaped Darcy under the assault of those memories, Henrietta jabbed a vicious beak into her extended hand.

With a startled yelp of pain, Darcy exited backwards from the coop, her dogs barking frantically at her heels.

'*Sta zitto!*' That command slashed through the air like a whip.

Darcy twisted round in dismay. In the light of her recent thoughts she was truly appalled to see Luca poised on the path several feet away. Her face flamed. There he was, six feet four inches of staggeringly attractive, sleek and powerful masculinity, luxuriant black hair smooth, charcoal-grey suit shrieking class and expensive tailoring. But, disconcertingly, Darcy's defiant subconscious threw up a much more disturbing image of Luca. Luca sprawled gloriously naked across white sheets, a magnificent vision of golden-skinned male perfection, a life-sized fantasy toy entirely at her mercy.

Far, far too late had she learnt that Luca had inspired her with something infinitely more dangerous than desire. He would laugh longest and loudest if he ever realised that truth.

Suddenly sick with pain and regret at her own stupidity, Darcy twisted her bright head away under the onslaught of those fiercely intelligent dark eyes.

As Humpf and Bert grovelled ingratiatingly round his feet, Luca scanned Darcy's bedraggled appearance. Her jeans were streaked with dirt, her sweater liberally adorned with pieces of straw. Dawning disbelief in his grim appraisal, he breathed with admirable restraint, 'You have exactly ten minutes to change and board the helicopter.'

'I can't!' Darcy protested, her evasive eyes whipping back in his general direction. 'I have to go to the bank—'

'Why? Are you planning to rob it?' Luca enquired sardonically. 'If I was your bank manager, nothing short of an armed assault would persuade me to advance you any further credit!'

Darcy compressed her lips in a mutinous line.

'No bank,' said Luca. 'We have a take-off slot to make at the airport.'

'I *can't* miss this appointment—'

Luca caught her by the elbow as she attempted to stalk past him. 'You're bleeding…what have you done to yourself?' he demanded.

Darcy flicked an irritable glance down at the angry scratch oozing blood on the back of her hand. 'It's nothing. Henrietta's always attacking me.'

'Henrietta?'

'Queen of the coop—the hen with attitude. I ought to wring her manic neck, but she'd come back and haunt me. In a strange way, I'm sort of fond of her,' Darcy admitted grudgingly. 'She's got personality.'

Luca's intent dark eyes now held a slightly dazed aspect. He was no Einstein on the subject of hens, she registered.

Darcy took advantage of his abstraction to pull free. 'I'll be back before you know it…I promise!' she slung over her shoulder as she sped off.

It took her ten minutes to change into the tweed skirt and tailored blouse she always wore to the bank.

Studiously ignoring the helicopter sitting on the front lawn, and the pilot pacing up and down beside it, she jumped into the Land Rover and rattled off down the drive.

Two hours later, having been to the bank, and then arranged for a local farmer to pick up and stable Nero, Darcy walked into Karen's kitchen to ask her to look after the dogs, feed the hens from a safe distance and keep an eye on the Folly.

Zia bounced up into her mother's arms. Darcy studied her daughter's clear dark eyes, smooth golden skin and ebony curls. A sinking sensation curdled her stomach. From her classic little nose to her feathery but dead level brows, Zia looked so *like* her father. Darcy buried her face in her daughter's springy hair and breathed in the fresh, clean scent of her child while she fought to master emotions and fears that were dangerously near to the surface. In fact, all she wanted to do at that instant was collapse into floods of overwrought tears, and the knowledge appalled her.

'Benito's been down twice to see if you're here...talk about fussing!' Karen told her above the toddler's animated chatter. 'What's all this about you going to Italy?'

'Don't ask,' Darcy advised flatly. 'I've just been to the bank. My bank manager says he's not a betting man.'

'I could've told you that without seeing him. He's so miserable, he wouldn't bet on the sun rising tomorrow!'

'He said that in six months' time, when I actually inherit, it'll be different, but that it would be wrong to allow me to borrow more now on the strength of what are only expectations.' That Luca had made the same forecast right off the top of his superior head infuriated Darcy.

'I'm really sorry...' Karen's eyes, however, remained bright with curiosity. 'But if you've got five minutes could you possibly tell me where the swanky limo and the helicopter have come from?'

'They belong to Luca.'

'So he *was* a dark horse. How very strange! People usually pretend to be more than they are rather than *less* than they are. Was Nina right, after all? Has he married you to gain a British passport?' Karen pressed with a frown. 'Why all the heavy secrecy? He's not one of these high-flying international criminals, is he?'

If Luca *had* been a criminal, the police might just have been able to take him away, Darcy thought helplessly. But then that wouldn't have suited her either. No matter how obnoxious he was, she needed to hang onto her husband for the next six months. What shook her even more at that moment was the sudden shattering awareness that in spite of the manner in which Luca was behaving, the threat of him disappearing altogether made her feel positively sick and shaky.

'Darcy...?' Karen prompted.

She averted her attention from her friend. 'There was a confidentiality clause in our pre-nuptial contract. I'd like to tell you everything,' she lied, because there was no way she wanted to tell a living soul about how stupid she had been, 'but I can't... Will you look after the Folly while I'm away?'

'Of course I will. I'll move in. Don't look so glum, Darcy...six months won't be that long in going by.'

But the Folly might well be repossessed long before that six months was up. Karen's purchase of the gate lodge had bought some time, by paying off the most pressing debts against the estate, but Darcy was still a couple of months behind with the mortgage repayments.

She drove back up to the house and clambered out. Luca emerged from the entrance, strong, dark face rigid, dark eyes diamond-hard with exasperation.

'Have you any idea what time it is?' he launched at her.

Zia skipped forward. She was unconcerned by that greeting. She had grown up with a grandfather who bawled the length of the room at everybody, and volume bothered her not at all. She extended a foot with a carefully pointed toe for Luca's inspection. 'See... pretty,' she told Luca chirpily.

'*Accidenti...*' Luca began, reluctantly tearing his attention from Darcy to focus with a frown on the tiny child in front of him.

'If you want peace, admire her frilly socks.'

'I beg your pardon?' Luca breathed grittily.

'Zia...' Darcy urged, holding out her hand.

But her daughter was stubborn. Her bottom lip jutted out. She wasn't used to being ignored. In fact, Darcy reflected, if Zia had a fault, it was a pronounced *dislike* of being ignored.

'Has you dot pretty socks?' Zia demanded somewhat aggressively of Luca.

'No, I haven't!' Luca ground out in fierce exasperation.

There was no mistaking that tone of rejection. Zia's eyes grew huge and then flooded with tears. A noisy sob burst from her instantaneously.

Darcy swept up her daughter to comfort her. 'You really are a cruel swine,' she condemned feverishly. 'She's only a baby...and if you think I'm travelling to

Italy with someone who treats my child like that, you're insane!'

Discovering that even the loyal Benito, who had come to an uneasy halt some feet away, was regarding him in shocked surprise, Luca felt his blunt cheekbones drench with dark colour. He strode back into the house in Darcy's furious wake.

'I'm sorry...I'm not used to young children,' he admitted stiltedly.

'That's no excuse—'

'Bad man!' Zia sobbed accusingly from the security of her mother's arms.

'Never mind, darling.' Darcy smoothed her daughter's tumbled curls.

'You could *try* contradicting her—'

'She'd know I was lying.'

But, mollified by the apology and the certain awareness that Luca had just enjoyed an uncomfortable learning experience, Darcy went back outside and climbed into the helicopter.

'Is she asleep?' Luca skimmed a deeply cautious glance into the sleeping compartment of his private jet to survey the slight immobile bump on the built-in divan, his voice a positive whisper in which prayer and hope were blatant and unashamed.

Darcy tiptoed out into the main cabin, her face grey with fatigue. In all her life she had never endured a more nightmare journey.

Zia had been sick all the way to London in the helicopter. The long wait in the VIP lounge until the jet could get another take-off slot had done nothing to improve the spirits of a distressed, over-tired and still nauseous little girl. Zia had whinged, cried, thrown hysterical tantrums on the carpet beneath Luca's utterly stricken and appalled gaze, and generally conducted herself like the toddler from hell.

'She's never behaved like that before,' Darcy muttered wearily for about the twentieth time.

By now impervious to such statements, Luca sank down with a shell-shocked aspect into a comfortable seat. Then he sat forward abruptly, an aghast set to his lean, dark features. 'Will she wake up again when we land?'

'Heaven knows...' Darcy was afraid to make any more optimistic forecasts, but maternal protectiveness prompted her to speak up in further defence of her daughter. 'Zia's not used to being sick. She likes a secure routine, her own familiar things around her,' she explained. 'Everything's been strange to her, and then when she was hungry and we could only offer her foreign food—'

'That was definitely the last straw,' Luca recalled with a shudder. 'I can still hear those screams. *Per meraviglia...*what a temper she has! And so stubborn, so demanding! I had no idea that one small child could be that disruptive. As for the embarrassment she caused me—'

'All right...*all right!*' Darcy groaned in interruption as she collapsed down into the seat opposite.

'Let me tell you, it is no trivial matter to have to trail a child screaming that I am a *bad man* through a crowded airport!' Luca slammed back at her in wrathful recollection. 'And whose fault was that? Who allowed that phrase to implant in the poor child's head? What I have suffered this evening would have taxed the compassion of a saint!'

Darcy closed her aching eyes. A policeman, clearly

alerted by a concerned member of the public, had intervened to request that Luca identify himself. Then a man with a camera and a nasty raucous laugh had taken a photo of them.

The flash of the powerful camera had scared Zia. Darcy had been shaken, it not having previously occurred to her that Luca might be a target for such intrusive press attention. Bereft even of the slight protection that might have been offered by Benito, who had left the Folly in the limousine, Luca had seethed in controlled silence. A saint he was not, but he *had* made a sustained effort to assist her in comforting and calming Zia.

Luca released his breath in a stark hiss. 'However, the original fault was of my own making. When I demanded an immediate departure from your home, I took no account of the needs of so young a child. It was too late in the day to embark on such a journey.'

Kicking off her shoes, Darcy curled her legs wearily beneath her. Such a concession was of little comfort to her now. She was wrung out.

'But this *is* our wedding night,' Luca reminded her, as if that was some kind of excuse.

Darcy didn't even have enough energy left to expel a grizzly laugh at that announcement. She sagged into the luxurious comfort of the seat and rested her head back to survey him with shadowed green eyes.

The sight of Zia asleep and the sound of silence appeared to have revived Luca. His dark eyes glittered with restive energy. He looked neither tired nor under strain, but he was no longer quite so immaculate, she noted, desperate to find comfort in that minor show of human fallibility. He now had a definable five o'clock shadow on his hard jawline. He had also loosened his tie and undone the top button of his shirt to reveal the strong brown column of his throat. And, if anything, he looked even more devastatingly attractive than he had looked at the altar, she acknowledged, and instantly despised herself for noticing.

With great effort, Darcy mustered her thoughts and breathed in deep. 'I have the right to know *why* you're doing this to me, Luca,' she told him yet again.

'But what have I done?' An ebony brow elevated. 'I agreed to marry you and have I not done so?'

Darcy groaned in unconcealed despair. 'Luca... *please!* I hate games. If I'd had the time and the peace at the Folly...if I hadn't been in so much shock at your threats...I wouldn't have allowed you to browbeat and panic me into this trip at such short notice.'

'I planned it that way,' Luca admitted, with the kind of immovable calm that made her want to tear him to pieces.

As her temper flared, colour burnished her cheeks and her eyes sparked with the fire of her frustration. 'You still have to tell me *why* you're doing this to me!' Darcy reminded him with fierce emphasis. 'And if you don't, I will—'

'Yes...what *will* you do?' Luca interposed deflatingly. 'Fly back to the UK alone and accept the loss of that house on which you place such value?'

It was the same threat which had intimidated Darcy into acquiescence that afternoon. But she was now beyond being silenced. 'You insinuated that I had done something dishonest that night in Venice...and that is an outrageous untruth.'

'Theft is a crime. It is never acceptable. But when theft is linked to deliberate deception, it is doubly abhorrent and offensive.' Luca delivered that condemnation with unblemished gravity.

Darcy's temples were beginning to pound with tension again. Her strained eyes locked to his cold, dark gaze. 'Let me get this s-straight,' she whispered, her voice catching in her throat. '*You* are actually accusing *me* of having stolen something from you that night?'

'My overnight guests don't as a rule use a small rear window as an exit,' Luca responded very drily. 'I was downstairs within minutes of the alarm going off!'

Darcy's face flamed with chagrin at the reminder of the manner in which she had been forced to leave his apartment. She had crept out of his bed while he was still asleep. When that horrible shrieking alarm had sounded as she'd climbed out of the window, she had panicked. Dying a thousand deaths in her embarrassment, she had raced down the narrow alley beyond at supersonic speed. 'For heaven's sake, I just wanted to leave quietly…but I couldn't get your blasted front door open!'

'Not without the security code,' Luca conceded. 'It would only have opened without the code if there had been a fire or if I had shut down the system. I was surprised that a thief ingenious enough to beat every other security device in that apartment *and* break into my safe should make such a very clumsy departure.'

'Break into your safe,' Darcy repeated, wide-eyed, weakened further by the revelation that this insane man she had married believed she was not only guilty of having stolen from him but also equal to the challenge of cracking open a safe.

'As a morning-after-the-night-before experience, it was unparalleled,' Luca informed her sardonically.

'I've never stolen anything in my life…I *wouldn't!*'

It was a strangled plea of innocence, powered by strong distaste. 'As for breaking into a safe, I wouldn't even know where to *begin!*' Darcy emphasised, eyes dark with disbelief that he could credit otherwise.

Luca searched her shaken face with shrewd intensity and slowly moved his arrogant dark head in reluctant admiration. 'You're even more convincing than I expected you to be.'

In an abrupt movement, Darcy uncoiled her legs and sprang upright to stare down at him. 'You've got to believe me...for heaven's sake...if someone broke into that apartment and stole from you as that day was dawning, it certainly wasn't me!'

'No, I made the very great misjudgement of taking the thief home with me so that she could do an easier inside job,' Luca commented with icy exactitude, his strong jaw clenching. 'And in a sense you're right; it wasn't you. You wore a disguise—'

'Disguise?' Darcy broke in weakly.

'You made the effort to look like a million dollars that night. You had to look the part.'

'Luca—'

'You gatecrashed an élite social function attended by some very wealthy people and were careful not to draw too much attention to yourself,' Luca continued grimly, his expressive mouth hard as iron. 'You refused to identify yourself in any way and you ensured that I brought you home with me...after all, with the number of staff around your chances of contriving to steal anything from the Palazzo d'Oro were extremely slim.'

'I didn't do it...do you hear me?' Darcy almost shrieked at him. *'I didn't do it!'*

Luca dealt her a withering glance of savage amusement. 'But you've already confessed that you did steal *and* sell the ring. Or had you forgotten that reality?'

Darcy's lashes fluttered in bewilderment. Left bereft of breath by that staggering assurance, she pressed a weak hand to her damp brow and tottered backwards into her seat again.

CHAPTER SEVEN

'DON'T you recall that sleepy and foolish little confession at the inn?' Luca prompted with a scathing look of derision. 'You admitted that the sale of an antique ring financed roof repairs for your family home and indeed may well have staved off the enforced sale of that home.'

'It was a *ring* which was stolen from your safe?' Darcy breathed shakily, belatedly making that connection. 'But that's just a stupid coincidence. The ring that my father sold belonged to my family!'

'The Adorata ring is stolen and only a few months later the Fieldings contrive to rescue their dwindling fortunes by the judicious discovery and sale of *another* ring?' Luca jibed, unimpressed by her explanation. 'There *was* no other ring! And, since your family estate is still in financial hot water, you must've sold the Adorata for a tithe of its true worth!'

'I've never heard of this Ador-whatever ring that you're talking about, nor have I been involved in any way in either stealing or selling it!' Darcy's taut voice shook, her growing exhaustion biting deep.

'You were wise enough to wait a while before selling it and you ensured that it was a private sale. Now I hope you also have sufficient wit to know when your back is up against a brick wall,' Luca spelt out icily. 'I want the name of the buyer. And you had better hope and pray for your own sake that I am able to reclaim the Adorata without resorting to legal intervention!'

'It wasn't your wretched ring. I swear it wasn't!' Darcy protested sharply, appalled by his refusal even to stop and take proper account of her arguments in her own defence. 'I don't know who bought it because my father insisted on dealing with the sale. He was a very proud man. He didn't want *anybody* to know that he was so short of money that he had to sell an heirloom—'

'Why waste my time with these stupid stories?' Luca subjected her to a hard scrutiny, his contempt and his impatience with her protests palpable. 'I despise liars. Before I put you back out of my life, you will tell me where that ring is…or you will lose by it.'

It occurred to Darcy then that no matter what she did with Luca, he intended her to lose by it. He had hemmed her in with so many threats she felt trapped. And the shattering revelation that he believed her to be a thief equal to safe-cracking just seemed to stop her weary brain functioning altogether.

Only two thoughts stayed in her mind. Luca might still be walking around as if he was sane, but he couldn't be. And possibly he had been watching too many movies in which incredibly immoral calculating women seduced the hero and then turned on him with evil intent. Safe-cracking? A glazed look in her eyes, Darcy contemplated the fact that she couldn't even operate a washing machine without going step by painful step through the instructions…

'Do you still find it magical?' Luca demanded, above the roar of the motorboat which had collected them from Marco Polo Airport to waft them across the lagoon into the city.

A woman in a waking dream, Darcy gazed out on

the Grand Canal. The darkness was dispelled by the lights in the beautiful medieval buildings and on the other craft around them. The grand, sweeping waterway throbbed with life. It was like travelling inside a magnificent painting, she thought privately. She assumed that they were heading to his apartment, but as far as she was concerned they could happily spend the rest of the night getting there.

When the boatman chugged into a mooring at the Palazzo d'Oro, with its splendid Renaissance façade, Darcy was astonished. 'Why are we stopping here?'

'This is my home,' Luca informed her.

'But it c-can't be...' Darcy stammered.

Deftly detaching Zia's solid little body from her arms, Luca stepped out onto the covered walkway semi-screened from the canal by an elaborate run of pillars and arches. At the entrance to the *palazzo,* an older woman in an apron stood in readiness. She made clucking sounds and extended sturdy arms to receive the sleeping child.

Darcy snatched at Luca's hand and stepped out onto the walkway. 'Who's that?'

'My sister Ilaria's old nursemaid. She will put Zia to bed and stay with her.'

'But I—'

As Luca urged her into the spectacular entrance hall, with its glorious domed ceiling frescoes far above, Darcy stilled. 'You *can't* live here—'

'My ancestors *built* the Palazzo d'Oro.'

Just as Luca finished speaking, a startling interruption occurred. Two enormous shaggy dogs loped noisily down the fantastic gilded staircase pursued by a shouting middle-aged manservant.

'*Santo cielo!*' Luca rapped out a sharp command that

forestalled the threatening surge of boisterous animal greeting. The deerhounds fell back, tails drooping between their impossibly long legs, great narrow heads lowered, doggy brown eyes pathetic in their disappointment.

The manservant broke into a flood of anxious explanation. Luca turned back to Darcy, exasperation etched in his lean, strong features.

'What are they called?' Darcy prompted eagerly.

'Aristide and Zou Zou,' Luca divulged reluctantly, his nostrils flaring. 'They belong to my sister.'

'Aren't they gorgeous?' Darcy began to move forward to pet the two dogs.

As a pair of very long tails began to rise in response to that soft, encouraging intonation, Luca closed an arm round his bride to restrain her enthusiasm. 'No, they are *not*,' he stressed meaningfully. 'They are undisciplined, unbelievably stupid and wholly unsuited to city life. But every time Ilaria goes away, she dumps them here.'

As Luca's manservant gripped their jewel-studded collars to lead them away, the two dogs twisted their heads back to focus on Darcy with pleading eyes. She was touched to the heart.

'Are you hungry?' Luca asked then.

'I couldn't eat to save my life.'

'Then I will show you upstairs.'

'If this is really your home,' Darcy whispered numbly about halfway up the second flight. 'That means...that means that you were the *host* at the masked ball.'

'You wouldn't let me tell you who I was. And since the ball invariably lasts until dawn, I could scarcely bring you back here for the remainder of the night. At the time, I had been using the apartment regularly while renovations were being carried out here.'

'There's so much I don't know about you—'

'And now you have all the time in the world to discover everything you ever wanted to know,' Luca pointed out in a tone of bracing consolation.

'I don't think I want to find out any more.'

'This has not been the most propitious of wedding days,' Luca conceded smoothly. 'But I'm certain you have the resilience to rise above a somewhat difficult beginning. After all, *cara mia*...I'm prepared to be very generous.'

Darcy gawped at him. *'Generous?'*

'If you satisfy my demands, I *will* allow you to inherit that one million. I'm not a complete bastard. There are those who say that I am,' Luca admitted reflectively, 'and I would concede that I am no bleeding heart, but I am always scrupulously fair in my dealings.'

'Is that a fact?' Darcy passed no opinion because she didn't have the energy to argue with him.

Passing down a corridor lined with fine oil paintings, Luca flung open the door of a superb bedroom full of ornate gilded furniture. One stunned glance was sufficient to tell Darcy that in comparison Fielding's Folly offered all the comfort of a medieval barn in an advanced state of decay.

'Your luggage will be brought up.'

'I want to see Zia. Where is she?'

'In the nursery suite on the floor above. Most mothers would be grateful for a break from childcare on their wedding night.'

'What is with this ''wedding night'' bit you keep on mentioning?' Darcy enquired with stilted reluctance.

Luca treated her to a slow, sensual smile. Dark golden eyes of intent gleamed below luxuriant black lashes. 'You are not that naive. Whatever else you may be, you are still a Raffacani bride, and tonight in the time-honoured tradition of my ancestors we will share that bed together.'

Darcy thought about this nightmare day she had enjoyed at Luca's merciless hands. She studied him in honest disbelief.

'You should congratulate yourself.' His exquisitely expressive mouth quirked. 'Only the memory of that incredibly passionate night we once shared persuaded me to go to the extremity of marrying you. The prospect of six sexually self-indulgent months played a major part in that decision.'

'I can imagine,' Darcy mumbled weakly, and she *could*.

Luca saw life's every event in terms of profit and loss. Almost three years ago he had suffered a loss for which he had falsely blamed her. Now he planned to turn loss into vengeful profit between the bedsheets. It was novel, she conceded. But for a rogue male to whom everything probably came far too easily, anything that supplied a challenge would always be what he wanted most.

Dear heaven, had she been that exciting in bed? She had been imaginative, she was prepared to admit, but that night had been a one-off. Heady romance, bitter rebellion and fiery desire had combined with champagne to send her off the rails. She had lived out a never to be repeated kind of fantasy and lived on to regret every single second of her reckless misbehaviour.

'I'll give you an hour to rediscover your energies and ponder the reality that a marriage that is *not* consummated is worthless in the eyes of the law.'

'What are you talking about?'

'Aren't you aware that sex is an integral part of the

marriage contract? And the lack of it grounds for an-
nulment?'

Darcy's jaw dropped.

'You see, I'm not a complete bastard,' Luca contended, smooth as glass. 'A complete bastard would
have left you to sleep in ignorance and gone for non-
consummation at the end of the six months.'

Leaving her to reflect on that revelation of astounding
generosity, Luca strolled back out of the room.

That is one happy man, Darcy thought helplessly. An
utterly ruthless male with the persistence of a jugger-
naut, punch-drunk on the belief that he had her exactly
where he wanted her. He was destined to discover that
he had a prolonged battle ahead of him. Although she
was currently at a very low ebb, Darcy was by nature
a fighter.

A thief. He thought she was a thief. He genuinely
believed that she had stolen that wretched ring with the
stupid name. And, truth to tell, if it had been stolen the
same night, he had some grounds for that suspicion.
Indeed, when that theft was combined with her flight at
dawn, her status as a gatecrasher and her flat refusal to
tell him who she was throughout the evening, she had
to concede that his conviction that she was the guilty
party *was* based on some pretty solid-looking facts.

However, those facts were simply misleading facts.
Obviously she had been in the wrong place at the wrong
time. But Luca wasn't the type of male likely to question his own judgement. In fact, unless she was very
much mistaken, Luca prided himself on his powers of
logic and reasoning. That being so, for almost three
years he had staunchly believed that she was the culprit.
By now, the real thief and the ring had to be long gone.
Luca's mistake, not hers.

In the meantime, only by finding some proof that the ring her father had sold had been a different ring entirely could she hope to defend herself. Had her father kept any record of that sale? And what the heck was the use of wondering that when she was stuck in Venice and unable to conduct any sort of search? Why, oh, why had she allowed Luca to steamroller her into flying straight to Italy?

And the answer came back loud and clear. If she had refused, Luca would have gone without her. Challenged at the very outset of their marriage, Luca would have carried through on that threat.

An hour later, Luca sauntered back into the marital bedroom and stopped dead only halfway towards the canopied bed.

Contented canine snores alerted him to the presence of at least one four-legged intruder. And there was no room for a bridegroom in the bed, vast as it was. Darcy lay dead centre, one arm curved protectively round her slumbering daughter, the other draped across two enormous shaggy backs.

Zou Zou was snoring like a train. Aristide opened his eyes, and in his efforts to conceal himself did a comic impression of a very large dog trying to shrink himself to the size of a chihuahua. Pushing his head bashfully between his paws, perfectly aware that he was not allowed on the bed, he surveyed Luca pleadingly, unaware that the child on the other side of the bed was his most powerful source of protection.

Luca drew in a slow, steadying breath and backed towards the door very quietly. He had learnt considerable respect for the consequences of *not* letting sleeping toddlers lie...

*   *   *

Darcy was nudged awake at half past six in the morning by the dogs.

After a brisk wash in her usual cold water in the *en suite* bathroom, she trudged downstairs in her checked pyjamas and old wool dressing gown, startling the dapper little manservant breakfasting in the sleek, ultra-modern kitchen on the ground floor. Beneath the older man's aghast gaze, she fed and watered the dogs and refused to allow him to interrupt his meal. She then insisted on charring two croissants and brewing some not very successful coffee for herself. She wrinkled her nose as she ate and drank. Cooking had never been her metier, but her digestion was robust.

Finding Zia still soundly asleep when she returned to the bedroom, she succumbed to the notion of returning to bed to give her daughter a cuddle, but while in the act of waiting for the toddler to awaken naturally she contrived to drift off to sleep again.

The second time she woke up, she stretched luxuriantly. Then, as she recalled rising earlier, she was seized by instant guilt and wondered with all the horror of someone who never, ever had a lie-in what time it was.

'It's a quarter past nine, *cara mia,*' a deep, dark drawl responded to the anxious question she had unwittingly said out loud.

That reply so alarmingly close to hand acted like a cattle prod on Darcy. Eyes flying wide in dismay, she flipped over to her side to confront her uninvited companion. 'Good heavens…a q-quarter past nine?' she stuttered. 'Where's Zia?'

'Breakfasting upstairs in the nursery suite.'

His clean-shaven jaw supported by an indolent hand, Luca gazed down at Darcy's startled face with a slow, mocking smile that made her pulses race. Her shocked appraisal absorbed the width of his bare brown shoulders above the sheet. Instantly she knew that he wasn't wearing a stitch.

'This bed was busier than the Rialto at high season last night,' Luca remarked.

'Zia needed the security of being with me. She was too cranky to settle somewhere strange on her own,' Darcy rushed to inform him, heart banging violently against her breastbone as she collided with flaring eyes as bright as shafts of golden sunlight in that lean, dark, devastating face.

'Were the dogs insecure too?'

'They cried at the door, Luca! They were really pathetic...'

'I wonder if I should have tried getting down on all fours and howling. I could have pretended to be a werewolf,' Luca suggested, taking advantage of her confusion to snake out an imprisoning arm and hold her where she was before she could go into sudden retreat. 'Then you would've had every excuse to tie me to the bed again.'

Darcy turned a slow hot crimson. Every inch of skin above the collar of her pyjama top was infiltrated by that sweeping tide of burning colour. *Again!* That single word was like a depth charge plunging into her memory banks to cause the maximum chaos. And, worst of all, he was exaggerating. With the aid of his bow tie, she had only got as far as anchoring one wrist before laughter had got the better of her dramatic intentions.

'Speaking as a male who until that night had never, ever relinquished control in the bedroom, I was delightfully surprised by your creativity—'

'I was *drunk!*' Darcy hissed in anguished self-defence.

'With a passionate desire to live out every fantasy you had ever had. Yes, you told me,' Luca reminded her without remorse as he leant over her and long fingers flicked loose the button at her throat without her noticing. 'You also told me that I was your dream lover…and you were undeniably mine. I don't have dream aspirations, but what I didn't know I was missing, I had in abundance that night, and since then no other woman has managed to satisfy me.'

'You're not serious,' Darcy mumbled shakily, mesmerised by the blaze of that golden gaze holding her own.

'So that is why you are here,' Luca confided with husky exactitude. 'I want to know *why* I find you so tormentingly attractive when my intelligence tells me that you are full of flaws.'

'Flaws?'

'You don't give a damn about your appearance. You're untidy, disorganised and blunt to the point of insanity. You hack wood like a lumberjack and you let dogs sleep on my bed. And, strange as it is, I have to confess that none of those habits or failings has the slightest cooling effect on my libido…' Lowering his imperious dark head on that admission, Luca skimmed aside the loose-cut pyjama top to press his mouth hotly to the tiny pulse flickering beneath the delicate skin of her throat.

'*Oh*…what are you doing?' Darcy yelped.

Involuntarily immobilised by the startling burst of warmth igniting low in her belly, she gazed up apprehensively at Luca as he lifted his head.

'Don't do that again,' she muttered weakly, her voice failing to rise to the command level required for the occasion. 'It makes me feel peculiar and we have to talk about things—'

'What sort of things?' Luca enquired thickly.

'That wretched ring for a start—'

'No.'

'I didn't steal it, Luca! And you should be trying to find out who *did!*' Darcy told him baldly.

His heated gaze cooled and hardened in the thumping silence.

Darcy gave him a weary, pleading look. 'I wouldn't *do* something like that…and as soon as I get home I'll be able to prove that the ring my father sold wasn't yours!'

'What do you hope to gain from these absurd lies and promises?' Luca demanded with raw impatience. 'I *know* that you took the Adorata! It is not remotely possible that anyone else could have carried out that theft. An idiot would confirm your guilt on less evidence than I have!'

'Circumstantial evidence, Luca…nothing more concrete.'

'While you refuse to admit the truth, there's nothing to discuss.' Luca studied her flushed and frustrated face with smouldering dark golden eyes. With cool deliberation, he smoothed the tumbled curls from her brow. 'All I want to do at this moment is make passionate love to you.'

'No!'

Luca let a teasing forefinger trail along the taut line of her mutinous lips, watched her shiver in shaken reaction to that contact. 'Even when you want to?'

'I don't want to!'

Suddenly alarmingly short of breath, Darcy looked back at him. Little prickles of tormenting awareness were filling her with tension. She was shamefully conscious of the raw, potent power of his abrasive masculinity, and of its devastating effect on her treacherous body. Already her breasts felt heavy and full, her nipples wantonly taut.

The silence pulsed.

'I *don't!* You think I'm a thief!' Darcy cried, as though he had argued with her.

Luca's smile was pure charisma unleashed. 'Possibly that's the most dangerous part of your attraction.'

Thoroughly disconcerted by that suggestion, Darcy frowned.

And, in a ruthless play on her bewilderment, Luca bent his well-shaped dark head and kissed her. He plundered her mouth like a warrior on the battlefield in a make-or-break encounter. She jerked as if fireworks were going off inside her. The hot, lustful thrust of his tongue electrified her. As she responded with all the answering hunger she could not suppress, nothing mattered to her but the continuance of that passionate assault.

In an indolent movement Luca sat up and carried her with him. He pushed the top down off her shoulders and trailed it free of her arms, freeing her hands to rise and sink into his luxuriant black hair. He released her reddened mouth, burnished golden eyes dropping lower to take in the tip-tilted curves of her small breasts and the bold thrust of her rosy nipples.

'You are so perfect,' he savoured huskily.

Perfect? *Never,* she thought, but in the pounding silence Darcy still found herself watching as he curved appreciative hands to her aching flesh. With a stifled moan, she shut her eyes tightly, but felt with every quivering fibre the shockwave of shatteringly intense sensation as expert fingers toyed with the tender peaks. She trembled, her heartbeat thundering in her eardrums.

'*Dio…*' Luca drew in an audible breath. 'You always do exactly what excites me most…'

With a distinct lack of cool, he pushed her back against the pillows and closed his mouth urgently to the source of his temptation. As he tugged at the shamelessly engorged buds with erotic thoroughness she flung her head back, every muscle tensing as a low, keening sound of excitement escaped her. With every carnal caress he sent an arrow of shooting fire to the tormenting ache between her trembling thighs.

Her fingers knotted tightly into the glossy thickness of his hair, holding him to her, desperately urging him on. A moan of impatience left her lips as he abandoned her breasts to tug up her knees and free her restive lower limbs from the pyjama bottoms.

'Kiss me,' she muttered feverishly then.

'Want me?' Shimmering golden eyes welded to her darkened gaze and the longing she couldn't hide from him. 'How much?'

'Luca…' she whispered pleadingly, shivering with need.

'I find you incredibly sexy, *cara mia.*'

Rising over her, he slid a lean, hair-roughened thigh between hers and crushed her mouth with passionate fervour under his. There was no room for thought in her head. Passion controlled her utterly. Her body writhed beneath his, a flood of hungry fire burning at the very heart of her. Feeling the bold promise of his manhood pulsing against her hip, she pushed against him in instinctive encouragement.

Luca pulled back from her, eyes smoky with desire. 'You're too impatient…the pleasure is all the keener when you wait for what you want. And didn't you make me wait that night?' A tantalising hand slowly smoothed over the tense muscles of her stomach. He listened to her suck in oxygen in noisy gasps of anticipation. 'In fact, you pushed me right over the edge when I was least expecting it.'

Instantly she was lost in that imagery. Luca, helpless in her thrall, driven to satisfaction against his own volition, disconcerted, reacting by suddenly reasserting his masculine dominance and driving her crazy with desire. She reached up to him, finding his sensual mouth again for herself, parting her lips to the stabbing invasion of his tongue. He shuddered violently against her, his control slipping as he kissed her back with raw, hungry force.

His hand skated through the damp auburn curls crowning the apex of her thighs and discovered the satin sensitivity of the moist flesh beneath. Mastered by a need that overwhelmed every restraint, she felt her spine arch, her body opening to him as the terrible ache for satisfaction blazed up, making her whimper and writhe, hungrily craving what he had taught her to crave in a torment of excitement.

'When you respond like that, all I can think about is plunging inside you,' Luca groaned, sliding between her thighs.

The hot, hard thrust of his powerful penetration took her breath away. Nothing had ever felt so good. Her whole being was centred on the feel of him inside her, boldly stretching and filling, and giving such intense pleasure she would have died had he stopped.

'You told me I was absolutely brilliant at this,' Luca reminded her, gazing down at her with a staggering mixture of lust laced with reluctant amusement as he plunged deeper still and watched her eyes close on a wave of electrified and utterly naked pleasure. '"Gosh, you're incredibly good at this too…" you said, in such surprise. I wondered if you were going to score my technique on a questionnaire afterwards—'

'Shut up!' Darcy moaned with effort.

'You said that too.'

She stared up at him, at a peak of such extraordinary excitement she was ready to kill him if he didn't move.

And Luca vented a hoarse laugh. He *knew* how she felt. And his own struggle to maintain control was etched in his taut cheekbones, the sheen of sweat on his dark skin and the ragged edge to his voice. With a muffled groan of urgent satisfaction, he drove deeper into her yielding body. Her heart almost burst with the force of her own frantic response.

Mindless, she clung to him as he took her with a wild vigour that destroyed any semblance of control. Her release brought an electrifying explosion. As the paroxysms of uncontrollable pleasure overpowered her, her nails raked down his damp, muscular back. Luca cried out her name and shuddered over her, as lost in that world of physical sensation as she was.

The most unearthly silence reigned in the aftermath of that impassioned joining.

Luca disentangled himself and rolled over to a cooler part of the bed. Darcy stared fixedly at the footboard. Even before the last quakings of sated desire and intense pleasure faded, she felt rejected.

So you slept with him, a little voice said inside her blitzed brain. Did you do it to make this a real marriage that couldn't be annulled? Did you do it to hang onto the Folly? Or did you do it because you just couldn't summon up sufficient will-power to resist him? After all, you knew how fantastic he would be.

Darcy flipped her tousled head over to one side to anxiously scan Luca. He looked back at her, his strikingly handsome face taut but uninformative, expressive eyes screened. Darcy's throat closed over. At that moment she wanted very, very badly to believe that she had sacrificed her body for the sake of her home. It might have been a morally indefensible move, but her pride could have lived with such a cold-blooded decision...

It would be an infinitely greater challenge to co-exist with the ghastly knowledge that she had made love with Luca because she found him totally and absolutely irresistible, even when she ought to hate him...but, unhappily for her, that was the dreadful truth. And any denial of the fact would be complete cowardice.

It was equally craven to lie in the presence of the enemy behaving like a victim, drowning in defeat and loss of face. Darcy flinched from an image infinitely more shameful to her than any loss of control in Luca's arms. It was unthinkable to let Luca guess that making love with him could reduce her to such a turmoil of painful vulnerability.

'Right,' Darcy said flatly, galvanised into action by that awareness and abruptly sitting up with what she hoped was a cool, calm air of decision. 'Now that we've got *that* out of the way, perhaps we can talk business.'

'*Business?*' Luca stressed in sharp disconcertion, complete incredulity flaring in his brilliant dark eyes.

CHAPTER EIGHT

'BUSINESS,' Darcy confirmed steadily.

'We have no mutual business interests to discuss,' Luca delivered rather drily.

'That's where you're wrong.' Her eyes gleamed at that dismissive assurance. 'As you were so eager to point out yesterday, the Folly estate is still on the brink of bankruptcy.' She breathed in deep. 'I only married you because I assumed that my bank manager would increase my overdraft limit once I explained to him about my godmother's will. However…he refused.'

From beneath dense ebony lashes, Luca surveyed her with something akin to unholy fascination.

'So as things stand,' Darcy recounted tautly, 'not only am I in no position to re-employ the staff laid off after my father's death, but I am also likely to have my home repossessed before that six months is even up.'

'One small question,' Luca breathed in a slightly strained undertone. He was now engaged on a fixed surveillance of the elaborate plasterwork on the ceiling above. 'Did you happen to mention my name to your bank manager?'

'What would I have mentioned your name for?' Darcy countered impatiently. 'I told him that I'd got married but that my husband would be having nothing to do with the estate.'

'Honesty is wonderful, but not always wise,' Luca remarked reflectively. 'I doubt that you need worry about any imminent threat of repossession. If you're only a little behind on the mortgage repayments, it's unlikely.'

'I disagree. I've had some very nasty letters on the subject already. Heavens, I'm scared to open my post these days!' Darcy admitted ruefully, thrusting bright curls from her troubled brow.

'Tell me, in a roundabout, extremely clumsy way, is it possible that you are trying to work yourself up to asking *me* for a loan?' Luca enquired darkly.

'Where on earth did you get that idea? I wouldn't touch your money with a barge-pole!' Darcy told him in indignant rebuttal. 'But I *need* to go home to visit all the other financial institutions that might help. I have to find somewhere prepared to invest in the future of the Folly!'

Luca now surveyed her with thunderous disbelief. 'That's a joke...isn't it?'

'Of course it's not a joke!' Darcy grimaced at the idea. 'Why would I joke about something so serious?'

As Luca sat up in one sudden powerful movement the sheet fell away from his magnificent torso. Outrage blazed in his dark eyes, his lean features clenched taut. 'Are you out of your tiny mind?' he roared back at her, making her flinch in shock from such unexpected aggression. 'I'm an extremely wealthy man...and as *my wife,* you dare to tell me that you plan to drag the Raffacani name in the dirt by scuttling round the banking fraternity begging for a *loan?* Are you trying to make me a laughing-stock?'

Darcy gazed back at him in stunned immobility. That possibility hadn't occurred to her. Nor, at that instant, would the prospect have deprived her of sleep.

'Accidenti...' Luca swore rawly, thrusting back the sheet and springing lithely from the bed to appraise her

with diamond-hard eyes of condemnation. 'I now see that I have found a foe worthy of my mettle! You are one cunning little vixen! And if you dare put one foot inside the door of *any* financial institution, I will throw you out of my life the same day!'

A foe worthy of his mettle? An unearned compliment, Darcy conceded abstractedly, her attention wholly entrapped by the glorious spectacle of Luca striding naked up and down the bedroom with clenched fists of fury. Gosh, he was gorgeous. Glossy black hair, fabulous bone structure, eyes of wonderful vibrance. Broad shoulders, powerful chest, slim hips, long, long legs. The whole encased in wonderful golden skin, adorned with muscles and intriguing patches of black curly hair. All male.

She looked away, cheeks hot, shame enfolding her. She was so physically infatuated with the man she couldn't even concentrate on arguing with him. It was utterly disgusting.

'OK,' Luca snarled, further provoked by that seemingly stony and defiant silence. 'This is the deal. *I* will take over temporary responsibility for all bills relating to the Folly estate!'

Shaken by so unexpected not to mention so unwelcome a suggestion, Darcy turned aghast eyes on him. '*No way…*why would you want to do that?'

'I don't want to…but that arrangement would be preferable to placing an open chequebook into those hot, greedy little hands of yours! *Porca miseria!*' Luca shot her an intimidating glower of angry derision. 'The bedsheets are not even cooled before you start trying to rip me off again!'

He had a mind as complex as a maze, Darcy conceded, lost in wonder at such involved logic. He was so incredibly suspicious of her motives. All she had tried to do was stress how very urgently she needed to return home to sort out those problems with the estate, but Luca had flown off on another tangent entirely. He honestly believed that she had just tried to blackmail him. Admittedly, it should have dawned on her that he might be sensitive to the idea of his wife seeking to borrow money when he himself was filthy rich, but the reason it hadn't dawned on her was that she didn't feel remotely married to him.

'I don't want your rotten money...I've already told you that.'

'*Dio mio*...you will not seek to borrow anywhere else!' Luca asserted fiercely.

'That's not fair,' Darcy protested.

'Who ever said that I would be fair?'

'You did....' Darcy said in a small voice.

Luca froze at the reminder.

An electrifying silence stretched.

'Suddenly I have a great need for the calm, ordered atmosphere of my office!' Luca bit out with scantily controlled savagery. He strode into the bathroom and sent the door crashing shut.

So that's the temper...*wow!*

The door flew open again. 'Even in bed, don't you ever think of anything but that bloody house?' Luca flung, in final sizzling attack.

The door closed again.

Wow...Darcy thought again helplessly. He's so passionate when he drops the cool front. He slams doors like I do. He's a suspicious toad, so used to wheeling and dealing he can't take anything at face value. But he also thought she had put one over on him, she registered. The beginnings of a rueful smile tugged at the tense, unhappy line of her mouth.

What was the matter with her? she questioned as she slid out of bed. Why was she thinking such crazy thoughts? Why did she feel sort of disappointed that Luca was planning to leave her? Why wasn't she feeling more cheerful at that prospect? She stared down at the empty chair where she had draped her clothes the night before. With a frown, she finally noticed that her open suitcase had disappeared as well. She wandered into the dressing room and tugged open the unit doors to be greeted by male apparel on one side and on the other unfamiliar female garments.

Pyjama-clad, she knocked on the bathroom door. No answer. She opened it. He was in the shower.

'Where are my clothes, Luca?' she called.

The water went off. He rammed back the doors of the shower cubicle.

'I got rid of them,' Luca announced, raking an impatient hand through his dripping black hair and snatching up a towel.

'*Rid* of them?'

'Rather drastic, I know, but surely not a sacrifice?' Luca gave her an expectant look. 'Since you need lessons on how to dress. *Porca miseria!*' He grimaced, watched her face pale and telegraph hurt disbelief. 'That was tactless. But I just thought it would be easiest if I simply presented you with a new wardrobe. The clothes are in the dressing room. You won't even need to go shopping now.'

Darcy's eyes prickled with hot, scratchy tears. She was appalled. Never had she felt more mortified. This was a member of the opposite sex telling her she looked absolutely awful in her own clothes, telling her that *he,* a man, knew more than she did about how she should be dressing. 'How could you do that to me?' she gasped strickenly, and fled.

'It's a gift...a *surprise*...most women would be over the moon!' Luca fired back accusingly.

'Insensitive pig!' A sob tearing at her throat, Darcy threw herself back on the bed.

The mattress beside her gave with his weight.

'You have a beautiful face and an exquisite slender shape...but your clothes are all wrong,' Luca breathed huskily.

Darcy was humiliated and outraged by such smooth bare-faced lying. *She* knew better than anyone that she wasn't remotely beautiful! Flipping over in a blind fury, she raised her hand and dealt him a stinging slap.

'*Not*...most...women,' Luca muttered half under his breath, like somebody learning a very difficult lesson. With a slightly dazed air, he pressed long, elegant fingers to the flaming imprint of her fingers etched across one hard cheekbone and blinked.

Instantly, Darcy crumbled with guilt. 'I'm sorry...I shouldn't have done that,' she muttered brokenly. 'But you asked for it...you provoked me...go away!'

'I don't understand you—'

'I *hate* you...do you understand that?'

Darcy coiled away from him. She hurt so much inside she wanted to scream to let the pain out. She hugged herself tight. When Luca put a hand on her shoulder, she twisted violently away. When he reached for one of her hands, she shook him off.

'I actually liked you before I realised who you were!' she suddenly slung at him in disgust. 'I actually *trusted* you! Gosh, I've got great taste in men!'

'Haven't you already got what you wanted from me?'

Luca raked back at her in cold anger. 'I have promised you my financial backing for the duration of our marriage. Your problems are over.'

Darcy regarded him with bitter outrage. 'I'm not something you can buy with your money.'

Luca shot her an icy unimpressed appraisal. 'If you're not...what are you doing in my bed?'

There was no answer to that question. She couldn't even explain that to her own satisfaction, never mind his. And that he should throw her sexual surrender in her face made her curl up and die deep down inside.

She listened to him dressing, and she was so quiet she barely breathed.

Luca forced himself under her notice again by coming to a halt two feet from the bed. Clad in a lightweight beautifully cut pearl-grey suit, he looked absolutely stupendous, but icily remote and intimidating...like someone who ate debtors five to a plate for breakfast. But now she knew that his black hair felt like silk when she smoothed her fingers through it, that his smile was like hot sunlight after the winter and that even his voice trickled down her spine like honey and made her melt, she thought in growing agony.

'This is not how I thought things would be with us. I'm civilised...I'm very civilised,' Luca informed her with unfeeling cool. 'We're supposed to be skimming along the surface of things and having a great time in bed. So tell me who bought the Adorata ring and we'll get that little complication out of the way. Then there is hope that peace will break out.'

'I've already told you that I did not take that ring,' Darcy whispered shakily.

'And repetition of that claim has an excessively aggravating effect on my normally even temper,' Luca drawled. 'We're at an impasse.'

Darcy studied him, cold fascination holding her tight but pain piercing her like cutting shards of glass—that same pain bright and unconcealed in her eyes. 'I can't believe that you're the same guy I met three years ago...I can't believe that we laughed and danced and you were just so romantic and warm and—'

'Stupid?' Luca slotted in glacially, deep-set dark eyes hard as diamonds but a feverish flush accentuating the taut slant of his high cheekbones. 'Absurd? Ridiculous? After all, outside my own élite circle, I wasn't streetwise enough to protect myself from a calculating little predator like you!'

Darcy was shaken by that response, dredged from her own self-preoccupation to finally think about how *he* must have felt when he'd believed he had been robbed by the woman he had spent the previous evening romancing in high style, the woman he had brought into his home, the woman he had made love to over and over again until they'd fallen asleep in each other's arms. And for the very first time she recognised the raw, angry bitterness he had until now contrived to conceal from her. He was very proud, hugely self-assured. The discovery that the ring had gone could scarcely have failed to dent his male ego squarely where it hurt most. Heavens, what an idiot he must have felt, she registered, with a belated flood of understanding sympathy.

'Luca...' she breathed awkwardly. 'I—'

Luca vented a harsh laugh. 'You were clever, but not clever enough,' he murmured with a grim twist of his mouth. 'I *was* a very conservative guy. I was twenty-eight and I had never felt anything very much for any woman. But with you I felt something special—'

'S-something special?' Darcy broke in helplessly.

Derision glittered in the look he cast her intent face. 'You could have got so much more out of me than one night if you'd stayed around.'

'I don't think so,' Darcy whispered unevenly, desperately wanting to be convinced to the contrary. 'I was playing Cinderella that night.'

'Cinderella left her slipper behind...she didn't crack open the Prince's safe.'

'But it wasn't *real*...those hours we spent together,' she continued shakily, still praying that he would tell her different, and all because he had said those two words 'something special'. 'You said all the right lines; I succumbed... Yes, well, maybe I more than succumbed. I guess I was a bit more active than that, but you had no intention of ever seeing me again...' She shrugged a slight shoulder jerkily, no longer able to meet his shrewd gaze, and plucked abstractedly at the sheet. 'I mean...I mean, *obviously* you never had the smallest intention of showing up on the Ponte della Guerra the next day.'

'You remember that?' Luca said, with the kind of surprise that suggested he was amazed that she should have recalled something so trivial.

Darcy remembered standing on that bridge for hours, and she could have wept at the memory. If there ever had been a chance that he would turn up, there had been none whatsoever after he had realised that he'd been robbed that same night. So it was all *his* fault. All her agonies could be laid at his door. And why was she thinking like this anyway? He couldn't possibly find her beautiful. Though he had behaved as if he did that night. True, she had looked really well, but surely his standards of female beauty had to be considerably higher?

'I have bright red hair,' Darcy remarked stiltedly.

'I could hardly miss the fact, but it's not mere red, it's Titian, and I'd prefer to see a lot more of it,' Luca proffered after some hesitation.

'But you must've noticed that I have a…a snub nose?'

'Retroussé is the word…it's unusual; it adds distinction to your face… Why am I having this weird conversation with you?' Luca demanded freezingly. He strode to the door, glanced grudgingly back over one broad shoulder. 'I'll see you later.'

Emptied of his enervating presence, the room seemed dim and dull.

But Darcy lay where she was. Luca liked her nose; he liked her hair. What everybody else called skinny, he called 'slender'. Strange taste, but she knew she wouldn't have the heart to tell him that. So Luca, who resembled her every fantasy of physical male perfection, could get the hots for a skinny redhead with a snub nose. That fact was a revelation to Darcy. No wonder he was annoyed with himself, but all of a sudden she wasn't annoyed with him at all.

He hadn't made love to her just out of a desire for revenge. No, he wasn't as self-denying as that. Luca had really *wanted* to make love to her. There was nothing false about his desire for her. Everything he had said in bed must have been the truth…even the part about no other woman being able to satisfy him since?

Something special? Why did she feel so forgiving all of a sudden? Why was her brain encased in a fog of confusing emotion? That wretched, hateful ring that had been stolen, she reflected grimly. Take that problem out of their relationship and how might Luca behave then? But even if she contrived that miracle, exactly how would he react to the news that the toddler from hell was *his* daughter?

It was early days yet, Darcy decided ruefully. A lot could happen in six months. Telling him that he had fathered a child the night of the ball might presently seem like an impressive counter-punch, but she didn't want to use Zia like a weapon in a battle which nobody could win. In fact, she conceded then, unless their marriage became a real marriage, she was pretty sure she would never tell Luca that Zia was his child. What would be the point?

Right now she had much more important things to consider: the Folly estate and how she planned to save it in the short-term. Borrowing money appeared to be out of the question. And accepting Luca's financial help would choke her. So was she going to have to steel herself to sell some of the Folly's glorious Tudor furniture at auction? If she did so, the pieces could never, ever be replaced. But what alternative way did she have of raising the cash to keep her home afloat over the next six months?

An hour later, garbed in a figure-hugging sapphire-blue dress and horrendously high stilettos, Darcy bent down with extreme caution to lift Zia up into her arms, and *bang*—inspiration hit her the same second that her attention fell on the glossy gossip magazine the middle-aged nursemaid had left lying on a nearby chair. Didn't people pay good money for an insight into the lives of the rich and famous? Wasn't Luca both rich and famous? And didn't she have a second cousin who was a secretary on one of those publications?

What would an interview and a few photos of Gianluca Raffacani's bride be worth?

Darcy blinked, cringing from the concept but hardening herself against a sensitivity she could no longer afford. Luca had said that infidelity or desertion would be grounds for ending their marital agreement. But he hadn't mentioned publicity…

CHAPTER NINE

HAVING heard the commotion, Darcy rose from her seat in the drawing room and walked to the door that opened onto the vast reception hall. She froze there, taken aback by the scene being enacted before her startled eyes.

On his return home, Luca was being engulfed by his sister's dogs. It was like a rugby scrum. But astonishingly informative. Aristide and Zou Zou adored him, Darcy registered in surprise. And there he was, fondling shaggy ears and valiantly bearing up to the exuberant welcome he was receiving. Failing to notice her, Luca then took the stairs two at a time, a gift-wrapped package clutched in one hand.

Since Darcy was a very slow mover in the unfamiliar high heels, she didn't catch up with him. And she was perplexed when he strode past their bedroom to turn up the flight of stairs that led to the nursery suite. She came to a halt in the doorway of the playroom. By the time she got there, Zia had already ripped the paper off a box which she was now regarding with enraptured bliss.

'Dolly!' she gasped, squeezing the box so tight in her excitement that it crunched. 'Pretty dolly!'

Peer pressure and television had a lot to answer for, Darcy decided uncomfortably. All the other little girls Zia knew at the playgroup already had that doll, but Darcy had ignored all pleas to make a similar purchase. Why? Because that particular doll had always reminded her of Maxie. Now that seemed so inadequate an excuse when she saw Zia reacting like a deprived child suddenly shot into seventh heaven.

'Shall I take her out of the box?' Luca enquired helpfully.

While Zia pondered whether or not she could bear to part with her gift even briefly, Darcy studied Luca's hard, classic profile, which showed to even better advantage when he was smiling. She was frankly bewildered by what she was seeing.

Zia extended the box. Hunkering down on a level with the toddler, Luca removed the packaging and finally freed the soft-bodied version of the doll. '*See,* Mummy!' her daughter carolled with pride.

As Luca's well-shaped dark head whipped round to finally note Darcy's silent presence, Darcy reddened with awful self-consciousness beneath his lengthy appraisal. While unnecessarily engaged in smoothing down the skirt of her dress with damp palms, she strove to act unconcerned and evaded his scrutiny. 'Did you say thank you, Zia?'

'Kiss?' Zia proffered instantly, moving forward to land a big splashy kiss on Luca's cheek and then give him an enthusiastic hug.

'Isn't cupboard love great?' Luca mocked his own calculation with an amused smile and vaulted upright again. 'We got off on the wrong foot yesterday. A peace offering was a necessity.'

'It was a kind thought,' Darcy conceded stiltedly.

'I can be very kind, *bella mia,*' Luca countered huskily.

Darcy collided with his scorching dark stare. And quite without knowing *how* she knew it, she knew he was thinking about sex. That sixth sense awareness spooked her and plunged her into confusion.

As her skin heated her breath caught in her throat, and her heart gave a violent lurch. She couldn't look away from those stunning dark golden eyes. The impact of that look was staggering. She felt dizzy, unsteady on her feet and far, far too hot. The tip of her tongue skimmed along her dry lower lip in a nervous motion. Luca's intent scrutiny homed in on the soft fullness of her mouth. Something drew tight and twisted, low in her stomach, a sexual response so powerful it terrified her. Mercifully, Zia broke the connection by holding out her new doll for her mother's admiration.

'You haven't much time to say goodnight to her. My sister is joining us for dinner,' Luca advanced as he strode out through the door. 'I need a shower and a change of clothes.'

'Night-night, Luca!' Zia called cheerfully.

Luca paused and glanced back with a raised ebony brow. 'In the right mood, she's really quite sweet, isn't she?' His eyes became shadowed and his wide mouth compressed. 'I had nothing to do with Ilaria when she was that age…I was at boarding school. She was only seven when I went to university. I lived to regret not having a closer bond with her.'

Twenty minutes later, having tucked Zia into bed and read her a story, Darcy walked into their bedroom. Only his jacket and tie removed, Luca was in the act of putting down his mobile phone.

'You look fantastic in that dress…you know why?' A wolfish grin slashed his lean, strong face. 'It *fits*. It isn't two sizes too large or a foot too long!'

'Margo always helped me to choose my clothes,' Darcy confided. 'She said that I had to dress to hide my deficiencies.'

'You have none. You're in perfect proportion for your size.'

But Darcy's diminutive curves and lack of height *had* been deficiencies to a stepmother who was both tall and lushly female in shape. Margo had loathed red hair as well, insisting that Darcy could only wear dull colours. Growing up with Margo's constant criticism, and Nina's pitying superiority, Darcy had learned only to measure her looks against theirs. That unwise comparison had wrecked her confidence in her own appearance.

But now she gazed back at Luca and could not fail to recognise his sincerity. He'd told her she looked fantastic. And sensual appreciation radiated from the lingering appraisal in those intent dark eyes. If she didn't yet quite credit that she *could* look fantastic, she certainly realised with a surge of gratified wonder that Luca genuinely *believed* she did.

Her softened gaze ran with abstracted admiration over his long, lean, powerful physique. She was shaken to note the earthy and defiantly male thrust of arousal that the close fit of his well-cut trousers couldn't conceal. She reddened hotly, but she also felt empowered and outrageously feminine.

'Luca...' she whispered shakily.

Later, she couldn't recall who had reached out first. She remembered the way his gaze narrowed, the blaze of golden intent between black spiky lashes, and then suddenly she was crushed in his arms and clinging to him to stay upright. He parted her lips to invade her tender mouth with his thrusting tongue, dipping, twirling, tasting her with fierce, impatient need. He cut right through her every defence with that blunt, honest admission of desire. She trembled violently beneath that devouring kiss. He made her feel possessed, dominated, and utterly weak with hunger.

'I should never have left you...I've been in a filthy temper all day,' Luca confided raggedly, slumberous eyes scanning her lovely face with very male satisfaction, a febrile flush on his taut cheekbones. 'I want you *so* much...'

'Yes...' Darcy acknowledged a truth too obvious to be denied. She felt the same. Her heart was pounding, her whole body throbbing with intense arousal. It was like being in pain; it made her crave him like a drug.

'I can't wait until later...I'm in agony,' Luca gritted roughly.

Hard fingers splayed across her spine to press her into direct contact with his hard thighs. He shuddered against her with a stifled groan, kissing her temples, the top of her head, running his fingers through her hair and then bringing her mouth back hungrily under his again. She couldn't get close enough to him. He slid one hand beneath her skirt, skimming up a slender thigh to the very heart of her. The damp swollen heat of her beneath the thin barrier of her panties betrayed her response. Excitement made her squirm and moan against that skilled touch.

'Luca...*please,*' she gasped urgently.

He backed her down on the side of the bed. He leant over her, hands braced on either side of her head, and plunged deep into her mouth again, eliciting a low cry of surrender from her. Tugging down the zip on her dress, he removed it, skimming off her remaining garments with deft, impatient hands. He stilled for a second, reverent eyes scanning the pouting curves of her breasts and the silky dark red hair at the apex of her slender thighs.

'You are gorgeous, *bella mia*...how can you ever have doubted that?' Luca demanded as he stood over her, peeling off his own clothing at speed.

He came down to her, gloriously aroused. Cupping her breasts, he caressed the sensitive buds with his lips and his tongue, and then he kissed a slow tantalising trail down over the flexing muscles of her stomach, pushing her quivering thighs apart to conduct a more intimate exploration. She was shocked, but too tormented by her own aching need for his caresses to stop him. He controlled her utterly, pushed her to such a pitch of writhing, desperate excitement she was helpless.

He rose over her again, his breathing fractured. He dipped his tongue between her reddened lips in a sexy flick as he tipped back her thighs with almost clumsy hands, his own excitement palpable. Burnished golden eyes assailed hers. He hesitated at the crucial moment when she was braced for the hot, hard invasion of his body into hers.

'Luca!'

'*Dio mio*...I don't know myself like this!' he groaned ruefully. 'I feel wild...but I don't want to hurt you.'

'You won't...'

'You're so much smaller than I am.'

'I like it when you're wild,' she whispered feverishly.

Above her, Luca closed his eyes and slammed into her hard, releasing such a flood of electrifying sensation that Darcy moaned his name like a benediction. He withdrew and entered her again, with a raw, forceful sense of timing that was soul-shatteringly effective. Her entire being was centred on the explosive pleasure building inside her. Heart pounding in concert with his, she cried out in ecstasy as he drove her over the edge. Then she just collapsed, totally drained.

They lay together in a sweaty huddle. Luca released her from his weight but retained a possessive hold on her, pressing his mouth softly to her throat, lingering to lick the salt from her skin and smooth a soothing hand down over her slender back.

'That was unbelievable...that was paradise, *cara mia*,' Luca sighed in a tone of wondering satisfaction. 'I have never felt this good.'

'What time is your sister coming?' Darcy mumbled.

Luca tensed, relocated the wrist with a watch, and suddenly wrenched himself free. '*Porca miseria*...Ilaria will be here at any moment!'

Feeling totally brainless and lethargic, Darcy watched him spring off the bed.

'Darcy...' he gritted then.

'What?' she whispered with a silly smile, surveying him with a kind of bursting feeling inside her heart.

'You can share my shower.' Luca scooped her up into his powerful arms and strode into the bathroom with her.

'I'll never get my hair dry!' But still she watched him, trying desperately hard to work out why she felt so ecstatically happy.

'Your eyes are glowing like neon lights.' Studying her with a curiously softened look in his dark, deep-set gaze, Luca hooked her arms round his strong brown throat and kissed her again, holding her plastered to every inch of him beneath the gushing cascade of water. He raised his head again, a slight frown drawing his black brows together. 'I assume you're on the pill...'

'Nope.'

'I didn't use anything to protect you,' Luca told her

slowly as he lowered her back down to the floor of the cubicle. '*Santo cielo*...how could I be that careless?'

Darcy had stiffened. How could *she* be that careless *again?* Yet another time. The first occasion had resulted in Zia's conception. She had foolishly assumed that the course of contraceptive pills she had stopped taking the day she failed to marry Richard would still prevent a pregnancy. Naturally it hadn't. Her own ignorance had been her downfall.

'Very little risk,' she muttered awkwardly, avoiding his searching scrutiny.

'You would know that better than I.'

He was wrong there, Darcy conceded ruefully. Her monthly cycles caused her so little inconvenience that she never bothered to keep a note of dates. She hadn't a clue what part of her cycle she was in, but she had almost supernatural faith in the power of Luca's fertility. Suppose she did become pregnant again... Oddly enough, the prospect failed to rouse the slightest sense of alarm. Indeed, as Darcy looked up at Luca, mentally miles away while he washed her, she was picturing a small boyish version of those same features that distinguished Zia. A buoyant warm sensation instantly blossomed inside her. Only when she appreciated how she was reacting to that prospect of pregnancy was she shocked by herself.

'What's wrong?' Luca prompted.

In her haste to escape those frighteningly astute eyes, Darcy lurched out of the shower. Grabbing up a towel, she took refuge in the dressing room to dry herself. I can't be in love with him. I can't be, she told herself sickly. It was a kind of immature infatuation and it had its sad roots in the past. Karen had been right about her: she *had* spent too much time alone. Building romantic castles in the air around Luca Raffacani would be a very stupid move, and, having done it once and learnt her mistake, she was convinced she was too sensible to be so foolish again.

By one of those strange tricks of fate Luca found her attractive, and they were sexually compatible, but she would have to be an idiot to imagine that Luca might now develop some form of emotional attachment to her. He had said it himself only this morning, hadn't he? He had talked with outrageous unapologetic cool about how they should be 'skimming along the surface of things and having a great time in bed' rather than arguing. Suddenly Darcy was very glad she had slapped him so hard…

'Tell me about your sister,' Darcy invited Luca as they left the bedroom. Having donned an elegant black dress and fresh lingerie at speed, she had attempted to coax her damp curls into some semblance of a style, but she was out of breath and her cheeks were still pink with effort. 'It'll look strange if I know nothing about her.'

Luca, as sleek and cool and elegant as a male who had spent a leisurely hour showering, shaving and donning his superb dinner jacket and narrow black trousers, gave her a wry look. 'My parents died in a plane crash when Ilaria was eight. My aunt became her legal guardian. I was only nineteen. Emilia was a childless widow, eager to mother my sister, but she was very possessive. She made it difficult for me to maintain regular contact with Ilaria.'

'That was selfish of her.'

'She also refused to allow me to share in Ilaria's upbringing when I was in a position to offer her a more settled home life. And she was a very liberal guardian.

She spoilt Ilaria rotten. When my sister turned into a difficult teenager, Emilia saw her behaviour as rank ingratitude. Being a substitute mother had become a burden. She demanded that I take responsibility for Ilaria and within the same month she moved to New York.'

'Oh, dear...' Darcy grimaced.

'Ilaria was devastated by that rejection and she furiously resented me. We had some troubled times,' Luca conceded with a rueful shrug. 'She's twenty now, but I have little contact with her. As soon as she reached eighteen, she demanded an apartment of her own.'

'I'm sorry.' Seeing his dissatisfaction with this detached state of affairs, Darcy rested her hand on his sleeve in a sympathetic gesture. 'I always think the worst wounds are inflicted within the family circle. We're all much more vulnerable where our own flesh and blood is concerned.'

'You're thinking of your father?'

'It's hard not to. I spent my whole life wanting to be *somebody* in his eyes, struggling to win his respect,' Darcy admitted gruffly.

'Everyone's like that with parents.'

Tensing as she noticed his attention dropping to the hand still curved to his arm, she hurriedly removed it, thinking then with pain that the kind of physical closeness which he was at ease with *in* bed seemed a complete no-no *out* of bed.

'But I was reaching for something I could never have. I don't think my father ever looked at me without resenting the fact that I wasn't the son he wanted...but all that made me do was try harder,' she confided ruefully.

Luca reached for her hand and curled lean fingers tautly round hers. 'Was that why you took the Adorata?'

he demanded in a roughened undertone, shrewd dark eyes drawn to her startled face. 'Darcy impressively riding to the rescue of the family fortunes with a pretend lucky find?'

Caught unprepared, Darcy lost every scrap of colour in her cheeks, her green eyes darkening with hurt at that absurd suspicion. Once again she had forgotten what lay between them, and with too great a candour she had exposed herself to attack.

'You must've lied to your father. He may have been domineering and aggressive, but he had the reputation of being an honest, upright man. Did you tell him that you had found it in some dusty antique shop where you had bought it for a song?' Luca pressed with remorseless persistence.

A door opened off the ball. Both Darcy and Luca whipped round. A slim, stunning girl with shoulder-length dark hair and a sullen expression subjected them to a stony appraisal.

'I have no intention of wasting an entire evening waiting for you to show up at your own dinner table, Luca,' Ilaria said with brittle sarcasm. 'Just why did you bother to invite me?'

'I hoped that you might want to meet Darcy. I'm sorry that we've kept you waiting,' Luca murmured levelly.

Ilaria vented a thin laugh. 'Why didn't you give me the opportunity to meet her *before* you got married?'

'I left several messages on your answering machine. You never call back,' Luca countered calmly.

The combination of aggression and hurt emanating from Ilaria was powerful. But then her big brother had married a total stranger. In those circumstances, her hostility was natural, Darcy conceded. Tugging free of

Luca, she walked over to his sister, a rueful look of appeal in her eyes. 'You have every right to be furious. And I don't know how to explain why—'

'We got married in a hurry,' Luca slotted in with finality as he thrust open the door of the dining room. Atmospheric pools of candlelight illuminated the beautifully set table awaiting them. 'There's not much else to say.'

'I can't imagine you doing anything in a hurry without good reason, Luca,' Ilaria gibed. 'Have you got her pregnant?'

Darcy froze, and then forced herself down into the seat Luca had spun out for her occupation. While Luca shot a low-pitched sentence of icy Italian at his sister, Darcy drowned in guilty pink colour and glanced at neither combatant. The suggestion had been chosen to insult, but it was more apt than either of her companions could know. However, she recognised the position Luca had put himself in, and she wanted to help minimise the damage to his already strained relationship with his sister.

'We had a quiet wedding because my father died recently.' Darcy spoke up abruptly. 'I have to admit that we were rather impulsive—'

'Impulsive? *Luca?*' Ilaria derided, unimpressed. 'Who do you think you're kidding? He never makes a single move that he hasn't planned down to the last detail!'

'In this case, he did,' Darcy persisted quietly. 'But it was selfish of us to just rush off and get married without letting our families share in the event.'

'Your family wasn't there *either?*' The younger woman looked astonished, but was visibly soothed by the admission. 'So where did you meet...and when?'

'That's a long story—' Luca began.

Darcy rushed to interrupt him. Telling the truth, or as much of it as was reasonable, would be wisest in the circumstances, rather than that silly story of her having reversed into his car in London and shouted at him. This *was* his sister they were dealing with, and Ilaria had to know that Luca would have wiped the pavement with any female that stupid.

'I met your brother almost three years ago at a masked ball here,' Darcy admitted, an anxious smile on her lips.

The effect of that simple statement stunned Darcy. To her left, Luca released his breath in a stark hiss and shot her a look of outright exasperation. To her right, Ilaria's face locked tight. She gaped at Darcy in the most peculiar way, her mouth a shocked and rounded circle from which no sound emitted, her olive skin draining to a sick pallor which made her horrified dark eyes look huge.

'I seem to have—'

'Put a giant foot in your mouth,' Luca completed grimly.

And then everything went crazy. Just as Darcy realised with a sinking heart that naturally his sister had to be aware of the theft that had taken place that night, and that she had just foolishly exposed Luca and herself to the need for an explanation that would be wellnigh impossible to make, Ilaria flew upright. The focus of her stricken attention was surprisingly not Darcy, but her brother.

As Ilaria began ranting hysterically at Luca in Italian she backed away from the table. A look of astonished incomprehension on his taut features, Luca rose upright and strode towards his sister. '*Cosa c'e che non va...* what's wrong?' he demanded urgently, anxiously.

Crying now in earnest, Ilaria clumsily evaded her brother's attempt to place comforting hands on her shoulders. Tearing herself away, she gasped out something in her own language and fled.

Instead of following her, Luca froze there as if his sister had struck him. He raised his lean hands, spread them slightly in an odd, inarticulate movement, and then slowly dropped them again.

Darcy hurried over to his side. 'What's the matter with her?'

His clenched profile starkly delineated against the flickering pools of shadow and light, Luca drew in a deep, shuddering breath. He turned a strange, unfocused look on Darcy. 'She said... she *said...*' he began unevenly.

'She said... *what?*' Darcy prompted impatiently, listening to Ilaria having a rousing bout of hysterics in the hall.

'Ilaria said *she* stole the Adorata ring,' Luca finally got out, and he shook his glossy dark head in so much shock and lingering disbelief he had the aspect of a very large statue teetering dangerously on its base.

'Oh... *oh, dear,*' Darcy muttered, so shaken by that shattering revelation that she couldn't for the life of her manage to come up with anything more appropriate.

Ilaria was sobbing herself hoarse in the centre of the hall. Darcy tried to put her arms round the girl and got pushed away. Ilaria shot an accusing, gulping stream of Italian at her.

'I'm sorry, but I was absolutely lousy at languages at school.' Darcy curved a determined hand round the girl's elbow and urged her into the drawing room. 'I know you're very upset…but try hard to calm down just a *bit*,' she pleaded.

'How can I? Luca will never forgive me!' Ilaria wailed, and she flung herself face-down on a sofa to sob again.

Sitting down beside her, Darcy let her cry for a while. But as soon as Luca entered the room she got up and said awkwardly, 'Look…I'll leave you two alone—'

'No!' Ilaria suddenly reached out to grab at Darcy's hand. 'You stay…'

'Yes…because if you don't, Darcy,' Luca muttered in the strangest tone of eerie detachment from his sister's distress, 'I may just kill her.'

'You're nearly as bad as she is!' Darcy condemned roundly as Ilaria went off into another bout of tormented sobbing. 'You won't get any sense out of her talking like that.'

'I know very well how to get sense out of her!'

Luca rapped out a command in staccato Italian which sounded very much like a version of pull-yourself-together-or-*else*.

'I'm sorry…I'm really s-sorry!' Ilaria gulped brokenly then. 'I panicked when I realised that Darcy was the woman you met that night… Because you had *married* her I thought you had guessed…and that you had brought me over here to confront me with what I did!'

'Your brother wouldn't behave like that,' Darcy said quietly.

Luca shot her a curious, almost pained look, and then turned his attention back to his sister. 'How did you do it?'

'You shouldn't have been at the apartment at all that evening because it was the night of the ball.' Sitting bolt-upright now on the sofa, clutching the tissue that

Darcy had fetched for her use, Ilaria began to shred it with restive, trembling hands. 'I needed money and you'd cut off my allowance...refused to let me even see Pietro...I was so *angry* with you! I was going to run away with him, but we needed money to do that—'

'You were seventeen,' Luca cut in harshly. 'I did what I had to do to protect you from yourself. If you hadn't been an heiress that sleazy louse wouldn't have given you a second glance!'

'Let her tell her story,' Darcy murmured, watching Ilaria cringe at that blunt assessment.

'I h-had a key to the apartment. I knew all the security codes. One day when I had lunch there with you, you went into the safe and I watched you do it from the hall,' Ilaria mumbled shamefacedly. 'I thought there would be cash in the safe...'

'Your timing was unfortunate.'

'All there was...was the Adorata,' Ilaria continued shakily. 'I was furious, so I took it. I told myself I was entitled to it if I needed it, but when I took the Adorata to Pietro, he...he laughed in my face! He said he wasn't fool enough to try and sell a famous piece of stolen goods. He said he would have had Interpol chasing him across Europe in pursuit of it...so I planned to put the ring back the next morning.'

'That was a timely change of heart,' Darcy put in encouragingly, although one look at Luca's icily clenched and remote profile reduced her to silence again.

'But you see, you went back to the apartment that night and stayed there...you found the safe open and the Adorata gone...I was too *late!*' Ilaria wailed.

'What did you do with the ring?'

'It's safe,' his sister hastened to assure him. 'It's in my safety deposit box with Mamma's jewellery.'

Momentarily, Luca closed his eyes at that news. *'Porca miseria...'* he ground out unsteadily. 'All this time...'

'If you'd called in the police I would have had to tell you I had it,' his sister muttered, almost accusingly. 'But when I realised you believed that the woman you'd left the ball with had taken it...' She shot a severely embarrassed glance at Darcy, belatedly recalling that that woman and her brother's wife were now one and the same. 'I mean—'

'Me... it's all right,' Darcy cut in, but her cheeks were burning.

'You see...' Ilaria hesitated. 'You weren't like a real person to me, and it didn't seem to matter who Luca blamed as long as he didn't suspect me.'

Darcy studied the exquisite Aubusson carpet fixedly, mortification overpowering her. She could well imagine how low an opinion Ilaria must have had of her at seventeen: some tramp who had dived into bed with her brother the same night she had first met him.

Disconcertingly, Luca vented a flat, humourless laugh. 'Aren't you fortunate that Darcy disappeared into thin air?'

Darcy was more than willing to disappear into thin air all over again. She turned towards the door. 'I think you need to talk without a stranger around,' she said with a rather tremulous smile.

Distinctly shaky after the strain of the scene she had undergone, Darcy shook her head apologetically at Luca's manservant, who was now hovering uncomfortably in the dining room doorway, obviously wondering what was happening and whether or not any of them intended to sit down and eat dinner like civilised people. She had enjoyed a substantial lunch earlier in the day and now she felt pretty queasy.

Poor Luca. Poor Ilaria. Such a shaming secret must have been horrible for the girl to live with for so long. A moment's reckless bitter rebellion over the head of some boy she had clearly been hopelessly infatuated with. As Ilaria matured that secret would have weighed ever more heavily on her conscience, probably causing her to assume a defensive attitude to cover her unease in Luca's presence.

Guilt did that—it ate away at you. Little wonder that Ilaria had avoided Luca's company. She had been too afraid to face up to what she had done and confess. And the instant Ilaria had appreciated that her brother's wife was also the woman Luca had once believed to be a thief, she had jumped to the panic-stricken conclusion that Luca somehow knew that *she* was the culprit. After all, how could Ilaria ever have guessed that her lordly big brother might have married a woman he *still* believed to be a thief out of a powerful need to punish her?

And now Luca would finally get that wretched ring back. Could he really believe that any inanimate object, no matter how valuable, precious and rare, was worth so much grief? How did he feel now that he knew he had misjudged her? Gutted, Darcy decided without hesitation. He had looked absolutely gutted when comprehension rolled over him like a drowning tidal wave. His *own* sister.

Darcy heaved a sigh. Maybe, as Luca had said himself, peace would now break out. Naturally he would have to apologise...in fact a bit of crawling wouldn't come amiss, Darcy thought, beginning to feel rather surprisingly upbeat. Having checked on Zia, she wandered downstairs again and into the dining room.

She sat down at the table, appetite restored, and tucked into her elaborate starter. No, she didn't want Luca to crawl. He was having a tough enough time with Ilaria and his spectacular own goal of misjudgement. She had to be fair. The evidence had been very much stacked against her. And how could he ever have suspected his seventeen-year-old sister of pulling off such a feat?

She was halfway through the main course when Luca appeared. '*Santo cielo*...how can you eat at a time like this?' he breathed in a charged tone of incredulity.

'I felt hungry...sorry to be so prosaic,' Darcy muttered, wondering where that rather melodramatic opening was about to take him. 'How's Ilaria?'

'I persuaded her to stay the night. I'm sorry about that...'

'About what?' Conscious that the sight of the cutlery still in her grasp seemed to be an offence of no mean order in his eyes, she abandoned her meal. In fact, in the mix of shadow and dim light in which Luca stood poised, the dark, sombre planes of his unusually pale features lent him an almost lost, lonely sort of aspect.

'About what?' Luca echoed, frowning as if he was struggling to get a grip on himself. 'Aren't you furious with Ilaria?'

'Gosh, no...she was terribly distressed. She's rather young for her age—very...well, emotional,' Darcy selected, striving to be tactful for once in her life.

'Being emotional is not catching...is it? You must be outraged with me,' Luca breathed starkly.

'Well, yes, I was when all this nonsense started—'

'*Nonsense?*' Luca cut in with ragged stress.

Darcy rose to her feet, wishing she could just run over and put her arms round him, spring him out of this strange and unfamiliar mood he was in, but he looked so incredibly remote now. As if he had lost everything he possessed. But he would strangle the first person who had the bad taste to either mention it or show a single hint of pity or understanding.

'I *always* knew I didn't take the wretched thing,' she pointed out gently. 'I'm awfully glad it's all cleared up now. And I understand why you were so convinced I was the thief…after all, you didn't *know* me, did you?'

Luca flinched as if she had punched him in the stomach. He spun his dark head away. 'No…I didn't,' he framed almost hoarsely.

She watched him swallow convulsively.

Feeling utterly helpless, craving the confidence to bridge the frightening gap she could feel opening up between them, Darcy was gripped by a powerful wave of frustration. He was so at a loss; she wanted to hug him the way she hugged Zia when she fell over and hurt herself. But she thought she would crack their tenuous relationship right down the middle if she made such an approach. He was too proud.

'We'll talk later,' Luca imparted with what sounded like a really dogged effort to sound his usual collected self. 'You need to be alone for a while.'

He needed to be alone for a while, Darcy interpreted without difficulty. He's going to walk out on me…what did I do wrong? a voice screamed inside her bemused head. Here she was, being as fair, honest and reasonable as she knew how to be, and the wretched man was withdrawing more from her with every second.

'Tell me…would you have preferred a screaming row?'

'We have nothing to row about any more,' Luca countered, without a shade of his usual irony. In fact he sounded as if his only enjoyment in life had been wrenched from him by the cruellest of fates.

As the clock on the mantelpiece struck midnight, Darcy rose with a sigh. And that was when she heard the sound of footsteps in the hall. As the drawing room door opened, she tensed. For a split second Luca stilled at the sight of her, veiled eyes astutely reading the anxious, assessing look in hers.

'Would you like a drink?' he murmured quietly as he thrust the door closed.

'A brandy…' She watched him stride over to the ornate oriental drinks cabinet. Lithe, dark, strikingly good-looking, every movement fluid as poetry. He didn't look gutted any more—but then she hadn't expected him to. Luca was tough, a survivor, and survivors knew how to roll with the punches.

But *she* must have been born under an unlucky star. What savage fate had decreed that she should be involved up to her throat in the two biggest mistakes Luca had ever made? It was so cruel. He would judge himself harshly and he would never think of her without guilty unease again. She was like an albatross in his life, always a portent of doom. She hoved in to his radius and things went badly wrong. If he was like every other man she had ever known, he would very soon find the very sight of her an objectionable reminder of his own lowest moments.

Luca handed her the balloon glass of brandy, his lean, strong face sombre. 'I have come to some conclusions.'

Menaced by both expression and announcement, Darcy downed the brandy in one long, desperate gulp.

'You must have found the last few days very traumatic,' Luca breathed heavily, fabulous bone structure rigid. 'In retrospect, it is impossible to justify anything that I have done. I can make no excuse for myself; I can only admit that from the instant I found you gone from the apartment, the safe open, the Adorata gone, I nourished an obsessive need to run you to ground and even what I saw as the score between us—'

Predictably, Darcy cut to the heart of the matter. 'You thought I'd made a fool of you.'

'Yes…and that was a new experience for me. I must confess that there was nothing I was not prepared to do to achieve my objective,' Luca admitted with a grim edge to his dark, deep voice. 'If Ilaria hadn't confessed tonight, I'd still have believed you guilty, and since it would not have been possible for you to satisfy my demand that you help me to regain the Adorata…I would, ultimately, have dispossessed you of Fielding's Folly.'

Darcy was ashen pale now. 'No…you wouldn't have done that.'

Slowly, Luca shook his dark head, stunning dark eyes resting full on her disbelieving face. 'Darcy, you're a much nicer person than I have ever been…I *would* have done it. When I married you, I already held the future of the Folly in the palm of my hand.'

'What do you m-mean?' she stammered, moisture beading her short upper lip as she stared back at him.

From the inside pocket of his beautifully tailored dinner jacket, Luca withdrew a folded document. 'I bought the company which gave your father the mortgage on the Folly. This is the agreement. You're in default of the terms of that agreement now. I could have called in the loan and forced you out at any time over the next six months,' he spelt out very quietly. 'It would've been as easy as taking candy from a baby.'

Her shattered eyes huge dark smudges against her pallor, Darcy gazed back at him transfixed. 'You...you *bought* the company?' she gasped sickly.

As he absorbed the full extent of her horror at such calculated foreplanning, Luca seemed to pale too. 'I had to tell you. I had to be completely honest with you. You have the right to know it all now.'

Her lips bloodless, Darcy mumbled strickenly, 'I don't think I wanted to know that...how could anybody sink *that* low?'

'I wish I could say that I don't know what got into me...but I *do* know,' Luca murmured with bleak, dark eyes. 'My ego could not live with what I believed you had done to me that night. I had the power to take a terrible revenge and that was my intention when I replied to your advertisement.'

Darcy nodded like a little wooden marionette, too appalled to do anything but gaze back at him as if he had turned into a monster before her very eyes.

A faint sheen now glossed Luca's golden skin. 'Not a very pretty objective...when I think back to that now, I am very much ashamed. You have made such a valiant struggle to survive against all the odds.'

Darcy shook her pounding head with a little jerk. She felt as if she was dying inside, and now she knew what was really the matter with her—could no longer avoid knowing. She had fallen in love with him. How else could he be hurting her so much? She turned almost clumsily away from him, a mess of raw, agonised nerve-endings, and sank down onto a sofa. 'I *slept* with you,' she muttered, suddenly stricken.

'I definitely don't think we should touch on that issue

right now,' Luca contended without hesitation. 'I'm sinking faster than a rock in a swamp as it is. What I want to do now...what I *need* to do...is make amends to you in every way possible.'

'I hate you...' And she did. She hated him because he didn't love her, because he had made a fool of her, because she had made a fool of herself and, last but not least, because she could not bear the thought of having to struggle to get over him again.

'I can live with that.'

'I want to go home.'

'Of course. The jet is at your disposal. When were you thinking of leaving?'

'Now—'

'It wouldn't be a good idea to get Zia out of bed.' Since Darcy was still staring numbly at the rug beneath her feet, Luca hunkered down in front of her. 'Shout at me...hit me if it makes you feel better. I don't know what to do when you're quiet!' he murmured fiercely.

'I'll leave first thing in the morning,' Darcy swore.

Luca reached for her tightly coiled hands. 'When do you want me to fly over?'

Darcy focused on him for the first time in several minutes but said nothing, her incredulity unfeigned.

Brilliant dark eyes glittered. 'You're stuck with me for the next six months,' Luca reminded her gently. 'Surely you hadn't forgotten that...had you?'

Darcy *had*. Her brain felt as if it was spinning in tortured circles.

Luca contrived to ease up each small coiled finger during the interim, and gain a hold on both of her hands. 'I promise to fulfil our agreement. No matter what happens, I will not let you down.'

Darcy snatched her hands back in a raw motion of repudiation. 'I couldn't *stand* it!'

'I have tried to express my remorse—'

'I don't think you have it in you to *feel* remorse!' Darcy condemned abruptly, her oval face flushing with a return of healthier colour as she got her teeth into that conviction. 'You're sneaky, devious…and I can't abide sneakiness or dishonesty. The only two things in life that excite you are sex and money.'

A dark rise of blood had delineated the savagely taut slant of his cheekbones. 'Once there was a third thing that excited me, far more than either of those.'

'What?' she gibed with a jagged laugh as she sprang upright, no longer able to stand being so close to him, terrified her fevered emotions would betray her. 'The prospect of taking revenge? Gosh, I should be flattered! Was that stupid bloody ring really worth this much effort?'

Luca vaulted back to his full commanding height, but with something less than his habitual grace. 'No…' It was very quiet.

'And do you want the biggest laugh of all?' Darcy slung shakily at him, green eyes huge with pain, her slender body trembling with the force of her feelings. 'I fell like a ton of bricks for you that night, only I didn't realise until it was too late. I even tried to find my way back to your apartment but I couldn't! What a lucky miss! You'd have had me arrested for theft before I'd cleared the front door!'

Luca looked poleaxed, as well he might have done. Darcy hadn't meant to spill out such a private painful truth, but she flung her head back with defiant pride, meeting the sheer shock in his spectacular dark eyes without flinching.

'You went to the Ponte della Guerra,' he breathed with ragged abruptness, catching her by surprise. 'No...please tell me you *didn't!*'

'While you were ferreting like a great stupid prat round your empty safe!' Taking a bold stance, Darcy stalked to the door. 'Don't you dare show your face at the Folly for a few weeks!'

'As we are supposed to be a newly married couple that might arouse suspicion,' Luca pointed out flatly.

'Luca...you're not seeing the whole picture here!' Darcy informed him with vigour. 'A honeymoon that lasts less than three days has obviously been a wash-out! An absentee workaholic husband completes the right image for a marriage destined to fail. And when you do come to visit, and everyone sees how absolutely useless you are at being my strong right arm, nobody's going to be one bit surprised when I dump you six months down the line!'

CHAPTER TEN

DARCY closed the glossy magazine with a barely re-
strained shudder, undyingly grateful that Luca would
never read the interview she had given. At her request,
the magazine had faxed the questions to her. After carefully studying some old magazines to see how other
women had talked in similar interviews, Darcy had responded to those questions with a cringe-making
amount of slush and gush.

Anyway, Luca was in Italy, and men *didn't* read
those sort of publications, did they? The sizeable cheque
she had earned for that tissue of lies about her blissfully
happy marriage and her even more wonderful new husband was more than sufficient compensation for a little
embarrassment. With the proceeds she would be able to
bring the mortgage repayments up to date, settle some
other outstanding bills and put the Land Rover in for a
service.

It had been two weeks and three days since she had
seen Luca. Every day, every hour had crawled. She felt
haunted by Luca. Having him around to shout at or even
ignore would have been infinitely more bearable. She
ached for him. And she was angry and ashamed that
she could feel such an overpowering need and hunger
for a male who had entered her life only to harm her.

Impervious to all hints, and beautifully well-
mannered to the last, Luca had seen them off at the
airport. Zia had actually burst into tears when she realised that he wasn't coming with them. Lifting the little

girl for a farewell hug, Luca had looked strangely self-satisfied. But seeing those two dark heads so close together had had a very different effect on Darcy.

The physical resemblance between father and daughter was startling. The Raffacani straight nose and level brows, the black hair and dark eyes...Darcy was now confronting unwelcome realities. Zia had the right to know her father. And Luca had rights too—not that she thought he would have the slightest urge to exercise them.

But if she didn't tell Luca that he had a daughter, some day Zia would demand that her mother justify that decision. And the unhappy truth was that her own wounded pride, her craven desire to avoid a traumatic confession and her pessimistic suppositions about how Luca might react, were not in themselves sufficient excuse for her to remain silent.

Richard had phoned in the week to say that he would come down for a night over the weekend with his current girlfriend. Darcy had been looking forward to some fresh company, but unfortunately Richard arrived on Friday afternoon, just as she was on her way out with Zia. He was alone.

Tall, loose-limbed, and with a shock of dark hair and brown eyes, Richard immediately made himself at home on the sagging sofa by the kitchen range. 'If you're going out, I intend to drown my sorrows,' he warned, his mobile features radiating self-pity in waves. 'I've been dumped.'

Darcy almost said, Not *again*, which would have been very tactless. Managing to bite the words back, she gave his slumped shoulder a consoling pat. He was like the brother she had never had, and utterly clueless about women. He had a fatal weakness for long-legged glamorous blondes, and the looks and the money to attract them if not to hold them. He didn't like clubbing or parties. He lived for his horses. He was a man with a Porsche in search of a rare, horsy homebody hiding behind the façade of a long-legged glamorous blonde.

'Zia's been invited to a party and I offered to stay and help,' Darcy told him. 'I'll be a while, so you're on your own unless you care to ring Karen.'

'Pity *she's* not a blonde,' Richard lamented, stuck like a record in a groove. He pulled a whisky bottle out of a capacious pocket. 'None of the women I like are blonde...'

'Doesn't that tell you something?'

'I wish I'd done the decent thing and married you. I probably would've been quite happy.'

'Richard...' Darcy drew in a deep, restraining breath, reminded that she had yet to tell Richard that she was currently in possession of a husband. 'Why don't you put the booze away and go down to the lodge and keep Karen company?'

'I'm not telling *her* I've been dumped again...she'd *laugh!*'

Darcy called Karen before she went out. 'Richard's here,' she announced. 'He's been dumped.'

Karen howled with laughter.

'I thought I'd let you get that out of your system before you see him in the flesh.'

It was almost seven by the time Darcy arrived home. After all the excitement at the party, Zia was exhausted and ready only for bed. Richard was in a maudlin slump in the kitchen. Darcy surveyed the sunken level on the whisky bottle in dismay. 'You're feeling *that* bad?'

'Worsh,' Richard groaned, opening only one blood-shot eye.

Pity and irritation mingled inside Darcy. She, too, was miserable. Some decent conversation might have cheered her up, but Richard was drunk as a skunk. And, since he had never behaved like that before, she couldn't even reasonably shout at him.

She took Zia upstairs, gave her a quick bath, tucked her into bed and started to read her a story, but Zia fell asleep in the middle of it. Her eyes filled with guilt and love, Darcy smoothed her daughter's dark curls tenderly from her brow and sighed. She owed it to Zia to tell Luca the truth.

With a steely glint in her gaze, Darcy went back downstairs to sort out Richard. Since he'd chosen to get legless in her absence, he could jolly well go and sleep it off.

'Time for bed, Richard,' she announced loudly. 'Get up!'

He lumbered upright in slow and very shaky motion. 'Ish still light…' he muttered in bewilderment.

'So?' Darcy pushed him towards the stairs. 'You're lucky Karen's not here…you know how she feels about alcohol after her experiences with her ex.'

Richard looked terrified. 'Not coming, ish she?'

Reflecting on the awkwardness of having two close friends who occasionally mixed like oil and water, she guided him into the room beside her own, which she had once promised Luca. Richard lurched down onto the mattress like a falling tree.

'Met your hushband…when did you get a hushband?' Richard contrived to slur, with only academic interest.

In the act of throwing a blanket over his prone body

Darcy stilled, not crediting what she was hearing. 'My husband?' she queried sharply.

Grabbing her hand, Richard tugged her closer and whispered confidentially, '*Not* a friendly chap…tried to hit me…would've punched my lights out if I hadn't fallen over…'

He was rambling, out of his skull, hallucinating. He *had* to be.

'Now isn't this cosy?' A dark sardonic drawl breathed at that exact same moment from the doorway.

Darcy got such a shock she almost leapt a foot in the air. An incredulous look on her face, she wrenched herself free of Richard and whipped round. 'Where did you come from?' she gasped, totally appalled and showing it. 'I've been home over an hour!'

'Since you were out, I went for a drive,' Luca divulged grimly.

And she looked awful, she reflected in anguish. Before bathing Zia she had sensibly changed into a faded summer dress. Had she known Luca was coming, she would have dressed up—*not* because she wished to attract him, but because she didn't want him thinking, Gosh, what a mess she is. What did I ever see in her? She had her pride and now it was in the dust.

Luca, clad in yet another of his breathtakingly elegant suits, looked absolutely stupendous. Navy suit, white shirt with fine red stripes, red silk tie. Smart enough to stroll out in front of television cameras. Slowly, very slowly, she allowed her intimidated gaze to rise above his shirt collar. Jawline aggressive. Beautiful mouth grim. Spectacular cheekbones harshly prominent and flushed. Sensational eyes blazing like gold daggers locking into a target.

Her mouth ran dry, her heart skipping a beat.

The very image of masculine outrage, Luca continued to stare at her, the sheer force of his will beating down on her. 'Carlton is *not* staying the night here!'

Richard opened his eyes. 'Thash him,' he said helpfully. 'Speaksh Italian like a native...'

'Oh, do shut up and go to sleep, Richard,' Darcy muttered unevenly.

'He stays...*I go*,' Luca delivered in a charged undertone.

'Don't be daft...he's not doing you any harm!'

Luca spun on his heel. Darcy unfroze and flew through the door after him. 'Luca...where are you going?'

He shot her a scorching look of incredulous fury. 'I'm leaving. *Per amor di Dio*... I will not stay beneath the same roof as your lover!'

'Are you out of your mind?' Darcy demanded, wide-eyed. 'Richard is *not* my lover.'

His shimmering eyes murderous, Luca spread both hands in a slashing motion and shot something at her in wrathful Italian.

Darcy gulped, registering that she was dealing with a seethingly angry male, presently incapable of accepting reasoned argument or explanation and indeed at the very limit of his control. 'OK...OK, I'll get rid of him,' she promised in desperation, because she knew at that moment that if she didn't, it was the end of everything. Luca would depart never to return.

She lifted the phone by the bed and dialled the lodge. 'Karen...I need a very big favour from you...in fact, it's so big I don't quite know how to ask. Richard is drunk, Luca's here and he's got this ridiculous idea that Richard and I are lovers. He's really furious and he wants him out of the house, and I—'

'Richard, drunk…?' Karen interrupted that frantic flood. 'Helpless, is he?'

'Pretty much. Could you possibly give him a bed for the night?' Darcy felt awful making such a request.

'*Oh, yes…*' Karen coughed suddenly, evidently clearing her throat, and added very stiffly, 'Yes, I suppose I could.'

'Thanks.' Darcy sagged with relief.

'We're going to go for a little walk, Richard,' she said winsomely as she yanked the blanket off him again.

Running through his pockets, she extracted his car keys and, anchoring a long arm round her shoulder, tried to haul him off the bed. 'Richard…you weigh a ton!' she groaned in frustration.

'Allow me,' Luca breathed savagely from behind her.

In dismay, Darcy released her hold on Richard. In a display of far from reassuring strength, Luca accomplished the feat of getting Richard upright again.

'Where are you taking him?' Luca demanded roughly.

'Not far. Just get him down into his car. Don't… don't hurt him,' she muttered anxiously on the stairs, as Richard staggered and Luca anchored a hand as gentle as a meat hook into the back of his sweater.

Richard loaded up, Darcy swung into the driver's seat of the Porsche and ignited the engine.

'Where we goin'?' Richard mumbled.

'You'll see.' She didn't have the heart to tell him. He had found himself at the withering end of Karen's sharp and clever tongue too often. Handing him over drunk and incapable of self-defence was the equivalent of handing a baby to a cannibal.

Karen had heard the car. She walked out into the lane

and had the passenger door open before Darcy had even alighted.

'*Karen...?*' Richard was moaning in horror.

'Relax, Richard,' Karen purred, sounding all maternal and caring. 'I'm going to look after you.'

Darcy gaped at her friend over the car bonnet. 'Karen...what's going on?'

'Have you any idea how long I've waited for a chance like this?' Karen whispered back, her eyes gleaming as she reached up to smooth a soothing hand over Richard's tousled dark hair. 'Blondes are bad news for you, Richard,' she told him in a mesmeric tone of immense compassion.

'Yesh,' Darcy heard Richard agree slavishly as Karen guided him slowly towards the lodge.

Karen was either planning to lull Richard into a false sense of security before she turned a hose on him in the back garden to sober him up, or she was planning to persuade Richard that his dream woman had finally arrived in the unexpected shape of a small but very attractive brunette.

Darcy walked back up to the Folly. Luca was waiting in the hall for her. He didn't even stop to draw breath. 'What was that drunken idiot doing here tonight?' he demanded rawly.

'For goodness' sake, he often stays, and he doesn't normally drink like that. He brings his girlfriends here too,' Darcy proffered tautly. 'I don't know where you get the idea that we're lovers—'

'Three years ago, you almost married Carlton. *He jilted you!*' Luca reminded her savagely. '*Porca miseria*...do you expect me to believe that he's now only a platonic friend?'

'Yes, I do expect you to believe that.' Darcy met his burnished gaze levelly.

'Even though he's the father of your child?' Luca framed with driven ferocity.

Darcy turned pale as milk. 'I assure you that Zia is *not* Richard's child.'

The tense silence simmered, but she saw some of the tension ease in Luca's angry stance.

Desperate to know what Luca was thinking now that she had made that admission, Darcy murmured tautly, 'Until Richard and I both fell for other people, neither of us realised what was missing in our relationship. We stayed friends. He's a terrific guy, kind, caring...'

Luca's mouth twisted as he listened, hooded eyes hard as stones as he followed her into the drawing room. 'Mr Wonderful...Mr Perfect...'

'No...he does tend to tell the same horsy stories and jokes over and over again.'

Darcy was surprised that he had made no further comment on the subject of Zia's paternity. Heavens, did he still think there had been other men in her life, then?

'And he's thicker than a block of wood...don't forget that minor imperfection,' Luca slotted in drily. 'But why didn't you tell him that you're married? *Accidenti*...so close a friend and he didn't even know I existed!'

'Tonight was the first time I'd seen him since our wedding, but I didn't have time to talk to him because I had to go out. When did you arrive?'

'After six. I did not expect to arrive here and find another man in residence!'

Darcy blinked, and thought about the last enervating half-hour. Luca had behaved like a jealous, possessive husband and instinctively she had reacted like a foolish and insecure new wife, eager to placate him. Luca, jealous? It was a stunning concept.

'Were you jealous when you thought Richard was my lover?' Darcy asked baldly.

Luca stilled and sent her a gleaming glance from below inky black lashes. 'I am naturally jealous of my dignity.'

'Your dignity?' Her hopeful face had fallen by a mile.

'Is it unreasonable for me to expect you to behave like a normal wife?' Luca countered levelly. 'In the light of your previous relationship with him, inviting Carlton to stay here alone with you was most unwise—'

'Unwise,' Darcy parroted, thinking what a bloodless, passionless word that was.

'As my wife, you are now in the public eye, and a potential target for damaging gossip. Surely you can't want anyone to have cause to suspect at this early stage that there is anything seriously wrong with our marriage?'

Darcy slowly nodded. He wasn't jealous. He was just an arrogant, macho male, determined to preserve his own public image. People might laugh if they suspected his wife was being unfaithful, and he wouldn't like that.

'By the way, I settled your mortgage,' Luca remarked with stupendous casualness.

Darcy's lower lip parted company with her upper in shock.

Brilliant dark eyes intent on her aghast expression, Luca continued smoothly, 'As you're so independent, I imagine you'll wish to repay me once you inherit your godmother's money, but in the short term you are no longer burdened by those substantial monthly payments.'

Darcy stumbled into speech. 'But, Luca...what right—?'

'I haven't finished yet. I have also had a word with your bank manager. There is no longer a limit on your overdraft. Don't throw it all back in my face,' he urged almost roughly, openly assessing her shaken, troubled face. 'I had no *right* to interfere, but I had a very powerful *need* to offer you what help I could.'

Still reeling, Darcy swallowed hard. She understood, oh, yes, she understood. Luca felt guilty. This was his way of making amends. His intervention on such grounds filled her with pained discomfiture, but she was in no position to refuse his efforts on behalf of the estate. He was making it possible for her to survive and re-employ the staff.

'Thanks,' she said stiltedly.

'I would have liked to do a great deal more, *cara mia,*' Luca admitted steadily. 'But I knew you wouldn't have accepted that.'

At that respectful acknowledgement, a slow, uncertain smile drove the tension from her tense mouth. 'Did you park your wings outside?'

'My wings?'

'You'd make a really good guardian angel.'

'I was afraid you were about to say fairy godmother,' Luca confided.

'It did cross my mind.' Darcy wrinkled her nose and laughed for the first time in weeks. And then she remembered what she still had to tell him and her face shadowed. Tomorrow, she decided, she would tell him tomorrow...

It was half past eight when the Victorian bell on the massive front door shrieked and jangled.

Luca was in the library, having excused himself to make some calls, and Darcy had gone upstairs to slide into an outfit that magically accentuated her every slender curve. Green, with a fashionably short skirt and fitted jacket. She thought it looked kind of sexy on her. She slid her feet into high heels and fiddled anxiously with her hair in the mirror. And the whole time she was engaged on that transformation she refused to think about *why* she was doing it.

When Darcy opened the door, out of breath from rushing full tilt down the stairs, her sensitive stomach somersaulted when she saw Margo and Nina standing outside. Her stepmother elegant in black, and her stepsister dressed to kill in a sugar-pink dress so perilously short it made Darcy's skirt look like a maxi.

Both women did a rather exaggerated double take over her altered image.

'Is that a Galliano?' Nina demanded in an envious shriek.

'A...a what?' Darcy countered blankly.

'And those shoes are Prada! He got you out of your Barbour and your wellies fast enough!' Nina gibed thinly. 'It's such a dangerous sign when a man tries to change a woman into something she's not.'

On her lofty passage towards the drawing room, Margo winced. 'And green simply *screams* at your red hair, Darcy!'

'But Darcy doesn't have *red* hair,' a deep, dark drawl interceded across the depth of the hall from the library doorway. 'It's Titian, a shade defined by the dictionary as a bright, golden auburn.'

Darcy threw Luca the sort of look a drowning swimmer gives to a life jacket.

Margo and Nina weren't quite quick enough to conceal their dismay and surprise at Luca's appearance.

'I understood that you were still in Italy, Luca.' Her
stepmother's smile of greeting was stiff.

'I thought that might be why you were here.' As Luca
strolled over to the fireplace and took up a relaxed
stance there, he let that statement hang a split-second,
while their uninvited visitors tensed with uncertainty at
his possible meaning before continuing smoothly, 'How
very kind of you to think that Darcy might be in need
of company.'

'I'm sure Richard Carlton's been dropping in too,'
Nina said innocently.

'Yes, and what a very entertaining guy he is,' Luca
countered, smiling without skipping a beat while
Darcy's fascinated gaze darted back and forth between
the combatants. Margo and Nina had definitely met their
match.

'Nina and I were only saying yesterday what a coincidence it is that Darcy and Maxie Kendall should
have got married within weeks of each other!' Margo
exclaimed, watching Darcy stiffen with suspicious eyes.
'Now what was the name of Nancy Leeward's other
godchild?'

'Polly,' Darcy muttered tightly. 'Why?'

'Naturally I'm curious. That old woman left such an
extraordinary will! I expect we'll be hearing of Polly's
marriage next...'

'I doubt it,' Darcy slotted in. 'When I last saw her,
Polly had no plans to marry.'

Nina directed a brilliant smile at Luca and crossed
her fabulous long legs, her abbreviated dress riding so
high Darcy wouldn't have been surprised to see pantie

elastic. 'I bet you haven't a clue what we're talking about, Luca.'

Margo chimed in, 'I'm afraid it did cross my mind that Darcy might—'

'Might marry me to inherit a measly one million?' Sardonic amusement gleamed in Luca's steady appraisal. 'Yes, of course I know about the will, but I can assure you that an eccentric godmother's wishes played no part whatsoever in *my* desire to marry your stepdaughter.'

'Yes,' Darcy agreed, getting into the spirit of his game with dancing green eyes. 'I believe Luca would say that when he married me, he had his own private agenda.'

'Ouch,' Luca breathed for her ears alone, and her cheeks warmed.

But Margo was not so easily silenced. 'I don't know how to put this without seeming intrusive...but frankly I was concerned when I learnt from friends locally that Darcy had come home alone after spending only forty-eight hours with you in Venice—'

'Mummy...it's hardly likely to be her favourite place,' Nina said with a meaningful look.

'I love Venice,' Darcy returned squarely.

'I know you gave your poor child that silly name— Venezia—but I notice you soon gave up using it,' Margo reminded her drily.

'Venezia?' Luca queried abruptly.

Darcy's sensitive insides turned a sick somersault. She encountered a narrowed stare of bemusement from Luca and turned her head away abruptly.

'Such a silly name!' Nina giggled. 'But then Darcy never did have much taste or discretion.'

Darcy felt too sick to glance again in Luca's direc-

tion. Her nerves were shot to hell. She wanted to put a
sack over Nina and suffocate her before she said too
much.

'Your sense of humour must often cause deep offence,' Luca drawled with chilling bite, studying Nina
with contempt. 'I have zero tolerance for anything that
might distress my wife.'

Two rosy high spots of red embellished Nina's
cheeks. Heavens, Darcy thought in equal shock, he
sounded so incredibly protective. Her strain eased as she
realised that Nina had abandoned her intent to make
further snide comments about Zia.

'Yes, you were very thoughtless, Nina,' Margo
agreed sharply. 'That's all in the past now. I actually
came here today to express my very genuine concern
over something Darcy has done.'

'Really, Margo?' Darcy was emboldened by the supportive hand Luca had settled in the shallow indentation
of her spine.

'You brought Luca to the engagement party I held
and not one word did you breathe about his exalted
status,' Margo returned thinly.

Too enervated to be able to guess what her stepmother was leading up to, Darcy saw no relevance
whatsoever to that statement.

'So what on earth persuaded you to do *this?*' Her
stepmother drew a folded magazine from her capacious
bag, her face stiff with distaste and disapproval. 'Is
there *anything* you wouldn't do for money, Darcy? How
could you embarrass your husband like that?'

Instant appalled paralysis afflicted Darcy. Her green
eyes zoomed in on the magazine which contained that
dreadful gushing interview, and in the same second she

turned the colour of a ripe tomato, her stomach curdling with horror. Embarrassment choked her.

Margo shook her blonde head pityingly. 'I was horrified that Darcy should sell the story of your marriage to a lurid gossip magazine, Luca.'

'Whereas I shall treasure certain phrases spoken in that interview for ever,' Luca purred in a tone of rich complacency, extending his arm to ease Darcy's trembling, anxious length into the hard, muscular heat of his big frame. 'When I read about Darcy's ''mystical sense of wonder'' and her ''spiritual feeling of soul-deep recognition'' on first meeting me, I envied her ability to verbalise sensations and sentiments which I myself could never find adequate words to describe.'

'Luca?' Darcy mumbled shakily, shattered that he had actually read that interview and absorbed sufficient of her mindless drivel to quote directly from it.

But Luca, it seemed, was in full appreciative flow. 'Indeed, I was overwhelmed by such a powerful need to be with Darcy again I flew straight here to her side. I shall *always* regard that interview as an open love letter from my wife.'

For the space of ten seconds Margo and Nina just sat there, apparently transfixed.

'Of course, I'm very relieved to hear that the interview hasn't caused any friction between you. I was *so* worried it would,' Margo responded unconvincingly.

'You surprise me.' Fabulous bone structure grim, eyes wintry, Luca studied their visitors. 'Only a fool could fail to see through your foolish attempts to diminish Darcy in my eyes. She is a woman of integrity, and how she contrived to hang onto that integrity growing up with two such vicious women is nothing short of a miracle!'

'How dare you talk to me like that?' Margo gasped, rising to her feet in sheer shock.

'You resent my wife's ownership of an estate which has been within her family for over four hundred years. You're furious that she has married a rich man who will help her to retain that home. You hoped she would be forced to sell up because you planned to demand a share of the proceeds,' Luca condemned with sizzling distaste. 'That is why I dare to talk to you as I have.'

'I'm not staying here to be insulted,' Margo snapped, stalking towards the door.

'I think that's very wise.'

Luca listened to the thud of the massive front door with complete calm.

Stunned at what had just transpired, Darcy breathed. 'I need to check on Zia...'

'Venezia,' Luca murmured softly, catching her taut fingers in his as she started up the stairs. 'Obviously you chose that name because it held a special significance for you. You were happy with me that night in Venice?'

'Y-yes,' Darcy stammered.

'But we met in what was clearly a troubled and transitional phase of your life.' His lean, strong features were taut, as if he was selecting his words with great care. 'I understand now why you so freely forgave Carlton for jilting you. Evidently he wasn't the only guilty party. You went to bed with someone other than him before that wedding.'

'No, I didn't!' Angry chagrined colour warmed Darcy's face as she stopped dead in the corridor.

'*Accidenti!* What's the point of denying it?' Luca demanded in exasperation. 'You may well not have been aware of the fact that night, but you *were* pregnant when you first met me!'

'No...I wasn't,' Darcy told him staunchly, pressing open the door of Zia's bedroom. 'You're still barking up the wrong tree!'

'You must've been pregnant,' Luca contradicted steadily, as if he was dealing with a child fearfully reluctant to own up to misbehaviour. 'Your daughter was born seven months later.'

'Zia was premature. She spent weeks in hospital before I could bring her home...' Darcy held her breath in the silence which followed, and then steeled herself to turn and face him.

Luca had a dazed, disconcerted look in his dark, deep-set eyes. He stared at her. 'She was premature?' he breathed, so low he had to clear his throat to be audible.

'So you see, now that you've been through the butcher, the baker and the candlestick-maker, as they say in the nursery rhyme, we're running out of possible culprits,' Darcy pointed out unsteadily, her throat tight, her mouth dry, her heart thumping like mad behind her breastbone. 'And to be honest, there only ever *was* one possibility, Luca.'

In the dim light, his eyes suddenly flashed pure gold. 'Are you trying to tell me that...that Zia is mine?' he whispered raggedly.

CHAPTER ELEVEN

DARCY'S voice let her down when she most needed it. As Luca asked that loaded question she gave a fierce, jerky nod, and she didn't take her strained gaze from him for a second.

Black spiky lashes screened his sensational eyes. He blinked. He was stunned.

Darcy swallowed and relocated her voice. 'And there's not any doubt about it because Richard and I never slept together. We had decided to wait until we were married.'

'Never?' Luca stressed with hoarse incredulity.

Darcy grimaced. 'And, since we didn't *get* married, we never actually made it to bed.'

'That means...but that means that I would've been your first...*impossible—!*' Luca broke off and compressed his lips, studying her with shaken dark eyes.

Darcy reddened. 'I didn't want you to guess that night. You said virgins were deeply unexciting,' she reminded him accusingly.

'We both said and did several foolish things that night...but fortunately making Zia was not one of them.' With a roughened laugh that betrayed the emotions he was struggling to contain, Luca closed his hands on hers to draw her closer while he gazed endlessly down at Zia, and then back at Darcy, as if he was being torn in two different directions. *'Per amor di Dio*...the truth has been staring me in the face from the start,' he groaned. 'The fact that nobody knew who the

201

father of your child was. You wouldn't say because you *couldn't* say…you didn't even know my name!'

Her anxious eyes were vulnerably wide.

Slowly Luca shook his glossy dark head. 'I saw that photo of Carlton, and he's dark as well. I assumed he was her father and that you still loved him enough to protect him. Then, when you said he wasn't, it *still* didn't occur to me that she could be my child!'

'You didn't know Zia was born prematurely. She arrived more than six weeks early.'

'I want to wake her up to look at her properly,' Luca confided a little breathlessly as he suddenly released Darcy to look down at his daughter. 'But that's the first lesson she taught me. Don't disturb her when she's asleep!'

'She sleeps like the dead, Luca.'

'Where were my *eyes?*' he whispered in unconcealed wonder. 'She has my nose—'

'She got just about everything from you.' As she hovered there Darcy was feeling slightly abandoned, and, pessimist that she had been, she was unprepared for Luca's obvious excitement at the discovery that he was a father.

Excitement? No, she certainly hadn't expected that. But then nothing had gone remotely like any of her vague imaginings of this scene. Luca had been shocked, but he had skipped the mortifying protest stage she had feared and gone straight into acceptance mode.

'She's really beautiful,' Luca commented with considerable pride.

'Yes, I think so too,' Darcy whispered rather forlornly.

'*Per meraviglia…*I'm a father. I'd better get on to my lawyer straight away—'

'I beg your pardon? Your lawyer?'

'If I was to drop dead tonight before I acknowledge her as my daughter, she could end up penniless!' Luca headed straight for the door. 'I'll call him right now.'

Drop dead, then, Luca. Darcy's eyes prickled and stung. She sniffed. Of course she didn't mean that. In fact just thinking of anything happening to Luca pierced her to the heart and terrified her, but it was hard to cope with feeling like the invisible woman.

'Aren't you coming?' Luca glanced back in at her again.

She sat in the library, watching him call his lawyer. Then he called his sister, and by the sound of the squeals of excitement Ilaria was delighted to receive such a stunning announcement.

'Zia is mine. Obviously it was meant to be,' Luca drawled, squaring his shoulders as he sank down into the armchair opposite her. 'Now I want to hear everything from the first minute you suspected you might be pregnant.'

'I was about five months gone before I worked that out.'

'Five *months?*' Luca exclaimed.

'I didn't put on much weight, didn't have any morning sickness or anything. I *was* eating a lot, and I got a bit of a tummy, and then I got this *really* weird sort of little fluttery feeling…that's what made me go to the doctor. When he told me it was the baby moving I was shocked rigid!'

'I imagine you were.' Luca's spectacular dark eyes were brimming with tender amusement. Rising lithely from his chair, he settled down on the sofa beside her and reached for her hand to close it between his long fingers. 'So you weren't ill?'

'Healthy as a horse.'

'And how did your family react?'

'My father was pretty decent about it, but I think that was because he was hoping I'd have a boy,' Darcy admitted ruefully. 'He didn't give two hoots about the gossip, but Margo was ready to kill me. She went round letting everyone believe the baby was Richard's because, of course, that sounded rather better.'

'What did you tell your family about Zia's father?'

'More or less the truth…ships that pass…said I'd *forgotten* your name,' Darcy admitted shamefacedly.

'How alone you must have felt,' Luca murmured heavily, his grip on her small hand tightening. 'But that night you gave me to understand that you were protected.'

'I honestly thought I was. I didn't realise that you had to take those wretched contraceptive pills continuously to be safe…and, of course, I'd tossed them in the bin the first morning I was in Venice!'

'If *only* you hadn't run away from the apartment—'

'You'd have stuck the police on me instead.'

'I wouldn't have. Had you stayed, your innocence would never have been in doubt. *Why?*' Luca emphasised, intent, dark golden eyes holding her more evasive gaze. 'Why did you run away?'

'It's pretty embarrassing waking up for the first time in a strange man's bed,' Darcy said bluntly. 'I felt like a real tart—'

'You don't know the first thing about being a tart, so don't use that word,' Luca censured with frowning reproof.

But a split second later he was smiling that utterly charismatic smile of his, sending her heartbeat bumpety-bumpety-bump as he asked all sorts of questions about

Zia, demonstrating a degree of interest that was encyclopaedic in its detail. At the end of that session, he murmured with considerable assurance, 'Well...there'll be no divorce now, *cara mia.*'

Even though that development was what Darcy had hoped for from the instant she knew that she loved Luca, she didn't like the background against which he had formed that instant arrogant supposition. She tugged her hand free of his, her face frozen. 'Why? Do you know something I don't?'

Luca dealt her a startled, questioning look. 'We have a child. She needs both of us. I simply assumed—'

'I don't think you should be assuming anything in that line!' Darcy told him roundly. 'It may be important that Zia has a father, but I'm concerned about what *I* need too.'

'You need me,' Luca breathed a shade harshly, all relaxation now wiped from his taut features and not a hint of a smile left either.

Darcy flew upright. 'Don't look at me like that!'

'In what way am I looking at you?' Luca enquired forbiddingly.

'Like I'm a bad debtor or something, and you're...you're trying to work out my Achilles' heel!' Suddenly frightened by the awareness that she was heading for an argument with him and that she didn't want that, didn't trust her own overwrought and confused emotions, or her too often dangerously blunt tongue, she said tightly, 'Look, I'm very tired. I'm going up to bed.'

From the foot of the stairs she glanced back into the library. Luca was standing by the window, ferocious tension screaming from his stillness. Her heart sank at the sight. Everything had gone wrong from the moment she questioned his conviction that they should now view their marriage as a real marriage. And why the heck had she done that? Why, when she herself longed for that stupid agreement they had made to be set aside and totally wiped from both their memories? Why had she refused the offer of her own most heartfelt wish?

And she saw into herself then, was forced to confront her own insecurity. She feared that Luca only wanted their marriage to continue for Zia's benefit. Hadn't she felt threatened and excluded by his unashamed absorption and delight in Zia? How foolish and selfish that had been, on the very night he first learned that he was a father!

Feeling considerably less bolshie, Darcy made up her bed with fresh sheets. She took the dogs down the service stairs to sleep in the kitchen. Then she donned a strappy oyster-coloured satin nightie and slid between the sheets to wait for Luca.

But an hour later, when she heard footsteps in the corridor and tensed with a fast-beating heart, Luca passed by her room. In the silence of the old house she listened to him enter the room Richard had briefly occupied earlier and close the door.

She fell back against the pillows then, shaken, hurt and scared...utterly out of her depth with this Luca who was not even tempted to make love to her after an absence of three weeks.

'Fabulous apartment,' Karen sighed when she arrived for lunch, scanning the fantastic view of London from the penthouse. 'And Luca...he is *the* perfect man; I am totally convinced of that. The guy that clears off without a murmur so that you can have lunch with your best friend is special, and when he takes the toddler with him, he zooms up the scale of perfection and hits the bell at the top!'

'He's a very committed father.'

'I wouldn't say he was a slow starter in the husband stakes either. In one month, he has transformed your life. He even brings you flowers and cute little gifts... Richard's not into flowers, but he gave me a sweater covered with embroidered horseshoes for my birthday. It is the most *gross* garment you have ever seen, but he phones me about five times a day, and he's so scared I'm going to dump him, it's unbelievable,' Karen shared with a rather dreamy smile.

'I'm glad you're happy.'

'Well, you don't look glad enough to satisfy me,' Karen responded drily. 'I hope you're not turning into one of those spoilt little rich madams who can't appreciate what she's got!'

Darcy managed to laugh. 'Can you see the day?'

'No, but I know by your expression that there's something badly wrong, and that was an easy way to open the subject!'

Darcy thought back over the last four weeks. The Folly estate was now employing a full quota of staff, not to mention giving added employment to all the local firms engaged in the repairs and improvements which Luca had insisted the house required without further delay. While that work was going on they had set up temporary home in London at Luca's apartment, and when the summer was over they were shifting to Venice, where they would make their permanent home.

'Has he got another woman?'

'Of course he hasn't!' Darcy said, aghast.

'He's not violent or alcoholic or anything like that, is he?'

'*Karen!*' Darcy took a deep breath. 'He just doesn't love me.'

'*This* is the problem that has you moping about like a wet weekend?' Karen breathed incredulously. 'Luca arranges to fly me up here in a helicopter to have lunch with you as a surprise...he hangs on your every word, watches your every move...I mean, the guy's so besotted he's practically turning somersaults to impress!'

Darcy shrugged, unimpressed, gloom creeping over her again. They were sleeping in separate bedrooms. He hadn't made the slightest move to change that. It was as if sex didn't exist any more. And she couldn't forget that he had once admitted that possibly his belief that she was a thief had been the most dangerous part of her attraction. And it *was* as if her sex appeal had vanished overnight. Yet, aside from that, loads of really positive things were happening in their relationship...

Although she wasn't sure that being more hopelessly in love with Luca than ever was a positive thing. He was being caring, kind, supportive and considerate of her every need bar the one. He never lost his temper— no, not even when Zia had drawn all over a set of important business documents that had had to be replaced at supersonic speed before a big meeting. He took her out to dinner all the time. He took her to parties. He behaved as if he was very proud of her and paid her lots of compliments. He laughed, he smiled, he was a dirty great ray of constant sunshine, but when night fell he climbed into his *own* bed.

'Have you mentioned that you love *him* yet? I don't think it would be immediately obvious from your current demeanour,' Karen opined rather drily. 'Or maybe he's just not very good with the words.'

An hour after Karen's departure for home, Zia

bounced into her mother's bedroom to show off the latest pair of new frilly socks on display. They had three layers of handmade lace round the ankle. She was tickled pink with them. Zia was just one great big sunny smile these days. She had her mother, her adoring father and a devoted nanny, not to mention shelves groaning with toys. As she danced out again, a restive bundle of energy, Luca strolled in.

'Did you enjoy seeing Karen?' he enquired.

'Yes, it was great...I should've invited her up myself, but I knew she wouldn't want to be away for long, not with her romance with Richard hotting up the way it is.'

Just looking at him, she felt her mouth run dry and her pulses race. So she had learnt *not* to look at him directly. One quick, sneaky glance and then away again. If he didn't find her attractive any more, then the very last thing she needed was for him to guess that she was suffering withdrawal symptoms of the severest, cruellest kind. But that one sneaky glance she stole was enough to send her dizzy. Either Luca literally *did* get more gorgeous with every passing day, or she was more than usually susceptible.

In her mind's eye, she summoned him up. Casual silver-grey suit, superbly fitted to his wide shoulders, lithe hips and long powerful legs, worn with a cashmere sweater the colour of charcoal. He radiated sex appeal in waves she could *feel*. In much the same way that secret radar could feel the impact of those stunning dark eyes of his watching her.

'Darcy...I invited Karen here in the hope that you would relax with her,' Luca imparted tautly. 'But it doesn't seem to have done much good.'

'You can't put a plaster on something that isn't broken.'

'Is that one of those strange English nursery sayings?' Luca enquired.

Darcy didn't even know why she had said it, except to fill the tense silence, so she wasn't able to help him there. She twisted back to him but didn't meet his eyes.

'You know something, *cara mia?*' Luca breathed in a dangerous tone. 'I have decided that tact, patience and sensitivity do not work with you.'

'Probably not,' Darcy conceded, wondering why he had raised his voice slightly.

'In fact any man foolish enough to devote himself to the hopeless task of winning your trust would probably hit his deathbed before he got there.'

'Winning my trust?' Darcy repeated.

'What the hell do you think I've been doing for the past month?' Luca suddenly splintered at her in raw frustration.

And the strands of pain in that intonation made her look straight at him. She saw the same lonely ache there that she saw in her own face every time she stared in the mirror, and she stilled in shock.

Luca spread his hands in a familiar gesture that tugged at her heart. 'One minute you give me hope, the next you push me down,' he groaned. 'I don't need you to tell me that I made an appalling hash of our relationship, but I've been trying really hard to make up for that...only you seem to be getting further and further away from me, and I can't *bear* that when I love you so much!'

'You...you *love* me?' Darcy whispered shakily.

'You told me that you fell for me, too, that night in Venice, and that gave me hope.'

'If you love me why have you been sleeping in another room?' Darcy demanded accusingly. 'Why don't you touch me any more?'

Luca gave her a sincerely pained appraisal. 'I wanted you to appreciate that I *really* loved you.'

'Bloody funny way of showing it,' she mumbled helplessly, not knowing whether she was on her head or her heels. 'I've been so miserable.'

In one stride, Luca closed the distance between them. 'I was waiting for you to give me some sign that you still wanted me...I couldn't afford to take *anything* for granted about this marriage!'

'If you love me,' Darcy breathed headily, 'you can take me for granted all you like.'

With a muffled groan, Luca brought his mouth down hard on hers and set off a devastating chain reaction of lust through her entire quivering body. He crushed her so close she couldn't breathe, backed up towards the door to turn the lock and then lifted his dark head again. 'I've never been so frustrated in my life...I *ache* for you, *cara mia.*'

She let her hand travel up over one blunt cheekbone in a caress and framed his face, her eyes full of love. 'Me too... I've been pretty stupid, putting my pride ahead of everything, closing you out when I needed you instead of showing it. I love you loads...and loads...and loads,' she told him a little tearfully, because her emotions were running so high they were right up there with the clouds. 'You should've been able to tell that a mile off!'

'You wouldn't even look at me any more!'

She gave him a flirtatious scrutiny from below curling lashes as he drew her hand down from his face and planted a kiss in the centre of her palm. 'You're a minx,' he told her huskily.

'I like the guy to do all the running. You see, the one time I did it the other way round, I ended up climbing out of a window with a burglar alarm screaming—and I also ended up pregnant,' she pointed out in her own defence.

'Zia's so precious, she could never be a source of regret,' Luca countered. 'I really fell for you in a very big way that night three years ago.'

'I find that so hard to believe—'

'That's because you don't think enough of yourself,' he scolded. 'You knocked me for six. You were so different from every other woman I had ever met. I fell asleep that night with you in my arms, and I felt pretty damned smug and self-satisfied—'

'And then it all went horribly wrong.'

'And I spent three insanely frustrating years trying to track you down... Make no mistake, I *was* totally obsessed,' Luca confided ruefully. 'I never admitted to myself how I really felt about you, but I could hardly wait for our wedding...all I allowed myself to think about was getting you back into bed.'

'I noticed that was a fairly big issue straight off.'

Luca flushed. 'I just didn't know what was going on inside my own head, but I was incredibly happy I had you back in my bed, under my roof, *trapped*... Then Ilaria confessed, and it was like being plunged into a big black loser's hole.'

'I know,' she sighed, sympathetically.

'And that was when I finally realised I loved you,' he groaned. 'I'd blown it every way possible. All I had to hang onto was that stupid agreement we'd made for a platonic marriage...what else did you need me for?'

'Gosh, I never thought of that…'

'So I decided you could comfortably do without being reminded of what a bastard I'd been for a couple of weeks. But it was hell without you,' Luca confessed as he bent and swept her possessively up into his arms and carried her over to the bed. 'And then Benito handed me that magazine interview to read. I know you don't truly think that I'm *that* wonderful, but by the time I'd read it about ten times…'

Darcy kicked off her shoes. 'So that's why you knew it by heart.'

Luca unzipped her dress, spread the edges back and planted his mouth almost reverently on a smooth bare shoulder. 'I decided that if you really hated me, the odd sour note would've crept through. So, inspired by hope—'

'And a certain amount of ego…'

'I jumped straight on the jet,' he completed, tugging her round in his arms to give her a reproachful look. 'And when I realised that Zia was my child, I was ecstatic…it meant I had another hold on you.'

'But you jumped the gun, saying that because of Zia we should stay married. Much as I love my daughter, I need to feel wanted for myself.'

'I was clumsy. I pushed for too much too fast. I didn't dare tell you I loved you that soon because you would never, ever have believed me,' Luca informed her ruefully.

'I might've done…I'm more credulous and trusting than you are,' Darcy teased, her heart singing with love and happiness as she collided with his brilliant dark eyes and the open tenderness there.

From the inside pocket of his jacket, Luca withdrew a miniature gold box the shape of a casket. He snapped it open and removed the ornate gold ring within. The star-shaped ruby caught the light in its rich depths.

Darcy caught her breath and gasped, 'This is *it,* isn't it...that wretched ring you thought I'd nicked?'

With a wolfish grin, Luca lifted her hand and slid the medieval ring onto her wedding finger. 'The Adorata...'

'It really is gorgeous,' Darcy whispered.

'Tradition holds that the Adorata is given to a Raffacani wife on the birth of the son and heir,' Luca shared huskily. 'But this is the nineties, and I think it's time it was awarded simply for the birth of the *first* child.'

'Yes, I like that,' Darcy told him appreciatively. 'None of that sexist rubbish about sons being more important in *our* family.'

Luca pressed his lips tenderly to the corner of her smiling mouth. 'I didn't quite have the nerve to ask before now but...is there any chance you might be expecting another baby?'

'Not unless you've come up with some very kinky way of ravishing me mentally...no, not this time, but maybe some other time,' she conceded softly, tenderly, as she laced her fingers blissfully through his luxuriant black hair. 'Gosh, I love having the right to mess up your hair...it's so tidy all the rest of the time!'

'I didn't like it when you said bankers were boring,' Luca confided. 'And then in that interview you said I was the most passionate man you had ever met.'

'You *are*...about me, about Zia. You're so intense beneath that cool front.' Darcy gave a little feeling wriggle to stress how much she liked that.

'Has anybody ever told you how unbelievably sexy you look in wellington boots?'

She giggled, something she never did. 'I really, really believe that you love me now!'

Reaching up to claim his sensual mouth for herself again, Darcy gave herself up to the promise of a future full of blissful contentment and joy.

The Greek Tycoon's Ultimatum

Lucy Monroe

CHAPTER ONE

"THE coldhearted bitch."

Flinching as the words flew venomously from her sister-in-law's lips, Savannah Marie Kiriakis forced her gaze to remain fixed on the emerald-green grass in front of her.

The traditional Greek Orthodox graveside service was over and everyone had paid their final respects, everyone but her. Poised on the edge of the grave, a single white rose in her hand, she tried coming to terms with this—the final end to her marriage.

Relief warred with guilt inside her, forcing out the pain of Iona's verbal attack.

Relief that her own torment was over. No one would ever again threaten to take her children. And guilt that this should be her reaction to the death of another human being, particularly Dion—a man she had married in good faith and youthful stupidity six years ago.

"What right has she to be here?" Iona continued when her first insult was not only ignored by Savannah, but also by the other mourners.

Dion's younger sister had a flair for the dramatic.

Unbidden, Savannah's gaze sought the reaction of Leiandros Kiriakis to his cousin's outburst. His dark eyes were not set on Iona, but focused on Savannah with a look of such contempt if she'd been a weaker person, she would have been tempted to jump into the grave with her dead husband.

She could not turn away, though her heart and emotions were screaming inside for her to do just that. Leiandros's contempt might be justified, but it hurt in a way that Dion's frequent infidelities and bouts of violent temper had not.

The smell of fresh earth mixed with the floral offerings covering the now closed casket assailed her nostrils and she managed to shift her gaze to her husband's grave.

"I'm sorry," she whispered soundlessly before dropping the rose she carried onto the casket and stepping back.

"A touching gesture, if an empty one." More words meant to wound, but these delivered directly to her with the sharp precision of a stiletto aimed at her heart.

It took every bit of Savannah's inner fortitude to turn and face Leiandros after the way he had looked at her a moment ago. "Is it an empty gesture for a wife to say her final goodbye?" she asked as she lifted her head to make eye contact.

And wished she hadn't. Eyes so dark, they were almost black, blazed with a scorn she knew she had earned, but nevertheless grieved. Of all the Kiriakis clan, this man was the only one with legitimate reason to despise her. Because he had firsthand knowledge of the fact she had not loved Dion, not passionately and with her whole heart as a man like her husband had needed to be loved.

"Yes empty. You said goodbye to Dion three years ago."

She shook her head in instinctive denial. Leiandros was mistaken. She would never have risked saying good-bye to Dion before fleeing Greece with her two small daughters in tow. Her only hope of escape had been to board the international flight for America before Dion realized she was gone.

By the time he had tracked her down, she had filed for a legal separation, thus preventing him from spiriting their children from the country. She had also filed a re-straining order, citing her healing bruises and cracked ribs as evidence that she was not safe in Dion's com-pany.

The Kiriakis clan knew nothing of this. Even Leiandros, head of the Kiriakis Empire and thus the fam-ily, was ignorant of the reasons for the final break in Dion and Savannah's marriage.

Leiandros's sculpted face hardened. "That's right. You never did say a final goodbye. You wouldn't give Dion his freedom and you wouldn't live with him. You were the kind of wife nightmares are made of."

Each word pierced her heart and her sense of self as a woman, but she refused to bow in shame under the weight of his ugly judgments. "I would have given Dion a divorce at any time over the last three years." He had been the one to threaten to take their daughters if she made good on her intention to file for permanent dis-solution of their marriage.

Leiandros's face tightened with derision and she felt the familiar pain his scorn caused. His opinion of her had been cast in stone the night they met.

She'd been nervous attending a party given by a man she didn't know, a man Dion had raved about and stressed she had to impress in order to be accepted into the Kiriakis family. If that pressure had not been enough to make her tremble with anxiety, the fact that Dion had abandoned her in a crowd of strangers speaking a language she did not understand was.

Attempting to be unobtrusive, she hovered near a wall by the door to the terrace, away from the other guests.

"*Kalispera. Pos se lene? Me lene Leiandros,*" A deep, male voice speaking in Greek penetrated her isolation.

She looked up to see the most devastatingly attractive man she'd ever encountered. His lazy smile all but stole her breath right out of her chest. She stared at him, mesmerized by a rush of inexplicable feelings toward him, unhindered by societal conventions or even unfamiliarity.

Feeling horribly guilty for such a reaction to a man who was not her husband, she blushed and dropped her gaze. Using the only Greek phrase she knew, she told him she could not understand his language. "*Then katalaveno.*"

He placed a finger under her chin and forced her head up so she had no choice but to look in his eyes. His smile had turned vaguely predatory. "Dance with me," he said in perfect English.

She was shaking her head, trying to force her frozen vocal chords to utter the word *no* even as he put a possessive arm around her waist and pulled her out onto the terrace. He then drew her into his arms, his hold anything but conventional. She struggled while their bodies swayed to the seductive chords of the Greek music.

He pressed her closer. "Relax. I'm not going to eat you."

"But I shouldn't be dancing with you," she told him.

His hold grew even more possessive. "Why? Are you here with a boyfriend?"

"No, but—"

Demanding lips drowned her explanation that she was with her husband, not a boyfriend. Her struggles to get free increased, but the heat of his body and the feel of his hands caressing her back and her nape were already seducing her good intentions.

And to her everlasting shame she felt her body melt in helpless response. The kiss drew emotions from her Dion had never tapped into. She wanted it to go on forever, but even under the influence of a wholly alien passion, she knew she had to break away from the seduction of his lips.

The hand on her back moved to her front and cupped her breast as if he had every right to do so. The fact that he was touching her so intimately was not nearly so appalling as her body's reaction to it. Her breasts seemed to swell within the confines of her lacy bra while their tips grew hard and aching. She'd never felt this way with Dion.

The thought was enough to send her tearing from Leiandros, her sense of honor in tatters while her body actually vibrated with the need to be back in his arms. "I'm married," she gasped.

His eyes flared with the light of battle and she stood paralyzed for a solid minute, their gazes locked, their breathing erratic.

"Leiandros. I see you've met my wife."

And Leiandros, whose body was turned away from Dion so her husband could not see his expression had glared at her with a hate filled condemnation that had not diminished in six years.

"Do not fool yourself into believing that since my cousin is not here to defend himself, your behavior can be dismissed with lies."

Leiandros's voice brought her back to the present, to a woman no longer capable of any kind of response to a man. For a moment she grieved the memory of those awesome feelings she had not experienced since and knew she would never experience again. Dion had seen to that.

Leiandros's six-foot-four-inch frame towered over her own five feet, eight inches, making her feel small and vulnerable to his masculinity and the anger exuding off of him. She took an involuntary step backward and finding refuge in silence, she merely inclined her head before turning in order to leave.

"Do not walk away from me, Savannah. You won't find me as easy to manage as my cousin."

The implied threat in his tone halted her, but she did not turn around. "I do not need to manage you, *Leiandros Kiriakis*. After today, all necessity for communication between myself and your family will be at an end." Her voice came out in an unfamiliar husky drawl when she had meant to sound firm.

"In that, you are mistaken, Savannah." His ominous tone sent shivers skating along her nerve endings.

She whirled to face him, taking in the stunning lines of his masculine features, the way the sun glinted off his jet-black hair and the aura of power surrounding him even as she tried to read the expression in his enigmatic gaze.

"What do you mean?" Had Dion betrayed her in the end?

Leiandros's sensual lips thinned. "That is something we will have to discuss at a later date. My wife's graveside service begins in a few minutes. Be content with the knowledge that as sole trustee for your daughters' inheritance, you and I must of necessity talk occasionally."

Pain assailed her—a sympathetic pain for the grief this strong and arrogant man must be feeling at the death of his wife in the same car accident as his cousin.

"I'm sorry. I won't keep you."

His eyes narrowed. "Aren't you coming?"

"I have no place there."

"Iona thought you had no place here, yet you came."

Because of the phone call. She never would have come if Dion had not made that call the night before his accident.

"Regardless of what the Kiriakis clan would like to be true, I married Dion. I owed my presence here to his memory." Both the memory of the Dion who had courted her and the man who had called that one last time.

"Then do you not owe me your attendance at Petra's service as a member of my family?"

"Why in the world would you want me there?" she asked, unable to hide her complete bewilderment.

"You claim your place in my family. It is time you paid the dues accompanied by that status."

Humorless laughter fought to break free of the constriction in her throat. *Paid her dues?* Hadn't she done that for six long years? Hadn't she paid dearly for the privilege of wearing the Kiriakis name?

Leiandros watched emotions chase across Savannah's usually expressionless face. She hadn't been that way the first time they met. Then, she had seemed achingly vulnerable and sweet. So sweet she allowed another man to kiss her, to touch her while married to his cousin, he reminded himself.

Although she avoided eye contact with him on the few occasions they met after that, she'd still had an appealing vibrancy and beauty which made him understand why Dion stayed with her even after she had shown herself unworthy of her husband's respect and love. At least for the first year, but the one time Leiandros had seen her the second year she lived in Athens, she had changed beyond recognition.

Her green eyes had dulled to the point of lifelessness. Had guilt over her lovers done that? Her demeanor had completely lacked emotion—except when she looked at her daughter. Then a love Leiandros had envied—and hated himself for doing so—had suffused her face and brought life back to her green eyes. No wonder Dion ran wild with his friends. His wife had reserved all her emotion for the daughter she bore as the result of a liaison with one of her lovers.

Leiandros had chided Dion for showing so little interest in fatherhood after Eva's birth. Dion had cried when he told Leiandros that his wife had claimed the baby was not his. If Leiandros had ever doubted

Savannah's culpability in their shared kiss the night they met, he doubted no longer.

Remembering that encounter, his body tensed with anger. "Perhaps you are right. You have no place at my wife's funeral. One display of false grief within our family is enough."

Her eyes widened with what he could have sworn was fear before she took yet another step away from him. "I'm sorry Petra died, Leiandros."

The apparent sincerity in her soft voice almost touched him, but he refused to be taken in by her act a second time. She was no more the vulnerable innocent than he was a gullible fool. "I think you will be, Savannah."

"What do you mean?" she asked, her voice quavering in a way that annoyed him while she brushed a lock of wheat-colored hair away from her face.

What did she think he was going to do? Hit her? The thought was so ridiculous, he dismissed it out of hand. She had reason to be concerned, if not afraid. He did have plans for her, but they had to wait. "Never mind. I have to go."

She nodded. "Goodbye, Leiandros."

He inclined his head, refusing to utter a farewell he did not mean. After he expressed his respect for Petra with a year of mourning, Savannah would be seeing him again.

Then she would be made to pay for all that she had cost his family...all she had cost *him*.

CHAPTER TWO

SAVANNAH could hear the happy chatter of her daughters
playing in their bedroom as she settled into the creaking
desk chair in the small, cluttered study of her home in
Atlanta, Georgia.

She stared at the letter from Leiandros Kiriakis, feeling as if it were a black moccasin ready to strike. In it
he *requested* her presence in Greece for a discussion
regarding her financial future. Worse, he had demanded
Eva and Nyssa's presence as well.

He would be freezing Savannah's monthly allowance
until such a discussion occurred.

Panic shivered along her consciousness.

After the trial of attending Dion's funeral a year ago,
she had promised herself she would never have to see
anyone Kiriakis again. Okay, if not never, then at least
for a very long time.

The girls would have to be introduced to their Greek
family someday, but not before they were old enough to
deal with the emotional upheaval and possible rejection
of doing so. In other words, not until they were confident, mature adults.

She wished. She knew that wasn't realistic. Not after
the revelations Dion had made in that final phone call,
but she *had* intended to put the trip off for a while. Like
until she had a secure job and her Aunt Beatrice no
longer needed her.

14

Her mouth firming with purpose, she decided Leiandros would have to have his discussion with her over the phone. There was no earthly reason for her to fly all the way to Greece merely to talk about money.

Savannah's confidence in Leiandros's reasonability was severely tested ten minutes later when his secretary informed her he would not take Savannah's call.

"When would you like to fly out, Mrs. Kiriakis?" the efficient voice at the other end of the line enquired.

"I don't wish to fly out at all," Savannah replied, her southern drawl more pronounced than usual, the only indicator the conversation was upsetting her. "Please inform your boss that I would prefer to have this conversation by telephone and will await a call at his convenience."

She rang off, her hands shaking, her body going into fight or flight mode at the very thought of confronting Leiandros Kiriakis again in the flesh.

The phone rang ten minutes later.

Expecting Leiandros's secretary, Savannah picked up the receiver. "Hello?"

"You are due to receive your monthly allowance tomorrow." Although he had not bothered to identify himself, there was no mistaking the deep, commanding tones of Leiandros's voice.

It was a voice that haunted her dreams, erotic dreams that woke her in the middle of the night sweating and shaking. She could control her conscious mind, stifling all thoughts of the powerful, arrogant businessman, but her subconscious had a will of its own. And the dreams did nothing but torment her, as she knew without question she would never again experience those feelings outside the subconscious realm.

"Hello, Leiandros."

He didn't bother to return the greeting. "I won't be sanctioning that deposit, or any other until you come to Greece." No explanation, just an ultimatum.

The exorbitant prices Brenthaven charged for her aunt's care and the expense of attending university had prevented Savannah from accumulating more than a few weeks of living expenses in her savings. She needed the deposit to make her monthly payment to Brenthaven, not to mention to buy mundane items like food and gas.

"Surely any discussion we need to engage in can be handled via the phone."

"No." Again, no explanation. No compromise.

She rubbed her eyes, glad that he could not see the gesture that betrayed both physical weariness and emotional weakness. "Leiandros—"

"Contact my secretary for travel arrangements."

The phone clicked quietly in her ear and she pulled it away to stare at it. He'd hung up on her. She said a word that should never pass a lady's lips and slammed the phone back into its cradle. Shocked rigid by her own unaccustomed display of temper, she stood motionless for almost a full minute before spinning on her heel to leave the now stifling study.

She'd reached the door and opened it when the phone rang again. This time it wasn't Leiandros or his secretary. It was the doctor in charge of Aunt Beatrice.

Savannah's beloved aunt had had another stroke.

Savannah tucked her daughters into bed, telling them their favorite rendition of the Cinderella tale for their bedtime story before ensconcing herself in the study to make the dreaded call to Leiandros.

She pulled up her household budget spreadsheet on the computer and ran the numbers one more time. Nothing had miraculously changed. She *needed* the monthly allowance. Even if she could manage to land a full-time job the very next day, starting wages in spite of a degree in business were not going to be enough to cover their household expenses and the increased cost of Aunt Beatrice's medical care.

Savannah picked up the phone and dialed Leiandros's office.

His secretary answered on the first ring. The conversation was short. Savannah agreed to fly out the following week, but she refused to bring her daughters. The secretary hung up after promising to call back within the hour with an itinerary.

Savannah was making herself a cup of hot tea in the kitchen when the phone rang only minutes later.

A sense of impending doom sent goose bumps rushing down her arms and up the backs of her thighs. She just knew the secretary wasn't calling back with travel plans already.

After taking a steadying breath, she picked up the phone. "Yes, Leiandros?"

If she'd hoped to disconcert him, she was disappointed as there wasn't even a second's pause before he started talking.

"Eva and Nyssa must accompany you."

"No."

"Why not?" he demanded, his Greek accent pronounced.

Because the thought of taking her daughters back to Greece terrified her. "Eva has almost two weeks left of school."

"Then come in two weeks."

"I prefer to come now." She needed the money now, not in two weeks. "Besides, I see no reason to disrupt the girls' schedule for what will amount to an exhausting, but short trip."

"Not even to introduce them to their grandparents?"

Fear put a metallic taste in her mouth. "Their grandparents want nothing to do with them. Helena made that clear when Eva was born."

She'd taken one look at Savannah's blue-eyed and blond-haired baby and decreed the child could not possibly be a Kiriakis. Eva's eyes had darkened to green by the time she was a year old and her baby fine hair had been replaced by a thick mane of mahogany waves by the time she was four.

It was too bad Helena had refused point-blank to even come to see Nyssa. Savannah's youngest had been born with the black hair and velvet brown eyes of her father.

Unmistakably a Kiriakis.

"People change. Their son is gone. Is it so strange Helena and Sandros should wish to know his offspring?"

Savannah sucked in much needed oxygen and marshaled her thoughts. "Do they now acknowledge Eva and Nyssa as Dion's?"

"They will when they meet them."

No doubt. Both her daughters had enough physical characteristics of the Kiriakis clan that once seen their parentage could not be challenged, but that did not mean she was ready to introduce them to their family in Greece.

"How can you be so sure?" she asked, wondering how he knew of her daughters' physical resemblance to their relatives.

"I have seen pictures. There can be no question Eva and Nyssa are Kiriakises." The words sounded like an accusation.

"Dion's pictures, you mean?"

She'd sent him frequent updates on the girls' progress along with photos, hoping that one day he would show some inclination to acknowledge them. She'd felt her own lack of family and mourned her inability to know her own father and did not want the same grief visited on her daughters.

"Yes. I supervised the disposal of his effects from his Athens apartment." Again Leiandros's voice was laced with censure, as if she should have done the job herself.

After three years of separation and living independent lives on two different continents, she hadn't even considered such a thing. "I see."

"Do you?" he asked, his voice silky with unnamed menace and that awful sense of dread washed over her again.

"Have Helena and Sandros expressed a desire to meet them?"

"I have decided the time has come."

And as the head of the Kiriakis clan, he expected the rest of the family to go along with whatever decision he made.

"No."

"How can you be so selfish?" Condemnation weighted each word with bruising force.

"Selfish?" she asked, feeling anger roiling in her stomach, making it churn. "You call it selfish for a mother to wish to protect her children from the rejection of people that are supposed to love them, people that should have loved them since birth, but decided for their own obscure reasons not to?"

She knew she wasn't being entirely fair. For six years, Savannah had believed Dion's family had hated her because she was not the suitable Greek bride they had chosen for him to wed and therefore rejected her children. His phone call the night before he died effectively obliterated that theory.

Along with other stunning revelations, her dear husband had admitted that he'd been poisoning their minds with his insane jealousy, accusing her of infidelity, from almost the very start of their marriage. Helena and Sandros had what they believed to be legitimate reasons to question the parentage of Savannah's daughters, but that didn't make her any more willing to expose Eva and Nyssa to possible rejection and pain.

"Sandros and Helena will accept the girls with open arms."

"Who do you think you are. God?"

Funny, she could actually sense the fury sizzling through the phone lines. He was not used to being questioned. He'd been in charge of the huge Kiriakis financial empire since his father's unexpected death when Leiandros was twenty. At thirty-two, his arrogance and sense of personal power were as ingrained and natural to him as making his next million.

"Do not be blasphemous. It is unbecoming in a woman."

She almost laughed out loud at how stilted he sounded, like someone's maiden aunt giving lessons in etiquette. "I'm not trying to be offensive," she replied, "I simply want to protect my daughters' best interests."

"If you expect those interests to include further financial support from the Kiriakis family, you will bring them to Greece."

Savannah tried to draw in a breath, but it seemed to get stuck somewhere between her windpipe and her lungs. The edges of her vision turned black and she wondered with a sense of detachment if she were going to faint. Leiandros didn't know it, but he was forcing her to choose between the elderly aunt who had raised her and the safety of her daughters' emotions along with her own sanity.

It was her second worse nightmare. The first had already happened. She'd married Dion Kiriakis.

"Savannah!"

Someone was shouting in her ear. Her hand instinctively tightened on the phone and the room came slowly back into focus.

"Leiandros?" Was that thready voice hers?

How pathetic she must sound to the self-assured man on the other end of the line, but then she doubted anyone had ever forced him to do anything he did not want to.

"Are you all right?"

"No," she admitted. The last of her emotional reserves seemed to have dissipated with his overt threat.

"Savannah, I'm not going to let anyone hurt Eva and Nyssa." His voice reverberated against her ear with conviction and assurance.

But would he let them hurt her? "How can you prevent it?"

"You will have to trust me."

"I don't trust people named Kiriakis." Her words came in the flat monotone she couldn't seem to shake.

"You don't have a choice."

Leiandros hung up the phone, satisfied.

The opening gambit had gone to him. It would only be a matter of time before he captured her.

Savannah and her daughters would be flying to Greece the day after Eva's school let out for the summer. Savannah had agreed only after extracting a promise from him not to instigate any meeting between Eva, Nyssa and their grandparents before she had an opportunity to speak to Helena and Sandros.

How could she now show such concern for her daughters' emotional well-being when her lies about their parentage had denied them the love of their family since birth?

No doubt, her arguments were an attempt at manipulation. Perhaps she intended to try to use the girls as bargaining chips for a larger allowance. While her current stipend was substantial, it would hardly support the designer clad, jet setting lifestyle she had experienced while living with Dion.

He put through a call to his secretary. "Arrange for my jet to land in Atlanta to transport Savannah Kiriakis and her children to Athens two weeks from today."

He cut the connection after giving his secretary other necessary details.

Savannah had balked at flying on his jet, but after he

told her the plane had a bedroom the girls could use to sleep in comfort, she had agreed. If she'd remained insistent he would have given in to her. The first step in his plan was the most important: getting Savannah and the girls to Greece.

Savannah had to be on the chessboard in order to engage her in the game.

He would not allow an ocean and two continents to prevent him from exacting full payment from her for all that she had cost his family, all that she had cost *him*.

Savannah had committed the gravest of all sins against his family, that of withholding her children, using lies and manipulation to cheat Dion out of his fatherhood and Helena and Sandros out of their rightful role as doting grandparents.

That would end in two weeks time.

When he had first met Savannah, he had been drawn to her apparent innocence, to the impression of untouched sensuality she had exuded. So drawn he had kissed her without knowing her name or anything else about her.

She had struggled at first, but within seconds had gone up in flames. Her response had been more exciting than any other sexual experience he'd ever had. Then, she'd yanked herself from his arms and told him she was married. His first, primitive instinct had been to tell her she had married the wrong man. And then her husband had arrived. *His cousin.*

Leiandros's body still remembered the feel of hers. His mouth still hungered for her taste. His sex still ached for the release denied him that night. No matter how he tried to forget the forbidden desire for his cousin's wife, she was always there, in his dreams, in his mind.

Even knowing she was a scheming, heartless witch, he wanted her. Now, he would have her. She would replace what he had lost and in the process, he would sate his body's urge to possess her.

CHAPTER THREE

SAVANNAH carried a sleeping Nyssa toward customs, following Leiandros's personal flight attendant who led an equally worn-out, but barely awake, Eva by the hand. Exhaustion dragged at Savannah and she looked forward to a shower with almost religious fervor.

She could have taken one on the plane, but had not wanted to wake Eva and Nyssa any sooner than she had to. Wound up by the excitement of flying in an airplane, they had not made proper use of the plane's bedroom until an hour before landing.

When they reached customs, she was given VIP treatment and rushed through, an example of Leiandros's power and far reaching influence. It increased the sense of a trap closing around her she'd had since stepping onto his private jet.

As she stepped into the main terminal, she forced her weary eyes to focus on the scene around her. The new airport was all modern glass and streamlined walkways, but still incredibly crowded. She sighed and shifted her grip on Nyssa. Her arms felt like two strands of pasta cooked al dente.

Even as her gaze swept the crowded terminal, she felt the fine hairs on the back of her neck stand on end. Turning her head slightly to the right, she met the dark, inscrutable gaze of Leiandros Kiriakis himself and she stopped. Not voluntarily. Her legs simply quit working.

She hadn't expected to see him until the next day.

The flight attendant paused beside her, forcing the stream of air passengers to break and flow around them. "Mrs. Kiriakis? Is something wrong?"

Savannah could not make her lips form words. Her entire being was caught up in this first sight of Leiandros Kiriakis in a year. His black hair had been cut to lie close to the sculpted lines of his head. His sensual lips set in a grim line, his eyes betrayed nothing. He made no move to come toward them, but seemed content to wait, towering with unconscious arrogance above the sea of humanity that welled around him.

Taking a tighter hold on her sleeping daughter, she stepped forward only to bump into another passenger. "Excuse me. I'm sorry."

The woman she'd bumped ignored Savannah and scurried away toward the luggage carousel.

A large man who looked like a Greek Sumo wrestler barreled into her from behind. Stumbling, she feared she would lose her hold on Nyssa when two strong hands gripped her upper arms and steadied her. How had he gotten to her so quickly?

"You're dead on your feet, Savannah. Let me take the child." Leiandros moved one hand from her arm to Nyssa's back.

Without conscious volition, Savannah yanked herself and her daughter out of touching distance from Leiandros. "No. I can carry her, but thank you," she tacked on belatedly.

His eyes narrowed.

"Mama…" Eva's tentative interruption saved Savannah from whatever Leiandros had planned to say.

Savannah turned her attention gratefully to her daughter. "Yes, sweet pea?"

"I'm tired. May I go to bed now?"

"It will be a little while before we reach your bed, but you can sleep in the car. The seats are big enough for a little girl like you to treat them like a bed," Leiandros said.

"I'm five," Eva announced.

His mouth quirked. "If you are five, you must be Eva. I am Leiandros Kiriakis."

Eva's head tipped back and she measured him with a drowsy but direct look. "Kiriakis is my name, too."

He squatted down until his face was almost level with that of Savannah's serious little daughter. He matched Eva's grave expression. His mouth curved into a devastating smile. "So it is. That is because we are family."

Eva tugged her hand away from the flight attendant's and sidled next to Savannah, taking a grip on the loose fabric of her crushed silk trousers. "Is he my family, Mama?"

Leiandros's eyes blasted Savannah with sulfuric fury briefly as he straightened to stand at his full impressive six feet four inches. He seemed to be daring her to deny the link to her daughter, which she had no intention of doing.

She hadn't been the one to deny her daughters' family ties. "Yes, darling, your father was his cousin."

"Does he look like my father?" Eva asked.

Leiandros speared Savannah with another look of censure.

"You've seen pictures, what do you think?"

Savannah replied, letting her daughter draw her own conclusions.

She felt Eva's head shift against her thigh as the little girl nodded her head. "But maybe he's bigger."

Eva put her hand on Nyssa's small leg dangling over Savannah's arm. "This is Nyssa. She's four."

He acknowledged the introduction with a devastating smile.

"Now that we are acquainted, it is time we left. Felix will take care of the luggage," he said, indicating a short, stocky man standing several paces away near another very muscular man, only a couple of inches shorter than Leiandros.

Leiandros led them outside and Savannah blessed the lightweight nature of her crushed silk pantsuit when the hot Greek air blasted her as they stepped out of the air-conditioned environs of the recently completed airport. While the heat wasn't so very different from Georgia, the sun's impact felt stronger.

As they approached a black limousine with darkly tinted windows, the chauffeur opened the back door while another man stood sentry on the driver's side. He and the man with Felix were no doubt part of Leiandros's security team.

Savannah motioned Eva to climb in first. She did, taking Leiandros at his word and making herself comfortable for sleep on the far side of the seat, leaving enough space for Savannah to lay Nyssa's dozing form down as well. Another wave of exhaustion rolled over her and Savannah wished she could join Nyssa in her peaceful slumber. Within fifteen minutes of leaving the airport, Eva had done so.

"Sleep if you wish. I will not be offended," Leiandros offered. "The trip is a long one from the airport."

Savannah swallowed a yawn. "I didn't think it was that far from the city."

"It is not, but there is road construction." He shrugged. "It will take us at least two hours to reach the villa."

She'd been relaxing against the seat, preparing to take him up on his advice to pass the time sleeping when he made that comment. She sat straight up and twisted her body until she could look him full in the face.

"What villa? I thought we were staying at a hotel."

"You are family. You will stay with family."

There was that word again, but Savannah had had enough experience her first time around in Greece with the dutiful ties of the Kiriakis family not to trust them.

"You promised me the girls would not have to see their grandparents until we discussed it," she accused him in a fierce whisper, not wanting to wake her daughters to hear this particular argument. "I insist you take us to a hotel."

"No."

"No? No! How dare you do this? You promised." She settled back against the seat with her arms crossed. "I knew I couldn't trust a Kiriakis."

That seemed to get him, because his hands curled into fists at his side and his face looked hewn from rock.

"You will not be staying with Helena and Sandros."

"You said we'd be staying with family, at the villa." As the words left her lips, an awful thought occurred to her. "You want us to stay at *your* villa on Evia Island? *With you?*"

His brows rose in sardonic challenge. "My mother is also staying at the villa. She will be sufficient chaperone."

"*Chaperone?* I don't need a chaperone. I need privacy. I need to stay in a hotel."

"Relax, Savannah. There is no reason to shout about it. With two active children, you will find the villa much more comfortable than a hotel, I promise you."

In that respect, she had no doubt he was right, but it wasn't her daughters she was worried about at the moment. It was herself. She shuddered inwardly at the prospect of sharing living space with Leiandros.

"I suppose you still keep an apartment in Athens and spend most of your time there," she said hopefully.

"Yes."

She couldn't quite stifle her sigh of relief.

"Of course, I've arranged to work from the villa for the next few days so I can spend time with *my family.*"

Savannah's throat went tight in reaction to the threat in his voice, despite the innocence of the sentiments expressed.

"How long did you plan our visit to last?" It was something he'd refused to discuss on the phone.

If she'd been in her right mind, instead of riddled with worry over her aunt, Savannah would have forced the issue.

Leiandros looked at her as if trying to read her mind. "We'll discuss that tomorrow."

"I'd rather discuss it now." She kept her expression purposefully blank.

"Very well." He shrugged again, his face wearing a strangely watchful air. "Permanently."

"Permanently?"

The grim line of his mouth went even more taut. "Yes. You've spent enough time running from your family. It's time you came home, Savannah."

Home? She wanted to shriek at him and pound her fists, but even with rage coursing through her veins like molten lava, she held onto her temper. She'd learned that lesson much too well to forget it, even with the current provocation.

She'd lost her control once with a Kiriakis male and opened herself to physical reprisal from her husband. She still had nightmares about her last meeting with Dion, the feeling of bruising male fists landing against her unprotected flesh.

"America is my home," she said, spacing the words evenly, keeping her voice flat.

"It was your home before you married a Kiriakis, yes. But now Greece is your home, specifically my villa."

"Your villa? You expect me to live in your villa permanently?" She was in a waking nightmare.

He reached out and opened the minifridge, pulling out a bottle of water, handing it to her before taking one for himself. "Yes."

She stared at the cold plastic bottle in her hand, wondering for a second how it had gotten there. "I can't."

He didn't bother to argue with her. In fact, he didn't answer her at all. Instead, he pulled a buzzing cell phone from his pocket and answered it.

*   *   *

Savannah slowly regained consciousness, uncertain what had wakened her, and shifted in the cocooned warmth of her make shift bed. She burrowed her face into the pillow, which felt strangely hard against her cheek. Unsated exhaustion tugged at her, tempting her back into an unconscious state.

Her bed moved and the blanket pressed against her back in a soft caress. "Wake up *pethi mou,* we have almost arrived."

Her eyes flew open. For the space of several seconds she couldn't even breathe. The blanket caressing her back was in fact a large, male hand and her firm pillow, a muscular chest. Frozen into immobility by shock, she further discovered that her arms were wrapped tightly around his torso.

The subtle fragrance of fresh, clean male and expensive aftershave teased her senses. Familiar and yet unknown. She blinked, trying to focus, but her vision was clouded by crisp white silk and her mind could not quite come to grips with the first intimacy shared with a man in well over four years.

And not just any man.

She was wrapped up like an early Christmas present in the arms of Leiandros Kiriakis.

Reality so closely matched the dreams that had tormented her subconscious for seven long years that she spent several precious seconds trying to determine if she were still asleep.

"Eva, how come Mama is hugging that man?" Nyssa's voice unlocked Savannah's frozen limbs.

She was definitely awake. Her daughters had never played a role in the dreams she had had about Leiandros. Yanking her arms from their snug nest in his suit coat, she launched herself from Leiandros with such a violent movement she bounced against the opposite door and nearly fell off the seat.

He reached out to steady her and she recoiled violently from the possible touch. "I'm fine," she all but snarled, her usual polite reserve a forgotten ideal.

"He's our family," Eva said, as if that explained everything. She had that much in common with her uncle.

Savannah couldn't help but wonder if he had thought the familial claim justified the intimacy of their position as well.

"Mama?" Nyssa asked, her brown Kiriakis eyes wide with curiosity.

Savannah settled herself more firmly on the large limousine seat. Not caring what Leiandros thought of the action, she scooted as close to the door as she could get without sitting on the armrest. "Yes, sugar?"

"Why did you hug the big man?"

"I wasn't hugging him." She turned and glared at Leiandros. This situation was all his fault. "I was asleep."

"Oh." Nyssa turned her interested gaze to Leiandros and stared at him in silence for several seconds before turning back to her mother. "Were you sitting in his lap to sleep?"

The heat of embarrassment crawled over Savannah's skin like ants on a picnic blanket. She couldn't look at Leiandros. She had no idea how she'd ended up sleeping with her body plastered against his and feared finding out she had been the instigator.

The last thing she remembered was letting her head rest against the back of the seat. She'd closed her eyes in weariness as she tired of waiting for him to finish the latest of his numerous business calls on the cell.

She'd obviously fallen asleep. That she could understand. She'd been nearly comatose from exhaustion before the plane had landed. The last two weeks had been peppered with sleepless nights and emotionally draining days visiting her aunt.

Even so, she found it difficult to believe she'd allowed herself to get that close to a man, asleep or not. Her subconscious mind might crave Leiandros Kiriakis, but her conscious mind rejected even the hint of intimacy with any man.

The evidence, however, was irrefutable. Her skin still tingled from where she had touched him.

Before she got a chance to form a reply to Nyssa's question that wouldn't betray the rawness of her nerves, her daughter smiled at Leiandros. "Sometimes I sit on my mama's lap for sleeping, but she says I'm getting too heavy. Isn't she too big for your lap?"

Savannah wanted to groan out loud at her daughter's logic. Nyssa's nap had clearly been long enough to rejuvenate her mind as well as her spirits. Savannah wished she had been so lucky. Her mind felt too sluggish to deal with the current situation. Unbelievably, her traitorous body craved return to the warm, muscular resting place of Leiandros's chest.

"I'd say she's just right." His low, sensual tone caressed Savannah's insides, making them tighten and interrupting her chaotic thoughts.

Awareness of his masculinity bombarded her. Along with something else, something elemental that left her feeling hot and strangely edgy. *Impossible.* She had spent the last four years believing she would never again experience sexual desire and here she was as jittery as a mare being bred for the first time. Wanting it, but terrified at the same time.

"Where are we?" she asked in a desperate bid to change the direction her thoughts were taking.

"Very near Villa Kalosorisma. We have just crossed the bridge to Evia Island." His eyes told her he knew exactly why she'd asked the question and found the knowledge amusing.

The car slid to a halt and seconds later, the door next to Savannah opened. The chauffeur helped first Eva, then Nyssa from the car. By the time Savannah swung her legs around to climb out, Leiandros had exited from the other side and come around to take her hand in his.

He pulled her from the sleek chauffeured car, the heat of his hand branding her as intimately as if he'd kissed her. She tried to ignore the sensation and swiftly stepped away from him.

The girls stood a few yards away, staring at the villa's front with identical expressions of surprised awe. Savannah identified with the feeling.

She had never been to Villa Kalosorisma. Dion had kept her separated from the rest of his family as much as possible, even his parents and sister. He'd told her at the time it was his way of protecting her from their disapproval until they came to accept the marriage. She now knew differently. He'd been afraid of having his ugly lies about her morality revealed. She still cringed at what a gullible idiot she had been then.

The pristine whiteness of the villa's stucco exterior dazzled her eyes, contrasting beautifully with the red tile roof. Three levels of terraces outlined by arches fronted the mansion. Surrounded by immaculate gardens and green trees, through which she could see glimpses of sparkling blue sea, Villa Kalosorisma simply took her breath away.

"It's a real pretty hotel," Nyssa announced.

"It's not a hotel," Savannah felt impelled to say.

"This is my home." Leiandros had come to stand behind Savannah without her realizing it.

She once again stepped away, impatient to put distance between herself and his disturbing presence. She'd almost grown accustomed to the anxiety a man's nearness caused in her, but that anxiety mixed with unmistakable sexual awareness was a cocktail mix guaranteed to corrupt her sanity.

"I thought we were staying in a hotel, Mama." Eva said.

"In Greece family is everything. It would be considered a grave insult were I not to offer my home to you all and equally offensive if your mama refused to accept it." Leiandros's words seemed laced with warning and Savannah turned her head to see him more clearly.

Was he trying to intimidate her and if so, why? She'd already agreed to stay at his villa and in fact felt a small measure of gratitude that she hadn't been forced to play this scene with Helena and Sandros. She would have refused any invitation extended by them regardless of the offense taken.

The very thought of being forced to accept her in-law's hospitality was enough to make her feel slightly nauseous.

"Our house is lots smaller because we've just got a

mommy and me and Eva. You must have an awful lot of kids. You're house is like Cinderella's castle." Typically, Nyssa had spoken again while Eva silently watched the adults, letting her serious green gaze flicker between them and the big white villa.

Bitterness and pain reflected briefly in his dark chocolate eyes. "I have no children."

"Oh. Don't you like kids?" Nyssa asked before Savannah thought to caution her daughter to silence.

This time the pain was more pronounced and even slipped into his voice as he answered. "I like children very much."

Had he and Petra planned to have them right away? It must have been a horrible shock to lose her so soon after marriage. Leiandros and Petra had only been married about a year when Dion crashed his car with Petra in it, killing them both instantly. Knowing it was ridiculous, Savannah still felt guilty by association. It had been her estranged husband responsible for the crash.

Eva stepped forward and laid her little hand on Leiandros's forearm. "It's okay. Someday, you'll have some. Mama says you've got to believe in your dreams for them to come true."

He squatted down in front of Eva and reached out to brush her cheek. "Thank you, *pethi mou.* You and your sister staying at the villa will be like having children of my own."

In a wholly uncharacteristic move, Eva let her small fingers trail down Leiandros's face to his chin, her green eyes full of both compassion and a wistfulness that surprised Savannah. "I'll play checkers with you if you like. Daddies do that with their little girls sometimes."

"You can help Mom tuck us in at night, too," Nyssa added, not willing to be outdone by her sister.

Savannah watched the entire scene with a sense of unreality intensified by her tiredness. Her daughters had spent very little time around men, which usually made even the more gregarious Nyssa timid with them. And yet, here was Savannah's extremely cautious eldest daughter reaching out to touch Leiandros.

Even more shocking than her daughter's response to Leiandros were *his* words. Did he truly want her and the girls to move to Greece to fill a void that had opened in his life since his young wife's death?

She'd never considered Leiandros Kiriakis vulnerable in any way. The man spent his time running a multibillion dollar corporation. He couldn't seriously need the company of two small girls to complete his life.

Savannah curled her hands around the oversized woven bag she carried. It felt like a link to sanity, its casual American styling a reminder of the life she'd made for herself and her daughters. A life far removed from that of privileged wealth exemplified by Villa Kalosorisma.

A life she and her daughters *would* return to.

CHAPTER FOUR

LEIANDROS sipped his neat whiskey and waited for Savannah to join him in the fireside reception room before dinner.

The villa, built by his grandfather, boasted two large reception rooms as well as two formal dining rooms, one of which his father had turned into a study after losing the smaller area dedicated to that purpose to a TV viewing room at his wife's request. There was also a breakfast nook, eight bedrooms with en suites and full staff quarters on the ground level.

In other words, his home had plenty of space for Savannah to find the privacy she said she craved, but such privacy would not extend to her avoiding his company. That was not part of his plan. Tonight, he intended to make it clear to her he would be an intrinsic part of her life from now on.

He was so hungry for her, he had been unable to resist the growing temptation to pull her into his arms after she fell asleep. He'd watched her for several miles of travel before giving into the urge to pull her into his arms.

He had not held her, even in an embrace of greeting, since the hot kiss they had shared the night they met. He could not risk his own body's reaction. Touching her then had been wrong. She'd belonged to another man.

Dion had died and now Savannah belonged to Leiandros, even if she did not yet realize it.

Her body had known it. She'd curled around him like a lover of longstanding and his physical reaction had been predictable if surprisingly swift. He'd wanted to touch her, to remove her soft silk blouse and see the breasts pressed so tantalizingly against his chest, but even Greek tycoons had their sense of honor, he thought cynically.

When he touched Savannah, she would be awake and wanting it as much as he did.

As she had wanted his kiss seven years ago.

He took another sip of his whiskey as she appeared in the arched doorway. She'd changed into a knee length sheath in emerald green raw silk and pulled the multicolored, golden brown strands of her hair into an elegant twist on the back of her head. Her only jewelry was a necklace of hammered silver medallions and matching earrings.

It was a lovely look, but hardly the designer labeled couture he'd expected from her based on the monthly allowance she received. Nyssa had also said their house was small.

Was that the unrealistic view of a child, or had she been stating a fact? If Nyssa had spoken the truth, what did Savannah spend the ten thousand dollars a month she received from the Kiriakis coffers on?

Savannah hovered in the doorway, wanting to flee. The girls had been fed and put to bed an hour ago. They had invited Leiandros to help tuck them in, but he'd had to take an international call and had promised to do so the following night.

Savannah hadn't minded one bit. She found his presence distinctly disturbing.

"Come in, Savannah. I'm not going to eat you."

She forced a slight smile to her lips and a light tone to her voice. "Of course not. Billionaire Greek tycoons have too much discernment to eat houseguests, even reluctant ones."

His black brow raised in cynical amusement. "What would you like to drink?"

"Something nonalcoholic. I have no head for spirits and in my current state of jet lag, I'd probably pass out after a sip of your most innocuous sherry." And she needed her wits.

He turned toward the drink trolley, his gorgeous body graceful in movement and yet exuding power. He poured her a tall glass of chilled water over ice, adding a twist of lime to it.

She accepted the drink, making sure their fingers did not touch and then took a step back. "Isn't your mother joining us for dinner?"

He moved forward, closing the small gap she had created. "She's visiting friends. She'll be home in a couple of days."

"So much for her suitability as a chaperone," Savannah muttered under her breath.

He laughed softly. "You said you didn't need one. Have you changed your mind, Savannah?"

His deep, masculine voice vibrated through her, causing her insides to tighten in a frightening way and she felt her cheeks heat at the reaction and the import of his words. She took a long, cooling sip of water. "Mr. Kiriakis, we need to talk."

"Leiandros. Not Mr. Kiriakis. Not *Kyrios* Kiriakis. Leiandros. We are family. You will not address me so formally again."

Her intention had been to create distance between them mentally, if not physically, but clearly she'd managed to annoy him as well. She gritted her teeth. It just wasn't worth making an issue over. "Leiandros then. This idea you have of the girls and I making a permanent home in Greece is unfeasible at the present time to say the least."

His eyes narrowed while he indicated with a gesture of his hand she should sit down on one of the almond leather sofas on either side of the fireplace. "Why?"

"I have obligations, commitments, back home that I cannot dismiss." She chose a seat on the far end of the sofa located on the other side of the room from him.

His smile was predatory as he followed her and took a seat on the same sofa, his body turned toward hers. "What kind of commitments?" he asked with obvious suspicion.

She felt his presence like a physical force and she had to concentrate to answer his question. "The usual kind." She crossed her legs at the ankle while taking another sip of her drink. "Relationships. Work. My commitment to Eva and Nyssa's well being."

"You do not have a job."

She acknowledged the truth of his statement with a brief nod. "But I do need to have one if I'm ever to be free of my dependence on the monthly allowance." Surely he must see that.

"If independence is so important to you, why have you made no move to get a job in the last four years?" he demanded, skepticism lacing every word.

Her free hand curled into a fist and she felt her face tighten with anger before she made herself relax and her face go blank of emotion. "I've spent the last four years going to university. I now have a degree in business and plan to use it to support myself and my daughters.''

He looked absolutely stunned and she felt satisfaction at the reaction.

''Did you bring your diploma with you?'' he asked.

Had he lost his mind? ''Why would I bring it with me?''

''So I can verify you are telling me the truth.''

Unaccustomed and unwelcome anger filled her. ''Your arrogance is astounding. Why should I have to prove myself to you? My degree is immaterial to the discussion at hand.''

''Which is what?'' he asked, his voice laced with sensual innuendo.

She swallowed, trying to ignore the way her heart reacted to that particular honeyed tone. ''We are discussing my need to return home. Soon. I'll stay long enough for the girls to meet their grandparents if my discussion with them proves satisfactory, but then I'm going home and there's not a blessed thing you can do about it.''

''You'd be surprised at what I have to say about it.''

She gritted her teeth. How could she feel threatened by him and attracted to him at the same time? ''You can *say* what you like, but I'm still going.''

''If you really are interested in gaining your independence from the monthly allowance I provide, why have you come to Greece at all? You didn't want to come, but you agreed when I refused to pay it.''

That was not a question she was willing to answer. ''You don't provide our allowance. It comes from the girls' trust.'' She set her now empty glass down on a small table.

"I haven't touched Eva and Nyssa's trust in the past year."

"But..." She let her words trail off, nonplussed. *He'd* been paying their allowance for the past year? The knowledge made her feel strange, as if he had intruded into her life in an intimate way without her being aware of it.

"There are no buts. I have supported you for the past year and if you wish me to continue to do so, certain conditions must be met."

She'd had it up to her neck with conditions from Dion. She wasn't going to go that route with Leiandros. "I don't want to be supported. I'm perfectly willing to get a job."

"Then why have you come to Greece?" he asked again, his disbelief palpable.

"I need our allowance for another few months, until I'm on my feet financially."

"Do you honestly believe you'll be able to get a job starting out at ten thousand dollars a month?" He made it sound like she was the world's biggest idiot.

"No. Of course not, but I won't need that much money to live on in a few months." Her heart contracted with a spasm of grief at the thought of why she wouldn't need so much money.

The doctors did not expect her aunt to live to the end of the year. Without the monthly payments to Brenthaven, she and the girls could easily live on her income.

"Again I ask why?"

"You're like a dog with his favorite bone."

He shrugged. "So, answer me and I'll quit asking."

She met his gaze, hers level and as impassive as she could make it. "The answer is none of your business."

He didn't like that. His dark eyes flared with affronted pride. "Since I am paying your allowance I think it is."

"But I didn't *know* that."

"You do now."

Desperation edged her voice. "It can't change anything. I still need the money right now. Perhaps, we could make it a loan and once I've gotten a job I could pay you back in monthly installments."

She'd been forced to pull her entire savings to pay the increased costs of the round-the-clock care her aunt needed since the last stroke, but another payment would be due in only a couple of weeks.

Brenthaven had a strict policy requiring advanced payment for services. If she did not keep up-to-date, they would transfer Aunt Beatrice to the nearest state nursing home. They might regret the need to do so, but would do it nonetheless as she had discovered four years ago when she had separated from Dion without a financial support agreement.

Felix announced dinner before Leiandros responded to her suggestion of a loan.

Savannah tried to do justice to the excellent dinner Felix's wife had prepared, but jet lag and the stress of trying to spar verbally with Leiandros had stolen her appetite. Not to mention the strange vibrations that shivered through her whenever she let her eyes meet Leiandros's. Even her favorite moussaka tasted like sawdust in her mouth.

Leiandros pushed his empty plate aside while eyeing her nearly full one. "You should have taken a tray in your room. You're too tired to enjoy a full course dinner.''

''We needed to talk without interruption.'' Or witnesses. She did not want her daughters to know that Leiandros sought to have the Kiriakis women back in Greece permanently.

''So, talk. You can begin by telling me what significant change you anticipate in your circumstances that will make it possible for you to go from living on ten thousand dollars a month to a fraction of that.''

She didn't like the speculative look in his eyes. Nor did she have any intention of telling him what he wanted to know. If he found out about Aunt Beatrice, he would have the same stick to beat her with Dion had used so effectively.

''My financial needs are my concern. If you won't lend me the money, I'll take out a mortgage on my house.'' There was no reason to let him know that option was an iffy one at best without a proven source of income.

She had to hope Leiandros's pride would not allow a Kiriakis to go to a bank for what the family had been providing up to date.

He said nothing as the housekeeper removed their dinner plates and put small crystal bowls of fresh fruit and cream in front of them.

She smiled at Savannah. ''I think you'll eat this, yes?''

Savannah returned her smile. ''Yes. It looks very refreshing.''

Silence reigned as she and Leiandros ate their dessert.

When they were finished he told the housekeeper they would take their coffee on the terrace and led Savannah outside. The view from the back terrace was every bit as spectacular as it was from the bedroom windows. The sea glistened gold and red and even the pool shimmered with exotic color in the sun's setting light. She gave an involuntary sigh of appreciation.

"There is nothing more beautiful." Leiandros pulled a chair out for her from the white wrought-iron patio set.

She sat down, her gaze shifting from the vibrant sunset to the tall, dark man at her side. "Sunrise in a grove of Magnolia bushes isn't such a paltry sight, either."

His teeth flashed in the waning light before he took the chair nearest her own, putting his back to the spectacular Heavenly display and focusing his entire attention on her. "One day I may have to see that."

The thought of Leiandros in Georgia was enough to unsettle her nerves and send her stomach into cartwheels. "I can't imagine you finding sufficient business incentive to make the journey," was all she said.

Felix's wife arrived with a tray bearing two demitasse cups filled with the traditional aromatic, spiced Greek coffee. She also turned on the outside lights, illuminating the pool and the garden surrounding it, before returning to the house.

Several lighted pathways led into the orchards and olive grove surrounding the house. Savannah longed to explore their quiet solitude, but she had to remain with Leiandros and impress upon him her seriousness about returning home and her need for the monthly allowance to be deposited immediately into her account.

"Kiriakis International does not dictate every aspect of my life." The timbre of his voice and dark chocolate depths of his eyes spoke a sensual message that both frightened and excited her.

''I find that difficult to believe considering the amount of time you have always spent working.'' She took a sip of her coffee, allowing her senses to savor the unique flavor. She had missed this little luxury back in Georgia.

''And yet I found time to marry.''

The thought of Leiandros married to another woman made her feel raw inside, mitigating the effectiveness of her usually stringent guard on her tongue. ''To a traditional Greek girl who undoubtedly never questioned her role in your life.''

His scowl said he did not appreciate her view. ''Is that why you abandoned my cousin? Wasn't he willing to cater to your need to be the center of his universe?''

Savannah felt her emotions and thoughts close down as they always did at any mention of her disastrous marriage. ''I had no desire to be the center of Dion's life.''

She had in fact wished fervently that he had been less focused on her, particularly when that focus came in the guise of irrational jealousy and his desire to impregnate her with his child. His *male* child.

''I imagine that is true. Dion's obsessive love must have been an unexpected cramp in your pursuit of *friendships* outside of your marriage.''

The way he sneered the word friendships left her in no doubt about just what nature he believed those relationships had taken. Savannah had learned from Dion that denial was useless and defending herself only left her open to further accusations and insults. So, she didn't even bother to try.

She simply said, ''Obsessive is a very good name for the feelings Dion had for me.''

''The poor fool loved you.'' Leiandros made it sound

as if only an idiot would have such tender feelings for his wife.

"I suppose you were too much in control of your emotions to make the same mistake with Petra."

His jaw tightened. "I cared for my wife. She had a life most women envied, but you are right. I never subjugated myself to her the way Dion did with you."

Subjugated? Dion? Leiandros's view of her marriage would be laughable if the truth didn't hurt so much. "I prefer not to discuss my marriage."

"So sensitive. Are you trying to convince me that the subject is painful for you, or merely distasteful?"

Once again, she took refuge in her coffee. She needed time to collect her emotions before speaking. When she did, she was proud of the even tenor of her voice. "Dion and I were estranged for years prior to his death. I consider my marriage a part of my past that has no place in my present or future."

"You forget your daughters. They are a product of that marriage that preclude you dismissing it completely from your life." It was as if he was challenging her to deny Eva and Nyssa were Dion's daughters.

"Surely after seeing my daughters, you cannot doubt that Dion was their father."

"I do not deny it, no. It is you that have withheld the girls from their Greek relatives practically since birth." The accusation in his voice was unmistakable.

Anger, usually suppressed, burned through her reserve. "I was not the one who questioned their Kiriakis heritage. If you wish to lay blame for that, look to your cousin and his unreasonable jealousies. It was because of them that his mother pronounced Eva a cuckoo in the family's nest and refused to acknowledge her. She and

Sandros never even made the effort to see Nyssa. Not once in the six months before I left Greece or the years since.''

"How convenient. You can dismiss your role in your daughters' estrangement from their family because Dion no longer lives to give lie to your claims of innocence."

The pig. Of course he doubted her. After all, his male cousin would never have lied to him. Dion's jealous delusions were taken as gospel by his staunchly loyal family. She could admire that loyalty, but she didn't have to become a victim to it. She'd fought too hard to make something of herself and her life to allow Leiandros to tear away at her carefully constructed foundation with his cruel words.

Discussion over the monthly allowance would have to wait.

She stood up. "I'm tired. I believe I'll go to bed."

"So regal when running away. What's the matter, Savannah? Does the truth distress you so much?"

Her hands clenched at her sides while she willed the anger inside her to remain hidden. "I have discovered that Kiriakises are not interested in truth so much as their own delusions. I have no hope of changing yours so I refuse to try, but I also refuse to sit and listen to a character assassination based on those delusions. Good night."

She turned to walk away.

Suddenly he was there beside her, his long, masculine fingers wrapped securely around her upper arm. "Oh, no. You aren't walking away from me so easily. Dion may have let you dismiss him like a tame lapdog, but be warned I am a wolf in comparison."

Her heart had started to accelerate at the first touch of

his fingers and her breath shortened to panicky pants as the threat in his voice washed over her.

"Please, let me go." She didn't sound regal any longer. Her voice had come out weak and way too soft.

"Not yet. There is something I need to do first."

Was he going to hit her? She refused to cower, but she also hesitated to use the self-defense techniques she'd learned to dislodge his grip. She did not wish to hurt him and her heart denied vehemently any notion he would physically hurt her. Which led her to ask herself where her heart had gotten such an idea? The answer terrified her more than the memory of Dion's rage. On some level she did not understand, she trusted Leiandros physically in a way she did not trust any other man.

For the moment, she stood immobile in his arms. "What?"

"I neglected to kiss you in greeting at the airport. It is time I rectified that omission, don't you think?"

His words paralyzed her. She and Leiandros had not shared so much as a handshake since their disastrous first meeting. Of course he would not have greeted her in the traditional Greek manner at the airport.

"There is no omission to correct."

He propelled her around to face him and placed his free hand under her chin. "Ah, but there is."

She would have argued further, but he lowered his head and touched one of her cheeks briefly with his warm, firm lips. "Welcome home, Savannah."

She waited for the panic, which typically accompanied such close proximity to a male, but as in the limo, her body did not react with its usual desire to flee. Her mind *was* panicking however because as he kissed her other cheek, she had an inexcusable urge to turn her face so instead of the platonic salute to her cheek, she would receive a kiss full on the mouth. She fought the impulse, managing to remain immobile in his hold.

He didn't step away after kissing her second cheek, but remained close to her for several, tense, silent seconds.

"Don't you wish to return my greeting?"

She did. The desire was such a new experience after years of experiencing nothing but fear and distrust in the company of a man that she acted on it without thought. He released her chin and she kissed him on first his left cheek, then his right.

She could taste the clean saltiness of his skin and smell his distinctive cologne. She wanted to kiss him again, but she didn't. She waited to see what he would do next.

He didn't leave her in suspense long. He made an inarticulate sound deep in his throat and then covered her still tingling mouth with his own.

Her eyes slid shut and fireworks exploded in and around her. One second she was standing a safe distance from his virile male body and the next she was plastered against him with her hands locked fiercely behind his neck.

She opened her mouth for his invading tongue without a second's hesitation and eagerly entered the erotic duel he initiated. It was as if her body could not resist the feast of his touch after the famine she had imposed on it for so many years. It felt so good to be close to him.

He tasted like ambrosia to her passion starved mouth and she lost all conscious volition to control her actions. She operated on instinct and desire, both of which urged her to hold nothing back from this volatile kiss.

His large hands moved down her back to cup her buttocks. He squeezed and an involuntary moan of pleasure exploded from her mouth into his. He used his hold on her to lift her and press the apex of her thighs against his throbbing hardness.

She couldn't help arching into him any more than she could wrench her mouth from his marauding one.

It felt too delightful. It was even more devastating than the kiss they had shared the night they met because she had no voice of conscience telling her that she was a married woman who had no business feeling passion with a man not her husband.

Dion was gone and her body knew it.

She wanted Leiandros with a strength that overwhelmed her good sense, her fear of a man's nearness, even her sense of self-preservation that she had spent four years honing. Her nipples hardened into rigid peaks that strained against the soft lace of her light bra and she could feel moisture gathering between her legs in anticipation of the kiss's outcome.

Leiandros kneaded her bottom with his hands, helping her achieve maximum friction between his hardened maleness and her aching femininity, while sucking on her tongue and playing erotic biting games with her lips.

She rocked harder against him, overwhelmed by the sense of bliss his body gave to hers.

Pleasure began washing over her in waves and she whimpered, frightened of these new and overpowering feelings. He made approving sounds as his mouth continued to devour hers, but he lifted one hand from her bottom to caress the aching rigidity of her right nipple. He pinched it gently through the layers of raw silk and lace and something exploded inside of her.

She went rigid while her body convulsed in his hold, her cry of fear mingled with pleasure getting swallowed by his hot, hungry mouth. She shook and shook before her body went boneless. If he had not held her, she would have melted into a dazed puddle at his feet.

So that was what it felt like. She'd never known pleasure so glorious, nor sensations so intense. She could not prevent herself from wondering what it would be like with his body joined to hers. Could it possibly be better?

His arms wrapped around her, pressing her body close in an embrace that comforted her devastated emotions, while he drew his mouth away to kiss her eyelids, her cheeks, her nose, and even her chin.

She started to cry, quiet sobs so alien to her that they were almost as frightening as the mind-blowing pleasure.

He kissed the wetness from her cheeks, acting as if the tears were his due. "There can be no doubt our marriage bed will be a satisfying one."

CHAPTER FIVE

Savannah stared in disbelief at Leiandros. Had he just said they were going to get married?

She shook her head, but her mind refused to clear.

Without warning, he swung her high against his chest and carried her into the house and up the stairs to her room where he deposited her on the side of her bed. Her mind vaguely registered that he wasn't even breathing hard.

He cupped her nape and pressed his lips briefly and gently against hers, which clung without volition. "Good night. We'll discuss plans for the future tomorrow."

It was a measure of her bemusement that instead of disabusing him of any ideas of a shared future together, she merely nodded and watched quietly as he left the room, closing the door behind him. It took ten full minutes of silent contemplation of that same closed door before the enormity of what she had done hit her.

She had let Leiandros kiss her and touch her intimately on a well lit terrace where anyone could have seen them. Worse, her body had betrayed her by finding the ultimate pleasure at his touch. She hadn't even considered fighting him off or denying him access to her femininity. If he had undressed her and offered to share her bed, she would have let him.

She didn't think she could ever look Leiandros in the

eye again. How on earth was she supposed to discuss money and her now even more necessary return to America with him?

An involuntary smile curved her lips because her shock and dismay were tinged with a sense of elation she could not deny. The essence of her womanhood, the part of her she had believed destroyed by her husband's violence the last time they saw each other, was alive and well. She'd reclaimed her femininity and she'd done it with Leiandros Kiriakis.

She pushed herself into a standing position beside the bed, somewhat surprised when she remained vertical. She should take a shower. Yes, that's what she should do. Wash away the evidence of her desire and the effect of Leiandros's kisses. She walked over to the white wicker dresser and removed her jewelry, laying it on the glass top.

Unzipping her dress with fingers that still trembled, she moved toward the closet. She slid the dress from her body, sucking in a breath of shocked air at the way her nipples and thighs responded to the movement of the raw silk. Pressing the dress to her heated cheeks, she could smell her own perfume, but the faint fragrance of Leiandros's sexy cologne lingered on the fabric as well.

She stood there inhaling the evocative scent until she realized what she was doing and hastily hung the dress up. If she had thought removing her dress had been erotic, it was nothing compared to the reaction she had to taking off her underclothes. By the time she had tossed them in the round wicker clothes hamper, she recognized that a hot shower was the last thing her sexually awakened body could handle.

She slipped into a sleeveless white cotton nightdress with embroidery on the three button yoke. She'd always considered the nightgown rather innocent, but tonight it reminded her of a virgin waiting to be ravished on her wedding night.

Groaning at her wayward thoughts, she climbed between the Jasmine scented polished cotton sheets of her bed. Wasn't Jasmine supposed to be some kind of aphrodisiac? She certainly didn't need any more stimulation. Maybe she could ask the housekeeper for some plain sheets that smelled like good old-fashioned fabric softener tomorrow.

She snuggled into her pillow, sure she'd never get to sleep after the shattering events of the evening, but her eyes were heavy and her body felt replete in a way it never had before.

Her last drowsy thought was that Leiandros was more effective than a sleeping pill.

Leaving Savannah alone in her bedroom had been one of the more difficult tasks Leiandros had set for himself, perhaps even the most difficult task to date. He wasn't going to make love to her when she was suffering from exhaustion and jet lag. He would not allow her the out that she hadn't been in her right mind when she finally gave her body to him.

Besides, there was something he needed to do.

Picking up the phone, he dialed a well-used number. It answered on the second ring. "Raven here."

"Leiandros Kiriakis. I need some information."

"Person or company?"

"Person. Savannah Kiriakis of Atlanta, Georgia."

"Isn't she your cousin's widow?"

Leiandros leaned against the edge of the desk. "Yes."

"I see."

"I doubt it."

"What do you want to know?"

"Everything. I want to know who she sees. If there's a man in her life. She claims she's recently graduated from university. I want verification of the claim. But most of all, I want to know about her financial situation. She's been getting ten thousand American dollars a month in allowance, but she doesn't dress like it. According to her daughter, they live in a modest house. I want to know where that money is going and why she thinks she won't need it a few months from now."

"Is that all?" Raven asked with more than a little sarcasm tingeing his distinct British accent. "And I suppose you want the information yesterday."

"Yes." Leiandros didn't explain why. He didn't have to. He paid Raven well to find information and rarely shared his motive for wanting it with the private investigator.

"Lucky for you it's the afternoon in the States. My contacts there shouldn't have any problem tracking down this information for you."

"Good."

"Do you want it in a phone call or fax when I get it?"

"Fax. There could be pictures." He was thinking of the possibility that Savannah was seeing a man.

He'd taken that for granted considering how she had behaved while still married to Dion, but after the way she'd exploded like a roman candle in his arms tonight, he had to wonder if her social life had been as active as he'd imagined.

"Right." Raven hung up.

Leiandros put the phone down as well before going to his own room to take a cold shower and go over the details of his plan. It had to be airtight. After what he had shared with Savannah on the terrace, he was even more determined to bind her to him in marriage and establish her in his bed.

He would never let go of her again.

"Watch me, Mama. Watch!" Nyssa's demand brought Savannah's gaze from the aquamarine depths of the sea to the clear glistening water of the swimming pool.

Nyssa stood poised on the edge of the deep end, while Cassia, the nanny Leiandros had hired to help with the children, swam a few feet away. Leiandros had apparently been quite serious about her and the girls making their home with him, to the extent he had hired a permanent, full-time nanny. When the housekeeper had introduced Cassia to Savannah at breakfast, Savannah's first reaction had been to refuse any help with her daughters. However, the young Greek girl's obvious eagerness to please had stilled the words on Savannah's tongue.

As soon as she saw that Savannah was indeed watching, Nyssa launched herself toward Cassia, landing in the water with a huge splash. Savannah clapped her appreciation as her daughter went down, touched bottom and bobbed back to the surface before swimming to the side of the pool and climbing out to do it again.

Swinging her gaze to Eva, Savannah smiled in encouragement at her older daughter. Eva, who had been waiting quietly for her mother to notice she was on the verge of doing her own trick, did a standing dive in the water at the shallow end and brought her legs together straight up in the air. She proceeded to spread them in a V and then bring them together once more.

"Cool," Nyssa said, "I want to do a handstand, too."

Eva came up for air.

"That was wonderful," Savannah called.

"I agree."

The deeply masculine voice acted like a shot of adrenaline to Savannah's senses and she jerked in reaction. She could not make herself lift her eyes to meet his, certain she would see mocking disdain for her total loss of control the night before in the dark chocolate depths.

He came to stand behind her, so close she felt the electric charge zinging between them and did her best to ignore it, while reveling in the new experience of not wanting to back as far away from a man as possible.

"They're a couple of water babies," he said approvingly.

She inclined her head toward him, her gaze focused on the first level terrace near the house and realized her mistake almost immediately. But it was too late to block the memories the white wrought iron patio set invoked. She could feel her skin heating with embarrassment and something else. *Desire.*

"Yes. Eva and Nyssa have both always loved the water. They had swimming lessons when Nyssa turned two." She hoped the small quiver in her voice had not betrayed her mixed up emotions.

He picked up the paperback she'd brought outside, letting his hand skim her leg as he did it. "Savannah?"

She tensed, her thighs clenching against the feelings that even such a slight, careless touch could produce. She did not believe for one second the touch had been accidental. "Wh-what?"

What did he want with her book? He wasn't even looking at it, from what she could tell. She could be wrong because she still couldn't make herself meet his gaze.

"I do not like talking to the top of your head." He tapped the paperback against his palm.

Well she didn't like talking to him period. "Oh."

"Would it be so difficult to look at me?" The condescending humor in his voice chipped at her pride.

She mentally steeled herself to face the man whom she'd shared herself so intimately with without any sense of true intimacy between them and raised her head. Her mental steel felt more like melting aluminum. He looked even more devastating in his white polo and khaki linen trousers than he had in his suit. Every line of muscle was revealed by the knit fabric and cleverly cut linen.

Her fingers itched to trail over the defined muscles of his chest. She wished her sunglasses were mirrored, but though they were very dark, they were still revealing. Could he see the impact just looking at him had on her?

Why was she worried about her eyes? Her nipples would give her away any second. Already, they were growing tight and achy. She crossed her arms protectively over her chest, glad she'd done so when she could feel the tight points of her breasts drilling into her forearms. "What did you want?"

"To talk."

About last night? About her allowance? About her

staying in Greece or more alarmingly, about his shocking remark concerning marriage?

"This isn't a good time or place," she replied, indicating Cassia and the girls playing together in the pool.

"I agree the place is inappropriate. Interruptions will only make our discussion more difficult. But the time is, I think, ideal. Cassia can watch the girls and they all appear content to play in the pool for a bit longer."

"I don't want the girls overexposed to the sun," she said, desperate for an excuse to put off a confrontation between them.

"I'm sure Cassia is capable of taking them inside for showers and a snack at the appropriate time. She is a trained nanny."

"One you hired without my consent or input."

"Is there a problem with Cassia? If so, we can find an alternative nanny."

"I have a problem with you trying to dictate my life."

He laughed softly. "Are you coming?"

Savannah acknowledged defeat and her own cowardice at the same time. Leiandros wasn't going to forget her hedonistic pleasure in his arms the night before any more than she would. Putting off talking to him would only prolong the inevitable, not change it.

"All right." She stood up, putting the lounger between them. "Just let me talk to Cassia and then I'm all yours."

As the words left her mouth, she realized the connotation they could take and nearly bit her tongue.

Leiandros just smiled, *his* eyes hidden behind mirrored sunglasses. "You already are."

She felt like letting loose a string of very unladylike

expletives at his arrogance. She glowered at him, wishing glares really could singe their recipients.

"I'm not," she said, sounding like an angry six-year-old and not all that convincing.

His smile did not dim and he didn't bother to argue with her, which was a much more effective form of disagreement than words would have been.

She spun away, her foot hitting a patch of water on the tile that hadn't evaporated since Eva had come to stand next to her earlier. One foot went forward while the other remained sedentary and she felt herself falling backward toward the lounger, but once again like at the airport, Leiandros was there to catch her.

His big hands curved around her ribcage as he leaned over the lounger to hold her upright. "Careful, *yineka mou.*"

The endearment shocked her as much as the feel of his long fingers pressing against the underside of her unfettered breasts. She'd worn a loose India cotton summer dress cut straight and long and dyed in shades of brown so she could take advantage of the cooling affects of not wearing a bra. She regretted that decision deeply as his forefingers shifted slightly against her breasts and their tips went hard and pointed again in the space of two seconds.

Both the endearment and the action spoke of a possession she didn't want to acknowledge.

"Did you dress this way for me?" he asked in a quiet, sexy voice close to her ear.

"No," she denied quickly, too quickly. "It's hot. I'm not very big, so it's not usually a problem to go without…without…'' For the life of her, she could not say the word *bra* to him.

What did that make her? She'd behaved like a crazed wanton in his arms last night and today stumbled over a perfectly normal word like a blushing virgin. Did that make her sexually schizophrenic, she wondered wildly?

He allowed his palms to cup her intimately for just a second before sliding his hands back to their former, more respectable, position. "I'd say you are just right."

She gasped and darted a look at the pool. Cassia and the girls were playing a game in the shallow end, their backs to her and Leiandros.

"Don't do that." The words sounded breathless and wispy.

Leiandros not only seemed to have a hold over her body that frightened her, but he also decimated her control in a way that one else did. Even her daughters in a temperamental mood could not agitate her the way he did.

"But your body is so responsive to my touch. Any man would find that irresistible. I am no different."

She wanted to hit him. She really did. Preferably with a brick bat. Responsive? Irresistible? He could at least have the decency to find her attractive, instead he was all over conceited about her response to him. She called him several choice names in her head before she felt calm enough to speak.

"Let me go. I can stand on my own now."

Surprisingly he did.

She walked to the side of the pool and gave Cassia

instructions on what to do with the girls over the next hour or so, hoping Leiandros's big discussion would not take more time.

Leiandros led her into the study and closed the door behind them. "I've informed Felix we are not to be disturbed."

Savannah licked nervously at her bottom lip. "I see."

Great. Not only did he make her hard earned self-control disappear but he had her speaking in inanities as well.

"Sit down." He indicated a burgundy leather covered wing chair in front of the large polished mahogany executive desk at one end of the room.

She sat.

"Drink?" he asked, opening up a mini bar fridge cleverly disguised as one of the richly lustrous mahogany cabinets that made up the lower portion of the bookcases lining most of the room's interior walls.

"Yes, please. A wine spritzer."

"Since you do not usually drink alcohol, I have to assume you think you need a fortifier for our upcoming discussion." His sardonically raised eyebrow made a mockery of her carefully neutral expression.

He knew she was nervous, darn him. "I could have a mineral water just the same."

He ignored her, pouring a small amount of wine into a glass and then adding club soda to it. He handed her the glass with a faintly mocking expression. She immediately took a sip.

He poured himself chilled fruit juice and somehow she felt as if she'd made another mistake. His thinking wasn't going to be clouded by alcohol during this discussion. At least she'd eaten a substantial lunch only a little over an hour ago.

She waited in silence for him to open the dialogue. He would not intimidate her into asking questions that might give away her own inner anxieties. And if marriage was going to be discussed, she sure as heck wasn't going to be the one to bring up that disastrous subject.

He moved to lean against the desk in front of her chair, almost sitting on the edge. His legs were far too close to her own. Taking several sips of his fruit juice, he watched her with his damnably compelling eyes.

She took matching sips of her spritzer while forcing herself to meet his gaze, to show him she wasn't going to be cowed by his silence, though she doubted her green eyes were compelling so much as frightened. This situation would be so much easier if last night's proceedings had never happened.

Embarrassment played havoc with her need to remain cool, in control of herself and the situation.

When about half of his juice was gone, Leiandros spoke. "We can be married next Sunday. I've already seen to the legal formalities and booked a priest. Naturally we will be married in the chapel on the villa's grounds."

Her glass dropped to the Turkish carpet and though she noticed the spreading stain of white wine and club soda on the colorful rug, she did nothing to stop it. She couldn't. Her mind had gone numb. Leiandros Kiriakis had just said he wanted to marry her and this time she was sure she wasn't imagining it.

The thought was both tantalizing and overwhelmingly frightening. The fear she understood. The fear made sense. What woman who had suffered through the marriage she had had with his cousin would look forward to the prospect of marrying again? But the allure of the idea completely flummoxed her.

She couldn't seriously *want* to marry another Kiriakis. Could she? Did this mean she loved him? The thought made her feel ill. She had absolutely no illusions that such an emotion was motivating Leiandros. He did not respect her. He thought she'd had affairs while she was married. No way could he love her, but she didn't know what *was* motivating him, either.

She said the only thing she could say. "No."

He didn't look offended. In fact, he laughed. Not uproariously, not even with any real humor. His laugh sounded dark and if she were in a melodramatic frame of mind, she would think diabolical.

"I did not ask you a question. I told you of certain upcoming events." His voice was strangely gentle.

It sent shivers skittering the length of her spine and made all her fine body hairs raise in acknowledgment of true terror. He sounded so confident of her agreement.

She took several deep breaths focused on calming herself. "This is not the middle ages. You have to have my agreement for any marriage to take place and I'm not giving it."

His black eyebrow quirked. "You think not?"

"I know not."

"I believe you will change your mind when all the facts of the situation are made known to you."

"What facts?" she could not help asking.

"You are aware that Dion's will named me sole executor and trustee of his estate?"

"Yes." Did he think he could blackmail her with the money?

"Are you also aware that Dion named me Eva and Nyssa's guardian in the event of his death?"

"What do you mean? I'm their mother and sole guardian."

He bared his white teeth in a semblance of a smile. "In the States that is true, yes. But in Greece, I am their other guardian. You cannot take the girls out of the country without my consent. I assure you, I will keep much better track of you than my cousin. You will not sneak out in the middle of the night and spirit them back to America without my knowledge."

She had to breathe shallowly for several seconds to combat the nausea roiling in her stomach. She could actually feel the blood draining from her face. "You can't mean to keep my daughters from me."

He shook his head, his mouth grim. "No. I mean to marry you and keep you all in Greece. Together."

"I can't stay here." She thought of her aunt, stable for the moment, but with only months, perhaps weeks to live. "I need to return to Atlanta. I have responsibilities there."

"Responsibilities you will not be able to fulfill if you do not get an immediate influx of cash."

"No," she whispered. He couldn't know about Aunt Beatrice. "Why are you doing this to me? You can't want to marry me."

"You are wrong. I consider it a matter of justice."

"Justice?" For Dion?

"Because of you, I lost both my cousin and my wife."

"How... How do you make that out? I wasn't even in Greece when the accident happened."

His entire body tensed with rage that burned out of his eyes almost black with the emotion. "Exactly. You weren't here to be a proper wife. You stole his daughters. You stole his manhood. Dion went off the rails, looking for solace in parties and wild living. He took Petra with him."

She shook her head. "If Dion was so unstable, what was your wife doing with him?"

"They were friends. He was my cousin. His accident was caused because he had been drinking, trying to drown his sorrows that his latest request for you to bring his daughters to Greece had been rejected."

How could he believe such tripe? "You think Dion was a saint, don't you?" she asked with helpless despair.

"Not a saint, but a man who had been sorely mistreated by his wife." The accusation was there in his voice, in his eyes, in the way he leaned over her with intimidating fury.

Her hands trembled and she clasped them together tightly in her lap to stop the telltale sign. "I told him he could visit the girls. He didn't need to drown his sorrows."

"You expect me to believe this?"

"If you think I'm so hateful and dishonest why would you want to marry me?"

"You owe me."

"What? What do I owe you?"

"You owe the Kiriakis family your daughters to replace the loss of their father. You owe me a wife. You owe me a child."

"A child?" she asked faintly.

"Petra was four months pregnant with our son when she died."

Savannah shot clumsily to her feet, her body feeling sluggish from the shock of his words. "No."

"Yes," he hissed. "You are going to marry me and give me a child to replace the son I lost."

Her skin felt cold and red lights danced in front of her eyes. "No."

"Yes." Implacable. Angry. Determined.

The world went black around the edges and she felt her muscles falter before a welcome dark oblivion claimed her.

CHAPTER SIX

"WAKE up, *moro mou.* Come on, Savannah. Come back to me."

The alluring voice pulled her to consciousness along with the sensation of cool wetness caressing her face and neck.

Her eyes fluttered open. She was lying on the burgundy leather sofa at the opposite end of the study from the desk. Leiandros sat next to her supine form, bathing her neck with a cold, damp cloth, his touch incredibly gentle.

She stared at him, bemused. Her mouth felt cottony. Her head felt light, like she'd had too much champagne. But she hadn't been drinking champagne. Had she? No. A wine spritzer. And she'd only drunk about half of it before...

Her stomach started to churn as memory came flooding back.

She went stiff and pushed Leiandros's hand away. "You blame me for your wife and baby's death." Just saying the words increased the sick feeling in her stomach.

He put the cloth down on a table, his expression enigmatic. "Apportioning blame is unimportant, now. Justice will be served when you marry me and become pregnant with my child."

She struggled to sit up and he helped her, the strange

71

gentleness she'd woken to still in evidence. He had managed to lift her without shifting his own position, so now the hard muscle of his thigh brushed against her legs trapped on the sofa next to him. She tried to edge away, but had nowhere to go. "I won't marry you, Leiandros. I won't let you use my body as a broodmare to prove your own masculinity."

She'd had enough of that with Dion.

Leiandros reached out and tucked a wisp of hair behind her ear, allowing his long, male fingers to caress the sensitive skin there before removing them. Her breath caught even as she jerked her head away.

He smiled. "I have no need to prove my masculinity, but I do desire children and you are going to give them to me."

Another wave of dizziness passed over her. *"No."*

"You have no choice," he said, reminding her of the threats he'd made before she was swallowed up in the black void.

"You're wrong," she said, refusing to give into the fear his words invoked. "You can force me to stay in Greece by holding my daughters hostage, but only until I convince the court to allow them to return to Atlanta. *You cannot force me to marry you.*"

She could only hope if he saw his goal of marriage and procuring Savannah as a baby incubator as unattainable, he would let her and the girls go home. He had never struck her as the kind of man to pine after lost causes. He would find another nice traditional girl, like Petra, marry her and give *her* his babies. Savannah ignored the unexpectedly unpleasant image of a faceless brunette pregnant with his child biting into her consciousness.

"I think I can." Leiandros laid his hand on her thigh in a gesture that was both intimate and intimidating. "Consider this, Savannah. You have no money, but that which I give you. No means to hire a reputable Greek lawyer to argue your case, no resources with which to fight for sole guardianship of Eva and Nyssa. And I will fight. You cannot doubt it."

The insidious seductiveness of his voice almost blinded her to the content of his words. "No. It's not worth it to you."

His masculine lips tilted in a mocking smile as he began moving one finger on her thigh in small geometric patterns. "Isn't it?"

She couldn't think. The feel of his hand on her, even through a layer of clothing brought forth the most electrifying sensations in her body. Her gaze moved from his unrevealing features to the sight of his hand on her thigh. She should stop him, but all she wanted to do was take that hand and place it where her flesh ached the most. What was happening to her?

Her body had been dead for four long years. How could it come alive for a man who threatened her peace and stability?

"Eva and Nyssa belong in Greece," he was saying and her scattered attention found its way back to his mouth.

She watched the lips move in paralyzing fascination, knowing she should be listening to the words, but too enthralled by glimpses of the interior of his mouth to focus on anything so mundane. Memories of how those warm depths tasted tormented her mind and titillated her body.

"Any case brought before a Greek judge will naturally be heavily swayed in my favor. In Greece, family is everything and I am not seeking to separate you from your daughters, merely to see them raised among their only known extended family."

Finally his words penetrated and she came crashing to the reality of the present with a thud even as his hand came dangerously close to the apex of her thighs. Her body galvanized into action and she grabbed his wrist. She tried to wrench it away, but he was as movable as a rock. At least, he stopped the disturbing little caresses.

She tried to school her features into a familiar blank mask, but felt cracks around the edges. "I'll sell my house to finance the fight," she bluffed with an edge of desperation.

"What about your aunt?" he asked, his voice silky with both threat and smug certainty. "By the time your house is sold, she will have been moved to a state nursing facility."

Everything inside her went still. He'd discovered the stick and now he meant to beat her with it. Defeat stared her in the face. "You're worse than Dion," she grated.

That seemed to startle him. His eyes narrowed. "What do you mean by that?"

She shook her head, unwilling to expose her deepest hurts for him to exploit to his own advantage. "How did you find out about Aunt Beatrice?"

"I made a call last night to a private investigator. I received his report this morning."

He'd had her investigated. Her entire body went stiff

until each individual muscle felt like a rubber band pulled to its limit. "What else did he tell you?"

"Many interesting things." He squeezed her thigh.

Using both hands this time, she jerked at his wrist again, and managed to slide his hand a couple of inches away from her most vulnerable flesh. "I don't want you touching me."

"Really?" Pitiless brown eyes mocked her. "You like it. A minute ago you were practically begging for more."

"I wasn't."

He laughed, the sound more ominous than amused. "You were." He leaned toward her, his hand once again moving inexorably closer to her femininity and even under two layers of fabric, she felt unprotected against his imminent assault. "Shall I prove it to you?"

She shook her head. "No. Don't." She was begging him and she didn't care. If he kissed her, she would be lost.

His mouth was only millimeters from hers, his warm breath caressing her lips while his masculine scent surrounded her. "Admit it."

She leaned back until her neck was stretched beyond comfort. "No." No defiance in that whispered little word, just despairing appeal.

He smiled as if she already had and pulled back. "Do you want to know what the investigator said?"

He obviously hadn't discovered the reason for her flight to the States, or Leiandros wouldn't still be blaming her for Dion's death. Or, would he? Her body trembled and she despised the outward sign of her susceptibility to his words and his touch. "Yes."

He moved his hand, but only to rest it on her hip. He cupped her nape with his other hand, effectively trapping her within his arms. "You don't date. Ever. Not once in the three years since a certain window watching, elderly neighbor moved into the house across the street from your own."

Savannah felt vulnerable by his knowledge of her social life. "Who I date, or if I date is no concern of yours."

She hadn't dated at first because she'd been married, but even after Dion had died, her fear of men had not. Where was that fear now? Why wasn't it protecting her from Leiandros's potent attraction?

The hand on her nape squeezed. "Everything about you is my concern. You are going to be my wife and the mother of my children."

"I'm not." If she said it often enough, perhaps he would believe her.

He didn't bother to argue. "She also said you are on the verge of nervous collapse."

"Ridiculous!"

He shook his head. "According to her, you sleep very little, spend too much time driving to and from Brenthaven and need more help with the girls than the full-time university student you hired."

Savannah felt exposed, as if her every secret had been laid as bare as a baby's bottom in the bath. "I can handle taking care of my daughters and a few sick room visits."

Okay, so maybe she'd looked a little worn around the edges by the time she and the girls had left for Greece, but saying she was on the verge of nervous collapse was just plain silly.

"Can you not see that marriage to me will benefit you? You have pushed yourself too hard for too long. I will take care of you. Here you have Cassia to help you care for the girls and they will have both a mother and a father, the way it should have been from the beginning."

Leiandros could not possibly know how strongly he had tapped into her deepest desire. She wanted a whole family, had always longed for one and had even married too young and foolishly in order to make her dream a reality. Only marriage to Dion had turned her dreams into nightmares. Was Leiandros offering anything different?

His hand felt warm and improbably comforting against her neck. "I can also finance your aunt's stay at Brenthaven."

"She needs me with her."

"The doctor said she does not remember who you are from one day to the next. She needs care, but not at *your* hand."

The words wounded because Savannah could not deny their truth. She bit back the sob welling in her throat, blinking to dispel the moisture gathering behind her eyes. She never cried and she wouldn't start now, in front of her enemy.

Last night's anomaly, she tried to forget.

"You need a resting period. You are tired and worn-out emotionally. Even I can see that and you've been in Greece no more than twenty-four hours."

She laughed bitterly. "Right. So, now you're motivated by consideration for me. Your vengeance has nothing to do with it and my frazzled emotions are all because of Aunt Beatrice. They have nothing to do with you and your attempt to *blackmail* me.''

The specter of being forced to play the part of a human incubator loomed larger in Savannah's mind than anything else at the moment. She could not face going through that kind of pain again. Every month she didn't conceive she would be accused of being a failure as a woman, of taking something to prevent conception, of emasculating her husband.

And she'd learned that conception had not ended the humiliating litany of woes against her. She had to have a *boy* baby. A Kiriakis heir. Leiandros would be as equally determined as Dion had been. He had lost a son and expected her to replace what he had lost.

He brushed his thumb over her ear and then, finally, pulled his hand away from her. ''I will have justice, Savannah. I am not looking for revenge. Justice does not negate the reality that you too will find certain benefits in our marriage.''

''Benefits…'' She let her voice trail off.

Is that how he saw it?

''Yineka mou.'' There was that endearment again. But she wasn't his woman. She wasn't his wife. ''Your body goes up in flames at my slightest touch. It will be no hardship for you making a child with me.''

Humiliated color stained her cheeks and she glared at him. ''What if I *can't?*'' she asked, hopelessness edging her voice.

''You have already given birth to two precious little girls. The evidence indicates that you will have no trouble conceiving. Petra was pregnant within two months of our decision to try for a baby. Why should it be any different for you?''

Savannah curled her arms protectively around her stomach, over her womb. "But what if it is? What then?''

"Why are you worried about such a thing? Did you have surgery or something?'' Outrage at the thought laced his voice.

She sighed. "I haven't had surgery. I've never taken the pill or had any device implanted to prevent conception,'' she listed off, remembering Dion's accusations when her menses had come month after month the first year they were married.

"Then we have nothing to concern us in this regard.''

If only he knew, but even now, Savannah felt shame when she thought of the placating role she'd played in her marriage and a part of her *had* felt less of a woman when she hadn't conceived easily that first time. "I don't *want* to marry you.''

He shook his head and stood up. "You're very stubborn.''

"Yes. And I won't marry you,'' she said, more forcefully.

"You will. You owe it to me. You owe it to Helena and Sandros. You owe it to Eva and Nyssa.''

She swung her feet around and stood. His last assertion had finally penetrated the wall she kept her anger safely locked behind. She owed her daughters safety and love. She did not owe them a place in a family which had rejected them once already and her as well.

"I don't owe anyone anything.'' She glared at him when he opened his mouth to speak and made a slicing

gesture through the air with her hand. "Be quiet. You've had your say. Now, I'll have mine."

She could feel cleansing fury vibrating through her body. "It's not my fault that Dion drove while under the influence of alcohol. He made that decision. You made the decision to allow your young wife to maintain a friendship with an unstable man. If friendship was all it was."

She remembered too well Dion's favorite method of proving his masculinity when she failed to provide him with a son.

Leiandros seemed to swell with indignation and his six-foot-four-inch frame became even more intimidating than usual. *"Are you implying my cousin had an affair with my wife?"*

"Maybe. How would you know? By your own admission, you didn't love her. A woman finds emotion a seductive force." Who better than she to know how adept at projecting ardent affection Dion had been? She'd been taken in, hadn't she?

"You probably spent the minimum amount of time in Petra's company, Kiriakis International taking priority. No wonder she hooked up with Dion. He was closer to her age, good at the role of charming companion and was available where you were not."

Two slashes of red scored Leiandros's sculpted cheekbones and rage flashed out of his now almost black eyes. He took a step toward her and she flinched, but she didn't back away.

She was still too angry.

His hand swung up and she made a quick evasive maneuver, but he hadn't been about to strike her. His eyes narrowed and his finger pointed toward the door of the study. *"Get out."*

"Why? Is the truth so hard to hear? You want to blame me for your failure? Okay. Fine. But don't think I'll accept it. Don't think I'll marry you and become your broodmare because of it. You want another baby? Marry another Petra!"

"Leave. Now. Before I say something we both might regret." Each word shot out like a bullet from between his gritted teeth.

What could he say that would be more painful than what had already transpired? "Don't you mean do? Should I leave before you *do* something *I'll* regret?"

The need to taunt him beyond control rode her hard. What would he do in a towering rage? Would he use his fists when words did not work? "What will you *do*, Leiandros, if I refuse to leave? What will you *do* if I maintain my belief that your wife and my husband might have been more than friends?"

Her words seemed to infuriate him further. His expression turned deadly furious. "Are you implying now that I would strike you? Is it not enough that you seek to sully the memory of Petra and Dion with your vicious tongue without making me out to be some monster that would hit a woman?"

"Wouldn't you?" she goaded him further.

"No," he bit out. "I might kiss you to shut you up, but you like my kisses. I would never physically harm you."

His entire body radiated with incandescent fury. She had smeared his Greek honor, insulted his family and refused to take the words back. Still, he made no move to hurt her. He didn't even force the kiss on her he had threatened. He simply stood there, his anger like a living thing between them. His eyes demanded she acknowledge his words.

Something that had been locked tight inside Savannah for the past four years, opened and she said, "I believe you."

He could not know how difficult the words had been to say.

"Then believe me also when I tell you to go."

She went. Not because she feared him physically, but because she needed time to think.

Once Savannah left the study, she gave up any hope of time for contemplation. Eva and Nyssa wanted to explore the grounds, so Savannah found herself walking the pathways that had seemed so interesting to her the night before.

They were in an orchard of fig trees when Leiandros joined them. "I see you've found my favorite orchard." His smile did not include Savannah, but was focused on Eva and Nyssa.

"Theios!" Nyssa hurtled herself at him and was swung up in the air for a twirl before being lowered to the ground.

He ran his hand over Eva's hair. "Hello, quiet little girl. Do you and your sister like figs?"

Eva's eyes shone as she looked up at Leiandros. "Yes. May we try one? Is it safe?"

"Yes, *Theios,* please, can we try one?" Nyssa chimed in.

"It is safe. We do not use spray pesticides in our

groves or orchards.'' He picked two ripe figs for the girls.

He turned to Savannah. ''Would you like one?''

''No, thank you.'' She met his gaze levelly. ''Did you tell them to call you uncle?''

''Yes.'' He didn't elaborate, or ask her if that was all right with her, but then he wouldn't.

Leiandros believed he knew what was best for everybody.

Typically Eva finished her fig first. Nyssa had been too busy chattering away, uncaring if anyone was listening. Eva moved close to Leiandros and touched him on the arm. Savannah still had difficulty believing how comfortable her shy daughter acted around the tall, powerful male.

''*Theios?*''

''Yes, little Eva?''

''I'm tired.''

''Then I think I should carry you.''

Eva smiled dazzlingly at this obviously correct response to her broad hint. ''That would be nice.''

Nyssa's face twisted with a frown. She silently watched as Leiandros hoisted Eva's shorts clad figure to his shoulder. ''I think Eva will not be tired in a little while and then you can carry me, *Theios*.''

Savannah felt herself sharing Leiandros's obviously amused reaction to Nyssa's logic. ''If you are tired, sweetie, I can carry you now.''

Nyssa's brow furrowed. ''I don't think I'll get tired till Eva's turn is over.'' Proving the truth of her words, she turned to skip along the path between two rows of fig trees. Leiandros followed, talking in low tones to Eva.

Alarmed at the ready acceptance her daughters were showing Leiandros, Savannah trailed behind. Would they be just as taken with Helena and Sandros? Was she wrong to want to take them back to Georgia, away from an extended family that could love them?

Eva and Nyssa didn't have any other close adult ties in their lives. Their school and Sunday school teachers changed every year. They had no grandparents, no aunts and uncles. Aunt Beatrice, who had been the lynchpin of Savannah's childhood had had Alzheimer's since before the girls were born. Savannah had been too busy and admittedly too leery to make any other close friendships.

She could see why Leiandros's case might have a favorable reception in court, but even more importantly she felt a searing guilt that she hadn't done more to make lasting relationships for her daughters to share in.

She realized that she'd lagged quite a ways behind the threesome when Leiandros stopped and turned towards her. "Are you coming *moro mou?*"

She frowned at the endearment and hurried to catch up.

"Why did you call Mama your baby?" Eva asked.

Leiandros turned his head up toward Eva's face. "How did you know this is what I called her?"

Eva looked at Leiandros with an expression that said he wasn't very bright, but she was too polite to say so and Savannah couldn't help being amused by it. "Because I know."

"You speak Greek?" He sounded incredulous.

Eva shrugged. "Of course I do."

"I do, too," Nyssa announced.

He spun to face Savannah. *"You taught them Greek?"*

He didn't need to make it sound like the eighth wonder of the world. She had reached the others and stopped a few safe feet from his masculine form. "Yes."

"You speak the language?"

"It would be difficult to teach them otherwise."

He frowned at her sarcasm.

She refused to be cowed. The Kiriakis family had always been quick to believe the worst of her. Why cater to his surprise she had learned Greek and subsequently taught it to her daughters? In the three years she'd lived in Athens, she had worked very hard at becoming proficient in her new home's native tongue. The tutor she had hired for the purpose had pronounced her fluent six months before she had left Greece.

She'd never shared her new skill with Dion. By the time she was fluent enough not to fear his ridicule at her attempts in his language, she had not cared enough about his opinion to try to win it by telling him.

"It's Greek at breakfast and bedtime and English in between," Eva offered.

Leiandros looked at Savannah, his expression for once very decipherable. He looked as shocked as she'd felt when he'd announced his intention to marry her. "You are teaching your daughters to speak my language?"

Typically arrogant. *His* language indeed. *"Yes."*

"Why?" he demanded.

She'd done it because she had known the skill would be one more protection for her daughters from wholesale rejection by their Greek relatives. She had also believed it was important for the girls not to be denied half of their heritage as Savannah's paternal heritage had been denied her.

"I didn't want to lose my own fluency through lack of use and bilingual abilities could only enhance the girls' futures," she said dismissively, unwilling to share her more personal reasons with him.

"*Theios?*"

Leiandros turned. "Yes, Nyssa?"

"You like children, huh?"

He looked over her head at Savannah. "Very much."

"You want your own. You said so," Eva quietly inserted.

His gaze did not waver from Savannah, his eyes telegraphing a message she did not want to hear. "Yes."

"Would it be just as good to have little girls that were already born?" Nyssa asked.

Shocked to the core of her being, Savannah's throat felt locked in silence.

"Yes. I think having two little girls would be very good." He sounded so sincere and the way he looked at Nyssa spoke volumes.

"Me and Nyssa like babies," Eva announced. "Do you want more babies, too?"

"Definitely." This time Leiandros did more than look at Savannah, he reached out and touched her. Just a small brush of his fingers against the flat of her stomach but the implication was unmistakable to her. He was claiming possession and Heaven help her, she felt possessed.

"If you married Mama, you'd be our daddy wouldn't you?" Nyssa asked, while Eva looked hopefully on.

"You could call me *bampas* instead of *theios*."

Delight radiated from both her daughters and Nyssa turned to Savannah. "Eva and me decided that since our other father is dead, it would be okay for you to get married and get us a real one. One who wants to play games with us and will carry us when we're tired. I'm not too heavy to sleep in *Theios's* lap."

Savannah closed her eyes against the expectant expression gracing the two little faces and the smug expression on the man's. She felt trapped by her love for her daughters, by Leiandros's strength of will and her own weakness toward him.

"I think it would be an excellent idea for your mama and I to get married. Would you like to see the chapel where I plan to marry your mama?"

CHAPTER SEVEN

THEY spent another hour viewing the grounds, Eva and Nyssa enthusiastically agreeing to Leiandros's suggestion they see the chapel. The same white stucco structure under a red tile roof as the villa, it was the size of a country church back home. The bell tower and mosaic cross above the door indicated the building's purpose with simple dignity.

The girls made heavy hints about the suitability of such a church for a fairytale wedding. After Leiandros's blatant statement of intent, Savannah had quickly disabused her daughters of the notion she had agreed to marry him and informed all three conspirators she was unwilling to discuss the subject any more that day. But by the time they left the chapel, Savannah felt hunted.

Approaching the villa, an unfamiliar sense of welcome assailed her. True to its name Villa Kalosorisma. Welcome house. She had never felt welcome in a Kiriakis home, not even Dion's apartment in Athens. The quintessential bachelor pad, he'd resisted every change she made to it in pursuit of a family *home*. Yet this big white Mediterranean villa inexplicably felt like *her place*. A refuge.

When they got inside, Leiandros lifted Nyssa from his shoulders, having made the switch with the girls at the chapel.

Cassia appeared, with a shy smile on her face. "Did you enjoy your time outdoors?"

"It's great here," Eva enthused, "with lots of places to play and run and everything's so pretty. I want to live here always. I like the pool and the Mediter...the Mederanian. I could have my own bedroom."

Eva's voluble reply seemed to stun Cassia, maybe because the little girl had said it all in Greek. Savannah felt similarly poleaxed. Her daughter might not be able to pronounce Mediterranean, but she certainly had no trouble expressing her desires when the need arose.

"Don't you like sharing a room with Nyssa?" Savannah asked.

"Yes, Mama, but if we each had our own rooms then we could make up more games to play, like having our own houses for playing neighbors."

Nyssa piped up with, "When Eva wants to read, I could tell stories to myself and she wouldn't get mad."

Eva turned to Leiandros. "Nyssa only reads a little bit, but I read really well." She wrinkled her nose. "Greek is harder, but Mama says I'm getting better."

Leiandros's gaze caught Savannah's. "I suppose you taught them to read early as well."

She shrugged in reply.

He said, "It sounds like they both know what they want."

Savannah had no recourse but to nod in agreement.

"Isn't it lucky for me they want the same thing I do?"

"It's what I want in the end that counts." Brave words, but not necessarily true. How could she ignore her daughters' clear desire to stay in Greece, particularly after being ignorant for so long about their wish for a father?

"But you'll be swayed by the needs they've expressed this afternoon and by doing what is best for them."

She couldn't deny his assessment, so she didn't bother. Shrugging again, she broke eye contact.

She shifted her gaze to Cassia. "Would you mind taking the girls up and giving them their baths before dinner?"

"Of course, *Kyria*." Cassia led the girls up the stairs.

Savannah moved to go after them, craving a long, hot bath before overseeing her daughters' dinner and bedtime routine.

Leiandros stayed her with his hand on her shoulder. "I need to talk to you for a minute."

She refused to turn and face him, but the heat of his hand through her short cotton top resonated through her body. "If this is about the marriage vendetta, forget it. I've heard all I want on that subject."

"It is no vendetta." His hand gently squeezed her shoulder. If she didn't know better, she'd think he was trying to soothe the desperate edge to her voice. "I have arranged for us to dine with Helena and Sandros in Halkida this evening."

She felt her body turning of its own volition so she could see him once again. "Halkida?"

After a single caress of his thumb against her collarbone which sent her nerves tingling, he dropped his hand from her shoulder and nodded. He was always touching her and disturbing her equilibrium. "The island's capital. It is thirty minutes distant and close to their home."

She supposed she had known that, but right now she

really couldn't remember. With his attitude toward her and his certainty she would marry him, why bother trying to pretend he intended to keep his promise to let her determine whether or not Eva and Nyssa were to meet their grandparents?

She supposed this dinner was some sort of sop to his conscience. "What's the point?" she asked with resignation.

As her daughters' appointed guardian in Greece, he could force the issue and without doubt he would.

His mouth firmed in a straight line. "What do you mean?"

"You'll do what you want regardless of my feelings." She smoothed her hand down the bright yellow walking shorts that matched her top. "I don't see any point in a meeting them when you have already made the decision. I'm the wayward wife, the mother that took my babies to another country to live. I have no standing in your eyes and even less with Sandros and Helena."

His body went tense and she discovered he could exude just as much power in sexy tan polo and navy blue shorts as his handmade Italian suits. "I gave you my word."

Once again she'd insulted his Greek pride. She couldn't make herself care. "You also threatened me with all sorts of negative reprisals if I don't agree to your revenge scenario."

"Not revenge. Justice." He looked so darn serious, like he really believed his own justification.

He wasn't trying to hurt her, but right an imbalance. She'd have to marry him and have his baby to do it, but hey, that was the way the wheels of justice turned.

Sometimes they crushed, but they must roll to completion. He didn't even care if she loved him. Love played no part in his plans.

And if she did love him? If she had loved him for seven long years and he was the only man she would ever be able to trust her body with, what then? Talons of fear clawed her insides at the prospect that her inexplicable physical reaction to him and burgeoning trust in the face of his threats, indicated an altogether more devastating emotion than lust.

She didn't know if the panic she felt showed on her face, but she prayed it didn't. "You're saying if I feel it would be best for Eva and Nyssa *not* to meet their grandparents, you'll support my decision?"

"That is not going to happen." Such confidence.

"How can you be so sure? Because you believe no Kiriakis could do wrong? You weren't there the day Helena dismissed my baby, but I'll never forget it. I won't let my daughters face that kind of rejection again. Not ever."

He shook his head, negating her words with a gesture and she wanted to stomp her feet and scream. What did he know? She glared at him instead, surprising herself. Since her return to Greece, but particularly after their confrontation in the study, she'd felt her rigid emotional control slip away bit by bit. Especially when she was angry.

"When I showed them the pictures you had sent Dion, they both became emotional," he said. "They want very much to know their granddaughters."

"When did you show them the pictures?" she demanded, feeling oddly betrayed.

"Two weeks ago after our telephone call."

"You mean the call where you *blackmailed* me into bringing my daughters to Greece? The one where you promised me it would be *my choice?*" she asked, her voice dripping with sarcasm.

"It will be your choice," he said through gritted teeth.

"So you *will* support me if I refuse?" she pushed.

"Yes," he bit out.

The journey from Villa Kalosorisma to his cousins' home was accomplished in silence once Leiandros accepted that all of his overtures toward Savannah would be met with one-word answers and preoccupation. She acted like he was taking her to stand trial rather than dinner with family.

She perched stiffly on the opposite seat and looked out the tinted windows with such intense focus, he found himself following her gaze more than once to see what held her interest so completely. He saw only trees and stretches of coastline, nothing that electrifying.

Nothing worth ignoring him for, but then she would probably find any excuse to do that very thing.

She'd dressed in another of her simple, but elegant outfits, this time wearing an oversized sheer white shirt over her red sleeveless dress and racy red pumps with a tiny, high heel. She'd pulled her hair up into another of those loose, sexy styles that left a few soft brown strands flirting with her nape. His fingers stung with the need to touch her.

Even sitting with her knees so primly together, she could not hide her innate sensuality. The hem of her dress had ridden up to expose shapely thighs, but she did not fidget with the fabric. Just as earlier she had worn that enticingly short top that displayed glimpses of skin above the waistband of her shorts whenever she reached for one of the girls.

She blushed and could not bring herself to say the word ''bra'' in his presence and yet she showed no such embarrassment about her body. What a puzzle she was.

''We should be at Sandros's home in a few minutes.''

She nodded, her attention still on the scene out the window. ''I know. I recognize the road.''

''Dion did not take you to visit the family very often.''

''No.''

''Is that why you are so nervous tonight?''

She turned to face him, her eyes revealed nothing. She'd erected that emotionless façade of hers again. ''I'm not nervous so much as lacking in pleasant anticipation.''

He bit back a retort. He had to accept that she did not see his family as he did any more than she saw her own culpability in the events of a year ago. ''It will be fine. You must trust me, Savannah.''

''Must I?'' Her glorious green eyes fixed on him with the same intensity she had shown for her vigil at the window. ''I'm not sure that would be a smart thing for me to do.''

''I do not want to hurt you and I will not allow anyone to hurt Eva and Nyssa. I give you my solemn vow.'' He waited to see how she would respond to his words.

He didn't understand himself. Why should it matter to him if she trusted him? She'd already insulted his pride and his honor on several occasions. Would she continue with her stubborn unwillingness to recognize the role he was assuming in her life? That of protector and lover.

She licked her red tinted lips. "Thank you."

At last she had chosen to accept his words rather than challenge them. He wanted to kiss her luscious mouth to seal this new tentative bond of trust and had even started to move from his seat when the limo slid to a halt. His chauffeur got out to fetch Sandros and Helena.

Savannah paled and the red of her lips took on a garish glare against the now pallid complexion of her face.

"You will trust me," he told her, uncomfortable with this additional sign of vulnerability in a woman he had been convinced was completely lacking in that commodity.

She closed her eyes and took a deep breath, letting it out slowly before opening them again. "I think I do and that scares me more than this meeting with my former in-laws."

Why should she be afraid to trust him? He was head of his family, trusted by them all to act in their best interests. Why did she find it so difficult to do the same? Okay, so he'd used threats to back up his proposal of marriage. Any businessman would do the same. He had learned early to use every possible weapon or inducement at his disposal when going after something he wanted, whether in Kiriakis International or his personal life. So he'd done the same with Savannah.

He wanted marriage. He wanted his children planted in her womb. He wanted justice. So, he had found her weak spots and capitalized on them, but that did not negate the truth of the benefits she would find in marriage to him. And according to her friend back in the states, she needed looking after. He'd been looking after his family for years, he could look after Savannah and her daughters as well.

Sandros and Helena came toward the car, walking behind the chauffeur.

"Iona is with them," Savannah said with accusation.

Impatience with her constant mistrust of every member of the Kiriakis family but most particularly him edged his voice when he spoke. "I didn't invite her, but she is your sister-in-law and seven years your junior. She's hardly a threat."

Savannah's expression went blank and distant and she looked away from him toward the others. "It doesn't matter."

Damn it. Why did he feel like a heel, now? He hadn't said anything wrong and yet he felt as if he'd let her down. He went through a litany of curses in his head. He was getting too protective. Savannah would have to deal with her fears and accept that her family would no longer allow her to dismiss them from her life.

He nodded. "I'm glad you realize that."

She didn't bother to reply and the door opened. Savannah scooted to the far end of the seat. Helena stepped inside, greeted Leiandros with a hug and kisses before sitting at the far side of Savannah's seat.

Iona got in, her smile bright. "Good evening, cousin. Mama invited me to join you tonight. I hope you don't mind?"

He gave her a kiss of greeting. "Not at all."

She slid onto the seat next to him. "You're wonderful."

He laughed, so busy with Iona, it took him several seconds to realize Savannah had gone absolutely rigid as Sandros took the seat beside her and insisted on greeting her with the traditional kiss on each cheek. The expression on her face was a stiff imitation of a smile.

He could see her mentally preparing herself and then lean forward to return the old man's greeting with a hasty peck on one cheek and then pulling away completely. At that moment, Leiandros realized two things. One, Neither Helena, nor Iona had bothered to greet Savannah in any way and two, she did not want to be sitting next to Sandros.

He watched as she drew completely into herself and moved a little further away from Sandros, creating a separate space from the other occupants in the limo as effectively as if she had erected a physical barrier.

Why hadn't he considered this possibility? He knew how skittish around men she was. She'd practically fallen over in her haste to get away from his touch at the airport and when she'd woken in his arms later in the car, she'd vaulted away, literally bouncing against the far wall.

He took for granted her swift transition to accepting his touch, but now realized it did not mean she was any more comfortable forced into close proximity to another male. She showed every sign of being a woman who had been abused. Had one of her lovers hurt her?

The thought infuriated him. He wanted to demand an explanation immediately, but could not. Nor could he do anything about her skittishness with Sandros without causing grave offense to innocent people. He fixed his gaze on her, willing her to look at him. He wanted her to remember he was with her and he would protect her.

A man had an obligation to do that for his woman and it had nothing to do with maudlin emotions or even affection, he reminded himself.

During his ruminations, Helena and Iona had started a discussion of the latest fashions in Greek that was clearly meant to exclude Savannah. Iona made a comment about the coarseness of the way some American women dressed which Helena agreed with. They did not realize Savannah understood, but that did not excuse their behavior.

Sandros sat in silence, his expression faintly troubled.

Leiandros said, "Since the purpose of this evening is for Savannah to become reacquainted with the family, I think it would be best if you included her in your conversations, Helena."

"Yes, of course." Her voice lacked enthusiasm.

Iona snorted.

Sandros glared at his daughter and patted his wife's hand. "Remember, English."

Leiandros donned the expression he wore to deal with offending employees and met first Helena's eyes and then Iona's. "That won't be necessary. Perhaps you are ignorant of the fact, as I was, but Savannah worked very hard at becoming fluent in Greek and has even taught her daughters to speak our language. The oldest is learning to read in it as well."

"Did she tell you that?" Iona asked with sneering derision. "Really, Leiandros, I wouldn't expect you of all people to be so gullible. The oldest can be no more than five. A child that age simply isn't capable of such a thing.''

He saw Savannah flinch out of the corner of his eye and realized Iona would ruin any chances Helena and Sandros had for visitation with her youthful emotionalism. "You are wrong, Io. I can assure you both girls are fluent in our language because I've spoken with them at length in Greek and Eva does indeed read it as she proved to me when I tucked her in for the night."

Iona turned to regard Savannah for the first time. "How clever of you. Isn't it a tragedy you didn't bother to share your abilities with your *husband?*''

Feeling his frustration mount, he said, "Io, either decide to be a pleasant dinner companion, or accept that I will send you home in a taxi when we reach the restaurant.''

Her eyes filled with tears. "It's not fair! You're treating us like criminals when she's the one who's done everything wrong. It's sheer conceit for her to demand a meeting to determine whether my parents and I are worthy of having a part in Dion's daughters' lives.''

"Their names are Eva and Nyssa. They are human beings with thoughts, feelings and needs. They are not possessions to be fought over like some disputed piece of jewelry. Eva is the oldest. Your mother met her once. Nyssa is a year younger and did not have the benefit of even one meeting." Savannah's voice dripped with ice.

Helena's expression grew drawn and strained as Savannah's words penetrated, but Sandros looked as if he had the guilt of original sin on his shoulders. Iona opened her mouth to say something but Leiandros forestalled her.

"Let us get something clear. Savannah is not responsible for this meeting. I am. I am the one who extended the invitation to your parents. I am the one who allowed you to accompany us and I am beginning to wonder if that was a mistake. You're responding like an adolescent."

Iona gasped and instead of glaring at him, gave Savannah a look meant to wound. "I know Leiandros only agreed to this meeting because *you* forced him to."

Leiandros squeezed Iona's arm to warn her to silence. "As Dion's chosen legal guardian for his daughters and head of this family, it is my responsibility to make certain Eva and Nyssa's best interests are served."

Sandros nodded. "Exactly right."

Leiandros waited a second in silence to give his upcoming words impact. "I do not think encouraging a relationship with family members who dislike their mother and treat her with open scorn, would be beneficial in any way to Eva or Nyssa."

"Leiandros, you can't mean you would stand behind her scheming to keep us from our blood family," Helena said.

Iona nodded her agreement so vehemently, she looked like her head was attached to her body with a bobbing spring.

Sandros shifted in his seat, inadvertently moving closer to Savannah. "If Leiandros does not do as he's said, I will. No granddaughter of mine is going to be subjected to the kind of scene that's taken place in this car. Neither my wife nor my daughter exercised simple courtesy in greeting the mother of those little girls and the conversation so far has been distasteful." He subsided in silence.

"When have any of you ever known me to back down on my word?" Leiandros asked for Savannah's benefit.

"Never," Iona admitted grudgingly.

"Of course you keep your word," Helena replied, her voice expressing outrage at the question.

"Then accept that welcoming your granddaughters into your life will come after you have made your peace with Savannah."

Iona moved away from him, crossing her arms in a childish expression of defiance. Imagine she was of an age to marry. He pitied her future husband.

His eyes moved to lock Helena in his gaze.

"I will make every effort," she said.

Sandros once again patted her hand. "*Yineka mou,* you are a wife worthy of respect."

Savannah hadn't made a peep since Sandros had moved so close to her, but she was practically crawling onto the armrest.

"Iona, trade places with Savannah. You've made it clear you would be more comfortable sitting beside your father." He would normally ignore her little gestures of annoyance, but he could not stand that stiff lip and blank-eyed stare on Savannah's face for one second longer.

Io got up without deigning to answer. Savannah remained seated, clearly in a different world entirely.

"Savannah. *Pethi mou.* Come here."

Her eyes opened wide as if waking from a dream and she stared at him, their green depths dark with the emotions swirling through her. "Come to you?"

Iona made an impatient movement. "Don't act stupid. A woman capable of teaching her children to speak Greek and read before they are even six years old can understand a simple command."

Leiandros did not take issue with Iona because she had complimented Savannah, backhanded though it might be. He put his hand out toward Savannah and she vaulted off the seat, ducking under Io to take the spot next to him, her thigh touching his own.

He took her hand in his and brushed against her palm with his thumb. She shivered and pressed herself closer.

"Thank you," she whispered under her breath.

He squeezed her hand. He liked the way it felt when she aligned herself with him, too much. Her gratitude could become addictive.

CHAPTER EIGHT

AFTER the events in the car, it took several minutes for Savannah to become more than peripherally aware of her elegant surroundings. Sandros had suggested dining in a restaurant connected to a five-star hotel and it showed. Fine linen, crystal and delicate china graced the table at which they sat. She had no doubt the food would be up to the same standards of excellence. Not that she cared.

After the scene in the car and the humiliatingly tortuous experience of being forced to sit so closely to Sandros, she had no appetite and even less desire for the ordeal to come.

Leiandros laid a casual arm across the back of her chair, his fingers brushing her shoulder through the light silk of her overblouse. Did he have any idea the effect his touch had on her? Volts of electricity shot down her arm as his touch sparked something very different than the comfort he so clearly intended.

"Relax, *pethi mou*. All will be well."

She took a deep breath and tried to obey him, but she was fighting both trepidation over the meeting to come and her body's susceptibility to him. Under the cover of Sandros giving his order to the waiter, she asked, "How can you think so? They hate me. What hope is there for Nyssa and Eva?"

Almost black eyes burned into hers. "Your daughters

are separate people. Their grandparents love them already just from their pictures. Imagine how besotted they will become when they meet your sweet-natured daughters in person.''

Which meant what exactly? That all his fine words in the car meant nothing and it did not matter if Dion's family hated her guts as long as they could love Eva and Nyssa?

The waiter had turned to Leiandros, who requested a bottle of Greek wine and then proceeded to order for Savannah and himself with typical arrogance.

She had no opportunity to pursue her discussion with him before the waiter returned with their wine. Leiandros deferred tasting to Sandros and Savannah remembered Dion saying his father was something of an expert on wines, particularly those native to Greece. Sandros pronounced the wine acceptable and gave the waiter permission to pour.

As the waiter approached her, Leiandros asked, ''Would you prefer a spritzer?''

She needed to keep her wits about her tonight. ''Yes.''

''That's enough,'' he told the waiter when her glass was a third full. ''Please bring us a club soda.''

''Are our Greek wines too strong for your palate?'' Iona's voice was heavy with derision and Savannah's throat tightened.

Leiandros sighed. ''I think it is time for me to call you a taxi, Iona. You refuse to be civil and clearly do not have the maturity to realize that your sniping is only making a difficult situation worse.''

Did he think sending Iona away would solve the basic problem?

Shockingly, Iona's sarcastic mask crumbled and tears shimmered in her dark eyes. "I'm sorry."

Leiandros's expression did not soften. "I told you what would happen in the car if you continued to bait Savannah."

Iona turned her tear wet face toward her father. "Papa, please don't let Leiandros send me away. I am family, too."

If anything, Sandros's expression was even more forbidding. "Leiandros is well within his rights to send you home."

A small sob escaped Iona, now looking much younger and much more vulnerable than she had earlier. "Mama?" she pleaded.

When Helena remained silent, Savannah laid her hand on Leiandros's arm and spoke. "I prefer that Iona stay."

Leiandros's gaze turned to her, blasting her with censure. "You do not want this to work," he accused her in a tone so low only she could distinguish the words. "You are looking for a reason to withhold your daughters from their rightful family just as you withheld them for the past four years."

She supposed to his way of thinking, taking her daughters halfway around the world had effectively cut them off from their family, but pain at his words still coursed through her. He'd turned on her so easily. Was she right in believing he didn't care how repulsed Dion's family was by her?

Her feelings did not matter. Her pain could be dismissed. After all, she was the cuckoo. Everyone else at this table belonged. Even the volatile Iona. Savannah was the interloper and always would be. She'd never belonged, really belonged to anyone but Aunt Beatrice and then Eva and Nyssa.

Even that was being undermined here. Leiandros wanted Eva and Nyssa to belong to the Kiriakises as much as, or maybe more than, they belonged to Savannah and in a way she never could. They would never accept her. Would giving her daughters an extended family sentence her to a lifetime of rejection?

"Can you honestly say that any relationship between my daughters and their grandparents will not include Iona?" she whispered back, refusing to give into the despair boiling up inside of her.

Her only hope was to hold Leiandros to his word, even as he tried to manipulate her into letting him break it.

Surprisingly, his expression turned thoughtful.

She took her hand off his arm, her fingers still tingling from the contact. "You are wrong, you know. I *am* aware they are the only extended family my daughters can lay claim to. If I can bring Dion's family into Eva and Nyssa's lives without hurting them, I will be happy to do so." Even if it meant the sacrifice of her own feelings.

The waiter arrived with her club soda.

She broke eye contact with Leiandros to thank the waiter and then poured the soda water into her wine. "You're right, Iona," she forced herself to say civilly, "Greek wine has its own unique essence and requires adjusting of the palate to truly appreciate its flavor."

Iona, who looked stunned by Savannah's defense of her right to stay, gave a weak smile.

A low, but persistent beeping prevented further discussion as Leiandros pulled out his cell phone and answered with the traditional Greek words for greeting. He swiftly changed to a language that sounded like Italian.

Seconds later, he stood and gave them an encompassing glance of apology. "I'm sorry. I have to take this call. I'll make it as quick as possible." He leaned close to Savannah's ear. "Be good, *pethi mou.*"

She wasn't the one he had to worry about.

Sandros waved him away, while Savannah tried to hide the nervousness his abandonment was causing her. Even angry, she preferred Leiandros over dealing with Dion's family.

Silence reigned as she and the remaining guests at the table considered one another warily.

Helena put down her *dolmades* without taking a bite and looked across at Savannah with wounded eyes. "Why? Why did you tell my son the babies were not his? He missed so much. We all missed so much."

Resentment toward Dion welled up inside Savannah, but what good did anger toward a dead man do?

She met Helena's eyes, her own steady. "I never said any such thing. If you will recall, Helena, it was you who took one look at my beautiful Eva and declared her no Kiriakis." She turned to sear Iona with her gaze. "Is it any wonder I felt it necessary to meet with you all before I expose my daughters to possible rejection or revilement?"

"We would never do such a thing," Helena exclaimed.

"But Dion said you were unfaithful!" Iona said at the same time.

Savannah chose to answer Iona, ignoring Helena's blatantly untrue assertion. "I wasn't unfaithful. Ever."

Iona said, "But—"

Savannah cut her off, unwilling to travel this territory again. She'd already gotten bruised doing so with Leiandros. "I am not responsible for your brother's jealous delusions."

Feeling so brittle she thought she might shatter, Savannah bit back further, more precise words of self-defense. While an insidious voice in her mind demanded she acknowledge that in a way, Dion *had* been right. Oh, she had not encouraged other men. She hadn't been a flirt, but she had betrayed Dion. At least in her heart, because she had wanted his cousin.

She had wanted Leiandros Kiriakis with an obsession that had taken her entire strength of will to stifle, never allowing her fantasies to stray, ignoring the frisson of feeling his slightest touch could elicit, pretending her body did not hum with renewed life when he walked into a room she occupied.

She was shocked from her self-castigating musings when Sandros nodded in apparent agreement to her statement. "He was jealous because of his own feelings of failure, not because you gave him reason to be."

Sandros knew about Dion's low sperm count? Savannah could not believe it. Dion had been so adamant no one find out, ever, that he had made her life a misery in the pursuit of a son to prove his virility. After all that, had he told his father?

"Sandros! What are you saying?" Helena demanded, her cheeks flushed with distress.

Sandros gave a very heavy, very Greek sigh, looking

weary and sad. "Our son came to see me the morning of the accident."

"You never told me this," Helena said, her evident shock no greater than Savannah's.

"I could not." He squeezed Helena's hand. "He told me he had called Savannah the night before and asked her to bring their daughters to Greece. She refused."

Iona and Helena's hostility became a palpable entity.

Savannah did not want to defend herself to Dion's family, but if she refused to make an effort their current impasse could not be broken. "I invited Dion to come to Atlanta and visit the girls there." She had not trusted Dion not to take advantage of Greek family law to force her into keeping the girls in Greece.

Pity she hadn't been as savvy when dealing with Leiandros, but then deep down, she *had* wanted to see him again. She'd had no such desire regarding Dion.

"He told me this." Sandros grimly went on, "He said he considered the offer generous. I must admit I did not agree with him at first, but after he admitted to me that he had lied about Savannah's behavior and told me the separation was entirely his fault and why, I saw the truth in his belief that Savannah had behaved generously toward him."

"But she took the babies to America, so far away from family." Helena's voice cracked with emotion on the last word.

Sandros took both her hands in his own. "He admitted to me he refused to accept his role as a father because of his own self-doubt. He was obsessed with having a son."

He lifted his head and met Savannah's stricken gaze.

His eyes pleaded with her not to say anything more explicit. She was convinced he knew the whole truth about Dion's violent nature and it shamed him. He wanted to protect Helena and Iona from that shame.

She nodded her head slightly in acknowledgment and saw relief flicker in Sandros's eyes.

"Dion was young when we married, unprepared for his family's disapproval of his wife," she said, voicing the conclusion she'd drawn when trying to understand her former husband's behavior. "It is only natural that he sought to lay blame at my door. He didn't want to be alienated from those he loved so much."

She no longer believed Dion had ever loved her. She was convinced he had married her in an act of rebellion against having his entire future mapped out for him, including the choice of his bride.

Sandros grimaced. "You are too understanding, but my son guaranteed we would despise you from the beginning."

"What do you mean?" Savannah inquired, certain she was about to be regaled with another of Dion's lies.

"He told us you had gotten yourself pregnant and trapped him in marriage," Helena said, her voice questioning.

Savannah couldn't help laughing. "That would have been really something. The second immaculate conception on record." Though nothing Dion could have done could have surprised her, knowing he had undermined her relationship with his family in this way from the very beginning still hurt.

No wonder Leiandros had such a low opinion of her.

Helena and Iona gasped when the import of her words penetrated. Sandros looked pained.

"That's not possible," Iona practically shouted. "Dion told us he'd been a real chump, not requiring proof when you said you were pregnant. He said you'd lied to trap him, but if you were still chaste, he would not have believed you."

She took a sip of her spritzer, ignoring the humus and flat bread in front of her. "I guess he was trying to protect himself from his original lie being found out. I imagine he felt pretty desperate when I didn't conceive right away."

Only she knew how desperate.

She bit her tongue to prevent herself from saying more. Nothing would be served by accusing Dion of having been a selfish, manipulative, spoiled little boy during their marriage.

"Yes," Sandros said heavily. "The morning he came to see me, I told him the measure of a man is how he treats his family, not his ability to produce sons. I believe he was drinking later that day because of my words. It was the first time I was ever ashamed of him." Tears glistened in Sandros's eyes. "My son lied about his wife and he admitted those lies to me. We have all treated Savannah and her daughters shamefully because of the things Dion told us. The lies he told us."

Savannah couldn't help feeling compassion for his obvious feelings of guilt over his son's death. "You are not to blame."

"Papa, what is this you are saying?" Iona's voice shook.

"You said *nothing* of this a year ago." Helena reiterated.

His proud gray head bowed. "There are some things a man is not pleased to admit."

Savannah's heart ached for him as his head came up again and she saw the tears trickle down his cheeks, tears he wiped away with his thumb and forefinger.

Her half-formed idea that she would ask him to tell Leiandros the truth died a swift death. She could not ask Sandros to shred his pride in admitting Dion's weaknesses or his own to Leiandros. The Kiriakises had paid too high a price for Dion's sins already. None of which were their fault.

Helena's rejection of Eva had hurt Savannah, desperately so. Yet, how could Savannah blame the older woman for a reaction predestined by her beloved son's lies? The answer was that she couldn't. Nor could she withhold Eva and Nyssa from their Greek family when that family showed every evidence of wanting to love and cherish the little girls.

Surely now that Sandros had told Helena and Iona that Dion had lied about Savannah, their overt hostility toward her would end. Perhaps they would never be the best of friends, but they could maintain a relationship for the sake of two little girls who deserved more out of life than the loneliness Savannah had known.

One day, she would tell Leiandros the truth herself. All of it. He knew she hadn't dated in at least three years because her nosy neighbor had told his investigator as much. With that knowledge, he *couldn't* still see her as the unfaithful slut Dion had painted her.

Taking another fortifying sip of wine, she contemplated what to say next. "That is all in the past. We have to focus on the present. Eva and Nyssa deserve it. We all deserve it."

Sandros, more in control, nodded. "We all loved Dion, but he was no saint. We lost years of Eva and Nyssa's life because of mistaken beliefs. Let the anger and accusations end now." He spread his hands in a typically Greek expansive gesture.

It was Helena's turn to blink back moisture. She wasn't completely successful. "I want to hold my granddaughters."

Iona's eyes were troubled and she played with her fork. "I still don't understand why Dion would have lied to us."

Savannah didn't have an answer, so she said nothing. She'd gone as far as she could go in the reconciliation. The rest was up to Dion's family.

Leiandros chose that moment to return to the table, taking his chair beside Savannah. "My apologies I was gone so long."

"We hardly noticed," Savannah couldn't resist saying, though it was far from the truth. She noticed every moment she spent away from him and part of her wished he'd been there to witness Sandros's admissions about Dion. On the other hand, she had to wonder if Sandros would have hesitated to say anything in front of Leiandros. Male pride could be a very tricky thing.

Leiandros's dark brows rose in mockery. "Really?" Then he surveyed the table. "You haven't eaten anything."

"We have been talking," Sandros replied.

Leiandros's head twisted toward Savannah and he

searched her face, looking for she knew not what. Evidence of her capitulation, maybe? "We have all agreed it is time my daughters met their grandparents and aunt."

Rather than the satisfaction she expected to see, his expression became more probing. He reached out and laid his forefinger along her jaw. Even angry with him, she could not repress the immediate response of her body to his most innocent caress. "Are you okay with this?"

She jerked her face away. "Don't bother trying to pretend it matters to you," she said sharply, but in a very low voice she hoped the others could not hear. She still hadn't forgiven him for his earlier words.

His body tensed and he did not bother to whisper when he answered. "It does. I thought I convinced you of that before we left the house and did my actions not show you my sincerity earlier this evening?"

"Your actions showed me that you were intent on effecting a reconciliation even at the cost of protecting a woman you despise, but so you know, I *am* okay with this."

He looked like he wanted to say more, but Helena spoke up. "Savannah, do you think you could bring the children to our home in the next couple of days. I'm impatient to get to know them."

She stiffened at the prospect of visiting Helena's home with the girls, but she couldn't allow her own feelings stop her daughters from knowing important people in their lives who wanted to love them. "I'm sure they'd be happy to meet you tomorrow. Perhaps Leiandros would allow us to use his car to make the trip."

He shook his head and focused his attention on Helena and Sandros. "You are welcome at Villa Kalosorisma any time, but until Eva and Nyssa have come to know you and are sufficiently comfortable in your company, we shall hold off a visit for them to your lovely home."

While Helena nodded her agreement, her expression pained, Savannah tried to gather her thoughts scattered by Leiandros's unexpected announcement. He was putting Eva and Nyssa's needs above the feelings of his other family. She didn't fool herself into believing he'd done it for her sake.

He'd been as taken with her daughters as they had been with him.

CHAPTER NINE

LEIANDROS waited until Sandros and the other women had exited the limo before turning to Savannah. He touched her hand with his forefinger, running the tip along her soft skin. "The meeting was difficult for you."

She snatched her hand away. "Yes."

He stifled a sigh. She was back to bristling. She'd been angry with him since his return to the table from his phone call, accusing him of not caring whether or not she was okay with the results of the discussion which had occurred while he was gone. He had kept his word to her, but she didn't seem to see it that way. Angry he was forcing her hand about marriage, she gave him no credit at all.

"Yet you were kind to them, generous with the prospect of them getting to know the girls." It had surprised him after the way she had reacted to Io's sarcasm and his decision to send her home in a taxi.

She shrugged, her transparent shirt moving over the deep red of her dress. "My concerns were allayed in that regard."

"Your fear they would reject your daughters as they had once rejected you or your belief they would go on hating you?"

She bit her lower lip, breaking his concentration. He wanted to soothe that small wound with his tongue.

When she said, "Both," he could no longer remember

116

what the question had been. He had to concentrate to recall his words.

"They seemed to have dropped all hostility toward you, even Iona." The about face wholesale acceptance of Dion's family toward Savannah puzzled him.

He had expected a softening sooner or later. He knew how tenderhearted Helena and Iona really were. Their anger toward Savannah had been fed by their loyalty to Dion. With the advent of Eva and Nyssa into the family, new loyalties would be forged and regardless of Savannah's past treatment of Dion, she was now the mother of two little girls very much desired by their grandparents and aunt.

Yet, he had not expected the thaw to happen quite so quickly and had spent most of his phone call worried about the way his family was treating Savannah.

Something came and went in her expression. "You were right. They are very emotional at the prospect of getting to know Eva and Nyssa."

She shifted restlessly on the seat beside him and when she tried to move away, he anchored her against his hip with an arm around her waist. His hand curled over her lower rib cage and the feel of the sheer silk top against his fingers teased him. A slight upward move and his thumb would be caressing the delicate underswell of her breast.

He felt sweat break out on his brow. *He wanted to make that movement.* She knew it too. She had gone still and started breathing in short pants. He leaned down to nuzzle her ear, allowing his tongue to flick out and taste the tender flesh of her lobe as he bit it gently. "You taste good, *yineka mou.* Just as a woman should."

He wanted to taste more than this small morsel of her flesh. His body craved the opportunity to savor her lips and the silken warmth of her mouth, the golden softness of her skin, and her nipples. Most certainly, yes, her nipples. From there his tongue would travel a path to the womanly softness of her belly, to her inner thighs and the backs of her knees. He would take off her shoes and explore her dainty arches with his lips before returning to the secrets hidden between her thighs.

"We've been through this before. I'm not your woman. I'm not your wife."

It took him a second to retrieve his mind from the erotic journey it had been on and decipher what she had said. When he did, it was all he could do not to growl in frustration.

He kissed along the graceful line of her jaw while moving his hand up and under the transparent shirt, to cup her breast through the lightweight fabric of her dress. "You're wrong."

Her nipple puckered immediately and she sucked in air like a runner after a ten-kilometer dash. "Stop," she breathed.

He smiled in triumph and gently pinched the turgid nub.

She arched her back. "Leiandros! Please."

He tilted her face toward him so he could kiss her soft, sweet mouth. In the dark interior of the limo, her beautiful green eyes looked black and very, very wide.

He brushed her cheek. "Relax."

His lips prevented more half-hearted protests, not that she would have made any. The second his mouth touched hers, she melted against him in surrender. Her lips softened and parted to allow her delightful little tongue to dart out and trace his lips before teasing his mouth open. He let her explore, meeting her tongue with his own. She moaned and he pulled her closer, while squeezing her breast in his hand. He wanted to touch her without the fabric of her dress in the way.

He shoved her shirt off over her shoulders. The garment got stuck at her wrists and he left it there while atavistic excitement at her hampered movement coursed through him.

"I want you, Savannah." His voice sounded guttural and out of control even to his own ears.

His hands were busy with the zipper on the back of her dress when she responded.

"Do you really want *me,* or just an incubator for your baby?" she demanded in a passion raw voice.

Even in his desire clouded mind, he could tell the answer was important to her, and therefore to him. He would not let her go. "I want *you.*"

"Are you sure?"

The insecurity he heard in her voice told him she would not be satisfied with words. He would have to show her. He kissed her while lowering the zip on her dress. When it was open, he pulled back and she groaned her distress at the lack of contact.

A zing of primitive satisfaction shot straight to his sex and he yanked the dress down to her elbows, increasing the restriction of movement in her arms and hands. His carnal hunger grew as he realized she was so lost to her passion, she didn't even notice.

"*Pethi mou.* You are stunning," he whispered, as he looked his fill at her exquisite body.

Tight, pointed tips, rosy with sensual excitement crested her luscious, golden mounds.

She said nothing, her own gaze fixed on his face. Her nostrils flared in primal recognition of him and her mouth parted, her lips swollen and begging for his kisses.

He obliged her, devouring her mouth with unrestrained hunger. She didn't resist, but kissed him back with the same frantic energy, the same fundamental sexual craving. His hands traveled to the bare flesh of her breast and he cupped them, letting his thumbs brush back and forth, back and forth, over her taut nipples. He could explode touching her like this.

She pressed herself into his hands.

He moved his lips down her jaw toward the irresistible call of her naked flesh. "Yes. *Moro mou.* That's right. Just like that," he said as she moved side to side to increase the friction of his touch on her tender flesh.

She was his fantasy woman, the lover of his dreams. So responsive. So sensual. He wanted her. *He needed her.*

The constriction on her hands and arms seemed to register for the first time as she tried to lift them. She moved in agitation, her head tossing against the back of the seat.

She whimpered and primitive pleasure washed over him in crashing waves. "What is it?"

"I want to touch you," she moaned.

His lips closed over a hardened nub and he sucked it into his mouth in one strong, swift action. He played with her using his teeth and tongue and her whimpers grew, this time filled with obvious pleasure as well as frustration.

"Oh, Leiandros! Please. I need you," she cried.

He needed her too. So much that he didn't know if he could take the time to remove their clothes before taking her. He moved to her other breast and administered the same treatment, exulting in her wildly thrashing body and incoherent demands.

With impatient movements, he shoved her skirt to her waist and grabbed the side of her silk panties just as the car slid to a halt. She didn't seem to notice, her face contorted with feminine desire, her eyes closed, her entire body abandoned to the pleasure she found in his arms.

He wanted to curse in each of the five languages he spoke, but didn't have time. With more speed than finesse, he dragged her dress back into place and reached around her throbbing body to close the zip.

Her eyes opened. "Leiandros?"

"We have arrived at Villa Kalosorisma," he said in a voice made harsh by unsatisfied passion.

Her languid eyes looked blankly back at him for a full five seconds before they grew wide and she scrambled to a sitting position.

She struggled against her blouse, unable to pull it back up with the sleeves inside out over her hands. "Fix it. Hurry!"

He obeyed and had it back in place just as the chauffeur opened the door.

Leiandros got out, pulling Savannah from the limo with him. "We aren't finished."

Her eyes registered his statement of intent with a mixture of alarm and still smoldering desire. *"Good night."*

He gripped her shoulders. "Like hell it is good night."

Her eyes dilated. "I didn't mean—"

"Tonight, you become mine. You will never again say I have not the right to call you *yineka mou.*" No way was she dismissing him like some casual date after a party, not following the unrestrained response she'd given him in the limo.

Her lovely lips moved, but no sound came out. He didn't need her answer; he could read it in the way her body swayed toward his. He bent to kiss her as the front door swung wide.

"Leiandros! You have returned. And Savannah! My terrible son did not bother to tell me you were coming, or I would have been here to welcome you home." His mother stood, silhouetted in the light pouring from the open doorway, his worst nightmare when his body was aching to possess Savannah.

There would be no possession tonight, nor any other night until the wedding. Not if his mother had her say about it, and when had Baptista Kiriakis ever hesitated to have her say?

Savannah struggled to listen as Baptista rattled on in rapid Greek. Her welcome had been effusive with a warm hug and kiss of greeting on each of Savannah's cheeks.

"I'm so pleased you've come to stay." She patted Savannah's shoulder. "Having you and the little girls here will be so good for Leiandros. He works too much, that one.''

Baptista gave her son a censorious look.

His lips tilted cynically in reply.

''I'm very happy to be here,'' Savannah replied, unable to snub such open friendliness.

Baptista led them into the fireside reception room. ''Come, let us have a nightcap before we retire. I have so much I wish to say to Savannah. My words for my son will wait for a more opportune time,'' she said ominously.

Savannah could almost pity him, but it was his fault she had to face Baptista, wondering how unkempt her own appearance was after their loss of control in the limo. More than merely a loss of control, it had been a life-altering experience. Still she did not want Baptista to know what they had been doing.

After insisting Leiandros pour them all a glass of champagne, *to celebrate Savannah's return to Greece,* Baptista pulled Savannah onto one of the sofas beside her.

''I met your daughters. I told them they must consider me their honorary grandmother.'' She gave Leiandros another judicious look. ''That one may never get around to remarrying and providing me with grandchildren.''

Savannah choked on her champagne, coughing and turning bright red as the oxygen rushed back to her head. What would Baptista think if she discovered her son wanted exactly that and was willing to resort to blackmail to get it?

He was there in a moment, seated on her other side, angled to face both her and his mother, his legs brushing against her own in a very distracting way. "Are you all right, *pethi mou?*"

She nodded, feeling distinctly vulnerable. She tried a tentative smile on him and his mother. "I'm not used to champagne," she said by way of a very lame excuse.

She hoped to shout she could come up with something better than that, otherwise Baptista was going to go to bed a very suspicious woman. Savannah stifled a groan at the thought.

Baptista's thin, lovely face warmed with a smile. Her lithe figure couldn't have been more different from Helena's voluptuous one and the already graying hair complimented Baptista's olive toned skin, while attesting to her age. With her luxuriant black locks, Helena looked young enough to be Iona's older sister.

But then the two older women were not related by blood. They had married Kiriakis cousins, though Leiandros treated Sandros and Helena more like a favored uncle and aunt.

"Eva and Nyssa are darlings. The little treasures greeted me in Greek. How clever you are to have mastered our language and then taught it to your children."

"Thank you," Savannah replied.

The other woman smiled apologetically at her son. "I think you ought to run along to bed, Leiandros. Savannah and I have so much to catch up on."

Savannah couldn't imagine what. She'd seen very little of Baptista Kiriakis her first time in Greece, though the older woman had always been kind to her. She turned to Leiandros, her expression as pleading as she could make it. She didn't want to be left alone with his mother.

He gave her a wry smile and shrugged. He was going to leave her. The polecat.

He leaned forward to kiss her forehead and even that innocuous salute caused her heart rate to increase. "Sleep well, Savannah. Pleasant dreams." He imbued the age old bedtime farewell with significance and personal meaning that had her insides melting even as his mother smiled benignly on them both.

He kissed his mother's cheek and bid her good night before leaving the room without another murmur.

"So…" Baptista's eyes measured Savannah and then she smiled with something that looked like satisfaction.

"Are you sleeping with my son, or is it still in the flirting stage?" she asked as Savannah tried hard not to fall off the couch in shock.

The next morning, Savannah was still reeling from Baptista's frank inquiries and equally frank assurances that the older woman wholly approved of the evident affection between her son and Savannah.

Turning onto her back on the sun lounger, Savannah lifted the upper portion of the chair to support her in a semireclining position. She surreptitiously watched Leiandros and the girls play together in the pool. Savannah had been swimming with her daughters when he came onto the terrace dressed in nothing more than a very sexy set of swimming trunks. He dove into the pool and she climbed out, leaving him to the mercy of two little girls with enough energy to light a small city.

She simply could not face the intimacy of joining in the water play after the way she'd come apart in his arms the night before.

Eva laughed at something Nyssa did and Leiandros went after both of them with a mock growl of outrage.

If she decided to marry him, he and the girls' strong rapport would make them a family in the true sense of the word, but where did she fit in?

Was she just a sacrifice on the altar of his perception of justice or did he truly want her for herself as he had passionately declared last night in the limo?

She silently ticked off the cons of marrying him on her fingers. He was ruthlessly blackmailing her into marriage. He didn't love her. He held her responsible for his cousin's death and that of his pregnant wife. A chill brought goose bumps to the surface of her skin. *He wanted her to replace his lost son.*

How would he react if Savannah only ever had daughters and more daughters? Would he resent it and blame her the way Dion had done? The prospect made her feel ill.

She watched as Leiandros lifted Eva high in the air and then let her drop to the water with a big splash, immediately fishing her out and hugging her while they both laughed. Nyssa demanded the same treatment and when she hit the water, she squealed. Savannah's heart tripped.

Her daughters already loved him. They didn't just want a father figure; they wanted Leiandros. And unlike their real father, Leiandros responded to them with all the warmth and approval most Greek males found so easy to give to small children. Both Eva and Nyssa reveled in the open affection.

She couldn't blame them. She yearned for his touch as well, though on a very different level. She wanted his body joined with hers in the primeval act of love. He wanted her too. His arousal had been more than evident the night before. A big part of her mindless reaction had stemmed from the heady knowledge Leiandros could desire her so uncontrollably.

Their need was definitely mutual, but where hers stemmed from strong emotion, she couldn't help wondering if his was connected to his passionate thirst for revenge, or justice as he called it. She sighed, rubbing more sunscreen on her legs. She wasn't even sure she could satisfy him when it came down to consummating their relationship.

Dion had said she was frigid and even after the intimacy she'd already shared with Leiandros, she still half believed Dion. After all, she'd never been able to summon so much as a penny's worth of enthusiasm toward his amorous overtures. On the other hand, one touch from Leiandros and she went up in flames. She pondered the implication of her body's differing reaction to the two men and her mind shied away from acknowledging the reason behind it.

Yet, there were no more barriers now to her attraction to Leiandros, no more reasons to hide her feelings for him, except the fear those feelings would never be returned. Fear she would not measure up in the bedroom. Fear that once he'd had her, he would grow tired of her. Fear that she could not give him the baby son he craved.

The litany of worries running through her mind disgusted her. When had she become such a craven coward?

Watching her daughters bravely take plunge after plunge into the crystal clear waters of the odd shaped pool, something inside of Savannah snapped. *She'd spent four years of her life living under the shadow of fear.*

Hadn't she stayed married to Dion long after she wanted to because she feared he would take away her daughters? She had avoided any semblance of intimacy with a man because she'd been terrified where it might lead. She'd hesitated to bring the girls to Greece because she dreaded their grandparents' reaction to them. If she were being honest with herself, she'd also have to admit that she had been anxious about returning to Greece because of the strong feelings Leiandros invoked in her.

A pathetic creature, holed up in her own little world, letting no one else in for fear they would hurt her, she was even afraid to give those feelings a name.

Her attention returned to Leiandros. If she refused to marry him, would he really refuse her the money to continue her aunt's care? Her instincts told her no, but she couldn't rely on them. They'd also told her to marry a young Greek playboy when she was a very innocent twenty. She had no doubts whatsoever that Leiandros would follow through on his threats regarding the girls. Family was too important to him to allow her to take them back to America, but as she'd told him the day before, she did not have to marry him to remain in Greece.

Eva made another splash, this time the result of diving from Leiandros's steady arms.

Savannah swallowed against a torrent of emotion welling within her. She had two options. Remain safe in her protected little world, or let Leiandros in and take a risk on marrying the man she loved.

Loved. Craved. Needed. Her feelings for him were so strong, it was no wonder she'd tried to sublimate them for seven long years. It hadn't worked. They'd come out in erotic dreams that tortured her sleeping hours. They'd come out in her capitulation about returning to Greece. She could have stayed in Georgia. She'd learned to cope at an early age with the curves life had a tendency to throw at her. No. She'd given up fighting Leiandros because that was what she had *wanted* to do.

Could she go back to her tiny house and lonely bed in Atlanta, even if by some miracle Leiandros allowed it? Her heart beat a steady negative. She loved Leiandros and the thought of losing him was worse than any other fear she'd ever experienced. It was a paralyzing terror. Marriage to a man who did not love her was a risk, but she made a discovery as she lay there soaking in the warmth from the Greek sun.

One emotion overcame fear, making her anxieties about the future seem insignificant. That emotion was love.

She would not give up a future with Leiandros because she feared what it might bring. She loved him and he wanted her. Badly. She would take any bet that he loved her daughters and he wanted *her* to have his babies.

She could build on such a foundation. She *would* build on it. Love would be the cornerstone of her new life, not fear.

CHAPTER TEN

"WHAT conditions?" Leiandros demanded, anger at the intense feeling of relief Savannah's surrender had evoked making his voice harsh.

She stepped back at his tone and her eyes widened before she narrowed them and tilted her elegant chin at an angle. "I need your assurance you will continue to give Eva and Nyssa attention and affection, even after I have your baby."

Offended at the implication he would ignore the precious little girls after the birth of his own child, he bit out, "That goes without saying."

"No, it does not." That stubborn little chin tilted another notch.

Why the hell not? What reason had she to believe he would reject her daughters? "*Eva and Nyssa will be my daughters.* The birth of other children will not negate that truth and as my daughters, they will always have claim to my affection."

She studied him as if weighing his sincerity. Her lack of trust infuriated him, but she finally nodded, her shoulders relaxing. He expected her to continue, but she looked away, her golden brown hair loose for once, falling in a silken mass to shield her expression from him.

"You said a *few* conditions?" he prompted.

Instantly, her entire body went taut with tension.

"Yes." Her pretty hands fisted at her sides. "You must also promise to be faithful."

She dared to demand this of him? "Look at me. I will not discuss this with the back of your head."

She seemed to brace herself and then turned, her face smooth and blank. Her eyes were a different matter. Their green depths had gone dark with some very intense emotion. "Well?"

Did she not realize she had once again questioned his honor? "When we marry, you become my wife, part of me. I would not so dishonor myself or you," he grated, feeling the rein on his temper slip a notch.

She flinched, but gave no sign of backing down. "Not all men consider marriage so binding and let's face it, you don't respect me. I need to know you will respect our marriage enough to compensate for that."

He wanted to kiss that antagonistic expression right off her face. "I have not said I do not respect you."

Her brow rose above challenging green eyes in obvious disbelief. "If you don't consider the numerous insults you have slung at my head testament to your lack of esteem toward me, then I would hate to be on the receiving end of what you do consider disrespectful comments."

"Sarcasm is not an attractive trait in a woman." He had only spoken the truth. His intention had not been to offend or wound her, but clearly he had.

"Evasiveness is even less attractive in a man. Do I have your promise of fidelity, or not?"

He bit back a derisive retort. He was not the partner in this deal that needed watching in this regard. "You have it."

Incredibly her eyes flickered with relief while some of the tenseness went out of her posture.

"I want no other woman, Savannah." He did not know why he offered the reassurance after the way she had insulted him, but needing to touch her, he reached out and pulled her closer to him. "Are there any other conditions?"

He scowled when she nodded again. *What else?*

"I'll marry you. I'll even try to have your baby..." she paused, biting her lip in obvious agitation.

She made the idea of having his child sound like a walk through purgatory. "Don't you want my children?" he demanded, experiencing a totally unaccustomed sense of uncertainty.

Her face suffused with color and she dropped her gaze. "Yes. Yes, I do."

"But?" he asked.

Her hands twisted together in front of her. "What will you do if we only have daughters? Will you divorce me? Or will you expect me to keep having children year after year until I produce your son and heir?"

The picture her words painted appalled him. "I have no intention of divorcing you. Ever. As to heirs...this is not the middle ages. Daughters can inherit as well as sons. I have little trouble seeing Nyssa running Kiriakis International."

Her eyes widened as if he'd shocked her. What did she think? He was some kind of dinosaur? So, perhaps he would prefer a son who shared his character and drive for business, but he would not love daughters any less. Had he not already proven that with Eva and Nyssa?

"Dion wanted sons." The words came out in a whisper he had to strain to hear.

Leiandros tensed at the sound of his cousin's name on Savannah's lips. He did not want to think about Dion being her husband before him, Dion wanting boy babies with her. "It is natural for a man to have this desire, but one cannot dictate the will of God. I want healthy babies and a wife who will love and nurture them as you have done with Eva and Nyssa."

"How many?"

"Be assured I do not wish you to be perpetually pregnant." He wanted a wife as much as he wanted a mother for his children.

Her hands rested against his chest, making it difficult for him to focus on their negotiations. "Give me a number."

A sudden thought occurred to him. "Was pregnancy difficult for you?" Some women struggled with a debilitating morning sickness. Petra hadn't been one of them, so he had not taken such an eventuality into consideration.

Savannah shook her head. "No. I liked being pregnant."

She muttered something under her breath. It sounded like she'd said she liked it when Dion hadn't been around. Leiandros didn't doubt it. A husband tormented by jealousies and the belief his wife carried her lover's child would not have been a pleasant companion or supportive mate during pregnancy.

"Then what is the problem?"

She met his gaze with green eyes filled with resolution. "The problem is gender and what you expect from me if you don't get the son you want to replace the one you lost.''

She wanted a number. Fine. He could give her a number. "Two. I believe raising four children will tax our patience and ingenuity sufficiently, particularly if the younger ones take after Eva and Nyssa.''

He'd meant to make her smile with that last remark and he succeeded. Her eyes twinkled at him. "Well, if they take after their father, I may just put in for early retirement.''

He drew her closer until their bodies were a breath away from touching. "No way. We are in this together, *yineka mou.*''

Whatever she would have said was lost between his lips and hers as he sealed their bargain with a kiss of commitment. She tasted so sweet, it took several seconds before he could lift his mouth from hers. He wanted more, but they were not alone in the house and he had no desire to explain certain matters to his inquisitive soon to be daughters.

"Are there any more conditions?''

To his chagrin, she nodded. "I need to return to Atlanta.''

His hold on her upper arms tightened convulsively. "Absolutely not." No way was he letting her leave him like she had left Dion.

She reached out and put her hand on his chest, in an apparent effort to comfort *him*. The touch shouldn't have soothed him, but it did. "I need to go back to take care of Aunt Beatrice. She won't last much longer." Pain reflected in her eyes and the downturn of her pretty mouth.

He moved his hands to cup both sides of her face, accepting her pain, even understanding it, but unwilling to be moved by it. "No." This was not negotiable.

She tried to pull away. "I *have* to go back, Leiandros."

He caught her mouth and kissed her lips softly. "No."

"You're being unreasonable."

"I'm being cautious. What good will marriage do me if you insist on staying in Atlanta? Dion learned that lesson the hard way. I refuse to be so trusting."

Her face drained of color, her eyes wounded. "It wasn't the same thing. I *had* to leave Dion. *I don't want to leave you,* but my aunt needs me."

"You can return after our honeymoon."

Her expression lightened to one of relief.

"But you must leave the girls here."

"Impossible!" She tore herself from his hold.

Her angry reaction had an immediate effect on the fit of his chinos. Her passion in any form wreaked havoc with his libido.

"I don't know how long I'll be gone! The girls *can't* stay here." She made an obvious bid to collect herself. *"Please."*

He didn't want her to beg. He wanted her to stay. "They will be my daughters too and I will care for them."

She shook her head wildly. "No. They must go with me."

"We've been through this before. You will not take them out of the country. Accept it."

She deflated like a parachute once the skydiver has landed, her stance one of defeat. "It won't work."

He agreed. Being apart was out of the question. She had to see that. According to the doctors, her aunt did not even recognize Savannah from one day to the next. Why was she so intent on returning to Atlanta to care for the other woman, or was it an excuse to get herself and the girls out of Greece?

"I can't marry you," she said baldly, her eyes filling with tears while a sense of dread caught hold of him.

"*Like hell.* You already gave your word. I won't allow you to change your mind."

"I said there were conditions." She blinked the tears away, rubbing the moisture under her eyes with her fingers.

He felt like cursing. She looked so vulnerable. And the worst of it was: he did not think she was attempting to gain his sympathy. She was trying too hard *not* to give into the tears.

"We can compromise." The very idea was alien to him. He did not usually approve or have need of the concept.

"Your compromises don't work for me." Her voice trembled.

He ignored that declaration. "I have spoken to the doctor in charge of your aunt's care. He says there is one nurse on staff that is a favorite of your aunt's. I can assure she is available for your aunt's personal care."

"I know who you are talking about and she's just discovered she's pregnant. What about when she goes on maternity leave? Will you allow me to go then?"

"According to her doctors, by then your aunt will no longer be with us." His own frustration came out in the cruel statement that he regretted the moment it left his lips.

Savannah did not look beaten any longer. She looked angry enough to attack him. "She is very special to me. She's the only family I've got."

"Do you discount me, my mother, Sandros, Helena and Iona so easily? Even your own daughters? Are we not all your family?"

"That is not what I meant." Some of the anger drained out of her. "She is *my* family. The closest thing to a loving mother that I've ever known."

"You are a Kiriakis." She had married into his family, made lifelong ties that could not be dismissed.

"I love her, Leiandros. I can't let her die alone."

The plea touched him when he wanted to remain unaffected. "According to her doctors, her condition is stable."

"At the moment," she agreed. "How did you know?"

"I call Brenthaven each day." Savannah was his, so her responsibilities were his also.

Her eyes widened and her pale face took on some much needed color. "You call Brenthaven every day?"

"Yes."

She took several seconds to digest this. "I want to go to her if her condition worsens. And even if it doesn't I want to visit her."

"Make them short visits and leave the girls here."

Savannah grimaced, but nodded. "And if she worsens?"

"We will deal with that when it comes, *pethi mou*."

He could not resist touching her any longer. Pulling

her into his arms, he kissed her. Strangely the feeling coursing through him was not passion, but unexpected tenderness and the light caress of her mouth against his once again soothed him when he least expected to be soothed.

He pulled his head away and rubbed her back. "Okay?"

She shuddered. "Yes."

This time he did not even try to stifle the feeling of relief washing over him like the Mediterranean at high tide.

Savannah waited nervously the next afternoon for the family to gather in the small reception room. Baptista had declared it more intimate, but to Savannah's eyes, it still looked big enough to swallow up most of her small house in Georgia. Leiandros intended to announce their upcoming marriage when everyone was together. Savannah was still trying to deal with her doubts, but accepted she had no real choice.

She loved her aunt too much to allow her to be moved to a state nursing home for the final weeks of her life and she loved Leiandros too much to let him go at all.

He caught her eye as he crossed the room to where she sat on the small settee near the window. He settled next to her, putting his arm casually around her waist and pulling her even closer than the small confines of the settee required. "Are you ready for the announcement?"

Was she? Focusing her attention on Eva and Nyssa sitting on either side of Helena and chattering a mile a minute she accepted the inevitable. "Yes." She could only hope the family responded more warmly to news of her marriage to Leiandros than they had when she married Dion.

Eva and Nyssa had taken to Dion's family with the exuberant affection of the young. They also adored their *honorary* grandmother, Baptista, who would be their real grandmother in less than a week's time.

Leiandros squeezed her and she turned to take in his sculpted features and the enigmatic dark chocolate gaze that made her heart flutter even in a room full of company. "They will all accept you as my wife."

"I hope so."

"They would not dare do otherwise."

She found herself grinning at his arrogance. "Of course not." Then she dropped her gaze in fear her love was shining a little too brightly in her eyes. Now that she'd acknowledged it, she discovered keeping her feelings from Leiandros was difficult indeed.

After everyone was seated, he stood and commanded their attention. Inevitably, he got it. Even her daughters sat perfectly still, their sweet faces turned toward him.

"Today heralds a new beginning for the Kiriakis family. Savannah has returned to us, bringing her daughters to renew relationships with the rest of their family."

Helena nodded, her eyes filled with tears. Baptista smiled approvingly at Savannah while both Sandros and Iona concurred with a Greek gesture of both joy and agreement.

Savannah felt her heart constrict at the obvious acceptance. Leiandros offered her far more than merely himself with marriage. He offered Savannah what she had always craved, had hoped to find with her first marriage, but it had been denied her...a family for herself and now for her daughters.

He nodded his proud head in an arrogant gesture, acknowledging the other's acceptance. "The only improvement which could be made on this new beginning would be for Savannah to once again join our family officially."

The air in the room crackled with expectancy.

Leiandros smiled down at Savannah and she returned the gesture, wondering if this was all just an act for the family's benefit. He wouldn't want them to know he had blackmailed her.

He returned his gaze to the family. "Do you not all agree?" he asked the room in general.

Every head nodded, except the girls who were looking perplexed.

"Then you will congratulate me on convincing Savannah to accept my proposal of marriage."

Pandemonium broke loose. The girls knew what it meant to get married and they jumped up from their seats like two tightly wound springs. Rushing across the room to throw themselves at Leiandros and Savannah, they squealed with delight.

"Does this mean you get to be my true daddy?" Eva asked, as he lifted her high in his arms.

Leiandros hugged her tightly and whispered something in her ear, which made her giggle and glow with happiness.

"Are you really going to marry *Theios?*" Nyssa demanded of Savannah, having crawled right into her lap.

Feeling overwhelmed with emotion, Savannah could only nod and smile, her lips wobbly. Nyssa squealed again and begged to be picked up by Leiandros as well. He stood there, six feet, four inches, of incredible male, holding one of her daughters in each arm and Savannah's heart swelled with so much love for all three of them that she thought it would burst.

Sandros came over and kissed Savannah's cheek before clapping Leiandros on the back. "I thought something like this was in the wind when we went to dinner." He grinned at the others. "Leiandros kept her so close to his side, the poor girl couldn't so much as take a breath and call it her own."

General laughter greeted Sandros's teasing.

As the laughter died, Leiandros set both girls down beside him and drew Savannah to her feet. "It is our custom to exchange rings upon announcing the intent to marry."

An expectant hush fell over the room. Savannah could not speak. He lifted her hand and slipped a ring with a large, deeply green, square cut emerald nestled between two clusters of diamond baguettes onto her finger. He brought her hand to his mouth and brushed his lips over the ring and her skin. His expression burned with possessiveness and she felt heat shooting up her arm from where the ring rested.

Then he slipped a ring into the center of her palm.

She looked down at it. Masculine and heavy, its recessed setting also bore an emerald along with two square cut smaller diamonds on either side. She trembled as she realized that he wanted her to put the ring on his finger, to announce before his family her intention to marry him.

Lifting his hand, she repeated his actions, including

the kiss. Afterward he announced that dinner would be the traditional betrothal feast and the room erupted into applause.

Baptista insisted on kissing and hugging each one of them. She kissed both of Savannah's cheeks. "I'm very pleased."

After many more congratulations, hugs and kisses, someone asked when the wedding was to take place.

"This Sunday," Leiandros replied.

"But that is only three days away!" Baptista cried. "There are so many things to be done, they cannot possibly be accomplished in so short a time."

"It is handled."

Evidently Leiandros's arrogance had no truck with his mother, because Baptista crossed her arms over her small bosom and gave him a glower worthy of an angry sailor. "Bah. What is everything? You could not have invited many guests and kept it such a secret. Do you wish to give your bride the impression you are ashamed of her?"

The haze of happiness surrounding Savannah melted and she shot a quick, questioning glance at Leiandros.

Was he ashamed of her?

His eyes narrowed and he took the two steps separating them before pulling her against his side. "Don't."

That was all he said, but she got the message. Don't worry. Don't doubt him. Don't be afraid, but how could she help it? He was marrying her for revenge and she was hoping it would turn into love. Heavens above! It was one thing to refuse to live a life constricted by fear, another entirely to be an incautious fool. Had she made an awful mistake?

"I am not ashamed of Savannah, but neither do I wish to wait to make her mine in every way."

Sandros laughed while Iona blushed, but Baptista's aggressive stance did not alter. Savannah tried to breathe while feeling like all the air in the room had gone on holiday, her cheeks burning with embarrassment at Leiandros's blatancy.

"You are no adolescent unable to control raging hormones. You are a man, my son. You can wait a few weeks. Your bride deserves to look back at her wedding with fond memories, not regret." Baptista's eyes dared her son to disagree.

His arm tightened around Savannah. "One week from Sunday. That gives you ten days to add whatever touches you and Savannah deem necessary to the wedding, but I will not wait one day longer."

Somehow, his implacability comforted her stressed nerves. He wanted to marry her, but he was willing to wait an extra week to make sure it was a wedding to be proud of. That did not indicate a man ashamed of his chosen bride.

Baptista agreed reluctantly and then launched immediately into plans for the next ten days. Helena and Iona offered their suggestions while Eva and Nyssa repeatedly proclaimed it had to be just like Cinderella in their mama's story.

The following days passed in a blur of activity, leaving Savannah dazed.

Baptista held the opinion that a mere man could know nothing of planning a proper wedding. She insisted on checking each one of her son's plans as well as taking

Savannah all over the island and to Athens in the helicopter for numerous shopping expeditions and lessons in traditional Greek dance. Baptista wanted Savannah to be able to perform the handkerchief dance to start at the reception.

Savannah saw little of Leiandros during these hectic days leading up to the wedding. Though he came home every evening from his office at Kiriakis International to spend time with her and the girls, he disappeared into his study to work after tucking them into bed. He said he needed to catch up on recently neglected work and clean his desk for their upcoming weeklong honeymoon.

She hadn't wanted to be parted for the girls for any longer and much to her surprise, he had acceded to her wishes. Even more surprising was the evident effort he had put into providing her with a dream wedding, effort he had to have expended before she had even come to Greece.

As the days progressed Savannah decided Leiandros was no ordinary man, because he knew quite a lot about weddings. The wedding gown he had chosen was declared fit for a princess. When she donned the simple veil, Baptista and the seamstress she had hired to make last minute alterations clapped their hands in approval.

He had brought in her favorite Southern magnolias along with fragrant gardenias to be mixed with traditional Greek flowers for her bouquet in one of the many efforts he had made to mix her customs with his. He had also taken an active interest in the expanded guest list, making sure they invited enough relations, friends and important business associates to fill the chapel and Villa Kalosorisma for the reception.

As each item fell into place and the wedding drew nearer, rather than bridal nerves, Savannah experienced a growing anticipation at the thought of linking her life with Leiandros.

She woke well before the maid came to deliver her breakfast on the day of her wedding. Baptista arrived with Eva and Nyssa in tow as Savannah was drinking her coffee. Baptista opened the terrace doors and the sound of aoud and fiddle music playing accompaniment to a male singer drifted in.

"What is that?" Eva asked as she climbed to sit on the bed next to Savannah. Nyssa was soon snuggled up to her other side.

"The music for dressing," Baptista replied. "It is tradition. The bridegroom arranges this treat for his bride."

Savannah warmed at Baptista's words and the rest of the morning was filled with happy chatter as the women prepared for the wedding in Savannah's room. A stylist came in and did everyone's hair and makeup. All too soon, it was time for Savannah to put on her wedding gown. As she slipped into the antique white satin, she felt like the princess her daughters kept calling her.

Someone knocked on the door and Baptista opened it.

"It is time," Savannah heard from the cracked doorway.

From then on, everything happened in a blur. A large group of wedding guests waited outside the villa's main entrance to join the procession to the chapel. Savannah sought Leiandros's commanding presence and her heart settled in her chest when she saw him. Dressed in morning coat with tails, he looked like the prince to her very own fairy tale.

They stopped outside the chapel in order for the priest to bless the rings before he led them inside.

The wedding itself was more like a church service, though the priest stopped to lead them in the traditional vows Savannah was accustomed to. Baptista had told her that Greek weddings rarely included vows as they were the union of two souls rather than a contract. Regardless of the reasoning, Savannah's heart rejoiced as Leiandros looked deeply into her eyes and promised to forsake all others.

He had done this for her and she smiled tremulously, her voice shaking as she promised to love and honor him.

When she saw the headpieces Leiandros had selected for the crowning, all the air left her lungs in one long gush. They truly were crowns fit for a king and queen, obviously made with real gold or at least overlay and encrusted with precious stones and gems. Several women sighed as the delicate tiara was settled on Savannah's head and the masculine counterpart placed on Leiandros.

They were pronounced man and wife and regardless of Greek custom, Leiandros kissed her with pent up passion and unmistakable possessiveness.

She could almost hear him saying, "You are mine now."

And she was.

CHAPTER ELEVEN

"You performed the handkerchief dance very well."

Savannah turned her head and smiled at Iona. They had developed a friendship of sorts, but neither woman mentioned the past or Dion.

"It was fun. Baptista wanted me to be perfect so she took me to lessons. I practiced until my legs felt like noodles and my arms threatened to fall off."

Iona grinned and winked. "Well, you got it right and from the sparks shooting between you and my cousin, Leiandros thought so as well."

Sparks? The feelings Leiandros incited in Savannah were more like a forest fire blazing out of control. Her entire body thrummed with anticipation for the upcoming night. He had done everything in his power to make her that way, too, at least that's how she felt. He'd been touching her constantly all day, nothing overt, a brush here, a caress there, but all of them fed the desire now raging through her blood.

The reception had been going on for what seemed like hours and she did not know how much longer she could wait to be alone with him without exploding on the spot.

"Look…"

Savannah looked where Iona had pointed. The men were gathering in a circle on the area by the pool that had been set aside for dancing.

Iona said, "The men are beginning the traditional dance."

Leiandros stood a head taller than most of the other men, his body rippling with muscles under the white shirt and pants he wore, all that remained of his wedding finery. He faced her across the large patio, his eyes holding hers as the dance began.

Soon, the eye contact was broken, but not Savannah's concentration. She knew peripherally other men were dancing and guests were clapping their hands, shouting their appreciation, but all she saw was him. Her husband. His body could feed the fantasies of the entire female population of Greece. He certainly fulfilled hers. With each turn and kick his muscles bulged against the single layer of fabric covering them.

Her body heated while her mouth went dry with desire. She didn't know how long the men danced before people started throwing plates, but when one was placed in her hand, she threw it down with passionate zeal, all the while her gaze never once moving from Leiandros. She felt powerless against the feelings coursing through her.

One by one, the men dropped out of the dance until Leiandros and two others were all that remained. For the first time since he had started dancing, Leiandros looked at her and she felt her throat constrict.

"Here, child." Was that Baptista's voice?

Enthralled with the movements of the dance and the sheen of sweat covering the V of chest exposed by Leiandros's shirt, Savannah couldn't make herself turn to find out. She took the plate and as Leiandros and the other two men went into a series of fast paced turns and steps, she threw it. It crashed onto the tile two feet in front of Leiandros.

Leiandros's eyebrows rose at the gesture.

She smiled brilliantly at him and took another plate from someone, throwing it to splinter into pieces near the other. The two men dancing with Leiandros moved away and he was the only dancer left, but then he'd been the only dancer in her eyes since the beginning.

She took another plate, this time from Iona, she thought, and tossed it with fervor. It broke directly in front of him. He smiled then, his eyes making sexual promises that made her body tremble. She'd broken three more plates when he started to dance in a pattern leading to her. He stopped when he reached her and she stared.

She could do nothing else.

He bent, placing one arm behind her knees and the other curved around her ribcage, then straightened lifting her high into his arms. The skirts of her dress billowed around them, while the guests yelled their approval and some of the men tossed suggestions to Leiandros that bordered on the risqué.

It all felt like a movie playing around her, muted and remote. The only reality was his hard chest against her side, his hand gripping her ribs, his thumb subtly brushing the side of her breast, the musky scent of his heated body and the promise in his dark as sin eyes.

He turned and shouted something to the guests and then carried her swiftly toward the helo pad. They had said goodbye to the girls earlier, while taking a break from the reception to tuck Eva and Nyssa into their beds.

There was nothing and no one to hinder their departure.

Aboard the helicopter, Savannah didn't even try to talk to Leiandros. The noise of the whirling blades made any sort of discussion impossible. She had expected to ride in the limo to the hotel attached to the restaurant they'd eaten at in Halkida. It took her several minutes to realize they weren't headed for Halkida at all.

She turned to Leiandros and shouted, "Where are we going?"

He smiled mysteriously and shook his head.

They'd been in the helicopter for about twenty-five minutes when she recognized the outskirts of Athens. Ten minutes later, they landed on the rooftop helo pad of a tall building in the business sector. Leiandros jumped out, grabbed her by the waist and lifted her out. Then he led her, running, away from the wind created by the blades.

When they got out of the radius of the blades, he once again swept her into his arms. A man opened a door leading from the roof to the interior of the building and Leiandros moved inside. He carried her down a short flight of steps, through another security door and into a waiting lift.

"Where are we?" she asked, breathless.

"Can you not guess, *yineka mou?*"

She probably could, if her brain could focus on something other than the fascinating play of light on his black hair.

He used the hand under her knees to press in a security code and the lift started moving. It stopped seconds later. The doors slid open and he carried her into a small foyer, keyed another security code outside the door and then pushed it open.

Finally it dawned on her where they were. "We're in your penthouse at the top of the Kiriakis building."

She'd only been here once before—the night of the fateful party. The night she had met him for the first time and allowed him to kiss her into almost complete submission.

Her gaze darted around her, taking in the entry hall and the living room as he carried her inside.

"It all looks the same," she whispered.

He nodded, his expression almost grim. "Petra was not interested in the penthouse. She spent most of her time living in a villa I bought near her parents."

Savannah knew right then and there, she never wanted to step foot in that villa. It belonged to another woman. "She didn't live at Villa Kalosorisma?"

He studied her face, his own expressionless. "Never."

Savannah let out a breath she didn't realize she'd been holding. Fiercely glad that her home was truly hers, she smiled involuntarily.

"You like that?" he asked.

She couldn't deny it. "Yes."

"You're possessive, but then so am I." He swung around and carried her out onto the terrace.

He lowered her to her feet, keeping her body molded to his. She couldn't see his face in the shadowy darkness and felt an atavistic shiver shake her. What was he thinking?

"Do you remember?" he asked, his voice almost harsh.

The kiss. He meant the kiss. "Yes." She had never been able to forget.

"I wanted you that night, Savannah. I was furious to find out you already belonged to another man. My own cousin."

She had sensed his fury at the time, but assumed it was directed at her for responding to him when she was married to Dion. "I belong to you now." He had to know it. He only had to brush against her and she lost touch with reality.

He growled something low in Greek and then he kissed her, just like that fateful night. His mouth moved on hers in tender exploration as if he'd never kissed her before, his tongue coming out to softly trace the outline of her lips. And just like before, she melted, her body going boneless against his. The kiss went on and on. Just like before, but unlike before, when he placed his hands on the outer curves of her breasts, she did not pull away.

She did not have to. He groaned his approval as his hands slid to her back and undid the zip cleverly hidden under a row of tiny buttons and loops. Her breath stopped in her throat as he undid her dress inch by tantalizing inch. Would he never finish? Her feminine flesh ached for him, and she pressed her thighs together, trying to alleviate the almost painful pleasure. It only made it worse.

She was going to expire from need before he even got her dress off.

"Leiandros…" his name came out a plea against his lips.

He hushed her with his mouth, taking possession of

the vulnerable interior of hers with his tongue. And the zip lowered another inch. She didn't feel boneless anymore, she felt desperate and her body squirmed against him, while his hands and tongue tormented her to higher levels of passion.

She loved him so much. She wanted to feel him inside of her, connected to her in the most fundamental way, their bodies joined, their souls one. She didn't care about preliminaries. She needed him now! But he acted like he had all the time in the world and kissed her lazily as he continued lowering that wretched zipper.

She would have screamed in frustration, but her mouth was too busy enjoying his.

Finally, the zipper gave completely and the edges of her dress parted under his expert fingers. Fingers that caressed the now incredibly sensitive skin of her back.

She moaned, wanting him to move those fingers to her front, her swollen breasts craving his touch, their tight peaks aching for his possession. She pressed herself against him, rubbing from side to side, but the friction of her gown only increased her torment.

She wanted the caress of his hands on her, not satin.

He stepped back and she tried to follow him, but he wouldn't let her. He looked down at her. "I burned for you that night, but my body had to go unsatisfied. I tried to drown the ache in another woman."

She didn't like hearing that and knew she had no right to feel that way. "Did it work?" she had to ask.

"She wasn't you." His voice sounded accusing.

Savannah let the bodice of her dress fall, to reveal her unrestricted breasts, her erect nipples jutting forth proudly. "I'm here now."

He swore, but instead of touching her as she expected, he swung her up in his arms and carried her back inside all the way to the master bedroom. When he got there, he dropped her legs and she stood against him, her bare breasts pressed against the silk of his shirt. But still he didn't touch her.

She whimpered her longing.

With another curse, he undressed her with barely suppressed hunger until she stood before him with not one stitch of clothing to hide behind, her body vulnerable to his dark gaze.

He stepped back. "Stay there."

His growled command rooted her to the spot, primal feminine fear curling around the edges of her desire.

He punched a button and recessed lighting illuminated the room. Although mellow, the light made her feel exposed. Still fully dressed, he stood a few feet away and stared at her, letting his eyes move over her body in a way that made her feel like a piece of artwork for sale and he the collector.

She started to lift her hands to cover herself.

"Don't!" he warned and her hands fell back to her sides of their own volition, her body shivering in response to his tone.

"What's happening?" She didn't think this was the sort of seduction most brides experienced on their wedding nights.

He was silent for several seconds before answering. "I wanted you here, like this. That night. I wanted you, naked in my bedroom, on my bed, under me."

His words sent arrows of sensations to her already moist feminine flesh, but his expression did something

else entirely. He looked enraged with some kind of male
sexual antagonism and tormented. It was the torment that
kept her still.

Yet under the oppression of his gaze, she shivered
again, the second time in as many minutes. She tried to
tell herself she was just tired, that she was imagining the
dangerous weight of his look, that he would not hurt her.
It had been a wonderful, but emotional day. Perhaps her
mind was playing tricks on her.

None of the arguments succeeded in dispelling the
gathering sense of doom surrounding her in its shadows,
bringing chills to her naked flesh and making her heart
beat like that silly little old jackrabbit.

But, she *wasn't* helpless. She was a woman, his
woman, his *yineka* and she would not cower to the fear
that dogged her like darkness chasing the sunset.

She let her eyes meet his now obsidian gaze.

He showed no expression as she began moving toward
him, her heart pounding against her ribs with a combination of apprehension and desire. "Well, I'm *here. In
your bedroom.*"

She veered her path as she came into touching distance of him and headed toward the oversized king bed.
White gauze draped from the ceiling, the excess folds
gathered with gold rope to each of the corners of the
four-poster bed.

She climbed onto the high mattress. Kneeling, she
faced him. *"On your bed."*

His jaw set in a hard line of uncompromising strength.
He said nothing. Nor did he move. His eyes did not
flicker.

She sucked in air and let it out again. "If you want

me *under you,* you'll have to take your clothes off and join me.''

She'd never been this bold. Had never wanted to be this wanton, but with this man, she felt no inhibitions. His manner caused small jolts of trepidation to skitter along her nerve endings, but instead of turning her off, she felt more excited, more ready to mate with her chosen lover.

Something was going on in his head, something to do with the night they'd kissed, but she knew with every fiber of her feminine being that Leiandros wanted her.

And he was going to have her, but not as some sorry little sacrifice. She intended to meet him equally, to give pleasure and to take it as well. So, she waited, waited for him to undress, waited for him to come to her.

They faced each other, both aggressors, both unwilling to bend. Until she started taking the pins from her hair. His eyes fixed on the movement of her fingers as strand by silky strand settled against her nape and shoulders, falling to the center of her back. She dropped the pins to the floor, each one landing silently against the thickly piled carpet.

When she finished, she moved to one corner of the bed and untied the gold rope. Two drapes swooshed down. She went to each corner, repeating her actions until the gauze completely enclosed the bed and Leiandros's figure was hazy through the sheer white fabric.

Then she laid down, lifting the leg closest to him, creating a visual barrier to her feminine secrets. In contrast, she stretched her arms above her head, arching her back so her breasts were shown to their best advantage. "Are you coming?"

The untamed sound he made thrilled her and she watched through the gauze as he stripped off his shirt, sending buttons flying all over the room. One landed against the bed curtains and slid to the floor.

He was more careful with his pants, easing the zipper down slowly over his obviously excited male flesh. She had a short glimpse of him standing gloriously proud in only his tiny male briefs before those, too, were dispensed with. She caught her breath at his full nudity.

Heavens, he was big. Her throat constricted with fear again, but this time it was the instinctual fear of a woman faced with her mate's full masculine strength for the first time. She knew her eyes were wide and her mouth parted in wonder as he approached the bed, his movements predatory and determined, but she couldn't help it.

She'd only actually seen male nudity a handful of times. Dion had preferred the dark and he'd never looked like this.

"You're magnificent," she whispered in awe and he faltered as he drew apart the curtains.

Laughter erupted from him as he launched toward her, landing with his huge body covering her, his weight pressing down her drawn up leg. The amusement in his eyes died as their naked bodies touched. She grabbed his head, trying to bring it down to meet her lips.

"You little torment! I hope you're ready for me. After that performance, I want to be inside you." He let her pull his mouth nearer and kissed her, his lips hot, his tongue intrusive. "Now," he said as if she didn't already get the picture.

Then, he grabbed her hands and kept them above her head with one of his, his expression tenderly menacing.

She answered with her body, letting her thighs spread apart and tipping her pelvis toward that magnificent male erection. She'd been ready since the final dance at the reception.

She'd wanted him outside on the terrace so badly she would have let him love her there, but he'd insisted on coming into the bedroom and playing that silly game.

"Take me," she demanded.

And he did. *Heavens,* how he did. For all his macho warnings, he didn't enter her with even a semblance of lust filled violence. He positioned himself against her opening and rocked himself inside her with a sensuous back and forth motion that had her insides swelling against him and her feelings spiraling toward that starburst of pleasure she had felt once before in his arms.

All the while his mouth pressed hot, salacious kisses all over her face down to the sensitive skin behind her ear and he rubbed the black curling hair on his rock hard chest against her oversensitive nipples.

She yanked her hands from his loosened hold and gripped his bottom, pulling him deeper inside with the strength of Samson as she felt the pleasure spin out of control. She heard a scream, followed by a guttural shout that would have deafened her if she hadn't been lost in wave after stupendous wave of mind-numbing pleasure. She floated in the aftermath until her heartbeat slowed and her eyes could focus again.

She smiled at him. "Am I dead?"

His eyes narrowed. *"No."*

"I must be," she teased and leaned up to kiss him. "I'm definitely in Heaven."

His too serious expression lightened to smug satisfaction. "Remember, it's only this *magnificent* male that can take you there. You belong to me now, *yineka mou,* and no one else will ever touch you this way again."

The underlying warning in his voice pricked at her heart. How could he think for one single, solitary second that she could *ever* go to another man's bed after sharing his?

"How did you know?" she asked, tongue in cheek, wanting to dispel the gloom settling over her.

He stilled, his semierect flesh hardening slightly inside her. "What do you mean?"

"I've never felt that way before." She played with the hair on his chest, pressing her fingers against the muscles underneath, their hardness attesting to his physical strength. She absolutely reveled in her freedom to touch him. "Well, except that time on the terrace. Couldn't you tell?"

"Never?" he demanded, sounding incredulous.

"Never," she repeated. "It was never you before."

He deserved that admission after the one he'd made on the terrace. His nearly black eyes burned into her, while his flesh went fully erect in the space of a heartbeat.

"Oh," she exclaimed. "Again? So soon?"

But he was too busy moving and touching every pleasure spot she knew of on her body and some she'd never suspected she possessed to answer.

Hours and repeated bouts of lovemaking later, he laid

with his head resting on her breast, his hand lazily moving over her skin, touching, branding, *knowing* her.

She tried to stifle a yawn, but couldn't quite accomplish the feat.

His head came up, his expression smug. "Tired, *moro mou?*"

Wanting to touch him some more, but too beat to move, she said, "Yes."

"That's too bad," he said in a voice that made her pulse leap, as spent as her body was.

"Is it?" she asked, her mind occupied with the way his fingers felt against her most sensitive flesh.

"Much, much too bad."

"Why?" she asked, her breath hitching in her throat.

"Because I haven't done everything I wanted to do yet."

There was *more?* "Like what?"

He kissed her nipple, teasing it with the tip of his tongue. "Like this." And his lips closed over the tender bud as he began a strong sucking motion that had her moaning.

Incredibly, he was right. He'd touched every inch of her flesh, licked most of it and nipped certain highly sensitive areas, but he hadn't once done this, the expected.

"I guess that means I don't get to go to sleep yet," she said, trying to sound disappointed, but failing miserably.

She couldn't have gone to sleep now for all the peaches in Georgia. She slid her hand onto his chest, finding the male counterpart of the flesh he was pleasuring so thoroughly, and lightly rubbed it. He arched against her hand and she made little circles around his flat male nipple before gently pinching it between her thumb and forefinger.

He nearly came off the bed. ''Yes. Little torment. Just like that. Don't stop.''

And she didn't.

They fell asleep, sweaty, sated and curled in one another's arms as the Greek sun started to rise, pouring diffused amber light through the gauze covered master bedroom's huge window.

CHAPTER TWELVE

"WAKE up, *yineka mou*. It is time to get up."

Leiandros's voice filtered through the layers of sleep fogging Savannah's brain.

"Why?" she muttered, not bothering to lift her head from the pillow. Her body ached in places she'd never recognized as having muscles and her eyes felt filled with sand.

"Come, *agapi mou*. Open your eyes."

Her eyes flew wide and she sat straight up, the white sheet falling around her waist. Had he just called her his love? She searched his face, but didn't see any sign of tenderness.

His eyes were serious, his mouth grim and the set of his shoulders stiff. "You must be strong."

Panic welled up in her chest. "Eva? Nyssa? My babies?"

"Are fine." He reached out and placed a warm hand on her bare shoulder. "It is your aunt."

Savannah could not make herself ask the question that needed to be asked.

He seemed to sense her hesitation and answered as if she'd voiced the words. "She is alive, but she has had another stroke. The doctor does not expect her to recover."

Savannah sagged against the pillows. "What do you mean?" Her words came out in an agonized whisper because she knew what he meant. Aunt Beatrice was going to die. "How long?"

"They do not know. Maybe a day, maybe a week."

"I need to go." She tensed for his refusal.

"The jet is at the airport as we speak. The helicopter is on the roof waiting to take us there. Take a shower and dress. You can eat on the plane. I've already packed for us."

"You're going with me? You're letting me go?" She couldn't take it in.

"Of course." He shrugged. "You are my wife. Your concerns are my concerns."

His words shocked her so much, she was in the shower when she thought of the girls.

Dressed in the clothes he had provided, her hair still damp, she left the bathroom in search of Leiandros. She ran him down in the study. He was on the phone.

When he saw her enter, he cut the call immediately and turned to face her. "Ready?"

"What about the girls?" She couldn't think, didn't know what to do.

"They are content with their grandmothers. The girls expect us to be gone a week. There is no reason to upset them with the news."

She nodded. She'd taken them to visit Aunt Beatrice only rarely because having the children around upset the older woman and therefore upset the girls as well. They had already said their goodbyes.

"I'm ready." She fingered the lightweight red fabric of her ankle length sleeveless dress. "This is very comfortable."

His smile was wry. "I admit comfort was not high on my list when I chose it."

The way he was looking at how the dress clung to her curves made her blush. "Oh. You picked it out?" Remembering his reaction to her dress the night they'd almost made love in his car, she thought she knew why he'd chosen this particular color.

"Yes." He didn't add anything else, but led her from the apartment back into the lift they had ridden the night before.

Leiandros insisted she try to sleep on the plane. She had no success until he joined her on the bed, pulling her tightly into the curve of his body and soothing her with his presence. They reached Atlanta in just over eight hours. When she expressed her surprise at the swift flight, he informed her that he'd had the pilot fly at the maximum speed allowed for the new jet without having to stop along the way for refueling.

Once again Leiandros had arranged VIP treatment through customs and had a limousine waiting for them at the airport to take them directly to Brenthaven. He kept her close to his side during the journey and her hand latched to his own as they walked down the quiet corridors of Brenthaven.

The room smelled like a hospital and Aunt Beatrice lay against the pillows, her translucent skin the color of the sheets. Savannah approached the bed, listening to the labored breathing of the woman in a coma lying there. Starting to shake, Savannah tried to stifle the pain filled moan that crawled up her throat.

She could no longer pretend to herself that one day Aunt Beatrice would come back to her.

Suddenly, Leiandros's arm was there, wrapped around her trembling shoulders. "Tell me about her."

So she did, through the interminable hours that followed she told him about her aunt, how she had raised a little girl orphaned by her mother's death and her father's desertion. Savannah shared the terror she'd experienced when her aunt was diagnosed with Alzheimer's when Savannah was nineteen, her desperation when near disaster had forced Savannah to put her aunt in a public nursing home.

"You married Dion so you could move your aunt here."

She didn't want to talk about her former marriage, so she just shrugged. "Nothing's quite that simple."

He didn't pursue it, but maintained his place beside her, ordering in food when he determined she should be hungry, cajoling her into drinking fruit juices when she'd have settled for black coffee and listening to her talk whenever she needed to. Ten hours later, her aunt quietly slipped away, never having regained consciousness.

Savannah's eyes remained dry as she listened to Leiandros make arrangements with the doctor. Her stoic expression did not waver when he led her from Brenthaven to the waiting limo, but when they got inside, he pulled her onto his lap and her defenses collapsed.

She burrowed into his chest, seeking a hiding place from her pain. She felt tears well and for the first time in almost two decades, she let them fall unrestrained.

Leiandros tightened his hold on her. "Cry, *pethi mou.* Let the grief out."

And she did. She cried out her grief over being alone in the world for so long. She finally mourned the lost years of her marriage, the pain of Dion's betrayal and Leiandros's contempt. But most of all, she wept for the woman who had been the closest thing to a real mother Savannah had ever had.

Through it all, he held her. When they reached her modest little house, he carried her inside while she continued to soak his shoulder and the front of his shirt.

"Our room?" he asked, implying his ownership of both her and her home.

She pointed down the hall.

He carried her through the bedroom into her private bath. She clung to him as he turned on the shower and began undressing them both. They were under the hot spray of water before her tears finally shuddered to a halt. She wrapped her arms around his waist and pressed herself against the warmth of his body. Even in the hot shower, she felt cold.

"She loved me when no one else would. I'm alone now."

He put his hands on her shoulders and pushed her far enough away that he could look into her face. "You are *not* alone. You are mine."

How could such possessive words sound so good to her battered soul?

After that, he remained silent, washing them both, then taking her out of the shower and toweling her dry like a baby.

"Go lie down. I'll get you a glass of water."

She obeyed without a murmur. She had climbed naked between the sheets, when he returned to the room with a tray. A carafe of chilled water, two glasses and two fresh peaches, sliced and peeled looked very enticing on the tray.

"Where did those come from?" She pointed to the peaches.

"I had the kitchen stocked and the house opened and aired while we were on our way here."

He had thought of everything. After drinking her water, she sat docile while he tenderly hand fed her peach slices. As he continued to feed her the mood around them subtly changed and he lingered over her lips with a gentle touch as she drew out every bite. She didn't know when her melancholy turned to desire, but soon she was feeding him succulent, slippery slices of peach, dipping her fingertips into his mouth with the fruit and sucking on his fingers when he returned the favor.

He shuddered. "Savannah?"

"I need you." So simple. So true. She needed assurance that she belonged to him, that she was not alone.

He placed the tray on the floor and then tumbled her back against the pillows, devouring her lips with his own. Though their kisses were passionate, hot and uncontrolled, at the first touch of his male flesh against her femininity, something in him changed. He took her with so much tenderness, so much gentle wooing, more tears seeped from her eyes, but there was no sadness in them.

She felt reborn by his touch and when the final pleasure came, it rolled over her in inexhaustible waves and still he did not stop. He continued to move in her and on her, kissing her eyelids, sipping her tears of passion and nuzzling her.

He carefully built the passion in her to a new crescendo, but this time when the cymbals crashed, he was with her. He did not withdraw for a long time and she did not want him to. This oneness was like an oasis to her thirsty soul.

When he finally moved out of her, he pulled her close to his side and kissed her temple. "You are not alone. I am with you, *yineka mou.*"

And he was. Through the funeral service, through the packing of her and the girls remaining personal possessions and in bed. Most definitely in bed. She slept cuddled to his body every night after making love and with each passing day her love for him grew and grew until she realized it had no bounds and exulted in the knowledge.

The night before they were to return to Greece, Savannah insisted on cooking, though Leiandros had hired a temporary daily cook and cleaner to make things easier for her. After they finished eating, she led him into the living room for coffee. She set the tray on the coffee table in front of the couch and poured the steaming brew into mugs before taking a seat beside Leiandros in the center of the sofa.

He took a sip of his coffee, his sensual lips pressing against the ceramic mug. "Your coffee is excellent, *pethi mou,* but I will be happy to drink Greek coffee again."

Not in the least offended, she smiled. Coffee didn't

really interest her right now, but then very little could compete with him.

She put her mug down and snuggled into his side. Would she ever grow accustomed to this freedom to draw comfort from his body whenever she wanted it? "I'm going to miss this house."

It had been a true refuge after the annihilation of her marriage.

He cupped her nape with long masculine fingers, letting his thumb rub a soothing pattern just below her ear. "Are you sorry to be returning to Greece?"

Her head popped up and she looked into dark chocolate eyes that shielded his secrets. "How can you ask that?" Couldn't he tell how much she needed him now? She'd never worked up the courage to tell him she loved him, but he had to know it.

He shrugged and pressed her head back to rest against his chest. "It does not matter. You belong to me now."

She smiled at his arrogance. "And you belong to me."

He didn't answer, but he did not deny it, either.

They finished their coffee, discussing last minute details of her permanent return to Greece, but Leiandros grew increasingly quiet until the conversation stopped altogether.

He drew away from her and looked at her with eyes that had gone black with some unnamed emotion. "Tell me about the lover that hurt you."

Bewildered by this totally unexpected change in topic, she asked, "What are you talking about?"

Then the full impact of his words hit her. He still believed she had taken lovers during her first marriage.

After the emotional and physical intimacy they had shared, she could not accept his clinging to such a belief. She had meant to tell him the truth, but somehow with all that he had done for her since the wedding, she'd come to believe it was unnecessary.

Obviously, she'd been wrong and their intimacy meant nothing in the face of his old resentments.

He took her hand in his, in what she assumed was supposed to be a comforting gesture, but she was too furious to feel anything but her anger. "There is no need to evade the subject. I know someone hurt you. You shied away from me when you first arrived in Greece. You are still uncomfortable in close proximity to other men, even Sandros."

Actually, she thought she'd done rather well at their wedding reception, giving and receiving numerous hugs and kisses of congratulations on her cheeks from one man after another as well as the women.

"And you believe one of my *many* lovers hurt me?" she asked, her voice scathing, her heart hurting.

His mouth tautened into a grim line. "Are you trying to convince me it did not happen? There is no need."

She sprang up from the couch, her body prickling with enraged tension. *"Damn you, Leiandros. Are you truly that blind?"* she shrieked at him.

His eyes widened in shock. "Do not swear at me."

She glared at Leiandros, her fury so great she had to take a deep breath before she could get the words out she wanted to say. "I can swear any damn time I want to!"

When he opened his mouth to speak, she rushed on, her voice loud enough to drown out anything he might utter. "Where is your evidence of my infidelity?" She swung her arms wide in a gesture of disbelief. *"Where?"*

He remained silent, his expression giving nothing away.

"That's right. You have none! You have only your cousin's word and he lied about me with horrific regularity. You accept that my daughters are Kiriakises. What chance is there if I were so promiscuous they would both be his?"

She inhaled another deep breath and went on. "Did you ever see me flirt? Did you ever see me make eyes at other men? Your investigator told you I hadn't dated in the last three years. What makes you think I was any different before?"

"The kiss." Just that. No more words.

She was so mad she wanted to spit, something a Southern lady was never to do. "Who pulled away first, Leiandros?" she demanded. "Who told you I was married? *Me!* Yes, I responded, but I didn't lead you on. I did not invite that kiss and after it happened, what did I do? I avoided you, to the point of ignoring instincts for my own safety."

"Explain that last remark," he barked at her, his unemotional façade cracking.

"You bet I'll explain. You just wait right there."

She whirled from the room, stormed into her tiny study, opened the safe and pulled out a large manila envelope.

She stomped back into the living room and threw the envelope on the coffee table in front of Leiandros. "Your answers are in there. Open it."

*   *   *

Savannah sat at the old-fashioned vanity, brushing the remaining dampness from her hair when Leiandros came into the room. She must have taken a shower. She'd wrapped her black velvet robe around her irresistible nakedness and tied the waist with a big knot.

He sighed. Her nonverbal communication was clear. *Don't touch.* But then he could not blame her. His stomach churned with nausea at what he had read and seen. Their eyes met in the mirror, hers still simmering with fury.

She didn't stop brushing her hair. "I suppose you've convinced yourself I deserved it, being such an immoral slut and all."

"*Theos mou.* Don't!" His voice was harsh with emotion. He could not stand the implication he could ever condone such a thing. He held the pictures toward her. "How many times did this happen before you left him?"

She put the brush down, but continued to face the mirror. "What difference does it make?"

"*How many?*"

"Once," she said defiantly.

What did she think? He would have expected her to stick around for more of the same?

"Tell me." He needed to know.

She spun to face him, her eyes burning accusation at him, but worse was the stark pain clouding their green depths. "Why? You think you know the story already. According to you, I was some kind of bed-hopping bimbo when I was married to your cousin. Obviously he got fed up and lost his temper."

Even if that were the case, there was no excuse for

what Dion had done to her. "Tell me the truth. Tell me how it really was," he practically begged.

Her eyes mirrored wariness. "Will you believe me?"

He no longer knew what to believe about his cousin's marriage to Savannah. The picture Dion had painted of her did not coincide with the woman Leiandros had come to know since her return to Greece.

This woman cared deeply for her children, reacted generously toward people who had hurt her in the past and had taken on responsibility for an elderly woman's care when she was barely old enough to be on her own.

His silence condemned him and before he could rectify the situation, she jumped up from the vanity chair.

"When you figure it out, let me know. Then *I'll* decide whether or not I want to tell you." She stalked over to the bed and grabbed one of the pillows, then opened the cedar chest at its foot, taking out a quilt and turned to leave the room.

Panic slammed through him, his superior brain not working for once. "Where are you going?"

She fixed him with that blank-eyed stare that said she was keeping her emotions under wraps. "I think I'll sleep on the couch tonight."

He said the first thing that came to mind. "Do not think you can manipulate me by withholding your body." As soon as the words left his mouth, he knew they were the wrong ones.

Not so much as a single facial muscle moved in the blank mask of her face. "I would not begin to dream that I could. In fact, I've finally wised up enough to stop dreaming completely."

And then she was gone, while he stood motionless

calling himself every kind of fool and a few words he
would never use in her company.

Savannah lay on the couch, dry-eyed and hurting so
much it was hard to breathe. She'd come to the couch
instinctively for comfort. It was one of the few pieces
of furniture she'd kept in storage when she moved to
Greece the first time. She'd slept on this same sofa for
the first year she had lived with Aunt Beatrice, but the
comfort she sought wasn't there.

Leiandros did not believe her. She had bared her soul,
showing him the pictures of her bruised body, her copy
of the doctor's report and the restraining order. And he
still believed his cousin had been the saint.

Her fists twined together, clenching the quilt as if it
were a lifeline, but there was no lifeline. Her dreams
were in ashes and her love mangled beyond recognition.

He'd demanded she tell him the truth, but what he'd
meant was her version of it. He'd retained the right to
judge the merit and honesty of her words. She bit her
bottom lip in an attempt to stifle the sobs demanding
release from her breast until she tasted blood. She'd
thought she could live with a one-sided love, that she
would eventually overcome his prejudices and mistrust.

She accepted now she never would.

If he could still believe Dion had been the victim after
seeing those pictures, there was no hope for her future
with Leiandros. His blindness toward his cousin's true
nature would always stand between them. She could ask
Sandros to tell Leiandros the truth, but to what purpose?
He didn't trust *her* and she couldn't live with that distrust.

A low moan of pain escaped her slightly parted lips and she curled into a fetal ball, her hands still clenched in the quilt.

A warm, slightly trembling masculine hand covered her clenched ones, and another hand cupped her cheek. "I'm sorry, baby. I'm so sorry, *moro mou*."

Startled, she opened her eyes to see the shadowed contours of his face and his glorious, naked body kneeling beside the couch.

"Come to bed, *yineka mou*." His husky voice sounded strangely pleading.

But she shook her head in denial. "I don't want to sleep with you."

She thought she detected red scorching his sculpted cheekbones in the dim light, but decided she was being fanciful. Leiandros Kiriakis was not capable of a vulnerable reaction like blushing.

"If you mean make love, I won't try to seduce you." He paused as if he found it difficult to get the next words out. "I only want to hold you. I *need* to hold you."

Need? He didn't need anyone, least of all her. She was just his "instrument of justice," the means by which he could have his precious heir and bring Eva and Nyssa back into the Kiriakis fold. "*Right*. Go to bed, Leiandros. It's late. We need our rest."

"But I cannot rest, not after my idiocy earlier."

Did he expect her mercy when he had given her none? She closed her eyes, blocking out the temptation of his body and the look of pleading in his eyes. It was probably a trick. He would never plead for anything, "I don't care."

His hand clutched in her hair. "But I do, Savannah.

I care very much. I care that I hurt you with my thoughtless reaction. I care that my cousin hurt you with his fists.'' He released her hair to brush his hand down the side of her neck to rest against her shoulder. ''Do you know what my first thought was when I saw those photos?''

She told herself it didn't matter. Whatever he'd thought, he hadn't *said* enough. She remained stubbornly mute.

He sighed and rubbed his thumb along her collarbone. In a voice husky with emotion, he said, ''I thought that if my cousin were alive, I would take pleasure in killing him.''

CHAPTER THIRTEEN

THE deadly intent in Leiandros's voice left no room for doubt in her mind that he meant what he said. Her eyes flew open. "But you—"

He closed her lips with his forefinger. "Shh... I was in shock. You cannot imagine how I felt reading the doctors report and then seeing photos of you bruised and your eyes reflecting every kind of inner devastation."

It was her turn to demand, "Tell me how you felt. Help me imagine it." Had she been wrong to think it was over between them? Did he trust her, but had been too shocked to say so?

His thumb stilled against the beating pulse in her neck. "I was furious, so furious, my mind could not take it in. I felt confused, shaken and somehow at fault. He was my *cousin*."

Her hands slowly unclenched from the quilt to take his hand between them. "Is that why you didn't say anything?"

"Yes." He rubbed her bottom lip with his thumb while turning his other hand to grasp hold of hers with a desperately strong grip.

She felt familiar sensations returning, but she could not give in to them. This was too important. "And now?"

He didn't help, brushing his lips across hers. "If you told me the sky was purple I would believe you."

As declarations went, that was a pretty good one. "Oh," she sighed as his lips touched hers again.

"Will you return to our bed?" he asked, sounding uncertain.

Leiandros sounding anything other than supremely confident was such an anathema, she was incapable of answering for several seconds. He obviously got tired of waiting because he lifted her, quilt, pillow and all. He stood motionless for almost a full minute and she neither moved, nor spoke.

Turning on his heel, he headed for the bedroom.

"I no longer have a choice?" she asked, thinking this behavior fit the man she'd married much better.

He squeezed her against his chest. "I gave you a choice, but you did not protest. You want to return to our bed and I need you to be there, so there you will go."

There was that word again. *Need*. Did he really need her? Even if it was as basic as desire, the prospect that he needed her, Savannah Marie Kiriakis, and no other woman rekindled another spark of the hope she had so recently abandoned.

Linking her hands behind his nape, she pressed her face into the hollow above his shoulder. "There I will go."

He shuddered and hugged her closer.

When they reached the bedroom, he laid her carefully on the bed and removed her bathrobe, his hands moving over her with trembling possessiveness.

"Have you changed your mind about the *no sex* part?"

"No." He glared down at her, his expression so fierce

she had to stifle an urge to roll off the bed and make a run for it. "We make love. It has never been just sex, some animalistic urge that could be satisfied by anyone else."

Oh, Heavens. He shouldn't say things like that. Her throat closed and her eyes filled with tears that seemed easier to shed since Leiandros had held her through the storm after Beatrice's death. She couldn't speak, but he stood their waiting for her acceptance, so she opened her arms and he came into them with gentle force.

They made love so tenderly, she wept from the sheer joy of it afterwards.

Touching her with a soothing motion, he asked, "What happened, *moro mou?*"

She didn't want to look at Leiandros while she told him, so she kept her face pressed against his chest where the beat of his heart soothed her.

"We hadn't had sex since I was four months pregnant with Nyssa and Dion found out she was a girl, too. I didn't mind. It wasn't anything like making love with you. And later, when I found out he had been having affairs all along, I was grateful. I didn't want to risk getting some disease because he felt the need to prove his virility by getting intimate with any woman who would spread her legs for him. Any love I felt for him died during those months."

Leiandros started to speak and then subsided.

"What?" she asked.

"I do not want to interrupt you, but why would he feel the need to prove his virility? He had married an incredibly beautiful woman and fathered two amazing daughters."

Her heart warmed at the compliment and this further proof that Leiandros's view of the world did not match that of his cousin. ''I guess he told you all I was pregnant and that's why we had to get married. He was pretty adamant about me getting pregnant immediately anyway. When I didn't, he took me to the doctor for fertility tests.''

She remembered the embarrassment she'd felt at that appointment. She didn't speak Greek yet and had no clue what Dion had instructed the doctor to do.

''They came back fine. There was nothing that should stop me from getting pregnant. I was mad at him for making me take the tests, humiliated at what I'd had to go through with a doctor I'd never met to get them done so I insisted he get tested as well. And did I learn to regret that.''

Leiandros's hand started rubbing soothing circles against her back.

''His tests came back saying he had a low sperm count. He was devastated and became fixated with proving his manhood. In his mind, impregnating me with a son would do the trick. Our two daughters were like a slap in the face to his thinking *and* I didn't even *conceive* Eva until eleven months into the marriage.''

She sighed and snuggled closer to Leiandros's body.

''If I thought going through his monthly temper tantrums when my menses came and being accused of doing everything from having surgery to taking the pill to prevent pregnancy was hard, I had no idea what it would be like when I did fall pregnant. He treated me like a walking incubator and I now realize his affairs started then.''

Leiandros made a distressed noise. "And I black-mailed you into trying to have my baby," he said, his voice thick.

She tried to comfort him with her hand against his heart. "I would never have agreed to your demands if I didn't want to fulfill them. I guess I realized somewhere deep in my heart that you truly wouldn't care if the baby was a boy or girl and I wanted your child. I still do," she admitted.

His hand jerked against her back in a hard hug. "Thank you. I don't deserve you." He leaned to kiss the top of her head. "Please tell me about that night."

"I'm leading up to it." She sucked in courage with her next breath to finish the story. She hadn't spoken of it to anyone since the doctor examined her on her return to Atlanta. "He came home one night, pretty drunk, when Nyssa was about six months old. He wanted sex. I said no. He screamed at me, the usual jealous diatribe, condemnation of my character and uselessness as a wife. He called me frigid and host of other names I won't repeat."

Her voice faltered to a halt.

Leiandros filled in the silence. "You said something about not having come to me when you needed me. Was it that night?"

She nodded, her face rubbing against chest. "I was afraid. I sensed that everything was escalating and I didn't know how to stop it. My mind screamed at me to go to you, that you could stop Dion from hurting me or my babies, but I'd gotten so used to stifling the need I felt for you in every way, I stifled that instinct, too."

"He beat you when you refused him sex?" The pain

and fury in Leiandros's voice both soothed her and tugged at her heart.

"No. I told him if he tried to force me, I'd leave Greece. He went out and came home later, this time he wasn't just drunk. He was high on something and terrifyingly not himself. He said more horrible things and started hitting me. I fought back, but I hadn't taken any self-defense classes then. You know, a Southern lady doesn't need them?"

She climbed on top of Leiandros, needing eye contact now when she had shied from it earlier. And she needed to feel her whole body in contact with his while she relived that awful time. "Anyway, he beat me pretty badly and then passed out. I've never been so grateful for anything in my life. You know the rest."

His eyes burned with tender emotion and searing regret. "Yes. I know the rest. You fled Greece and he told the family you hated living there and wanted to return to America. He put on a great show of grieving your loss."

She leaned down to kiss the male flesh that gave her such comfort. "He played the victim very well."

"But in reality you were the victim."

"No," she said fiercely. "I wasn't. I got away, but the rest of his family believed his lies and because of them, they missed out on the first few years of my daughter's lives. They were the real victims."

"*Agapi mou,* you are so generous with your heart, is it any wonder I love you?" He pulled her up until her mouth could meet his and kissed her so tenderly a lump formed in her throat. "*S'agapo.* I love you. *S'agapo.*"

That same heart he found so generous wanted to

pound out of her chest. *"You love me?"* she asked with awe and a little disbelief.

"So much. I know you cannot love me now. It will take a long time for you to forgive my blackmail and ruthlessness, if ever, but I can live with that as long as you don't leave me."

Leiandros in a humble mode was almost frightening. She thought about drawing it out, to get a little of her own back for the aforementioned blackmail, but the bleak look in his eyes undermined any such intention.

She tilted her pelvis toward him. "Do you really believe I would have let you touch me after what I went through with Dion, if I had not loved you?"

His flesh stirred against her, but he shook his head. "Perhaps you loved me then, but you cannot love me now. I've mistrusted you, hurt you and failed to protect you from my cousin's cruelty. I do not deserve it, but please promise me you will not leave me. I cannot face a future without you and our daughters."

Tears filled her eyes and spilled over onto her cheeks. "I don't want to leave you, you silly man. *I love you,* Leiandros. I've loved you since that first kiss, but refused to acknowledge it."

He looked at her like he wasn't sure he believed what he had just heard. "You had too much integrity to do so."

She smiled through her tears. "Just as you had too much honor to act on your desire for my body."

"It was more than desire. I fell in love with you that night. Just to be in the same room with you afterward was torture. I had to fight my feelings for six long years. I felt so much guilt I denied my heart and called my love sexual passion. You'll never know the torment I felt when Dion and Petra died in that crash.''

''I know. You lost your baby and your wife.''

He grimaced. ''I grieved that, but not as I should have. I grieved the loss of my baby more than Petra and it wasn't even twenty-four hours before my thoughts turned to making you mine. I told myself it was for justice, to replace what I had lost, but the truth is I couldn't live without you anymore. The barriers were gone and so was my self-control.''

She quickly pecked him on the lips for saying such very nice things and then smiled. ''So you decided to blackmail me into marrying you.''

He jerked his head in affirmative. ''Will you ever be able to forgive me and trust me knowing what a poor husband I was to Petra?''

''You were not a poor husband,'' she admonished him. ''If Dion had died and Petra had lived, you would have remained faithful to her and never allowed her to know you loved another woman. I know you, Leiandros. You are too principled to have done otherwise.''

He kissed her with a passion that seemed born of desperation and did not release her mouth until she was limp on top of him.

She smiled dreamily at his gorgeous features. ''You have nothing to reproach yourself for.''

His face contorted. ''My treatment of you. I believed everything my cousin said about you even though it didn't fit with the woman you had proved to be simply because I felt too guilty to do otherwise. I wanted my cousin's wife with a longing that would not die.''

"I forgive you. I love you. I will *always* love you," she assured him again.

His hands came up to cup her breasts as she leaned back to see his face more clearly. "*S'agapo,* Savannah. I love your spirit and your stubbornness. I love the way you smile when you are happy and hug your daughters when they are tired. I love the way you put up with my mother's craziness before the wedding and acted grateful to do so. But most of all, selfishly, I love your tender heart that can forgive a past wrong and keep loving."

She swallowed down the emotion welling up inside her at his words and gave him a wobbly, misty smile.

He returned the smile, reaching out to tuck a strand of her hair behind her right ear. He let his hand linger to caress the sensitive spot there. "I admire so much the way you reached out to care for an old woman when you were too young to be caring for yourself."

"I was nineteen," she protested.

"A mere babe."

"I'm twenty-seven now, does that make me old enough to take care of myself?" she asked with a saucy look.

His eyes turned grave. "Yes. You are old enough. You are smart enough. You are strong enough, but will you allow me the honor of taking care of you and our family?"

She pressed her breasts into his hot palms. "Yes," she said throatily, "You can take care of me any time you like."

His laughter rumbled up from his chest as he rolled over, pinning her body beneath his. She laughed with him until his movements made her draw her breath and then his mouth covered hers and she was lost.

A few months later, Savannah's Greek doctor, whom Leiandros had taken pains for her to get to know, pronounced her ten weeks pregnant. Ecstatic, she shared the news with Leiandros that night in bed.

Though he was thrilled, he immediately began listing off activities she'd have to curtail for her safety and pronounced she would have to start taking a long nap every afternoon. A nap he sometimes shared with her and provided less sleep than he intended, but Savannah had gotten very adept at getting her way with her Greek tycoon husband.

Eva and Nyssa were over the moon at the prospect of a baby and the grandmothers began fussing over Savannah like two clucking hens.

Six weeks after discovering she was pregnant, Savannah's ultrasound showed twins. They could only determine the sex of one baby, a girl. Leiandros's shell-shocked but obviously joyful response settled Savannah's doubts about his reaction to more daughters once and for all.

After Savannah's second contraction, five months later, Leiandros announced this would be her last pregnancy. He turned an interesting shade of gray as her labor progressed and promised never, ever to do this to her again. Savannah smiled through the pain, knowing the babies would be worth it.

Their third daughter was born first and named Beatrice, shortened almost instantly to Bea by her older sisters. Their son came out squalling and Leiandros came as close to fainting as he ever had in his life when he looked down at the two infinitely precious babies, knowing they were a product of his and Savannah's love. Savannah insisted on naming their son after his father and calling him Leo for short.

Later that day, Savannah lay in the private hospital bed, holding her son while Leiandros sat in a nearby chair and held their new daughter. Eva and Nyssa each perched on a grandmother's knee as Helena and Baptista sat side by side in the window seat.

Leiandros looked up from contemplation of their daughter and met Savannah's gaze. "*S'agapo, yineka mou.* You and our children are my world. My present. My future. My greatest treasure. Gifts from God."

His eyes grew suspiciously moist and his voice choked to a stop while Savannah's eyes sent the same message back to him before she asked if the older girls wanted to sit on the edge of her bed. Soon, they were all engrossed in the babies, the circle of their family complete.

Savannah once again looked deeply into the brown depths of her husband's eyes, eyes that no longer looked enigmatic or mysterious, but blazed with constant love for her and *all* their children.

"Thank you," she said, her heart too full to say any more.

He had promised her she would never be alone again and he had kept that promise, surrounding her with his love, his family and his friends, giving them freely until they became her own.

She would never regret her decision to live her life on the cornerstone of love instead of fear.

The Forced Marriage

Sara Craven

CHAPTER ONE

'TELL me something,' said Hester. 'Are you absolutely certain you want to get married?'

Flora Graham, whose thoughts had drifted to the ongoing knotty problem of informing those concerned that she didn't want her spoiled and brattish nephew as a pageboy, hurriedly snapped back to the immediate present, the crowded and cheerful restaurant, and her best friend and bridesmaid eyeing her with concern across the table.

'Of course I do.' She frowned slightly. 'Chris and I are perfect for each other; you know that. I couldn't be happier.'

'You don't look particularly happy,' Hester said judicially, refilling their coffee cups.

Flora rolled her eyes in mock despair. 'You wait until it's your turn, and you find yourself in the middle of a three-ring circus with no time off for good behaviour. My mother must have been having one of her deaf days when I said I wanted a small quiet wedding.'

'Then why don't you have one?' Hester met her astonished look steadily. 'Why don't you ask Chris to get a special licence, and slope off somewhere and do the business? I'll happily be one witness, and maybe Chris's best man would be the other.'

Flora went on staring at her. 'Because we can't. We're committed to all these arrangements—all that expense. We'd be letting so many people down. It's too late.'

5

'Honey, it's never too late.' Hester's voice was persuasive. 'And I'm sure most people would understand.'

Flora gave a wry shake of the head. 'Not my mother,' she said. *And, my God, certainly not Chris's.* 'Anyway, don't you want to do your bridesmaid thing? I've arranged for you to catch my bouquet afterwards.'

'Having observed you closely since the engagement party, I think I'll pass,' Hester said drily. 'I'm not ready for a nervous breakdown.' She paused. 'Talking of engagements, I see you're not wearing your ring. Would that be a Freudian slip?'

'No, I damaged a claw in the setting last week, and it's being repaired.' Flora's frown deepened. 'What is this, Hes? You're beginning to sound as if you don't like Chris.'

'That's not true,' her friend said slowly. 'But, even if you hate me for ever, I have to tell you I think you could do better.'

Flora gasped. 'You don't mean that. I *love* Chris, in case you hadn't noticed.'

Hester was silent for a moment. 'Flo, in all the years we've known each other I've seen you with various men, but never in a serious relationship with any of them. Although that's fine,' she added hastily. 'You've never slept around, and I admire you for sticking to your principles. *But* I always thought that when you fell, you'd fall hard. Passion to die for—heaven, hell and heartbreak—the works. And I don't see much sign of that with you and Chris.'

'I'm glad to hear it,' Flora said calmly. 'It sounds very uncomfortable.'

'But it should be uncomfortable,' Hester returned implacably. 'Love isn't some cosy old coat that you slip on because it's less trouble than shopping for a new one.'

'But that isn't how I feel at all,' Flora protested. 'I—I'm crazy about him.'

'Really?' Hester was inexorable. 'In that case, why aren't you living together?'

'The flat needs work—decoration. We want it to be perfect. After all, it's going to be my showcase, and it's taking longer than we thought.' Flora realised with exasperation how feeble that sounded.

'That,' said Hester, 'hardly suggests that you can't keep your hands off each other. And I suppose the cost of refurbishment prevents you sneaking off together for a romantic weekend in the country?'

'When we're married,' Flora said defiantly, 'every weekend will be romantic.'

'Be honest, now.' Hester leaned forward. 'If Chris came to you tomorrow and said he wanted to call it off, would it be the end of your world?'

'Yes.' Flora lifted her chin. 'Yes, it would.' She paused. 'Perhaps Chris and I aren't the most demonstrative couple in the world, but who says you have to wear your heart on your sleeve?'

'Sometimes,' Hester said gently, 'you simply can't help yourself.' She drank the rest of her coffee and reached for her bag, and the bill. 'However, if that's how you really feel, and you're sure about it, there's no more to be said.' She pushed back her chair. 'On the other hand, if you ever have doubts about what you're doing, I'll be around to pick up the pieces. Sal the demon flatmate is off to Brussels for three months, so I've a spare room again.'

'It's a sweet offer,' Flora said gently. 'And I don't hate you for making it, even though it's not necessary.'

She gave Hester an affectionate grin. 'I thought it was supposed to be the bride who got the pre-wedding jitters, not the bridesmaid.'

'I'd be happier if you were jittery,' Hester retorted. 'You act as though you're resigned to your fate. And there's no need to be. You're gorgeous and the world is full of attractive men waiting to be attracted.' She dropped a swift kiss on Flora's hair as she went past. 'And, if you don't believe me, check out the guy over there at the corner table,' she added in sepulchral tones. 'He's had his eyes on you all through lunch.' And, with a conspiratorial wink, she was gone.

Flora ought to have left too. Instead she found she was reaching for the cafetière and refilling her cup again. Maybe she should include sugar this time, she thought, biting her lip. Wasn't that one of the treatments for shock?

Because she couldn't pretend that Hester's blunt remarks had just slid off her consciousness like water off a duck's back.

Stunned, she thought wryly, is the appropriate word.

And all from an innocuous girlie lunch to make a final decision between old rose and delphinium-blue for Hester's dress.

Unbelievable.

And it wasn't the drink talking either. *In vino veritas* hardly applied to a glass of Chardonnay apiece and a litre of mineral water.

No, it was clear this had been brewing for some time, and, with a month to go before the wedding, Hester had decided it was time to speak her mind.

But I really wish she hadn't, Flora thought, biting her lip. I was perfectly content when I sat down at this table. And I've enough on my mind without doing a detailed analysis of my feelings for Chris, and seeing how they measure on some emotional Richter scale I never knew existed.

I love Chris, and I know we're going to have a good marriage—one that will last, too. And surely that matters far more than—sexual fireworks.

She felt her mind edging gently away from that particular subject, and paused quite deliberately. Because that would also be all right once they were married, she reassured herself, and that previous fiasco would be entirely forgotten.

She glanced at her watch and rose. Time was pressing, and she would have to take a cab to her next appointment.

On her way out of the restaurant she remembered Hester's parting remarks and risked a swift sideways glance at the table in question. Only to find herself looking straight into the eyes of its occupant.

He was very dark, she registered as she looked away, her face warming with embarrassment, with curling hair worn longer than she approved of. He was also startlingly attractive, in an olive-skinned Mediterranean way. The image of an elegant high-bridged nose, sculptured cheekbones, a firm chin with a cleft in it, and a mobile mouth that quirked sensuously under her regard accompanied her out of the restaurant and into the sunlit street beyond.

My God, she realised, half-amused, half-concerned. I could practically draw him from memory.

And, damn you, Hes. That was something else I didn't need.

She stepped to the edge of the kerb and looked down the street for an approaching taxi. But there wasn't one

in sight, so she started to walk in the required direction,
pausing every now and then to look back.

She didn't even see her assailant coming. The first hint
of danger was a hand in her back, pushing her violently,
and a wrench at the strap of her bag that nearly dragged
it from her grasp.

Flora felt herself go sprawling, the bag pinned underneath her, as she filled her lungs and screamed for help.
On the ground, she covered her head with her hands,
terrified that she was going to be punched or kicked.

Then she heard men's voices shouting, a squeal of
brakes, and the sound of running feet.

Flora stayed still, exactly where she was, the breath
sobbing in her throat.

She could hear someone speaking to her in husky,
faintly accented English.

'Are you hurt, *signorina*? Shall I call an ambulance
for you? Can you speak?'

'She may not talk, mate, but she can yell. Nearly took
me eardrums out,' said a deeper, gruffer voice. 'Let's
see if we can get her to her feet.'

'It's all right.' Flora raised her head dazedly and
looked around her. 'I can manage.'

'I don't think so.' The first voice again. 'I believe you
must accept a little help, *signorina*.'

Flora turned unwillingly in the speaker's direction, to
have all her worst fears confirmed.

Seen at close range—and he was kneeling beside her
so he could hardly have been any closer—the man from
the restaurant was even more devastating. His mouth
was set grimly now, but she could imagine how it would
soften. And his eyes, she had leisure to note, were green,
with tiny gold flecks. A whisper of some expensive male
cologne reached her, and, suddenly keen to get out of

range of its evocative scent, Flora hauled herself up on to her knees.

'Ouch.' Major mistake, she thought, wincing. She'd ripped her tights and grazed her legs when she fell. Her elbows and palms were sore too.

'Come on, ducks.' It was Voice Two. A burly arm went round her, lifting her bodily to her feet. 'Why don't I pop you in the cab and take you to the nearest casualty department, eh?'

'Cab?' Flora repeated. 'I—I wanted a cab.'

'Well, I could see that, and I was just pulling over when that bastard jumped you. Then this other gentleman came flying up, and the mugger legged it.'

'Oh.' Flora made herself look at the 'other gentleman', who stood, smiling faintly, those astonishing eyes trailing over her in a cool and disturbingly thorough assessment. 'Well—thank you.'

He inclined his head gravely. 'Your bag is safe? And he took nothing else?'

'He didn't really get the chance.' She gave him a brief, formal smile, then turned to the cabbie. 'I need to go to Belvedere Row. I'm supposed to be meeting someone there and I'm going to be late.'

'I hardly think you can keep your appointment like that,' her rescuer intervened firmly. 'At the least you require a clothes brush, and your cuts should also be attended to.'

Before she could protest Flora found herself manoeuvred into the back of the cab, with the stranger taking the seat beside her.

'The Mayfair Tower Hotel, please,' he directed the driver.

'I can't go there.' Flora shot bolt upright. 'My appointment's in the other direction.'

'And when you are clean and tidy, another cab will take you there.' An autocratic note could be detected in the level tone. 'It is a business meeting? Then it is simple. You call on your cellphone and explain why you are delayed.'

'So what's it to be, love?' the driver demanded through the partition. 'The Mayfair Tower?'

Flora hesitated. 'Yes—I suppose.'

'A wise decision,' her companion applauded smoothly.

She sent him a steely glance. 'Do you enjoy arranging other people's lives?'

His answering smile warmed into a grin. 'Only those that I have saved,' he drawled.

Deep within her an odd tingle stirred uneasily. She tried to withdraw unobtrusively, further into her corner of the taxi.

'Isn't that rather an exaggeration?'

He shrugged powerful shoulders that the elegant lines of his charcoal suit accentuated rather than diminished. The top button of his pale grey silk shirt was undone, Flora noticed, and the knot of his ruby tie loosened. For the rest of him, he was about six feet tall, lean and muscular, with legs that seemed to go on for ever.

He wasn't merely attractive, she acknowledged unwillingly. He was seriously glamorous.

'Then let's say I spared you the inconvenience of losing your credit cards and money. To many people, that would be life and death.'

She smiled constrainedly. 'And my engagement ring is at the jeweller's, so really I've got off lightly.'

That was clumsily done, she apostrophised herself silently, and saw by his sardonic smile that he thought so too.

She hurried into speech again. 'Why the Mayfair Tower?'

'I happen to be staying there.'

There was a silence, then she said, 'Then you must let me drop you off before I take this cab back to my flat, to clean up and change.'

'You are afraid I shall make unwelcome advances to you?' His brows lifted. 'Allow me to reassure you. I never seduce maidens in distress—unless, of course, they insist.'

Her mouth tightened. 'I dare say you think this is very amusing...'

'On the contrary, *signorina*, I take the whole situation with the utmost seriousness.' For a moment, there was an odd note in his voice.

Then he added with cool courtesy, 'You are trying to shrug off what has happened, but you have had a severe shock and that will bring its own reaction. I do not think you should be alone.'

'You're very kind,' Flora said tautly. 'But I really can't go with you. You must see that.'

'I seem to be singularly blind this afternoon.' He took a slim wallet from an inside pocket of his jacket and extracted a card. 'Perhaps a formal introduction may convince you of my respectability.'

Flora accepted the card and studied it dubiously. 'Marco Valante,' she read. And beneath it 'Altimazza Inc'. She glanced up. 'The pharmaceutical company?'

'You have heard of us?' His brows lifted.

'Of course.' She swallowed. 'You're incredibly successful. Whenever your shares are offered my fiancé recommends them to his clients.'

'He is a broker, perhaps?' he inquired politely.

'An independent financial adviser.'

'Ah, and do you work in the same area?'

'Oh, no,' Flora said hastily. 'I'm a consultant in property sales.'

His brows rose. 'You sell houses?'

'Not directly. The agencies hire me to show people how to present their properties to the best advantage when potential buyers are going round. I get them to refurbish tired décor—or tone down strident colour schemes.'

'I imagine that would not always be easy.'

She smiled reluctantly. 'No. We have a saying that an Englishman's home is his castle, and sometimes sellers are inclined to pull up the drawbridge. I have to convince them that their property is no longer a loved home but a commodity which they want to sell at a profit. Sometimes it takes a lot of persuasion.'

He looked at her reflectively. 'I think,' he said softly, 'that you could persuade a monk to abandon his vows, *mia cara.*'

Flora stiffened. 'Please—don't say things like that.'

He pantomimed astonishment. 'Because you are to be married you can no longer receive compliments from other men? How quaint.'

'That,' she said, 'is not what I meant.'

Totally relaxed in his own corner, he grinned at her. 'And you must not be teased either? *Si, capisce.* From now on I will behave like a saint.'

He didn't look like a saint, Flora thought. More like a rebel angel...

She glanced back at the card he had given her. 'You don't look like a chemist,' she said, and almost added *either.*

'I'm not.' He pulled a face. 'I work in the accounting

section, mainly raising funding for our research projects.'

'Oh,' she said. 'Well—that would explain it.'

Actually, it explained nothing, because he wasn't her idea of an accountant either, by a mile and a half.

'Does everything have to be readily comprehensible?' he enquired softly. 'Do you never wish to embark on a long, slow voyage of discovery?'

Flora had the feeling that he was needling her again, but she refused to react. 'I'm more used to first impressions—instant reactions. It's part of my job.'

'So,' he said. 'You know who I am. Will you grant me the same privilege?'

'Oh,' she said. 'Yes—of course...'

She delved into her misused bag and produced one of her own business cards. He read it, then looked back at her, those amazing eyes glinting under their heavy lids. 'Flora,' he said softly. 'The goddess of the springtime.'

She flushed and looked away. 'Actually, I was named after my grandmother—far more prosaic.'

'So, tell me—Flora—will you continue to work after you are married?'

'Naturally.'

'You are sure that your man will not guard you even more closely when you are his wife?'

'That's nonsense,' Flora said indignantly. 'Chris doesn't *guard* me.'

'Good,' Marco Valante said briskly. 'Because we have arrived at the hotel, and there is nothing, therefore, to prevent you going in with me.'

Flora had every intention of offering him a last haughty word of thanks, then hobbling out of his life for ever. But suddenly the commissionaire was there, helping her out of the taxi and holding open the big swing doors so she could go in.

And then she was in the foyer, all marble and plate glass, and Marco Valante had joined her and was giving soft-voiced orders that people were hurrying to obey— a lot of them concerning herself.

And suddenly the reality of making the kind of scene which would extract her from this situation seemed totally beyond her capabilities.

In fact, she was forced to acknowledge, all she really wanted to do was find somewhere quiet and burst into tears.

She didn't even utter a protest when she was escorted to the lift and taken up to the first floor. She walked beside Marco Valante to the end of the corridor, and waited while he slotted in his key card and opened the door.

Mutely, she preceded him into the room.

Although this was no mere room, she saw at once. It was a large and luxuriously furnished suite, and they were standing in the sitting room. The curtains were half drawn, to exclude the afternoon sun, and he went over and flung them wide.

'Sit down.' He indicated one of the deeply cushioned sofas and she sank down on it with unaccustomed obedience, principally because her throbbing legs were threatening to give way beneath her.

'I have told them to send the nurse here to dress your cuts,' he said. 'I have also ordered some tea for you, and if you go into the bathroom you will find a robe you can wear while your suit is being valeted.'

She said shakily, 'You're pretty autocratic for an accountant.'

He shrugged. 'I wish to make some kind of amends for what happened earlier.'

'I don't see why,' Flora objected. 'It wasn't your fault.'

'But I could, perhaps, have prevented it if I had been quicker. If I had obeyed my instinct and left the restaurant when you did.'

'Why should you do that?' Reaction was beginning to set in. She felt deathly cold suddenly, and wrapped her arms round her body, gritting her teeth to stop them from chattering.

'I thought,' he said softly, 'that I was not permitted to pay you compliments. But, if you must know, I wanted very much to make the acquaintance of a beautiful girl with hair that Titian might have painted.'

So Hes had been right, Flora realised with a little jolt of shock. He had indeed been watching her during lunch.

'Presumably,' she said, with an effort, 'you have a thing about red-haired women.'

'Not until today, when I saw you in the sunlight, Flora *mia*.'

For a moment her heart skipped a treacherous beat, before reason cut in and she wondered with intentional cynicism how many other women that particular line had worked with.

She closed her eyes, deliberately shutting him out. Using it as a form of rejection.

While at the same time she thought, 'I should not—I *really* should not be here.'

And only realised she had spoken aloud when he said quietly, 'Yet you are perfectly safe. For at any moment people will start arriving, and I shall probably never be alone with you again.'

And never, mourned a small voice in her head, is such

a very long time. And such a very lonely word. But that was a thought she kept strictly to herself.

She said, 'Perhaps you'd show me where the bathroom is.'

She had, inevitably, to cross his bedroom to reach it, and she followed him, her eyes fixed rigidly on his back, trying not to notice the kingsize bed with its sculptured ivory coverlet.

The bathroom was all creamy tiles edged with gold, and she stood at a basin shaped like a shell and took her first good look at herself, her lips shaping into a silent whistle of dismay.

Shock had drained her normally pale skin and she looked like a ghost, her clear grey eyes wide and startled. There was a smudge on her cheek, and her shirt was dirty and ripped, exposing several inches of lacy bra. Which Marco Valante was bound to have noticed, she thought, biting her lip.

Well, perhaps the valeting service could lend her a safety pin, she told herself as she removed her suit and carefully peeled off her torn tights.

She washed her face and hands, then did her best to make herself look less waif-like with the powder and lipstick in her bag, before turning her attention to her unruly cloud of dark red hair.

Usually, for work, she stifled its natural wave, drawing it severely back from her face and confining it at the nape of her neck with a barrette or a bow of dark ribbon. Although a few tendrils invariably managed to escape and curl round her face.

But today the ribbon had gone, allowing the whole gleaming mass to tumble untrammelled round her shoulders, and no amount of struggling with a comb could restore it to its normal control.

But then nothing was normal today, she thought with a sigh, as she put on the oversized towelling robe and secured its sash round her slim waist. It covered her completely, but she still felt absurdly self-conscious as she made her way back to the sitting room.

Only it was not Marco Valante awaiting her but the nurse, a brisk blonde in a neat navy uniform, clearly more accustomed to reassuring elderly tourists about their digestive problems. But she cleaned Flora up with kindly efficiency, putting antiseptic cream and small waterproof dressings over the worst of her grazes.

'You don't expect that kind of thing,' she remarked, giving her handiwork a satisfied nod. 'Not in a busy street in broad daylight. And why you, anyway? You're hardly wearing a Rolex or dripping with gold.'

Flora agreed rather wanly. The same question had been nagging at her too. After all, she wasn't the world's most obvious target. Just one of those random chances, she supposed. Being in the wrong place at the wrong time.

But, if it came to that, she was still in the wrong place, with no escape in sight.

Marco Valante had tactfully withdrawn while she was receiving attention, but now Room Service had arrived, bringing the tea, and he would undoubtedly be rejoining her at any moment.

And she would have to start thanking him all over again, she thought with vexation, because along with the tea had been delivered a carrier bag, bearing the name of a famous store, containing not only a fresh pair of tights but a new white silk shirt as well. Even more disturbingly, both of them were in her correct size, confirming her suspicion that this was a man who knew far too much about women.

Accordingly, her smile was formal and her greeting subdued when he came back into the sitting room.

'Are you feeling better?' The green eyes swept over her, as if the thick layer of towelling covering her had somehow ceased to exist. As if every inch of her body was intimately familiar to him, she thought as her heart began to thud in mingled excitement and panic.

'Heavens, yes. As good as new.' From some unfathomed corner of her being she summoned up a voice so spuriously hearty that she cringed with embarrassment at herself.

'And the hotel assures me your clothes will soon be equally pristine.' He seated himself opposite to her. 'They are being dealt with as a matter of priority.' He paused. 'But it seemed to me that your blouse was beyond help.'

Flora said a stilted, 'Yes', aware that her face had warmed. She reached for her bag. 'You must let me repay you.'

'With the greatest pleasure,' he said. He shrugged off his jacket and tossed it across the arm of the sofa, unbuttoned his waistcoat with deft fingers, then leaned back against the cushions, the lean body totally at ease. 'Have dinner with me tonight.'

Flora gasped. 'I couldn't possibly.'

'*Perche no?* Why not?'

'I told you.' Her colour deepened, seemed to envelop her entire body. 'I'm engaged to be married.'

He shrugged. 'You already told me. What of it?'

'Doesn't it matter to you?'

'Why should it? I might be *fidanzato* also.'

'Well—are you?'

'No.' Had she imagined an oddly harsh note in his voice? 'I am a single man, *mia bella*. But it would make no difference.' He paused, the green eyes sardonic. 'After all, I am not suggesting we should have our dinner served in bed.'

He allowed that to sink in, then added silkily, 'Do you feel sufficiently safe to pour the tea?'

'Of course.' Flora dragged some remaining shreds of composure around her. 'Milk and sugar?'

'Lemon only, I thank you.'

By some miracle she managed to manoeuvre the heavy teapot so that its contents went only into the delicate porcelain cups and not all over the tray, the table, and the carpet, but it was a close-run thing, and her antennae told her that Marco Valante was perfectly well aware of her struggles and privately amused by them.

She handed him his cup, controlling an impulse to pour the tea straight in his lap.

He accepted it with a brief word of thanks. 'Did you telephone your clients?'

'Yes.' An impersonal topic, she thought thankfully. 'They were very forgiving and rescheduled.'

'You do not think your *fidanzato* would be equally understanding, and spare you to me—for one evening?'

She gasped. 'I know he wouldn't.'

'Strange,' Marco Valante said musingly. 'Because he cannot be so very possessive.'

'Why do you say that?'

He smiled at her. 'Because he has never—possessed you, *mia bella*.'

Flora gasped in outrage. 'How dare you say such a thing?'

'When possible, I prefer to speak the truth. And I say that you are still—untouched.'

'You—you can't possibly know that,' she said hoarsely. 'And it's none of your business anyway.'

'Destiny has caused our paths to cross, Flora *mia*,' he said softly. 'I think I am entitled to be a little—intrigued when I look into your eyes and see there no woman's knowledge—no memory of desire.'

She replaced her cup on the tray with such force that it rattled. She said tautly, 'Actually, you have no rights at all. And I'd like to leave now, please.'

'Like that?' His brows lifted. 'You will be a sensation, *cara*.'

She said, her voice shaking, 'I'd rather walk down the street naked than have to endure any more of your—humiliating—and inaccurate speculation about my personal life.'

Marco Valante smiled. 'I am tempted to make you prove it, but I am feeling merciful today. I will arrange for you to have the use of another room while you wait for your clothes.'

He picked up the phone, dialled a number and spoke briefly and succinctly.

'A maid will come and take you to your new sanctuary,' he told her pleasantly when he had finished. He pulled a leather-covered notepad towards him and scribbled a few lines on the top sheet, which he tore off and handed to her. 'If you change your mind about dinner you may join me at this restaurant any time after eight o'clock.'

She crushed the paper into a ball and dropped it to the floor. She said, coldly and clearly, 'Hell will freeze over first, *signore*.'

His own voice was soft, almost reflective. 'So the flame does not burn in your hair alone. *Bravo*.'

She snatched up the shirt and tights, glaring at him, unbearably galled that she needed to use them, and crammed them into her bag.

'I'll send you a cheque for these,' she told him curtly.

Marco Valante laughed. 'I'm sure you will, *cara*. But in case you forget, I'll take a down payment now.'

Suddenly he was beside her, and his arm was round her, pulling her towards him. And for one brief, burning moment, she felt his mouth on hers, tasting her with a stark hunger she had never known existed.

It was over almost as soon as it had begun. Before she'd really grasped what was happening to her she was free, stepping backwards, stumbling a little on the edge of that trailing robe, staring at him in a kind of horror as her hand went up to touch her lips.

And he looked back at her, his own mouth twisting wryly. He said quietly, 'As hot as sin and as sweet as honey. I cannot wait for the next instalment, Flora *mia*.'

The note in his voice seemed to shiver on her skin. The silence between them tautened—became electric. She wanted to look away, and found that she could not.

It was the knock on the door that saved her. She went to answer it, holding up the encumbering folds of towelling, trying not to run.

His voice followed her. '*Ti vedro, mia bella.* I'll be seeing you.'

She said fiercely, 'No—no, you won't.'

And went through the door, slamming it behind her, because she knew, to her shame, that she did not dare look back at him. Not then. And certainly not ever again.

CHAPTER TWO

'I GOT you a herb tea,' Melanie said anxiously. 'As you still can't face cappuccino. They say shock can do that to you.'

Some shocks certainly could, Flora thought grimly as she took the container from her assistant with a word of thanks and a smile. Nor was it just cappuccino. She was also off espresso, latte and anything else tall and Italian.

Three jumpy days had passed since the aborted mugging and its even more disturbing aftermath. Out of the frying pan, she thought wryly, and into the heart of the fire. She was still screening her calls, and warily scanning the streets outside her flat and office each time she emerged.

'I'll be seeing you,' he'd said. The kind of casual remark anyone might make, and probably meaningless. An unfortunate choice of words, that was all. And yet—and yet...

He had made it sound like a promise.

Time and time again she told herself she was a fool for letting it matter so much. Her grazes, bumps and bruises were healing nicely, and she should let her emotions settle too. Put the whole thing in some mental recycling bin.

It had been obvious from that first moment that Marco Valante was trouble, and it was her bad luck that he should have been the first on the scene when she needed help. Because he was the kind of man to whom flirting

24

was clearly irresistible, and who would allow no opportunity to be wasted.

But—it was only a kiss, when all was said and done, she thought, taking a rueful sip of herb tea. And wasn't this a total overreaction on her part to something he would undoubtedly have forgotten by now?

He would have moved on—might even be back in Italy and good riddance—and she should do the same. So why on earth was it proving so difficult? Why was he invading her thoughts by day and her sleep by night? It made no sense.

And, more importantly, why hadn't she told Chris all about it? she asked herself, staring unseeingly at her computer screen.

Partly, she supposed, because his attitude had annoyed her. He'd been sympathetic at first, but soon become bracing, telling her she was lucky not to have lost her bag or been badly injured. She knew she'd got off lightly, but somehow that wasn't what she'd needed to hear. Some prolonged concern and cosseting would have been far more acceptable. And it would have been for her to tell him, lovingly, that he was going OTT, and not the other way round.

He was busy, of course, and she understood that. He was trying to build up his consultancy and provide a sound financial basis for their future; she couldn't realistically expect his attention to be focussed on her all the time.

But she had anticipated that he'd stay with her that evening at least.

Instead, 'Sorry, my sweet.' Chris had shaken his head. 'I've arranged to meet a new client. Could be big. Besides,' he'd added, patting her shoulder, 'you'll be much better off relaxing—taking things easy. You don't need me for that.'

No, Flora had thought, with a touch of desolation. But I could do with the reassurance of your arms around me. I'd like you to look at me as *he* did. To let me know that you want me, that you're living for our wedding, and the moment when we'll really belong to each other.

And that it won't be like that other time…

She bit her lip, remembering, then turned her attention firmly back to the report she was writing for a woman trying to sell an overcrowded, overpriced flat in Notting Hill. Although she suspected she was wasting her time and Mrs Barstow would not remove even one of the small occasional tables which made her drawing room an obstacle course, or banish her smelly, bad-tempered Pekinese dog on viewing days.

She would probably also quibble at the fee she was being charged, Flora decided as she printed up the report and signed it.

She turned to the enquiries that had come in recently, remembering that Melanie had marked one of them urgent. 'Lady living in Chelsea,' she said now. 'A Mrs Fairlie. Husband does something in the EU and they're having to move to Brussels like yesterday, so she needs to spruce the place up for a quick sale. Says we were recommended.'

'That's what I like to hear,' Flora commented as she dialled Mrs Fairlie's number.

She liked the sound of Mrs Fairlie too, who possessed a rich, deep voice with a smile in it, but who sounded clearly harassed when Flora mentioned she had no vacant appointments until the following week.

'Oh, please couldn't you fit me in earlier?' she appealed. 'I'd like you to see the house before matters go any further, and time is pressing.'

Flora studied her diary doubtfully. 'I could maybe call in on my way home this evening,' she suggested. 'If that's not too late for you.'

'Oh, no,' Mrs Fairlie said eagerly. 'That sounds ideal.'

Flora replaced the receiver and sat for a moment, lost in thought. Then she reached for the phone again and, acting on an impulse she barely understood, dialled the Mayfair Tower Hotel.

'I'm trying to trace a Signor Marco Valante,' she invented. 'I believe he is staying at your hotel.'

'I am sorry, madam, but Signor Valante checked out yesterday.' Was there a note of regret in the receptionist's professional tone?

'Oh, okay, thanks,' Flora said quickly.

She cut the connection, aware that her heart was thudding erratically—with what had to be relief. He was safely back in Italy and she had nothing more to worry about from that direction, thank goodness.

I've got to stop being so negative, she thought. Take some direct action about the future. I'll have a blitz on the flat this weekend, and persuade Chris to help me. Even if he hates decorating he can lend a hand in preparing the walls. And we'll finalise arrangements for the wedding too. A few positive steps and I'll be back in the groove. No time to fill my head with rubbish.

She took a cab to the quiet square where Mrs Fairlie lived that evening, appraising the house with a faint frown as she paid off the driver. It was elegant, double fronted, and immaculately maintained. And clearly worth a small fortune.

Flora would have bet good money that even if the entire interior was painted in alternating red and green stripes the queue of interested buyers would still stretch round the block.

And if Mrs Fairlie simply wanted reassurance that her property was worth the amazing amount the agents were advising, then reassurance she should have, Flora decided with a mental shrug as she rang the bell.

The door was answered promptly by a pretty maid in a smart chocolate-coloured uniform, who smiled and nodded when Flora introduced herself, and led her up a wide curving staircase to the drawing room on the first floor.

As she followed, Flora was aware of the elegant ceramic floor in the hall, the uncluttered space and light enhanced by clean pastel colours on the walls. As she'd suspected, she thought wryly, Mrs Fairlie was the last person to need style advice.

The maid opened double doors, and after announcing, 'Miss Graham,' stood back to allow Flora to precede her into the room.

She was greeted by the dazzle of evening sunlight from the tall windows, and halted, blinking, conscious that amid the glare someone was moving towards her.

But not the female figure she'd been expecting, she realised with a jolt, the confident, professional smile dying on her lips.

In spite of the warmth of the room she felt as cold as ice. She had to fight an impulse to wrap her arms across her body in a betrayingly defensive gesture.

'*Buonasera*, Flora *mia*.' As Marco Valante reached her he captured her nerveless hand and raised it swiftly and formally to his lips. 'It is good to see you again.'

'I wish I could say the same.' Her voice sounded husky and a little breathless. 'What is this? I came here to meet a Mrs Fairlie.'

'Unfortunately she has been detained. But she has delegated me to show you the house in her absence.'

'And you expect me to believe that?'

His brows lifted sardonically. 'What else, *cara*? Do you imagine I have her bound and gagged in the cellar?'

Something very similar had occurred to her, and she lifted her chin, glaring at him. 'I find it odd that you have the run of her house, certainly.'

'I am staying here for a few days,' he said calmly. 'Your Mrs Fairlie is in fact my cousin Vittoria.'

'I see.' Her heart seemed to be trying to beat its way out of her ribcage. 'And you persuaded her to trick me into coming here. Does your family claim descent from Machiavelli?'

'I think he was childless,' Marco Valante said thoughtfully. 'And Vittoria did not need much persuasion—not when I explained how very much I wished to meet with you again.' He smiled. 'She tends to indulge me.'

'More fool her,' Flora said curtly. 'I'd like to leave, please. Now.'

'Before you have carried out your survey of the house?' He tutted reprovingly. 'Not very professional, *cara*.'

She sent him a freezing look. 'But then I hardly think I've been inveigled into coming here in my business capacity.'

'You are wrong. Vittoria wishes your advice on the master bedroom. She is bored with the colour, and the main bedroom in her house in Brussels has been decorated in a similar shade.'

Flora frowned. 'She is genuinely selling this house, then?'

'It has already been sold privately,' he said gently.
'Shall we go upstairs?'

'*No!*' The word seemed to explode from her with such
force that her throat ached.

She saw him fling his head back as if she had struck
him in the face. Met the astonishment and scorn in the
green eyes as they held hers. Felt the ensuing silence
deepen and threaten, as if some time bomb were ticking
away. And realised with swift shame that she had totally
overstepped the mark.

Somehow, she faltered into speech. 'I'm sorry—I
didn't mean...'

He said grimly, 'I am not a fool. I know exactly what
you meant.' The long fingers captured her chin and held
it, not gently. 'Two things, *mia cara*.' He spoke softly.
'This is my cousin's house, and I would not show such
disrespect for her roof. More importantly, I have never
yet taken a woman against her will—and you will not
be the first. *Capisce?*'

Her face burned as, jerkily, she nodded.

'Then be good enough to carry out the commission
you've been employed for.' He released her almost contemptuously and moved towards the door. 'Shall I call
Malinda to act as our chaperon?'

'No,' she said huskily. 'That—won't be necessary.'
Her legs were shaking as she ascended another flight of
stairs to the second floor, and followed him into Vittoria
Fairlie's bedroom.

It was a large room, overlooking the garden, with
French windows leading on to a balcony with a wrought-
iron balustrade and ceramic containers planted brightly
with flowers.

The interior walls were the palest blush pink, with
stinging white paintwork as a contrast, and the tailored

bedcover was a much deeper rose. Apart from a chaise longue near the window, upholstered in the same fabric as the bedcover, and an elegant walnut dressing table, there was little other furniture—all clothes and clutter having been banished, presumably, to the adjoining dressing room.

'Well?' Marco Valante had stationed himself at the window, leaning against its frame. So how was it that everywhere she looked he seemed to be in her sightline? she wondered despairingly.

The image of him seemed scored into her consciousness—the casual untidiness of his raven hair, the faint line of stubble along his jaw, the close-fitting dark pants that accentuated his lean hips and long legs, the collarless white shirt left unbuttoned at the throat, exposing a deep triangle of smooth, tanned skin...

For a stunned moment she found herself wondering what that skin would feel like under her fingertips—her mouth...

Her mind closed in shock, and she hurried into speech. 'The room is truly lovely. I can't fault your cousin's taste—or her presentation.' She hesitated. 'Although I wonder if it isn't a touch—over-feminine?'

'That is entirely the view of her husband,' Marco acknowledged, his mouth twisting. 'He has stipulated for the new house—no more pink.'

'But it's difficult to know what to suggest without seeing the room in Brussels.' Her brow wrinkled. 'It may face in a different direction...'

'No. Vittoria says it is also south-facing, and very light.'

'In that case...' Flora gave her surroundings another considering look. 'There's a wonderful shade of pale blue-green, called Seascape, that comes in a watered silk paper. I've always felt that waking in sunlight with that on the walls would be like finding yourself floating in the Mediterranean. But your cousin may not want that.'

'On the contrary, I think it would revive for her some happy memories,' Marco returned. 'When we were children we used to stay at my grandfather's house in summer. He had this old *castello* on a cliff above the sea, and we would walk down to the cove each day between the cypress trees.'

'It sounds—idyllic.'

'Yes,' he said quietly. 'A more innocent world.' He paused. 'Have you ever visited my country?'

'Not yet.' Flora lifted her chin. 'But I'm hoping to go there on my honeymoon, if I can persuade my fiancé.'

'He doesn't like Italy?' The green eyes were meditative as they rested on her.

'I don't think he's ever been either. But he was in the Bahamas earlier this year, and that's where he wants to return.' She smiled. 'Apparently there's this tiny unspoiled island called Coconut Cay, where pelicans come to feed. One of the local boatmen takes you there early in the morning with a food hamper and returns at sunset to collect you. Often you have the whole place entirely to yourself.'

There was a silence, then he said expressionlessly, 'It must have happy memories for him.'

'Yes—but I'd rather go to a place where we can create memories together, especially for our honeymoon. We can go to the Bahamas another time.'

'Of course.' He glanced at his watch, clearly bored by her marital plans—which was exactly what she'd intended, she told herself.

'You will make out a written report of your recommendations for Vittoria? With a note of your fee?'

'I'd prefer it if you simply passed on what I've said.' Flora lifted her chin. Met his glance. 'Treat it as cancelling all debts between us.'

'As you wish,' he said courteously.

It wasn't what she'd expected, Flora thought as she trailed downstairs. She'd anticipated some kind of argument, or one of his smiling, edged remarks at the very least.

He'd clearly become bored with whatever game he'd been playing, she told herself, and that had to be all to the good.

She'd intended to continue down the stairs and out of the front door without a backward glance, but Malinda was coming up, carrying an ice bucket, and somehow Flora found herself back in the drawing room.

'Champagne?' Marco removed the cork with swift expertise.

'I really should be going.' Reluctantly she accepted the chilled flute and sat on the edge of a sofa, watching uneasily as the maid adjusted the angle of a plate of canapés on a side table and then withdrew, leaving them alone together. 'Are you celebrating something?'

'Of course. That I am with you again.' He raised his own flute. '*Salute.*'

He was lounging on the arm of the sofa opposite, but she wasn't fooled. He was as relaxed as a coiled spring—or a black panther with its victim in sight...

The bubbles soothed the sudden dryness of her throat. 'Even if you had to trick me into being here?'

'You didn't meet me for dinner the other night.' Marco shrugged. 'What choice did I have?'

'You could have left me in peace,' she said in a low voice.

'There is no peace,' he said with sudden roughness.

'There has not been one hour of one day since our meeting that I have not remembered your eyes—your mouth.'

She said in a stifled tone, 'Please—you mustn't say these things.'

'Why?' he demanded with intensity. 'Because they embarrass—offend you? Or because you have thought of me too, but you don't want to admit it? Which is it, Flora *mia*?'

'You're not being fair...'

'You know the saying,' he said softly. '"All is fair in love and war." And if I have to fight for you, *cara*, I will choose my own weapons.'

'I'm engaged,' she said, with a kind of desperation. 'You know that. I have a life planned, and you have no place in that.'

'So I am barred from your future. So be it. But can you not spare me a few hours from your present—tonight?'

'That—is impossible.'

'You are seeing your *fidanzato* this evening?'

'Yes, of course. We have a great deal to discuss.'

'Naturally,' he said softly. 'And have you told him about me?'

'There was,' she said, steadying her voice, 'nothing to tell.'

He raised his brows. 'He would not be interested to learn that another man knows the taste of his woman—the scent of her skin when she is roused by desire?'

'That's enough.' Flora got up clumsily, spilling champagne on her skirt. 'You have no right to speak to me like this.'

He didn't move, staring at her through half-closed eyes. She felt his gaze touch her mouth like a brand. Scorch through her clothes to her bare flesh.

He said quietly, 'Then give me the right. Have dinner with me tonight.'

'I—can't...' Her voice sounded small and hoarse.

'How strange you are,' he said. 'So confident in your work. Yet so scared to live.'

'That's not true...' The protest sounded weak even in her own ears.

'Then prove it.' The challenge was immediate. 'The day we met I wrote the name of a restaurant on a piece of paper.'

'Which I threw away,' she said, quickly and fiercely.

'But you still remember what it was,' he said gently. 'Don't you, *mia bella*?'

'Why are you doing this to me?' she whispered.

He shrugged. 'I am simply being honest for both of us.' He smiled at her. 'So, tell me the name of the restaurant.'

She swallowed. 'Pietro's—in Gable Street.'

He nodded. 'I shall dine there again this evening. As I told you before, you may join me there at any time after eight o'clock.' He paused. 'And it is just your company at dinner I'm asking for—nothing more. You have my guarantee.'

'You mean you don't...? You won't ask me...?' Flora was floundering.

'No,' Marco Valante said slowly. 'At least—not tonight.'

'Then why...?' She shook her head. 'I don't understand any of this.'

His smile was faint—almost catlike. 'You will find, *mia cara*, that anticipation heightens the appetite. And I want you famished—ravenous.'

She felt the blood burn in her face. She said, 'Then find some other lady to share your feast. Because, as

I've already made clear, I'm not available—tonight or any night.'

All the way to the door she was expecting him to stop her. To feel his hand on her arm—her shoulder. To be drawn back into his embrace.

She gained the stairs. Went down them at a run. Reached the hall where Malinda appeared by magic to open the front door for her and wish her a smiling good evening.

'It's all right,' Flora whispered breathlessly to herself as she crossed the square, heading for the nearest main road to pick up a cab. 'It's over—and you're safe.'

And at that same moment felt a curious prickle of awareness down her spine. Knew that Marco was standing at that first floor window, watching her go.

Yet she not dare to look back and see if she was right. Proving that she wasn't safe at all—and she knew it.

She got the cab to drop her at her neighbourhood supermarket and shopped for the weekend, spending recklessly at the deli counter and wine section.

She needed to get herself centred again, and what better way than a happy weekend with the man she loved, preparing for their future? she asked herself with a touch of defiance.

They could picnic while they worked, she thought, sweetening the pill by buying the things Chris liked best.

As she came round the corner, laden with bags, she saw that his car was parked just down the street from her flat, and felt her heart give a swift, painful thump.

She found him in the living room, sprawled in an armchair, watching a satellite sports channel, but the glance he turned on her was peevish.

'Where on earth have you been? I was expecting you ages ago.'

'I had a job to fit in on the way home, and I shopped.' She held up a bulging carrier. 'See? Goodies.'

'Ah,' he said slowly. 'Actually, I can't stay. That's what I called in to say. Jack Foxton is taking a golf foursome away this weekend and someone's dropped out. So he's asked me to go instead. I've got all my stuff in the car and I'm meeting them at the hotel.'

'Oh, surely not.' Flora stared at him distressfully. 'I had such plans for us.'

'Well, I couldn't turn him down,' he said with a touch of self-righteousness. 'He can put a lot of valuable business my way. You know that. I don't want to upset him.'

Flora lifted her chin. 'Apparently you have no such qualms about upsetting me.'

'Darling.' Belatedly he brought his charm into play. 'It was absolutely a last minute thing, or I'd have let you know earlier. And I'll make it up to you next week. You'll have my undivided attention each evening— promise.'

He got briskly to his feet, tall, blond-haired, blue-eyed and totally single-minded.

Armoured, Flora thought dispassionately, in his own concerns.

She said quietly, 'Chris—don't do this—please. Because I really need to spend some time with you. To talk...'

'And so you shall, sweetheart, when I get back.' He gave her a coaxing smile. 'Anyway, it will give you some space—let you get ahead on the work front—or do some of the girlie things you say you never have time for. Why not give Hester a call? She's probably not doing anything either.'

He aimed a kiss at her unresponsive lips on his way past. 'I'll ring you if I get the chance. If not—see you Monday.'

The door banged, and he was gone.

Flora stood, carriers at her feet, feeling completely deflated and more than a little lost.

Chris was her wall—her barricade against the invasion of all these disturbing thoughts and emotions that were assailing her. And suddenly, frighteningly, he wasn't there for her.

Anger began to stir in her as she recalled his dismissive parting comments. She said aloud, 'How dare he? How bloody *dare* he?'

What low expectations he had of her—and of Hester, come to that, assuming that her friend would have nothing better to do on Friday night than keep her company.

Was that how he had them down? she wondered incredulously. A couple of sad single women settling down with a takeaway and a video? Manless and therefore hapless?

Because, if so, he'd just made the biggest mistake of his life.

She stalked into her bedroom, flung open the wardrobe door and began to search along the hanging rail, pulling out a silky slip of a black dress with shoestring straps and a brief flare of a skirt. She'd bought it a few weeks before and had been waiting for a suitable occasion to wear it.

And tonight was the perfect opportunity, she thought defiantly, removing the price tag and ignoring the alarm signals going off in her brain. That small inner voice telling her that she too was about to commit a blunder that would leave Chris standing. That what she was planning was actually dangerous.

All my life I've played it safe, she argued back, rummaging for the black silk and lace French knickers that were all the dress would accommodate underneath. And where's it got me?

To a situation of being taken totally for granted—that was where.

This wasn't the first time that Chris's business interests had left her stranded at the weekend, she thought. Up to now she'd told herself that his ambition was laudable, that he deserved her whole-hearted support.

But there came a point when ambition became selfishness, and they'd reached it.

Because it wasn't only business which had taken him away from her. He could have cancelled that solo trip to the Bahamas, but he hadn't, even though it had come at a time when she'd desperately needed his love and support. When she hadn't wanted to be left alone.

She hurriedly closed down that train of thought, and the memories it engendered. That was all in the past, and for the moment the future seemed confused. Which left her with the here and now.

And she wasn't going to spend another Friday evening staring at her own four walls when, just for once, there was an attractive alternative.

For a moment she halted, looking at her own startled reflection in her dressing mirror as she acknowledged what she was contemplating. What she was risking.

Because Marco Valante was light years beyond being merely an attractive man. He was a force of nature, she thought, her body shivering in mingled apprehension and excitement.

From the moment she'd seen him that day in the restaurant she'd been drawn to him—a helpless tide to his dark moon.

All that stood between her and potential disaster was his own guarantee that tonight would involve dinner and nothing else. And how did she dare trust a stranger's promise?

Especially when instinct warned her that here was a man who lived by his own rules alone.

She lifted a hand and touched her lips, remembering...

She thought, I must be crazy.

Of course, all she need do was hang the dress back in the wardrobe and spend a blameless evening watching television. No one would be any the wiser.

Yet she already knew in her heart that eminently sensible course of action was not for her.

I'm going to have dinner with him, she thought defiantly. And I'm going to laugh and flirt and have fun in a way I haven't done for months. Just for this one evening. After all, he likes to play games, and I can do that too. And when it's over I'm going to thank him and shake hands nicely, and walk away. Nothing more.

Because I can. Because even if he breaks his word I have my own private armour. It may be called disappointment and failure, but it's very effective just the same. And it confers its own immunity against natural born womanisers like Signor Valante. End of story.

She showered and washed her hair, then finger-dried it so it sprang like an aureole of living flame around her head.

She applied the lightest of make-up, adding a touch of shadow and mascara to her eyes and a pale lustre to her mouth, then slipped her feet into high-heeled strappy sandals.

When she was ready she glanced at herself in the mirror, and gasped. A stranger was looking back at her, her skin milk-white against the starkness of the dress, her face flushed and her eyes bright with expectancy.

And tonight she was going to let that stranger live in her head, she thought, as she sprayed her favourite scent on to pulse-points and picked up her bag and pashmina.

'You still don't have to do this,' she whispered under her breath, as a cab drove her to the restaurant. 'It's not too late. You could always tell the taxi to turn round. But if you go through with it, and it shows any sign of getting heavy, you can leave. So there's nothing—not one thing—to worry about. Whatever happens—you're in control.'

Pietro's was small and quiet, the name displayed on a discreet sign beside the entrance.

Inside, Flora found herself in a smart reception area, confronted by a pretty girl with an enquiring smile.

She cleared her throat. 'I'm meeting someone—a Signor Valante.'

The smile widened. 'Of course, *signorina*. He is in the bar. May I take your wrap?'

'No, it's fine.' Flora maintained a firm grip on its silver-grey folds. 'I'll keep it with me.' In case I have to make a sudden exit, she added silently.

The bar was already busy but she saw him at once, lounging on one of the tall stools at the counter, looking like a man who was prepared to wait all night if he had to.

Only he didn't. Have to. Did he?

Because she was here, and she was trembling again, and that gnawing ache was back in the pit of her stomach.

And of course he had seen her, so it was too late to slip away. In her heart she knew it had always been too late. That something stronger than her own will—her own reason—had brought her to him tonight.

She felt his gaze slide over her. Saw his brows lift and his mouth slant in surprise and frank pleasure as he started towards her through the laughing, chattering groups of people.

And realised, with a pang of something like fear, that, contrary to her expectations—her planned strategy—it would not be as easy as she thought to turn her back and walk away from him when the evening came to an end.

Oh, God, she thought, dry-mouthed. I'm going to have to be careful—so very careful...

CHAPTER THREE

'CIAO.' His smile was in his eyes as he reached her side. He took her hand and raised it to his lips in a fleeting caress. 'You decided you could spare me a few hours of your life after all, hmm?'

She took a deep, steadying breath. 'So it would seem,' she returned with relative calm.

'Your *fidanzato* must be a very tolerant man.' His gaze travelled over her without haste, making her feel that he was aware of every detail of what she might— or might not—be wearing. Sending another flurry through her senses.

He said slowly, his lips twisting, 'But I think he would be wiser to keep you chained to his wrist—especially when you look as you do tonight.'

He had not, she realised, relinquished his clasp on her hand, and she detached herself from him, quietly but with emphasis.

'You gave me your word, *signore*, that I would be safe in your company,' she reminded him, trying to speak lightly.

His brows lifted. 'And is that why you came, *mia cara*?' he asked softly. 'Because you wished to feel— safe?'

She gave him a composed smile. 'I came because the food is said to be good here, and I'm hungry.'

'Ah,' he said. 'Then I must feed you.' He made a slight signal and Flora found herself whisked to a small table in the corner—which was somehow miraculously vacant—and supplied with a Campari soda and a menu.

Through an archway she could see tables set with immaculate white cloths and glistening with silverware and crystal, could sniff delectable odours wafting through from the kitchen.

To her own surprise she realised that her flippant remark had been no more than the truth. She was indeed hungry, and the plate of little savoury morsels placed in front of them made her mouth water in sudden greed.

'I am to tell you that my cousin was delighted with your suggestion for her bedroom,' Marco Valante said when they had made their choices from the menu presented by an attentive waiter and were alone again. 'But now, of course, she has asked who makes this particular wall-covering and where it is available.'

'Really?' Flora, who'd been convinced that Vittoria Fairlie's decorating problems were purely fictional, was slightly nonplussed. 'Then I'll send her a full written report with samples next week.'

'She would appreciate it.' He sent her a faint smile. 'It is good of you to take so much trouble.'

'I always take trouble,' she said. She paused. 'Even over commissions that don't really exist.'

He said slowly, 'I wonder if you will ever forgive me for that.'

'Who knows?' She shrugged. 'And why does it matter anyway?' She hesitated again. 'After all, you'll be going back to Italy quite soon—won't you?'

'I have fixed no time for my return.' He smiled at her. 'My plans are—fluid.'

'Your boss must be exceptionally tolerant, in that case.' She heard and hated the primness in her tone.

'We work well together. He does not grudge me a period of relaxation.'

He was silent for a moment, and Flora, conscious that he was studying her, kept her attention fixed firmly on the rosy liquid in her glass. At the same time wondering, in spite of herself, exactly what Marco Valante did for relaxation...

He said, at last, 'So what made you change your mind?'

She gave a slight shrug. 'My—plans didn't work out, that's all.'

'Ah,' he said softly.

She eyed him with suspicion. 'What does that mean?'

'How prickly you are.' His tone was amused. 'Does it have to mean anything?'

She spread her hands almost helplessly. 'How can I tell? I don't seem to know what's going on any more— if I ever did.' She made herself meet his gaze directly. 'And what I really can't figure out is why you're here this evening.'

'Because it's one of my favourite restaurants in London.' The green eyes glinted.

'That isn't what I meant,' Flora said. 'And you know it.' She paused. 'Clearly you know London well, and your cousin lives here and probably leads a hectic social life. I'm sure she could introduce you to dozens of single girls.'

'She has certainly tried on occasion,' he agreed casually.

'Exactly,' Flora said with some force. 'So why aren't you dining with one of them instead?'

He said reflectively, 'Perhaps, *cara*, because I prefer to do my own—hunting.'

She stiffened, eyes flashing. 'I am—not—your prey.'

He grinned unrepentantly. 'No, of course not. Just an angel who has taken pity on my loneliness.'

Her face was still mutinous. 'I'd have said, Signor Valante, that you're the last person in the world who needs to be lonely.'

'*Grazie,*' he said. 'I think.'

'So why, then?' Flora persisted doggedly. 'How is it that you're so set on having dinner with me?'

'You really need to ask?' His brows lifted. 'Are there no mirrors in that apartment of yours?' His voice dropped—became husky. '*Mia bella*, there is not a man in this restaurant who does not envy me and wish he was at your side. How can you not know this?'

Her skin warmed, and she took a hasty sip of her drink. She said stiltedly, 'I wasn't—fishing for compliments.'

'And I was not flattering.' He paused. 'Is the truth so difficult for you to acknowledge?'

She gave a small, wintry smile. 'Perhaps it convinces me that I should have stayed at home.'

'But why?' He leaned forward. Flora thought, crazily, that his eyes were filled with little dancing sparks. 'What possible harm can come to you—in this crowded place?'

She made herself meet his glance steadily. 'I don't know. But I think you're a dangerous man, Signor Valante.'

'You're wrong, *cara*,' he said softly. 'I am the one who is in danger.'

'Then why were you so insistent?'

'Perhaps I like to take risks.'

'Not,' she said, 'a recommendation in an accountant, I'd have thought.'

His grin was lazy. 'But I am only an accountant in

working hours, *carissima*. And now I am not working but relaxing—if you remember.'

Flora bit her lip, conscious of the fierce undertow of his attraction, how it could so easily sweep her out of her depth. If she wasn't careful, of course, she added hastily.

Thankfully, at that moment the waiter reappeared to tell them their table was ready.

And once the food was served, and the wine was poured, she would steer the conversation into more general channels, she promised herself grimly as she accompanied Marco sedately into the main restaurant.

She was faintly ruffled to discover that they were seated side by side on one of the cushioned banquettes. But to request her place to be reset on the opposite side of the table would simply reveal that she was on edge, she reflected as she took her seat.

There was a miniature lamp on the table, its tiny flame bright, but safely confined within its glass shade.

A valuable lesson for life, she thought wryly, as the waiter shook out her napkin and placed it reverently across her lap. She needed to keep the conflict of emotions inside herself controlled with equal strictness.

But she was already too aware of his proximity—the breath of cologne, almost familiar now, that reached her when he moved—the coolly sculptured profile—the dangerous animal strength of the lean body under the civilised trappings. The sensuous curve of the mouth which had once so briefly possessed hers...

This, she was beginning to realise, was a man to whom power was as natural as breathing. And not just material power either, although he clearly had that in plenty, she realised uneasily. His sexual power was even more potent.

She was glad to be able to focus her attention, deservedly, on the food. The delicate and creamy herb risotto was followed by scallops and clams served with black linguine, accompanied by a crisp, fragrant white wine that she decided it would be politic to sip sparingly.

The main course consisted of seared chunks of lamb on the bone, accompanied by a rich assortment of braised garlicky vegetables. The wine was red and full-bodied.

'I'm not surprised you come here,' Flora said after her first appreciative mouthful. 'This food is almost too good.'

He smiled at her. 'I'm glad you approve. But save your compliments for Pietro himself,' he added drily. 'He lives in a state of persistent anxiety and needs all the reassurance he can get.'

'You know him well?'

'We were boys together in Italy.'

'Ah,' she said.

'Now you are being cryptic, *mia bella*,' he said softly. 'What does that mean?'

She shrugged. 'I was just trying to imagine you as a child, with muddy clothes and scraped knees. It isn't easy.'

His brows lifted. 'Do I give the impression I was born in an Armani suit with a briefcase?' he asked lazily.

'Something like that,' she acknowledged, her mouth quirking mischievously.

'Yet I entered the world exactly as you did, Flora *mia*—without clothes at all.' He returned her smile, his eyes flickering lazily over her breasts, clearly outlined by the cling of her dress. 'Shall we indulge in a little— mutual visualisation, perhaps?'

Flora looked quickly down at her plate, aware that her

face had warmed. 'I prefer to concentrate on this wonderful food.'

They ate for a few moments in silence, then Flora ventured into speech again, trying for a neutral topic. 'Italy must be a wonderful country to grow up in.'

'It is also a good place to live when one is grown.' He paused. 'You should introduce me to your *fidanzato*. Maybe I could convince him to take you there.'

Her smile was too swift. Too bright. 'Maybe. But unfortunately he's had to go away this weekend.'

'Another visit to the Bahamas, perhaps?' There was an edge to his voice which she detected and resented.

'No, a business trip,' she returned crisply. 'Chris is his own boss, and that doesn't allow him a great deal of leisure—unlike yourself.'

'Cristoforo,' he said softly. 'Tell me about him.'

'What sort of thing do you want to know?' Flora drank some wine.

'How you met,' he said. 'When you realised that he of all men was the one. But no intimate secrets,' he added silkily. 'That is if you have any to tell...'

Flora bit her lip, refusing to rise to the obvious bait. 'We met at a party,' she said. 'I'd helped a couple sell their flat after it had been on the market almost a year, and they invited me to a housewarming at their new property. Chris was there too because he'd arranged their mortgage. We—started seeing each other and fell in love—obviously. After a few months he proposed to me. And I accepted.'

She saw a faintly derisive expression in his eyes, and stiffened. 'Is there something wrong? Because it seems a perfectly normal chain of events to me.'

'Not a thing,' he said. 'And you will live happily ever after?'

Flora lifted her chin. 'That is the plan, yes.' She paused. 'And what about you, *signore*? Do I get to hear your romantic history—or would it take too long?' She paused. 'Starting, I suppose, with—are you married?'

'No.' His tone was crisp and there was a sudden disturbing hardness in his eyes. 'Nor am I divorced or a widower.' He paused. 'I was once engaged, but it—ended.' He gave her a wintry smile. 'I am sure that does not surprise you.'

'So—you prefer to play the field.' Flora shrugged. 'At least you found out before you were married, so no real harm was done.'

'You are mistaken,' he said slowly. 'It was my *fidanzata* who found another man. Someone she met on holiday.'

'Oh.' This time she was surprised, but tried not to show it. 'Well—these things happen. But they don't usually mean anything.'

Marco Valante gave her a curious look. 'You think it is a trivial matter—such a betrayal?' There was a harsh note in his voice.

'No—no, of course not.' Flora avoided his gaze, her fingers playing uneasily with the stem of her glass. 'I—I didn't mean that. I just thought that if you'd—loved her enough it might have been possible to—forgive her.'

'No.' The dark face was brooding. 'There could be no question of that.'

'Then I'm very sorry,' she said quietly. 'For both of you.' She swallowed. 'It must have been a difficult time. And I—I shouldn't have pried either,' she added. 'Brought back unhappy memories. They say the important thing is to forget the past—and move on.'

'Yes,' he said softly. 'I am sure you are right. But it

is not always that simple. Sometimes the past imposes—obligations that cannot be ignored.'

Flora finished her meal in silence. She felt as if she'd taken an unwary step and found herself in a quagmire, the ground shaking beneath her feet.

There was a totally different side to Marco Valante, she thought. An unsuspected layer of harshness under the indisputable charm. Something disturbingly cold and unforgiving. But perhaps it was understandable. Clearly his fiancée's defection had hit him hard, his masculine pride undoubtedly being dented along with his emotions.

She felt as if she'd opened a door that should have remained closed.

I'll just have some coffee and go, she thought, sneaking a surreptitious glance at her watch.

But that proved not so easy. The waiter, apparently in league with her companion, insisted that she must try the house speciality for dessert—some delectable and impossibly rich chocolate truffles flavoured with amaretto.

And when the tiny cups of espresso arrived they were accompanied by Strega, and also Pietro, the restaurant owner, a small, thin man whose faintly harassed expression relaxed into a pleased grin when Flora lavished sincere praise on his food.

At Marco's invitation he joined them for more coffee and Strega, totally upsetting Flora's plans for a swift, strategic withdrawal.

'I had begun to think we would never meet, *signorina*,' Pietro told her with a twinkle. 'I was expecting you here a few nights ago. You have made my friend Marco wait, I think, and he is not accustomed to that.'

Flora flushed slightly. 'I can believe it,' she said, trying to speak lightly.

'You wrong me, *mia bella*,' Marco Valante drawled. 'I can be—infinitely patient—when it is necessary.'

She felt her colour deepen under the mocking intensity of his gaze. She hurriedly finished the liqueur in her glass, snatched up her bag, and with a murmured apology fled to the powder room.

Thankfully, she had it to herself. She sank down on to the padded stool in front of the vanity unit and stared at herself in the mirror, observing the feverishly bright eyes, the tremulously parted lips, as if they belonged to a stranger.

What in hell was the matter with her? she wondered desperately. She had a career—a life—and a man in that life. And yet she was behaving like a schoolgirl just released from a convent. Only with less sophistication.

And all this because of a man whose existence she'd been unaware of a week ago. It made no sense.

Well, you got yourself into this mess, she reminded herself with grim finality. Of your own free will, too. Even though you should have known better. And now you can just extract yourself—with minimal damage—if that's still possible.

It was hot in the lavishly carpeted, glamorously decorated room, yet Flora was suddenly shivering like a dog.

She felt light-headed too. Maybe she was just sickening for something—one of those odd viruses that kept surfacing in the summer months.

Or maybe she hadn't kept sufficient track, after all, of the number of times Marco Valante had filled and refilled her glass, she thought uneasily.

She'd started off well in control, but had definitely slipped during the course of the long meal—particularly when the conversation had got sticky. She'd tried to use her glass as a barricade, but it might well have turned into a trap instead. And those final Stregas hadn't helped at all.

She smoothed her hair, toned down her hectic cheeks with powder, and rose to her feet.

The dress had been a mistake, too. She'd worn it as a gesture of defiance, but it sent all the wrong messages. And her heels were suddenly far too high as well. They did nothing to combat that dizzy feeling.

She drew a deep breath and held it for a moment before releasing it slowly. Calming tactics before she went back into the restaurant and set about extricating herself from this self-inflicted mess with dignity and aplomb.

'I wish,' she muttered under her breath as she headed for the door, stepping out with more than ordinary care—which was, in itself, a dead giveaway.

She'd been dreading more coffee, more loaded drinks to go with the loaded remarks, but Marco was on his feet, standing by the table, putting away his wallet, his face withdrawn and grave.

It seemed he also wanted to call it a night, thought Flora, summoning relief to her rescue. And perhaps that oddly haunted look had been brought on by the size of the bill...

She paused, angered by her own flippancy when it was undoubtedly her desire to score points by cross-examining him over his love life that had revived too many unwelcome memories and driven him into intro-spection. After all, he was someone who had loved and lost, and in the bitterest circumstances, too, when all she had to do in life was count her blessings.

He glanced up and saw her, and his expression changed. Charm was back in season, and something more than warmth glinted in his eyes. Which she wasn't going to allow herself even to contemplate.

Accordingly, 'Well,' Flora said briskly, when she reached him, 'Thank you for a very pleasant evening, *signore*. And—goodbye.'

'It is not quite over yet,' he corrected her. 'Pietro has called a taxi for us.'

'Oh, he needn't worry about me. I'll be fine.' She reached for her pashmina. 'I'll pick up a black cab…'

'Not easily at this time of night, when the theatres are turning out.' He picked up the long fringed shawl before she could, draping it over his arm. 'And the streets are hardly safe for a woman on her own. I promise you, it would be better to wait.'

Better for whom? Flora wondered, her throat tightening. She stood, gripping her bag, looking down at the tiled floor, until a waiter came to tell them the cab was at the door. She wished Pietro a quiet goodnight, and forced herself to remain passive as Marco placed the pashmina round her shoulders.

Then she walked ahead of him into the street, stumbling a little on an uneven paving stone as the cool night air hit her.

'Take care, *mia bella*. You must not risk another fall.' His hand was under her elbow like a flash, guiding her to the waiting cab.

As she climbed in she heard with shock Marco give the driver her address.

'How do you know where I live?' she demanded, shrinking back into her corner as he took the seat beside her. 'It wasn't on the card I gave you.'

'True.' In the dimness, she saw him lift one shoulder in a shrug. 'But you were not so hard to trace, Flora *mia*.'

'So it would seem,' she said tautly.

It was not that great a distance, but traffic was heavy and the ride seemed to take for ever. Or was it just her acute consciousness of the man in the darkness beside her?

When they finally drew up in the quiet street outside her flat Flora moved swiftly, reaching for the handle. 'Thanks for the lift...'

'You must allow me to see you to your door.' His tone brooked no refusal.

She was concentrating hard on pursuing a steady path across the pavement, at the same time fumbling in her bag for her keys. Not easy when your head was swimming, she thought detachedly, and your legs felt as if all the bones had been removed.

'Let me do this.' There was faint amusement in his voice as he took the key from her wavering hand and fitted it into the lock.

'I can manage,' Flora protested. 'And the taxi's meter will be running,' she added, glancing over her shoulder. She gave an alarmed gasp. 'Oh—it's gone.'

'I hoped you would offer me some coffee.' He was inside now, accompanying her up the stairs, his hand under her arm, supporting her again. Taking it for granted, she thought furiously, that it was necessary. 'Isn't that the conventional thing to do?' he added.

'You wouldn't know a convention, Signor Valante, if it jumped out and bit you.' Not all her words were as clear as she'd have liked, but she thought she'd got the meaning across.

'On the other hand, I could make *you* some coffee,' he went on. 'You seem to need it.'

'I'm perfectly fine,' Flora returned with dignified imprecision. 'And our dinner date is over, in case you hadn't noticed.'

'Yes,' he said. 'But the evening still goes on. And I am curious to see where you live.'

'Why?' She watched him fit the flat key in the lock.

He shrugged. 'Because you can learn a great deal from someone's surroundings. You of all people should know that,' he added drily. 'And there are things I wish to discover about you.'

She gave him a brilliant smile. 'Good luck,' she said, and led the way into the living room.

Marco Valante halted, looking slowly round him, taking in the plain white walls, the stripped floorboards, the low glass-topped table, and the sofa and single armchair in their tailored smoky blue covers.

He said softly, 'A blank canvas. How interesting. And is the bedroom equally neutral?'

Flora walked back across the narrow passage and flung open the door opposite. 'Judge for yourself,' she said, and watched his reaction.

Here, there were no touches of colour at all. Everything from the walls to the fitted wardrobes which hid her clothes, and the antique lace bedcover and the filmy drapes that hung at the window, was an unremitting white.

'Very virginal,' Marco said after a pause, his face expressionless. 'Like the cell of a nun. It explains a great deal.'

'Such as?' she demanded.

'Why your *fidanzato* prefers to spend his time elsewhere, perhaps.'

'As it happens, Chris is here all the time. And he likes a—a minimalist look,' she flung back at him. 'And now that you've seen what you came for, you can leave.'

'Without my coffee?' He shook his head reproach-fully. 'You are not very hospitable, Flora *mia*.'

She said between her teeth, 'Please stop calling me "your" Flora.'

'You wish me to call you "his" Flora—this Cristoforo's—when it is quite clear you do not belong to him—and never have?'

She might not be firing on all cylinders, but she could recognise disdain when she heard it.

'You know nothing about my relationship with my fiancé,' she threw back at him, discomfited to hear her words slurring. 'And you're hardly the person to lecture me on how to conduct my engagement. I think it's time you went.'

'And I think you're more in need of coffee than I am, *signorina*.' He walked down the passage to the kitchen. Flora, setting off in pursuit with a gasp of indignation, arrived in time to see him filling the kettle and setting it to boil.

'You have no espresso machine?' He glanced round at her, brows lifted.

'No,' Flora said with heavy sarcasm. 'I'm sorry, but I didn't realise I'd be entertaining an uninvited guest.'

'If you think you are in the least entertaining, you delude yourself.' He reached for the cafetière. 'Where do you keep your coffee?'

Mute with temper, she opened a cupboard and took down a new pack of a freshly ground Colombian blend.

She said curtly, 'I'll do it.'

'As you wish.' He shrugged, and took her place in the doorway, leaning a casual shoulder against its frame.

'You give little away,' he remarked after a pause. 'No pictures—no ornaments or personal touches. You are an enigma, Signorina Flora. A woman of mystery. What are you trying to conceal, I wonder?'

'Nothing at all,' Flora denied, spooning coffee into the cafetière. 'But I work with colour all the time. When I get home I prefer something—more restful, that's all.'

'Is that the whole truth?'

She bit her lip, avoiding his quizzical gaze. 'Well, I did plan to decorate at first—perhaps—but then I met Chris, so now I'm saving my energies for the home we're going to share. That's going to be a riot of colour. The showcase for my career.'

'You say you plan to go on working after you are married?'

Flora lifted her chin. 'Naturally. Is something wrong with that?'

'You do not intend to have babies?'

She began to set a tray with cups, sugar bowl and cream jug. 'Yes—probably—eventually.'

'You do not sound too certain.'

She opened the cutlery drawer with a rattle to look for spoons. 'Maybe I feel I should get the wedding over with before I start organising the nursery.'

'Do you like children?'

'Boiled or fried?' Flora filled the cafetière and set it on the tray. 'I don't know a great deal about them, apart from my sort of nephew, and he's a nightmare—spoiled rotten and badly behaved. A real tantrum king.'

'Perhaps you should blame the parents rather than the child.'

'I do,' she said shortly. 'Each time I'm forced to set eyes on him.' She picked up the tray and turned, noting that he was still blocking the doorway. 'Excuse me—please.'

He made no attempt to move, and she added, her tone
sharpening, 'I—I'd like to get past.'

'Truly?' he asked softly. 'I wonder.' He straightened
and took the tray from her suddenly nerveless hands.

Taking a breath, Flora marched ahead of him back to
the sitting room, deliberately choosing the armchair.

He placed the tray on the glass table and sat down on
the sofa. 'I am beginning to accustom myself to your
unsullied environment.' His tone was silky. 'But I find
it odd that there are no photographs anywhere—none of
your Cristoforo—or of your parents either. Are you an
orphan, perhaps? Is your past as unrevealing as your
walls?'

'Of course not,' she said coolly. 'I have plenty of
family pictures, but I keep them in an album. I don't
like—clutter.'

His brows lifted mockingly. 'Is that how you regard
the image of your beloved?'

'No, of course not.' She bit her lip. 'You like to deliberately misunderstand.'

'On the contrary, I am trying to make sense of it all.'
He paused. 'Of you.'

'Then please don't bother,' Flora said swiftly. 'Our
acquaintance has been brief, and it ends tonight.'

'Ah,' he said softly. 'But the night is not yet over. So
I am permitted a little speculation.'

'If you want to waste your time.' Flora reached for
the cafetière and filled the cups, controlling a little flurry
of unease.

'My time is my own. I can spend it as I wish.' He
paused. 'So—are you going to show me these photographs of yours—if only to prove they really exist?'

For a moment she hesitated, then reluctantly opened

the door of one of the concealed cupboards beside the fireplace and extracted a heavy album.

She took it across to him and held it out. 'Here. I have nothing to hide.' She gave him a taut smile. 'My whole history in a big black book.'

He opened the album and began to turn the pages, his face expressionless as he studied the pictures.

Flora picked up her coffee cup and sipped with apparent unconcern.

He said, 'Your parents are alive and in good health?'

She paused, chewing her lip again. 'My father died several years ago,' she said at last. 'And my mother remarried—a widower with a daughter about my own age.'

'Ah,' he said softly. 'The mother of the tantrum king. Is that why you don't like her?'

'I have no reason to dislike her,' Flora said evenly. 'We haven't a great deal in common, that's all.'

He turned another page and paused, the green eyes narrowing. He said, 'And this, of course, must be Cristoforo. How strange.'

She stiffened. 'Why do you say that?'

'Because he is the only man to feature here.' His voice was level. 'Were there no previous men in your life, Flora *mia*? No minor indiscretions of any kind? Or have they been whitewashed away too?'

'I've had other boyfriends,' she said coldly. 'But no one who mattered. All right?'

He looked down again at the photograph, his mouth twisting. 'And he means the world to you—as you do to him?'

'Of course. Why do you keep asking me all these questions.'

'Because I want to know all about you, *mia cara*. Every last thing.'

Her throat tightened. 'But no one can ever know another person that well.'

'Then perhaps I shall be the first.' He closed the photograph album and laid it aside. He rose, taking off his jacket and tossing it across the back of the sofa, then walked across to her, taking her hands in his and pulling her to her feet. She went unresistingly, her heart beating a frantic, alarmed tattoo, her eyes widening in a mixture of panic and strange excitement.

He said softly, 'And I shall start with your mouth.'

'No,' Flora said hoarsely as his arms went round her, drawing her against the hard heat of his body. 'You can't. You said—you promised—that I'd be safe tonight.'

'And so you have been, *mia bella*.' There was laughter in his voice, mingled with another note, more dangerous, more insidious. 'But midnight has come and gone. It is no longer tonight, but tomorrow. And from this moment on I guarantee nothing.'

He added softly, 'You can command me not to touch you, but not to stop wanting you. Because that has become impossible.'

Then he bent his head, and his lips met hers.

CHAPTER FOUR

SOME distant voice in her mind was telling her that she should fight him. That she should kick, bite and punch, if necessary, before the warmth of his mouth on hers sapped every last scrap of resistance from her being.

That she should hang on, with every ounce of will she possessed, to her life—her safe, planned future with Chris.

And to her reason—her sanity.

But it was too late. Indeed, she realised helplessly, it had always been too late—from that first time she had seen him in the restaurant. And, even more, from that fleeting moment when his lips had first touched hers.

It was pointless to remind herself that she had no moral right to be doing this. That she was engaged—committed—soon to be married. That this was a madness she could not afford. Because logic, reason, even decency no longer seemed to matter.

And the most shaming thing of all was that he was using no force—because he didn't have to. Because her lips were already parting in acceptance, and welcome. And with a growing hunger she was no longer able to disguise, even had she wanted to.

Her mind—her will—was in free fall—cascading into surrender.

And the hands which had been braced in the beginnings of protest against the wall of his chest lifted and locked at the nape of his neck.

At first it was a gentle, almost leisurely exploration of

her mouth, as if he was learning the taste—the texture of her. Then, slowly, the kiss deepened, imposing new demands. Testing the outer limits of her control. And his.

Her body was pressed against him, making her aware that he was powerfully aroused. The hurry of his heartbeat seemed translated into her own being.

He pushed a hand into her hair, twining the silky strands round his fingers, drawing her head backwards so that the long, lovely line of her throat was exposed and vulnerable to the lingering passage of his caress. His lips found the pink shell of her ear, then travelled down to the frantic tumult of her pulse.

She gasped as she felt the heated, animal surge in her blood. As his lips encountered the delicate hollows at the base of her throat, pushing aside the narrow strap, baring the curve of her shoulder.

The long fingers found the rounded curve of her breast, moulding it gently as his thumb moved delicately, voluptuously on the hardening nipple. Flora leaned her forehead against his shoulder, eyes closed, lost in exquisite shuddering sensation.

Whatever coherency remained in her mind told her that she had never felt like this before. Never dreamed it was possible that she could *want* like this. That she could welcome every new intimacy and long for more.

She heard herself say hoarsely, 'What do you want from me?'

'Everything.' His voice was a husky whisper, the single word an affirmation. Almost a warning.

He kissed her again with slow, sensual purpose, while his hands continued their absorbed, teasing play with the heated peaks of her breasts, making her sigh her pleasure against his lips.

She wasn't even sure when he released the zip at the back of her dress, letting the soft fabric slide away from her shivering skin.

He lifted her into his arms, sinking back with her on to the sofa, holding her so that she was lying across his thighs, the black dress pooling round her hips, her entire body attuned—accessible—to the touch of his hands and mouth.

She heard him murmur in throaty appreciation as his dark head bent to adore the scented mounds he had uncovered, and she quivered as she felt the burn of his lips against her skin—the flickering glide of his tongue on her nipples.

She made a little stifled sound and he lifted his head, looking down at her, the green eyes warm and slumbrous.

'You don't like that?'

'Oh, yes,' she whispered. 'Too much—too much.'

He stroked each taut peak with a gentle finger. 'They are like tiny roses,' he told her softly. 'Only more sweet.'

Her own hands were pulling feverishly at the buttons on his shirt to free them, touch the heated, hair-roughened skin beneath, and he helped her, dragging the loosened edges apart, then lifting her triumphantly, almost fiercely, so that her naked breasts grazed his own.

His mouth closed on hers with renewed fire, and she clung to him, half dizzy with abandonment, aware of nothing but the pagan clamour of her flesh.

He moved suddenly, lifting her away from him, setting her on her feet, and for an instant she looked at him in mute bewilderment. He smiled slowly up at her, letting his hands drift down her body to disentangle her finally from the ruin of her dress.

When it was done Marco stared at her for a long moment, absorbing the contrast between the creaminess of her skin and the silken black of the tiny undergarment which was her sole remaining covering.

He said softly, 'All evening I have been imagining how you would look at this moment, and you are more beautiful than any fantasy, Flora *mia*.'

His fingers spanned her waist lightly. 'Because you are real.'

His touch lingered on her flat stomach. 'And warm.'

His hand moved downward, brushing over the fragile silk, until he reached the scalding secret core of her, where he lingered.

'And wanting me,' he added huskily.

With one lithe movement he was on his feet, lifting her effortlessly into his arms and walking with her out of the room, and across the passage into the stark whiteness of her bedroom.

Still holding her, he bent slightly, switching on the lamp beside the bed, then took hold of the immaculate bedspread, pulling it back and tossing it to the foot of the bed before lowering Flora to the mattress.

She looked up at him through half-closed eyes as he stood over her. She was aware of the thud of her heart, the rapid rise and fall of her breasts as sudden nervousness lent an edge to her excitement. And she was conscious too that it was a stranger's face that looked down at her in the lamplight, shadowed and almost feral in its intensity.

Her throat tightened. 'Is something—wrong?'

'Nothing.' The sound of her voice seemed to awake him from some spell. His smile banished the shadow— or had that just been a figment of her overwrought imagination? 'Except that you are still wearing too many clothes, *mia bella*.'

'So,' she whispered, 'are you.'

'You think so?' He gave a soft laugh. 'Well, that is easily remedied.'

He stripped with deftness and grace, and without apparent self-consciousness, although she knew he was watching her watch him.

Watching her widening eyes, and the swift, betraying flush that stained her cheeks as she absorbed his lean, strong, totally masculine beauty. The flutter of the muscles in her suddenly dry throat, as apprehension took hold. As she remembered…

Her eyes and her mind went blank. She wanted to run—to hide—to be a thousand miles from this place—this room—this bed—where pain and humiliation waited for her all over again.

The flame in her veins was cooling to ice. The swift, mindless rapture that had consumed her such a short time ago had burned itself out, leaving her with only the ashes.

She thought, Oh, God—what can I do? What can I say…?

She felt the bed dip as he came to lie beside her. Heard him say her name with a question in his voice.

Fingers as gentle as the brush of a feather stroked her hot cheek, then inexorably turned her face towards him.

He said quietly, 'Tell me.'

Pointless to pretend she didn't understand.

She said, falteringly, 'I'm not a virgin—at least, not completely.'

She'd been afraid he would laugh, or be scornful, but instead he nodded, the green eyes thoughtful.

'You are telling me that you have made love with your *fidanzato* after all?'

'Not—exactly.' She swallowed. 'This is—so difficult to explain.'

'No,' Marco said. 'You forget—I have seen your eyes, *mia bella*. And I do not believe that your first surrender was a happy experience for you. Is that what you are trying to say?'

'Yes—I suppose.' She flushed unhappily, avoiding his gaze. 'But it wasn't Chris's fault. I just didn't realise it would—hurt so much.'

She tried to smile. 'It's so ridiculous. I'm a twenty-first century woman, not some early Victorian. It never occurred to me...' Her voice trailed into silence.

He stroked her hair back from her forehead. 'And when the pain was over, did he give you pleasure?'

He sounded totally matter-of-fact—as if he was asking if she thought it would rain tomorrow, she told herself, bewildered.

She said stiltedly, 'He was very—kind about it. But, naturally, he was terribly upset that he'd hurt me. So he suggested it might be better—to wait—before trying again. So we—have...'

'Such amazing self-control.' The cool drawl held a sudden bite. 'I am filled with admiration.'

'He was thinking of me,' Flora defended swiftly.

He shrugged a negligent shoulder. 'Did I suggest otherwise?'

'And it was my problem—my failure,' she went on with determination.

'With lovers, there is no question of failure,' he said softly. 'Some times are better than others—that is all.' He paused. 'As for this problem you believe you have— we shall solve it together.'

Her voice shook. 'I don't think—I can...'

'Ah,' he said. 'But you will. And that is a promise, Flora *mia*. So, do you believe me? Say, ''Yes, Marco.'' '

A tiny shaken laugh escaped her. 'Yes, Marco.'

'Then why are you still trembling?'

She thought, Because no matter how scared I might be, you make me tremble—and burn—and shiver—and ache. And even if I had all the experience in the world you would still possess the power to do this to me. Because—with you—I cannot help myself.

She said, with a catch in her voice, 'I think you know…'

He said quietly, 'Perhaps.'

He framed her face in his hands and began to kiss her again, lightly and sensuously, making no further demands until her taut body began gradually to relax and her lips parted for him on a little sigh of acceptance. His kiss deepened, showing her a glimpse of hunger held well in check. Leaving her almost disappointed when he took his mouth from hers.

He held her for a long time, murmuring to her in his own language, his long fingers stroking her tumbled hair, her cheek, the line of her throat, his gentleness a reassurance. And a seduction.

When his lips next touched hers Flora responded like a flower turning to the sun, offering her mouth's inner sweetness without restraint.

As they kissed Marco began to caress her, the experienced hands slowly rediscovering the curves and planes of her body, revealing them to her anew through his touch.

She had never known there could be such excitement in the brush of skin on skin. She was warming deliciously, her body tinglingly alive to the subtle caress of his fingers, so intent on every new sensation he was offering that she hardly knew the moment when he slipped off her final covering and she was naked in his arms at last.

When his hand parted her thighs, her little gasp was lost under the answering pressure of his lips, as he kissed her deeply and with mounting sensuality. And any sense of shock or shyness was drowned in the flood of sensation which instantly assailed her.

His fingers stroked and tantalised, demanding her quivering body to yield up its most intimate secrets to him. Turning her slowly and deliberately to liquid fire.

She began to move in response to his caress, her body arching tautly towards him as his lips returned to her breasts, suckling the rosy peaks with voluptuous delight. At the same time his exploring hand discovered, then focused on another tiny hidden mound, moving gently and rhythmically on its moist, silken pinnacle.

She was making small helpless sounds in her throat, her head twisting involuntarily on the pillow. She was dissolving in pleasure, her attention absorbed, blindly concentrated on the delicate arousing play of his fingertips with an intensity that bordered on pain. Nothing existed but this man and what he was doing to her, she thought, as her breathing changed and even this last contact with reality slid away.

Even so, the final dark waves of ecstasy caught her unawares, lifting her to a sphere she had never known existed and holding her there, suspended in some rapturous vacuum, while she called out in a voice she didn't recognise and her body shattered into the uncontrollable spasms of her first climax.

She descended slowly, every inch of her body throbbing with a new languor yet feeling alive as never before.

She lifted heavy eyelids and looked up at her lover, and her hand went up to touch his face, feeling the taut jaw muscles clench under her fingers. He captured her questioning fingers and carried them to his lips, biting the tips gently.

She said softly, huskily, 'Is it appropriate to say thank you?'

'If you wish.' There was a smile in his voice, and his mouth was curving in disturbingly sensual appreciation.

Flora realised suddenly that he was moving—positioning himself over her without haste but with definite purpose. 'But I would prefer a more—tangible demonstration, *mia cara*,' he added softly, easing his way into her newly slackened and totally receptive body.

She looked up at him, her eyes wide and startled as she felt herself filled—possessed utterly.

'Hold me,' he instructed tautly, and she obeyed, her hands clinging to the smooth brown shoulders as he began to thrust into her, gently at first, his eyes watching hers for any sign of fear or reluctance, and then more powerfully—more urgently.

She had thought that he had taken her to the extremes of sensation, and beyond. That she was sated—content to be passive while he took his own satisfaction.

But, as she soon discovered with astonishment, she was wrong. Because her body was answering him—mirroring the strong, controlled rhythm of his lovemaking.

She lifted her legs, wrapping them round his sweat-dampened body, and he slid his hands beneath her, raising her towards him as he found her mouth with his.

His kiss was raw and passionate, and her surrender was total, dominated by the renewed demands of her own fevered flesh.

The rasp of his breathing was echoed by her own. She

felt as if she was poised on the edge of some abyss, and he must have felt it too, because he spoke to her, his voice hoarse and urgent. 'Come for me, *mia bella—mia cara*. Come now.'

And, deep within her, as if answering his cue, Flora felt the first sharp pulsation of rapture. She moaned aloud, burying her face against him, biting his shoulder, as the moment took her and sent her spinning out of control into some limbo where pleasure bordered on pain.

Marco flung his head back, his eyes closed, his face taut with the same kind of agony, and she felt his entire body shudder like a tree caught in a giant wind as he came in his turn.

When it was over, they lay together quietly. Flora tried to steady her breathing, to make sense of what had happened to her.

'I didn't know.' Her voice was a thread. He didn't answer, and she turned her head to look at him. He was lying, staring up at the ceiling, his profile as proud and remote as a Renaissance carving.

She felt her throat tighten. 'Marco—is something wrong?'

He turned his head slowly, and smiled at her. 'What could possibly be wrong, Flora *mia*?'

'You looked a thousand miles away.'

He shrugged a shoulder. 'I was thinking how ironic it is that I should have come all this way to find my perfect woman.'

'Truly?'

'You doubt me?'

'No,' she said slowly. 'It's just—that was a happy thought, and you didn't look very happy.'

'And you, *mia bella*, look as if you need to stop imagining things and sleep.' He gathered her closer, so that her head was pillowed on his chest. She could feel the beat of his heart, still slightly uneven, under her cheek.

He was not, she thought with satisfaction, as cool as he seemed. And she closed her eyes, smiling.

She slept deeply and dreamlessly, and awoke with reluctance. For a moment she lay still, feeling oddly disorientated—as if her faintly aching body no longer belonged to her. And then, like a thunderbolt, her memory returned and she sat up.

Oh, God, she thought desperately. I'm in bed with Marco Valante.

Except that wasn't strictly true. Because no sleeping man lay beside her. Nor, she realised, was there any sound from the bathroom, or any sign of his clothes either.

She said aloud, 'He's gone.' And her voice sounded small and desolate in the emptiness of the room.

She lay down again, pulling the tangled sheet up over her body, aware that her mouth was dry and her heart was thumping.

Well, Flora, she told herself. It seems you've just had your first one-night stand. Now you have to live with that, and I just hope you think it was worth it.

And, to make matters a million times worse, you've had unprotected sex with a stranger. A man who's probably left his notch on bedposts in every major capital of the world, and several small towns as well. And that's something else you'll have to deal with.

She pressed her clenched fist against her mouth, to stop herself from moaning aloud.

She had no one to blame but herself, whatever the consequences. After all, she'd gone out last night undressed to kill, flinging down a challenge to his sexuality that no red-blooded man could have ignored. And all because of a fit of pique.

She stopped right there. Because that was too easy—too glib an excuse for what she had done.

From that first glimpse of him, Marco had intrigued her. Had tantalised his way into her dreams, sleeping and waking. He himself had been the challenge—and the ultimate prize.

And she had hardly been short-changed. In a few brief hours Marco had taught her more about her body and its needs than she could have believed possible.

And she would never be the same again.

The girl who had had the rest of her life mapped out, with a sensible marriage and a secure future, had disappeared for ever—if she'd even existed at all.

What was it Hester had said? 'Heaven, hell and heartbreak'?

Well, she'd had the heaven, and now she was faced with the hell of knowing that, for him, it had been just a casual sexual encounter—another girl in another bed. And, although she was currently feeling numb, she knew the heartbreak would surely follow.

And then there was Chris, whom she had betrayed in the worst possible way.

I can't tell him, she thought miserably. I can't hurt him like that. He doesn't deserve it. I'll have to find some other excuse for calling off the wedding. Tell him I've been having second thoughts—that I prefer my career—my independence.

His mother will be pleased, anyway. She never thought I was good enough for him—always dropping hints about modern girls not knowing how to be homemakers.

She groaned, pressing her face into the pillow. No amount of self-justification was ever going to excuse what she'd done. She'd had no right to have dinner with Marco Valante, let alone allow him to make a feast of her in bed.

And now he'd walked away without a backward glance, and she knew she had no one to blame but herself.

Act like a tart and you'll get treated like a tart, she thought drearily.

She pushed away the encircling sheet and got up. It was the morning after the night before, and she simply had to get on with her life. She would have a bath—wash away the taste and touch of Marco Valante—get dressed, then start to dismantle the arrangements for the wedding that were already in place. Florists, caterers and printers would all have to be notified, and the church cancelled. She would need to make a list, she thought, trailing into the bathroom and turning on the taps in the tub.

And somehow she would have to tell her mother, and endure the inevitable wailings and recriminations.

On the plus side, she thought wanly, I will not have the nephew from hell following me up the aisle, although I expect that Sandra will have something to say about her little darling's disappointment.

She poured a capful of her favourite bath essence into the steaming water.

There was going to be a lot of music to face, she thought frowningly, but only if she chose to do so. She could always take the weeks she'd booked off for her honeymoon and move them up. Get right away for a while and put herself back together again.

Some of the clients she'd planned to see might not be

too happy if she went missing for a couple of weeks, but Melanie would simply have to make new appointments for them.

It'll be good for her, she thought, testing the water. Show what she's made of in a crisis.

And she was ready to bet that most of the clients would be prepared to wait for her return. Because she was good at her job.

I wish, she thought, as she stepped into the tub, that I was equally as good at life.

She settled back into the scented water with a little sigh and closed her eyes.

She'd made a monumental fool of herself, and taken a terrible risk, but she didn't have to allow it to cloud her entire future, she told herself firmly. Everyone was surely allowed one serious mistake—and Marco Valante was hers. That was all.

She heard a slight sound, and turned her head sharply.

Her serious mistake was standing in the bathroom doorway, one shoulder negligently propped against its frame. He was fully dressed, but tieless, and his shirt was open at the throat.

He said softly, *'Buon giorno.'* And began to walk towards her, discarding his jacket as he did so. 'I thought you would sleep until my return, *cara.*'

'Your return?' Her voice was a stifled croak. 'Where have you been?'

'Your refrigerator was full of food, but nothing for breakfast, so I went shopping.' He counted on his fingers. 'We have fresh rolls, orange juice, cheese and some good ham.' The green eyes glinted as they surveyed her. 'All of which we will have—later.'

Flora realised he was rolling up the sleeves of his

shirt. He reached down and took the soap from her un-resisting hand.

'Stand up, *mia bella*,' he directed quietly.

Somehow she found herself mutely obeying, her eyes fixed on his face, aware that her throat had tightened with mingled panic and excitement.

Marco lathered his hands with the soap and began to apply the scented foam to her skin, starting with her shoulders and working his way downwards, massaging it into her body very slowly, and very thoroughly.

His gaze was reflective—almost dispassionate—as he worked—like a sculptor judging his latest work, she thought confusedly as her senses began to riot.

Everywhere he touched her—and he didn't seem to miss an inch—was tingling and burning. An agonised trembling had ignited deep inside her.

Her breasts were aching with desire as his fingers lingered over their rosy tips. She quivered as he moved with exquisite precision down the length of her spine to her rounded buttocks.

When he touched her thighs, and the soft curls at their apex, Flora had to bite her lower lip to prevent herself from whimpering out loud.

When he'd finished, he took the hand spray from the shower unit and rinsed away the soap, just as carefully. The water droplets felt like needles piercing her over-sensitised skin as they cascaded over her small round breasts, making the nipples stand proud.

At last, when she was beginning to think she could bear no more, he turned off the spray and reached to the towel rail for a bath sheet. He took her hand and helped her out of the water, then wrapped the soft towelling round her.

'Dry yourself, *carissima*,' he ordered softly. 'I would not wish you to catch a chill.'

Chill? Flora thought, as she started, dazedly, to pat herself dry under his unwavering scrutiny. She was already running a high fever. Her legs were shaking so much that she thought she might collapse and her blood was on fire. And he had to know this.

When she had finished, she paused, her eyes asking a question. He nodded, as if she had spoken aloud. He took the edges of the bath sheet, using them to pull her gently towards him. His arms enfolded her and his mouth came down on hers in a slow, deep kiss that sent her already reeling senses into free fall.

When he raised his head, his own breathing was ragged. He drew the edges of the bath sheet apart and began to kiss her body, his lips drifting soft as thistledown from her throat down to her breasts, then travelling over her ribcage to the faint concavity of her abdomen.

He sank down on one knee, his hands holding her hips as the trail of kisses continued downward. When he reached the division of her thighs, and parted them, she gave a little startled cry as she felt his mouth on the burning core of her, the silken eroticism of his tongue as he pleasured her tiny secret bud.

She wanted to tell him that he must not do this—that he should stop. But she could not speak.

She was conscious of nothing but the exquisite sensations rippling through her as he continued his intimate caress. Every atom of her being was focused almost painfully on her growing delight. And then, almost before she was aware, her body imploded into orgasm, the pulsations so strong she thought she might faint.

There were tears running down her face. He wiped

them away with the edge of the towel, then picked her up in his arms and carried her towards the door.

'Where are we going?' Her voice was a breathless squeak.

'Back to bed.'

'But we were going to have breakfast.'

'I think now that is going to be—very much later.' He bent and kissed her mouth, fiercely, sensually. 'Don't you agree, *mia cara*?'

Flora pressed her lips against the triangle of hair-darkened skin revealed by his unfastened shirt. 'Yes, Marco.' Her voice was husky. 'Oh—yes—please.'

CHAPTER FIVE

A LONG time later, lying in his arms, Flora said dreamily, 'I think we've missed breakfast—but it could always become lunch.'

Marco tipped up her chin and looked down at her, brows raised austerely. 'You mean I am not enough for you? You want food as well?'

She gave a soft giggle. 'I think I need to keep my strength up—if this is how you mean us to spend our time.'

She felt the arm that encircled her harden with sudden tension, and realised, with shock, that she'd spoken as if they had a real relationship. That she'd made unwise assumptions about a future which almost certainly did not exist.

She turned away quickly as her face warmed in helpless embarrassment. 'Anyway—I—I'll get us something to eat...' she added with determined brightness.

She pushed away the covering sheet, then hesitated as she remembered that her robe was in the bathroom.

It was ludicrous, she thought with bewilderment. This was the man with whom she'd been intimately entwined for the best part of twelve hours, who had explored and kissed every inch of her body, and yet, in the space of a drawn breath, everything had changed. And suddenly she was reluctant to walk around naked in front of him.

Lack of inhibition was different when it was fuelled by passion. She'd given herself to him again and again

79

in unthinking delight. Learned to bestow pleasure as well as receive it.

But now reason had intervened.

And it was still nothing more than a one-night stand, no matter how she might try to justify it. There'd been no commitment of any kind between them. It had been—just sex. A transient pleasure. And now the sex was over she felt awkward and bewildered—unsure how to behave.

Because Marco, in so many ways, was still a stranger to her, she acknowledged unhappily. Someone who had walked into her life a few days ago and who would soon be leaving in the same casual way.

And it was naïve of her to have supposed—or hoped—that anything that had happened had any real importance in the great scheme of things.

As a lover Marco was gifted, patient and imaginative, luring her into areas of sensuousness she had not know existed.

But she knew that no amount of pleasure would ever be matched by the pain of watching him leave.

It's so easy for a man, she thought sadly. He can just get dressed and go. Whereas I—I've slept with Marco once, and now I want to make him a meal. Next I'll be wanting to have his baby.

Behind her, Marco moved. 'Is something wrong?' He brushed his lips gently across the small of her back. 'You are not having—regrets?'

'No—of course not.' She spoke bravely, not looking at him. 'I was just wondering—where I'd left my dressing gown.'

She heard the smile in his voice. 'Does that really matter?'

She said shortly, 'It does to me.'

There was a silence, then he said slowly, '*Cara*, are you trying to tell me you are—shy?'

She bit her lip. 'Is that so extraordinary?'

He said, 'A little, perhaps, considering what you and I were doing to each other a little while ago.' He paused. 'Would it make things easier for you if I promised to shut my eyes?'

'Yes,' she agreed with a touch of defiance. 'Yes, it would.'

He sighed. 'Just for you, then, *mia bella*.'

Flora slipped out of bed and made for the door. As she reached it something prompted her to look back over her shoulder.

Marco was propped up on an elbow, watching her with undisguised and shameless appreciation.

'Oh,' she choked furiously, and flew to the bathroom, followed by his laughter.

By the time she had prepared lunch, adding fresh fruit and a dish of black olives to the food he'd provided, and choosing a bottle of wine, she was feeling altogether more composed.

While he'd been in the bathroom she'd snatched the opportunity to dress, in a brief blue skirt and white tee shirt, and give her hair a vigorous brushing.

She looked different, she realised with a sense of shock as she glanced at herself in the mirror. There was a new glow to her creamy skin, a woman's shining secrets in her eyes. She was no longer the innocent of twenty-four hours ago, and everything about her proclaimed it.

All she needed to do now was develop a persona to go with her new-found sexual sophistication, she thought wryly. Find something hip and flippant to accompany her smile when she waved Marco goodbye. Proving beyond doubt, she hoped, that she'd always known this was a strictly casual encounter.

When she was alone she ate at the breakfast bar in the kitchen, but for guests she kept a folding table in the walk-in cupboard in the hall. She'd set this up in the corner of the living room, with the directors' chairs which accompanied it.

She was just opening the wine when Marco came to the door.

'*Bello,*' he approved softly. 'A feast.' He indicated the towel draped decorously round his hips. 'See, I am sparing your blushes, *cara.*'

Flora bit her lip. 'You must think I'm awfully stupid...'

'You are wrong. I find you a delight.' He held out a hand. 'Come to me.'

She went over to him and he drew her close, resting his cheek against the top of her head while she inhaled the clean, fresh scent of his skin.

After a moment she stood back, studying a discoloured mark on his shoulder. 'What's that?'

He grinned at her. 'Don't you remember?'

'Oh,' she said, discomfited. 'I—I'm sorry.'

'Then don't be. I like my battle trophy—and its memories.'

'Is that how you see making love—as a war?' She laughed, but she felt faintly troubled too. 'Then who is the victor and who the vanquished?'

He kissed her, his mouth moving on hers with tender warmth. 'At a moment like this,' he murmured, 'it hardly seems to matter.' He paused, stroking the hair back from her face. 'And don't look at me like that, Flora *mia,*' he added softly. 'Or lunch might become dinner.'

Her glance didn't waver. 'I wouldn't mind.'

'Then let me be wise for us both.' His smile was rueful. 'I think it is time I also put on some clothes.'

He kissed her again, and went soft-footed back to the bedroom.

It was a quiet lunch. Marco seemed lost in thought more than once. Or perhaps, thought Flora, he was just exhausted...

'What are you thinking ?' he asked.

'Nothing in particular.' She took a hasty swig of wine. 'Why?'

'Because you are blushing again. I thought it might be—significant.'

'Not really.' Flora fanned herself with her napkin. 'It's probably the heat. It's such a beautiful day.' She paused. 'Would you like some more wine?'

'No, I thank you.' He glanced at his watch. 'I must get back to my cousin's house. And I shall be driving later.'

Oh, Flora thought flatly. So—that was that, after all. And she couldn't pretend it was a surprise.

'It would be good to get out of the city,' he went on. 'I thought I would hire a car.' He smiled at her. 'Perhaps you could suggest a suitable destination.'

She sat rather straighter. 'I really couldn't advise you.'

'No? You disappoint me.'

'I don't really know your tastes.' She hesitated. 'Do you like—looking at things?'

'I like to look at you.' The green eyes met hers with cool directness. 'As for the rest, I am not a sightseer, but I thought we might find a pleasant hotel in some beautiful part of England and spend the remainder of the weekend together there.'

He paused, running a hand over his chin. 'I need to shave, and we both have bags to pack. When I return you can tell me where you would like me to take you.'

She said quietly, 'After paradise, anywhere else will seem rather tame.'

There was an odd silence. Flora saw his mouth tighten, and the green eyes become suddenly remote. It was as if she had made him angry, she thought in bewilderment.

But when he spoke his voice was light. 'You flatter me, *carissima*. But you should beware of paradise. It can so often conceal a serpent.' He rose to his feet. 'I should not be longer than an hour or two.' He came round the table and dropped a kiss on her hair. 'Have our route planned.'

There was a nightgown in her drawer, a sheer, lacy thing wrapped in tissue, that she had bought for her honeymoon with Chris.

The betrayal was complete now, she thought, as she put it carefully into her weekend case. And the wretchedness of telling Chris would be her punishment.

She thought of phoning Hes. You're a witch, she'd say lightly. You wished it on me and it's happened. Passion to die for. *And then loneliness to last a lifetime.* Only she wouldn't say that.

Nor did she make the call. There would be plenty of time for confession in the weeks to come, she thought without joy.

But she did not have time to brood because, surprisingly, Marco was back within the hour, driving a low, sleek open-topped sports car.

Flora gaped at it. 'Someone let you hire that?' she asked incredulously.

'It belongs to Vittoria,' he said. 'She has lent it to me.' He paused. 'She also suggested somewhere we might go—unless, of course, you have thought of a place.'

She spread her hands. 'I've been racking my brains, but I so rarely go out of London—except to Surrey, to stay with my mother and stepfather.' And very occasionally to Essex and Chris's family, she thought with a pang of guilt.

'It is called the Aldleigh Manor Hotel,' he said. 'Vittoria says it is very comfortable, with beautiful grounds, and wonderful food.'

'It sounds perfect,' she said. 'Like a dream.'

His brows drew together. 'You would prefer somewhere else? That's not a problem. We could tour around, maybe? Take our chances?'

'Oh, no,' Flora said swiftly. 'Aldleigh Manor sounds really wonderful. But it might be fully booked.'

'They have a room for us,' he said quietly. 'Overlooking the lake. I must confess I already made the reservation. Although it can always be cancelled if you wish?'

'Certainly not.' Flora threw him a wicked grin. 'I can't wait to see it. And if it's anything short of paradise I shall know who to complain to.'

'You're very quiet,' she commented as they edged their way out of London.

'I am concentrating on my driving,' Marco returned after a pause. 'Remember that for me the gear shift—the road—everything is on the wrong side. And if I scratch Vittoria's darling—*Madonna!*—I'll be a dead man. And I have people depending on me back in Milan.'

'Are accountants really that important?' she teased.

'Only when they are as good as I am, *mia bella*.' He slanted a grin at her.

He really had no need to worry, she thought. He was a marvellous driver, considerate with other traffic, and not using the powerful car as an extension of his virility.

All she had to do was sit back and admire his profile, and bask in the envious glances of people toiling along hot pavements.

The hotel was important enough to be signposted.

'Oh,' Flora said. 'It has a golf course.'

'Well, that need not concern us,' Marco said, turning the car between tall stone gateposts. 'Unless you wish to hire clubs and play?'

'No, thanks,' she said hastily. It was just a reminder of Chris that she didn't need, she thought, guilt piling in again. Well, perhaps she could find some reason to tell Marco she didn't like the place, and persuade him to drive somewhere else.

But it was difficult to know what she could possibly object to, she thought, as the building itself came into view from the long curving drive. It was three storeys high, its grey stones lit by the late afternoon sun which gave the mullioned windows a diamond sparkle. The commanding entrance was made more welcoming by the urns of bright flowers which flanked it.

As Marco drew into one of the parking spaces allotted to hotel guests a porter instantly emerged to take their bags.

They were shown into a vast foyer, made cool by arrangements of tall green plants and dominated by a massive central staircase.

Through an open door Flora could see people sitting in a pretty lounge, enjoying afternoon tea.

She touched Marco's arm. 'That looks nice.'

He smiled at her. 'I'll have some sent up to our room. Wait for me here, *cara*, while I register.'

As he went to the desk Flora took off the scarf she'd been wearing and shook her hair free. She looked around her, noting where the lifts were and spotting discreet signs indicating the cocktail bar, the dining room and the leisure club. According to the brochure that she picked up from a side table, as well as an outdoor swimming pool the Manor boasted an indoor pool, together with a gymnasium and a sauna in its basement.

Perhaps I can interest Marco in some other form of exercise, she thought, suppressing a grin. Or, on second thoughts, perhaps not...

She heard her name spoken, and turned, the smile freezing on her lips as she did so.

Because it wasn't Marco with the key, as she'd expected.

It was Chris. Standing there in front of her with three other men, all carrying golf bags. Looking astonished, and not altogether pleased.

'Flora,' he repeated. 'What on earth are you doing here? How did you find me? Is something wrong?'

'No, nothing.' *Or everything*, she thought desperately. 'I didn't know you were here.' She gave a wild, bright smile. 'But I'm not actually staying. So, please, don't let me interfere with your game. Do go on, and I—I'll see you on Monday.'

'Oh, we've finished for the day,' Chris said. 'Not a bad couple of rounds at all. But you haven't met the lads. Jack—Barry—Neil, this is my fiancée, Flora Graham, who seems to be just passing through for some reason.' And he laughed with a kind of boisterous unease.

There was a chorus of greeting which faded into a bewildered silence, and Flora realised, horrified, that she'd actually taken a step backwards.

'So nice to see you all,' she babbled. 'But I really must be going.'

If I can just get outside and find the car I can wait in it. Tell Marco I can't stay...

She turned to flee, and cannoned straight into Marco himself. He steadied her, hands on her shoulders, halting her flight.

'You are going in the wrong direction, *carissima*.' He sounded amused, every word falling on her ears with total clarity. 'The lift is over there, and we are on the first floor—in the bridal suite, no less.' He slid his arm round her waist and pulled her close. His voice became lower, more intimate. 'I have asked them to send up your tea, and some champagne for us, so that we can—relax before dinner. Would you like that, my sweet one?'

The silence seemed to stretch out until doom. Except that doom would have been preferable, Flora thought. She felt as if she was watching everything from a distance—Chris looking stunned, with his mouth open and his face brick-red—his companions exchanging appalled glances and trying to edge away—and Marco, his hand resting on her hip in unquestioned possession, smiling like a fallen angel.

At last, 'Who are you?' Chris burst out hoarsely. 'And what the hell are you doing with my fiancée?'

Marco looked in his direction for the first time, his glance icy and contemptuous. And totally unwavering. He said, 'I am Marco Valante, *signore*, and I am Flora's lover. Is there anything more you wish to ask me?'

Flora saw Chris's mouth move, and realised he was silently repeating the name to himself. The angry colour

had faded from his face and he was suddenly as white
as a sheet.

There was tension in the air, harsh, almost tangible,
filling the shaken silence.

'No,' Chris muttered at last. 'No, there's nothing.'
And, without looking at Flora again, he turned and stumbled away, followed by his embarrassed companions.

'I think, *mia bella*,' Marco said softly, 'that your engagement is at an end.'

'You know the old cliché about praying for the floor to
open and swallow you?' Flora threw a sodden tissue into
the wastebin and pulled another from the box. 'Well, it's
all true, Hes. I just wanted to disappear and never be
found again.'

'Yet once again the floor remained intact,' said Hester.
'So what did you do? Go for the sympathy vote and
throw up over Chris's shoes?'

'It's not funny.' Flora sent her a piteous look. 'Hes,
it was the worst moment of my life, bar none.'

Twenty-four hours had passed, and they were in
Flora's sitting room. Flora was stretched out on the sofa
and Hester was standing by the window, glass of wine
in hand.

She nodded. 'I believe you.' She whistled. 'Boy, when
you fall off the wagon, Flo, you do it in spectacular style,
I'll grant you that. No half-measures for our girl. So
what happened next? I presume Chris tried to kill him?'

'No.' Flora shook her head drearily. 'He just stood
there, looking at Marco as if he'd seen a ghost—or his
worst nightmare. And then—he walked away.'

Hester frowned. 'You mean he didn't even take a
swing at him? I'm not pro-violence, but under the circumstances...'

'Nothing,' Flora said tonelessly. 'And he didn't look at me, or say one word.'

Hester grimaced. 'Probably didn't trust himself.'

'I can hardly blame him for that,' Flora sighed. 'I can't forgive myself for the way I've treated him.'

'Let's talk some sense here.' Hester walked over, refilled her glass, then resumed her station at the window. 'I never felt that you and Chris were the couple of the year. You met and liked each other, and it—drifted from there.'

She shrugged. 'Maybe you'd both reached a stage where marriage seemed a good idea, and you were content to settle for just all right rather than terrific. It happens a lot, and in a lot of cases it probably works perfectly.

'But not for you, Flo. That red hair of yours gives you away. You're really an all or nothing girl, and sooner or later you'd have realised that. It's much better that it should happen now, before the wedding, even if the end-game was a bit drastic. But you didn't plan it that way, so stop beating yourself over the head. Ultimately it's all for the best.

'And, if it comes to that,' she added, frowning, 'why wasn't he here seducing you himself? If he hadn't been off with the lads, this Italian guy wouldn't have been able to get to first base with you.'

'We weren't joined at the wrist,' Flora objected.

'Or anywhere else, I gather,' Hester said drily.

She paused. 'Have you heard from Chris since it happened?'

'No,' Flora said bitterly. 'But I've had calls from practically all our families and friends. Clearly Chris recovered enough to get on the phone from the hotel and spread the bad word about me. By the time I got back here the answer-machine was practically bursting into flames. My mother—his mother—even my bloody step-sister banging on about little Harry's disappointment over the loss of his pageboy role.'

'Nightmare stuff,' said Hes. 'And universal condemnation, I suppose?'

Flora shrugged. 'My mother's disowned me completely. Says I've brought disgrace on the entire family and she'll never be able to hold her head up at the bridge club again. And, according to Chris's mother, in more right-thinking times I'd have been whipped at the cart's tail.'

'Prior to being stoned to death, I suppose,' Hester said acidly. 'Charming woman. Pity there isn't a public hangman any more. She'd have been ideal. Well, at least you've escaped having her as a mother-in-law. That's one bright spot amid the encircling gloom.'

She paused, then said carefully, 'And what about your Signor Valante? Has he been in touch since yesterday?'

'He drove me back here. I don't think either of us said a word. He brought in my bag and said he regretted the embarrassment he had caused me. And went.' Flora made a brave attempt at a smile. 'End of story.'

'Presumably because he's hideously embarrassed himself.' Hester sighed. 'After all, it was the most appalling coincidence to choose that hotel out of all the others you could have gone to.' She was silent for a moment. 'Whose decision was that, by the way?'

'It was Marco's suggestion, but he didn't pressure me into it. He said we could take pot luck somewhere else, if I wanted.' Flora shook her head. 'I should have obeyed my instincts and taken him at his word. Only Aldleigh Manor did sound lovely.'

'Wonderful,' Hester agreed drily. 'Just the place to meet one's friends.'

'Oh, don't.' Flora blew her nose, destroying another tissue. 'Anyway, it happened, and it's over. And Marco's gone. I just hope I never have to set eyes on him again,' she added, her voice cracking in the middle.

'Pity,' said Hester. 'I'd have liked to meet the man who finally made you into a woman. Because under all the woe, my lamb, there's a new light burning.' She gave her friend a worldly look. 'Nice, was it?'

'I don't want to discuss it.' Flora crunched another tissue in her hand.

'That good, eh?' Hester said reflectively. 'So what are your immediate plans, once you're over your crying jag?'

'I've got to get away for a while. I'd already been considering it, and now I'm sure. I feel bad enough about all this without having to field the angry phone calls,' she added, shuddering. 'I need to get myself back on track—somehow.'

'And you really don't want to see Marco Valante again?'

'Never—ever.'

'That's tough.' Hester came away from the window. 'Because he's outside, just getting out of a car.'

'Oh, God.' Flora scrubbed at her tearstained face. 'Don't let him in.'

'Nonsense.' Hester grinned at her as she went into the hall to answer the doorbell. 'I want to meet him, if you don't. I might even shake hands with him for his sterling efforts on behalf of repressed womanhood.'

'Hester!' Flora shrieked, but it was too late. The front door was being opened and there was a murmur of voices in the hall.

A moment later, Hester returned, her face wearing a faintly stunned expression. 'You have a visitor,' she said, standing aside to allow Marco to precede her into the room. 'And I have places to go and things to do, so I'm sure I leave you in good hands.'

'No—please. There's no need…' Flora began desperately, but Hester simply blew her a kiss, added an enigmatic wink, and departed.

Leaving Flora staring at Marco across the back of the sofa. She was horribly conscious of how she must look, in ancient jeans and a sweatshirt, her hair pulled back carelessly into a rubber band, her face pale without the camouflage of cosmetics, eyes reddened through weeping.

He, on the other hand, was immaculate, in another elegant suit, but his usual cool assurance was not as much in evidence. There was an odd tension about him, she realised. There were signs of strain in his face, the skin stretched tautly across the high cheekbones, and his eyes were watchful, even wary, as they studied her.

And yet, in spite of everything, she felt the familiar, shaming clench of excitement deep within her at the sight of him. The uncontrollable twist of yearning that she was unable to deny.

She felt more tears welling up suddenly—spilling over. He made a small, harsh sound in his throat and walked round the sofa to sit beside her. He took a spotless handkerchief from his pocket and began to dry her face, his touch gentle but impersonal.

When she was calm again he studied her gravely for a long moment. 'My poor little one,' he said quietly. 'Have you discovered you cared for him more than you knew?'

She shook her head. 'I wish I could say that,' she said

huskily. 'But it wouldn't be true. I—I would have broken off the engagement anyway, but I never meant it to happen like that. To publicly humiliate him in front of his friends.'

'Then why are you crying?'

Because, she cried out in her heart, I thought I would never see you again. Because I've just realised that, for me, it was never just sex. That, God help me, I've fallen in love with you. But I know you don't feel the same, so this has to be a secret I can never share—with anyone.

She gave a wavering smile. 'Perhaps because I've never had so many people concertedly angry with me before.' She swallowed. 'The general view is that I've done an unforgivable thing.'

He was silent for a moment. 'That is a harsh judgement,' he said at last. 'Engagements are broken every day.

'But not by me,' she said. 'I—I've always been so— well-behaved. And now I'm a bad lot. A scarlet woman, no less.'

He said her name, on a shaken breath, drawing her into his arms and holding her close. She flattened her hands against the breast of his shirt, absorbing the comforting warmth of his body, feeling the beat of his heart under her palm. Content, she realised, just to be near him. And how pathetic was that?

He took the band from her hair, running his fingers through the silky waves to free them, lingering over the contact. She could sense the pent-up longing in his touch, and her heart leapt.

'Your friend told me you are planning to go away for a while,' he said at last. 'Is that true?'

'Yes.' She bit her lip. 'I know I'm being a wimp, but

Chris seems to have told everyone about us, and I'd rather not face the music for a while.'

'Have you decided where to go?'

'Not yet.' She shook her head. 'I don't seem capable of active planning at the moment.'

'But your passport is in order?'

'Yes, of course.'

'Then that makes it simple,' he said. 'I shall take you back to Italy with me.'

Her lips parted in a soundless gasp. She stared up at him. 'You—can't be serious.'

'Why not?' He shrugged. 'I have to return there, and you need to escape. It solves several problems.'

And creates a hundred others. She thought it, but did not say it.

'Won't your family—your friends—find it—odd?'

'Why should they? I shall take you to the *castello*. I often have friends staying with me there.'

In translation, the *castello* was where he took his women, she told herself with a pang. She would be just another in a long line.

She ought to apply some belated common sense and return a polite but firm refusal, and she knew it. But he was leaving soon, and she wasn't sure that she could bear knowing this was the last time she would be in his arms, breathing the warm masculine scent of him, or feeling his lips touching hers.

She thought in agony, I can't let him go. I can't...

She said slowly, 'Marco—why do you want me with you?'

He put his lips to the agitated pulse in her throat. 'You have a short memory, *mia cara*.' The smile was back in his voice. That husky, sensuous note which sent her blood racing. 'Do you really not know?'

It was the answer she'd expected, so there was no point in regret or recrimination.

Heaven, she thought. Hell—and now heartbreak. Stark and inevitable, whether she stayed or went. But at least he would be hers—for a little while longer.

On a little whisper, she said, 'Do you think this is wise?'

'Ah, *mia bella*.' There was an odd note in his voice that was almost like sadness. 'I think it is too late for wisdom.'

'Yes,' she said, sighing. 'Perhaps so.' She tried to smile. 'In that case the answer's yes. I—I'll go with you, Marco.'

He took her hand and kissed it, then laid it against his cheek, his eyes closed, his face wrenched suddenly by some emotion that she did not understand.

But instinct told her it had nothing to do with happiness.

And she thought, Heaven help us both.

CHAPTER SIX

THEY flew to Italy three days later.

Flora had hardly had time to draw breath, let alone seriously question what she was doing.

She'd managed to reschedule the majority of her appointments. Only a few had taken umbrage and declared they would approach another company. So it seemed she would have a career to come back to when the bubble burst. As it surely would.

And, after an initial panic, Melanie had decided to enjoy being in charge for a short time, and was blooming under her new responsibilities.

One of the tasks Flora had considered essential had been to collect her engagement ring from the jeweller's and have it messengered over to Chris. So far he'd made no attempt to contact her, either at home or work, and she'd been thankful. But after that she'd expected an angry response, and had been surprised and relieved when there was only continuing silence.

Her mother, of course, had not been so reticent. Flora had called her reluctantly, to explain why she would not be available for the next couple of weeks, and had walked into another barrage of criticism and recrimination.

She was an embarrassment. She was ungrateful. She'd caused untold trouble and inconvenience over the wedding arrangements.

'And now you're actually going to Italy with this man.' Mrs Hunt's voice rose shrilly. 'Have you lost all sense of decency? My God, Flora, you know nothing about him. Why, he could be in the Mafia!'

Flora sighed. 'I don't think so, Mother,' she said with a touch of weariness. 'He's an accountant.'

'Well, that means nothing,' her mother said peevishly. 'They need people like him to—launder their money. I can't believe your behaviour, Flora,' she added. 'First you indulge in a sordid affair, and hurt your fiancé deeply. Now you could be mixing with criminals. You've disgraced us all, and I wash my hands of you.'

Flora bit her lip. 'Goodbye, Mother.' She spoke with resignation. 'I'll call you when I come back.'

'*If* you come back,' Mrs Hunt said ominously.

I'm glad I didn't mention Marco worked for a pharmaceutical outfit, Flora thought as she put the phone down, or she'd have said he was a drug dealer.

She decided to cheer herself with some retail therapy. However this stay in Italy turned out, it would be her first holiday in a considerable while. She had been too busy establishing her business to have time for overseas breaks.

For her honeymoon, of course, she'd have made an exception, she thought with a wintry smile.

But her wardrobe was seriously short of leisure gear, and she made a lightning raid on Kensington High Street to see what was available. There was some glamorous swimwear on offer, and she took her pick, choosing filmy sarongs and overshirts to go with her selection.

She packed with discrimination, reminding herself that she was packing for two weeks' holiday only—not a lifetime.

Now that the moment of departure was approaching, her nerves were bunching into knots.

She was stingingly aware that she'd hardly seen anything of Marco in the past forty-eight hours, although he had telephoned her several times. But he hadn't been round in person and there'd been no suggestion that he wished to spend the night with her.

And she missed him like hell.

All these years, she reflected wryly, she'd slept alone in her own bed, tranquil and untroubled.

Now, after those few brief hours in his arms, she was restless, forever reaching for him in the darkness and finding only an empty space beside her.

The words *Will I see you tonight?* had trembled on her lips more than once as they'd spoken on the phone, but she hadn't dared utter them.

Perhaps he was having serious second thoughts, she mused, wincing, and she would get a last-minute phone call making an excuse to withdraw his invitation.

If so, she decided proudly, she would be round to the nearest travel agent for a last-minute deal—anywhere but Italy.

She could not conceal her shock, however, when Marco arrived to collect her at the appointed time in a chauffeur driven car.

'You like to travel in style,' she commented, brows delicately lifted, as she watched the driver load her one modest case into the boot.

'So do you, *cara*.' Marco looked her over slowly, with an undisguised appreciation that played havoc with her pulses.

She was wearing a knee-length cream skirt, with a matching round-necked top in a silky fabric and a dark green linen jacket. She had her hair trimmed, and layered slightly too, so that it clung more smoothly to the shape of her head.

She might be trembling inside, but on the surface she looked confident—impeccable.

She tilted her chin, offering him a frankly sultry smile. 'I wonder what other surprises you have in store for me, *signore*.'

'Behave yourself, *mia bella*,' he warned softly. 'We have a plane to catch.'

And not just any old plane, Flora discovered. After being ushered with due deference into the VIP lounge at the airport, she found herself subsequently seated in the first-class area of the aircraft, with an attentive stewardess offering champagne.

She said shakily, 'Is this a company perk? They must think very highly of you.'

'I am revered,' Marco returned solemnly, but Flora had seen the flicker of amusement in his eyes and drew a deep breath.

'Marco,' she said, 'who actually owns Altimazza?'

He smiled ruefully. 'The Valante family, *cara*, and I am the chairman and principal shareholder.'

For a moment indignation held her mute, then she rallied. 'Then why have you been making a fool of me—letting me think you were just an employee—an accountant?'

'You didn't request to see my résumé, Flora *mia*.' He shrugged. 'And I *am* a qualified accountant. For the record, I have also studied law and business management,' he added. 'If you had asked, I would have told you.'

Wryly, he surveyed her flushed, mutinous face. 'Does it really make such a difference? We are both still the same people.'

'How can you say that?' Her voice shook a little. 'From the first you must have been laughing at me...'

'No,' he said quietly. 'That was never true—believe me.'

'Then what is the truth?' Flora asked stormily. 'That it amused you to play the prince in disguise, with me as some bloody Cinderella?'

His mouth tightened. 'I hardly found you in rags. But I admit that perhaps I had a foolish wish to be wanted for myself. It has not always been so in the past.'

'Oh, dear.' Her voice bit. 'You poor rich man. I bet you didn't turn down many of the offers, for all that.'

'What do you expect me to say?' Marco threw back at her. 'That I lived a celibate life while I was waiting for you? I will not insult you by such a pretence.'

It was her turn to shrug. 'What's one more among so many?'

'Why are you so angry?' he asked curiously.

'Because I feel stupid,' she said. 'And because I wonder what else you've been hiding.'

'One thing I never hid,' he said quietly. 'That I wanted you from the moment I saw you. And the only reason you are here at this moment is because we both wished it. And, for me, nothing has changed.'

He paused. 'However, I shall not force you to stay,' he added levelly. 'If it has become impossible for you to remain with me then I can arrange to have you flown anywhere else in the world you wish to go. The choice is yours, *carissima.*'

For a long moment she was silent, as her head and her heart fought a short, fierce battle.

Then she said in a stifled voice, 'There's nowhere else in the world I wish to go—and you know it.'

'Ah, *dolcezza mia,*' he said softly. 'Sometimes you tear me apart.'

She sat beside him, her hand clasped in his, and saw

the envy in the eyes of the pretty girls who waited on them. Who thought she'd won the jackpot—sexually, as well as in money terms.

And she smiled back, and thanked them for the lunch and hot towels, because they might be right. Because for the next two weeks she was going to be spoiled and cosseted by day, and taken to heaven each night.

And then it would be over. Midnight would strike and Cinders would be back in the real world.

But, for now, she was having a wonderful time—of course she was—with even better to come. And she had no illusions—no crazy naïve dreams about the possibility of a future with the man at her side. Or not any longer, anyway, she amended swiftly.

Her time with him was finite, and she accepted that.

So, there was no need for this niggling feeling of unease. No need at all.

And if I say it often enough, she thought, I may even begin to believe it.

But no uncertainty could cloud her first view of San Silvestro.

As the helicopter began its descent Flora saw the sun-baked stones of the *castello*, gleaming pink, grey and cream in the afternoon light as it reared up from the riot of greenery which surrounded it.

That first heart-stopping glimpse showed her a cluster of buildings, roofed in faded terracotta and surmounted by a square tower. Its clifftop setting had clearly been chosen with an arrogant eye for impact, and it lay, like a watchful lion, overlooking the azure sea.

For Flora, it was a fairytale image—a vision of Renaissance power—but for the man beside her, she realised, it was home. Emphasising the very different worlds they inhabited, she thought with sudden bleakness, picking out the turquoise shimmer of a swimming pool.

As the helicopter landed on a flat sweep of lawn at the rear of the *castello*, Flora could see people descending the steps from the imposing terrace and coming to meet them.

Her stomach clenched in swift nervousness.

The man leading the charge was tall, with silver hair. He was dressed in dark trousers and a discreet grey jacket, and the austerity of his features was relieved by a smile of sheer delight.

That must be Alfredo, Flora thought, remembering what Marco had been saying on the flight down.

'He is my *maggiordomo*, and Marta, his wife, is the housekeeper,' he'd told her. 'Alfredo's father worked for my grandfather, so he was born at the *castello*, like myself, and loves it as much.'

She found herself swallowing as Marco helped her alight from the helicopter, maintaining his firm grip on her hand.

'*Avanti,*' he said briskly, and they set off across the lawn towards the welcoming party, Flora struggling to match his long-legged stride.

After the warmth of his greeting for his master, Flora found Alfredo's calm correctness towards herself slightly daunting. She was also aware of the shrewdly assessing glances being directed at her by the rest of the staff as they were formally presented to her.

'This is Ninetta, *signorina*.' Alfredo indicated a plump, pretty girl in a dark dress and white apron. 'She will unpack for you, and attend you during your time with us.'

'*Grazie,*' Flora murmured, wryly reviewing the modest contents of her luggage.

Alfredo gave a stately inclination of the head. 'So, if you will follow me, *signorina*, I will show you to your room.'

As he went past Marco spoke to him softly and briefly in his own language. Just for a second the impassive mask slipped, and the major-domo let surprise show. But he recovered instantly, murmuring a respectful, '*Si, signore, naturalamente,*' as he set off for the house, snapping his fingers at Ninetta to pick up Flora's case.

Inside the *castello*, Flora received a whirlwind impression of large rooms with tiled floors, low ceilings and frescoed walls. Then she was ascending a wide stone staircase, walking along a gallery, navigating a long corridor and climbing another short flight of stone steps.

Alfredo opened the double doors at the top and bowed her into the room. Its square shape told her instantly that she was in the tower of the *castello*, and probably its oldest part, too.

She stared round her, her jaw dropping at the subdued magnificence of the tapestry-hung walls and vast canopied bed. There was little furniture, but the few pieces were clearly very old and valuable, and the ancient carpet spread on the gleaming wood floor was possibly priceless.

There were deep cushioned seats in the window embrasures, and on the wall opposite the bed long glass doors had been fitted into the stone, giving access to a balcony with a wrought-iron rail and a stunning view over the sea.

Alfredo, observing her reaction with discreet satisfaction, pointed to a door in the corner of the room. 'That is the *signore's* dressing room.' He opened another door in the opposite corner. 'And here—the bathroom, *signorina.*'

Peeping past him, Flora saw it contained a sunken bath as well as an imposing circular shower cubicle.

She said quietly, 'It's all—so beautiful. I can hardly believe I'm not dreaming.'

He bowed politely. 'Please tell Ninetta if there is anything you need, *signorina.*'

While the maid dealt speedily with the contents of her case Flora opened the balcony doors and went outside. Below her was a tangle of trees, the silvery shimmer of olives punctuated by the deep green of cypresses standing like tall sentinels, and she could see amongst them the paler line of a track going down towards the sea.

The air was warm, and heavy with the scent of flowers and the hum of insects. Slowly, Flora felt herself begin to relax.

When you're out of your depth—float, she told herself.

So when Marco came to stand behind her, and slid his arms round her waist, she leaned back in his embrace, smiling as his lips found the leaping pulse in her throat.

'Do you think you can like it here?' he whispered against her ear.

'It's really heaven on earth,' Flora returned softly. 'How can you bear to be away from it?'

'We all have work—other duties.' He paused. 'Sometimes they take us to places where we would rather not be.'

She pointed. 'Is that the path you used to take to the beach—you and Vittoria?'

'You remember that?' He sounded faintly surprised.

'Of course.' *I remember,* she thought, *every word you've ever said to me.* 'Will you show it to me?'

'Yes,' he said. 'I'll show you everywhere and everything. But later, *mia cara.*' His hands lifted, cupping her breasts. 'At the moment I have—other priorities.'

He drew her back into the shaded quiet of the room and she went unresistingly, raising her mouth to his.

As their lips met everything changed. Suddenly his kiss was a hunger—the fierce, driving need of a starving man. Gasping, Flora responded, her senses going wild under the onslaught.

They swayed together, as if caught in a storm wind. She felt his hands seeking her, running over her breasts, hips and thighs with a kind of desperation through the thin layer of clothing as his kiss deepened almost savagely.

At last he lifted his head, staring down into her flushed face, his eyes glittering like emeralds.

She heard herself say his name on a husky, aching sigh of pure longing.

Roughly Marco pushed the jacket from her shoulders, tugged at the zip of her skirt, dragging the loosened cloth down over her hips, lifting her free of it.

There was no sound in the room but the hoarse raggedness of their breathing and the rustle of clothing ruthlessly pulled apart and discarded.

Marco sank down to the floor, taking her with him. As he moved over her, her body opened for him in a demand as fierce as his own.

It was not a gentle mating. Their mutual desire was too wild—too urgent for that. Their hands and mouths clung, tore, ravaged, as their bodies fought their way to the waiting glory.

It was upon them almost before they knew it. Flora

cried out half in exhilaration, half in fear as she felt herself wrenched apart in a pleasure so dark and soaring that she thought she might die.

Almost fainting, she heard Marco crying out in an anguish of delight as he reached his own climax.

Afterwards she lay, supine, feeling the beloved weight of his head on her breasts, his arm across her body, his hand curved possessively round her hip. Lay very still, incapable of movement, speech or even thought.

Eventually it was Marco who stirred first. He raised himself and looked down at her, a sheen of moisture still clinging to his skin, his eyes remorseful.

'Did I hurt you?' he whispered. 'Tell me the truth, my sweet one, my heart.'

She smiled up at him, slowly, languorously, her lashes veiling her eyes. 'I don't remember,' she told him softly, her arms lifting to draw him down again. 'And I certainly don't care,' she added as her lips parted for his kiss.

After a while she said, 'Won't everyone be wondering where we are?'

'They are not paid to wonder,' Marco said lazily, his hand stroking her arm.

She gasped. 'Aren't you the autocrat? You just take all this for granted—don't you?'

'No, *mia bella*. I take nothing for granted. But I agree we cannot spend the rest of our lives here on the floor.' He got to his feet, pulling her up with him. 'We'll take a shower, then I'll show you the way down to the beach.'

'What about our clothes?' Flora looked with dismay at the crumpled garments strewn across the carpet.

'Leave them. They will be attended to.' Marco swept her briskly into the bathroom.

It seemed strange to share the shower with him. To

see her toiletries set out on the marble top beside his. To know that her clothes were hanging beside his and laid away in drawers in his dressing room.

She had never known this level of intimacy with anyone before, she realised blankly.

Even when she'd shared a flat with two other girls she'd had her own room. Up to now she'd kept her space inviolate—in more ways than one, she thought wryly, remembering the pristine white bedroom in London.

And then Marco had invaded her life, overturning all the careful structures and beliefs that she'd built up. Taking her to another dimension. But only on a temporary basis, she reminded herself, pulling on a black bikini and covering it with a black and white voile shirt.

And, she thought, thrusting sun oil and dark glasses into her pale straw shoulder bag, she must never let herself forget that.

The grounds of the *castello* were a riot of blossom. As they made their way down the path Flora was assailed by scent and colour on all sides. Roses hung in a lovely tangle over stone walls and the stumps of trees, studded by the paler shades of camellias. Terracotta urns, heavy with pelargoniums, marked each bend in the track, which occasionally became shallow stone steps.

At one point their way was blocked by a tall wrought-iron gate.

'My grandfather had it put there when I was a small child,' Marco explained, releasing the catch. 'He wanted to make sure I never went down to the beach to swim unsupervised.'

'Oh,' she said. 'And did it work?'

'No.' He slanted a grin at her, and for a moment she

glimpsed the boy he'd once been. Her heart twisted inside her.

The cove was bigger than she'd expected. At one end there was a boathouse, and a small landing stage, at the other, separated by a crescent of pale sand, was a platform of flat rock.

'You can dive from that rock,' Marco said. 'The beach shelves quickly and very deeply. It is easy to get out of one's depth.'

She thought, I'm out of my depth now—and drowning.

Aloud, she said, 'Then I'll have to be careful.'

There were sun loungers on the sand, two of them, under a large striped umbrella. And under the shadow of the cliff was a small pavilion painted pale blue, with a pretty domed roof.

'It has changing rooms and a shower,' Marco explained, as if it was all a matter of course. 'Also a refrigerator with cold drinks.'

'Yes,' she said. 'Naturally it would have.'

His brows lifted. 'You disapprove?'

'No.' She pulled a face. 'I was just thinking of the poor souls who have to schlep down here to arrange the sun beds and refill the fridge.'

'They provide a service for which they are well paid,' he said, after a pause, adding drily, 'As you do yourself, *mia cara*.' He gave her a meditative look. 'Would you prefer me if I lived in a city flat without air-conditioning and cooked for myself?'

'No.' Her tone was defensive. She gestured wildly around her. 'I'm just not prepared for—all this.'

'I hoped San Silvestro would please you.'

'It does. It's unbelievably beautiful and I'm totally knocked out by it. But I'm Flora Graham, and I do live in the city, without air-conditioning, and I do my own cooking—and I don't know what I'm doing here.'

'You are here because I asked you, Flora *mia*. Because I wanted you to spend some time with me in a place that I love.' He stripped off the shirt he was wearing and held out his hand to her. 'Now, let us go for a swim.'

The water felt like warm satin against her skin. She swam, then floated for a while, looking up at the unsullied blue of the sky, then swam again, making her way over to the rocks. She clambered up on to one of them and perched there, wringing the water out of her hair.

After a few moments Marco joined her, bringing the sun oil with him.

'You must use this, *cara*, or you will burn.'

She applied the fragrant oil to her arms and legs, then handed him the bottle. 'Do my back for me, please?'

He dropped a kiss on her warm shoulder. 'The pleasure will be all mine,' he assured her softly. He undid the clip of her bikini top, pushing away the straps, and began to rub the oil into her skin with deft, light strokes. She moved luxuriously under his touch, lifting her face to the sun, smiling when his hands moved to her uncovered breasts.

Then felt him halt, tensing suddenly.

'Don't stop,' Flora whispered protestingly, teasingly.

'Listen.' His tone was imperative.

Mystified she obeyed, and heard the throb of an approaching engine. Next moment a boat, low, sleek and powerful, appeared round the headland, a solitary figure at its wheel.

Flora saw an arm lifted in greeting, then the boat turned into the cove, heading for the landing stage.

Marco said something quiet, grim, and probably obscene under his breath. Then, 'Cover yourself, *cara*,' he ordered.

Flora retrieved her bikini top and he clipped it swiftly into place.

By the time they had clambered down from the rocks the boat had come to rest and its occupant was on the landing stage, making it secure.

He was of medium height, and stockily built, with a coarsely handsome face. He was wearing minuscule shorts and a striped top, and he strutted towards them, his full mouth grinning broadly.

'*Ciao*, Marco. *Come va?*' He burst into a flood of Italian, his bold eyes raking Flora as he did so.

'Tonio,' Marco acknowledged coolly, his fingers closing round Flora's.

A gesture not lost on the newcomer. '*Ciao, bella. Come ti chiami?*'

Flora lifted her chin. 'I'm sorry, *signore*, but I don't speak your language.'

There was an odd silence. Then, '*Inglesa, eh?*' their visitor said musingly. 'Well, well.' The black eyes surveyed her unwinkingly. 'And what is your name, *bella ragazza*?'

'This is Flora Graham,' Marco intervened coldly. 'Flora, allow me to present Antonio Baressi.'

'But you must call me Tonio.' He gave her another lingering smile, then turned to Marco. 'What a wonderful surprise to find you here, my friend. I thought, after your successful mission, you would be keen to get back to your desk in Milan. Instead you are entertaining a charming guest. *Bravo.*'

Marco's mouth tightened. 'What are you doing here, Tonio?'

'Visiting Zia Paolina, naturally.' He allowed a pause,

then smote a fist theatrically against his forehead. 'But of course—you did not realise she was in residence. She will be fascinated to know that you are at the *castello*. May I take some message from you?'

On the surface he was all smiles, and eagerness to please, but Flora wasn't deceived. There was something simmering in the air, here, a tension that was almost tangible.

'Thank you,' Marco said with cool civility. 'But I shall make a point of contacting her myself.'

Tonio turned to Flora. 'My aunt is Marco's *madrina*—his godmother,' he explained. 'It is a special relationship, you understand. Since the sad death of his parents they have always been close.' The black eyes glittered jovially at her. 'But I am sure he has already told you this.'

Flora murmured something polite and noncommittal. The sun was blazingly hot, but she felt a faint chill, as if cold fingers had been laid along her spine, and found herself moving almost unconsciously slightly closer to Marco.

'You must bring Signorina Flora to meet Zia Paolina,' Tonio went on. 'She will be enchanted—and Ottavia, too, *naturalamente*.' He dropped the name like a stone into a pool, then gave them an insinuating glance. 'Unless, of course, you would prefer to be alone.'

'*Si,*' Marco said softly, his hand tightening round Flora's. 'I think so.'

Tonio shrugged. 'How well I understand. In your shoes I would do the same.' He kissed the tips of his fingers, accompanying the gesture with a slight leer. 'You are a fortunate man, *compagno*, so why waste valuable time paying visits?'

Marco said, very softly, 'Or receiving them...'

'Ah.' The other's smile widened. 'A hint to be gone. You wish to enjoy each other's company undisturbed. *Si, capisce. Arrivederci, signorina.* I hope we meet again.'

That, thought Flora, is the last thing I want. But she forced a smile. 'Thank you.'

As they stood, watching the boat heading out to sea again, she stole a glance at Marco, aware of him rigid beside her, his face expressionless.

She said, quietly and clearly, 'What a squalid little man.'

There was a silence, then she felt him relax slightly. He turned to her, his smile rueful.

'Indeed,' he said. 'And today he was relatively well-behaved.'

She hesitated. 'We don't—have to see him again, do we?'

'I hope not.' Marco's mouth tightened. 'But, as you see, he does not always wait for an invitation.'

She said slowly, 'He'd need a hide like a rhinoceros to come back. You were hardly welcoming.'

'I have my reasons.'

She bit her lip. 'Are you going to tell me what they are?'

'Perhaps one day,' he said, after a silence. 'But not now. Not yet.' He moved his shoulders briefly, almost irritably, as if shaking off some burden. 'Do you wish to swim again, *cara*, or shall we go back to the house? Has that fool spoiled the afternoon for you?'

'He's spoiled nothing. And he's gone. So I'd like to stay for a while—catch the last of the sun.' Flora moved over to one of the sun loungers and lay down on it. As Marco stretched himself silently beside her she looked at him, aware of his air of preoccupation.

She said suddenly, 'Marco, if you feel you should visit your godmother, then that's fine with me. I'll be perfectly happy to stay here.'

'Do not concern yourself, *carissima*. I have more than fulfilled my obligations to her, believe me.'

He spoke quietly, but she could hear an underlying note of almost savage anger in his voice, and was shaken by it.

There were undercurrents here, she thought, staring sightlessly at the sky, that she could not begin to understand. But, then, her comprehension wasn't required, she reminded herself with a pang. His other relationships were none of her business. Because she was here to share Marco's bed, not his problems.

So she wouldn't ask any more questions about Zia Paolina.

Nor would she permit herself to speculate about the unknown Ottavia, and her place in the scheme of things. After all, Marco had enjoyed a life before he met her, and that life would continue after she was gone. She couldn't allow that to matter.

But then she remembered the satisfaction in Tonio's voice when he'd pronounced the name—the gloating relish in his black eyes—and she knew that Ottavia could not be so easily dismissed.

She thought suddenly, Tonio's the serpent that Marco warned me about—the serpent waiting for me here in paradise.

And found herself shivering, as if a dark cloud had covered the sun.

CHAPTER SEVEN

IT WASN'T really a cloud, Flora decided. It was more a faint shadow. Yet she was aware of it all the time.

It was there in the sunlit days, while she and Marco went to the beach, swam in the pool, played tennis, and explored the surrounding countryside.

While they dined by candlelight, or sat on the moonlit terrace, drinking wine and talking, or listening to music.

It was even there at nights, when he made love to her with such exquisite skill and passion, or soothed her to sleep in his arms.

And the time was long past when she could have said totally casually, Who is Ottavia?

To ask now would be to reveal that it was preying on her mind. That it had come to matter. And she couldn't let him know that.

Because she had no right to concern herself. The parameters of their relationship were in place, and there was no space for jealousy.

There had been no more unwelcome visitors. In fact, no visitors at all. The real world was hardly allowed to intrude.

Flora was wryly aware how quickly she'd adapted to life at the *castello*, where unseen hands seemed to anticipate her every wish.

It was the quiet, impassive presence of Alfredo, she knew, that made San Silvestro run with such smooth

efficiency. And, whatever his private views on her presence, he treated her invariably with soft-voiced respect.

Which was more than could always be said for
Ninetta, Flora acknowledged frowningly. And it was just
unfortunate that she had more to do with her than any
of the other servants at the *castello*.

Not that the girl was overtly insolent, or lazy. There
was just something—sometimes—in her manner which
spoke of a buried resentment. The occasional suggestion
of a flounce, and a faint curl of the full lips when Flora
requested some service.

Not that it happened often. However much Marco
might tease her about it, Flora could no more leave her
clothes lying around for someone else to pick up, or
abandon wet towels on the bathroom floor than she could
fly. But sometimes she felt that Ninetta might have
thought better of her if she'd done exactly that.

Or perhaps the girl was just tired of having to run
round after yet another of the *signore's* mistresses, she
thought, with a stifled sigh. Although she could never
ask her that, of course. Or whether Ottavia had ever been
one of them...

She firmly closed off that line of questioning. She had
to learn to live entirely for the present, she told herself.
It was pointless concerning herself about the past, or
even worrying over the future, because both were out of
her hands.

So, it would be one day at a time, and no more, and
what was the problem with that when she was so happy?

And no one, she thought, could ever take that away
from her.

The boathouse, Flora had soon learned, was not just for
show. It contained a speedboat, which Marco used

mainly for water-skiing, as well as his windsurfer, and a sailing boat—the *Beatrice II*.

'My father built the first one, and named it for my mother,' he told Flora when he took her sailing the first time, standing behind her, steadying her hands on the wheel. 'I decided to continue the tradition.'

'Did she like to sail?' Flora found she was revelling in this swoop along the coast, her ear already attuned to the slap of water against the bow and the song of the wind in the sails above her.

He shrugged. 'My father loved to—and she loved to be with him. She even watched him play polo, which terrified her. And she was his first passenger when he got his pilot's licence.' There was a taut silence. 'And, of course, his last.'

Flora was very still. Marco knew every detail of her family background, but up to now had said very little about his own. Perhaps this new candour would drive away the faint mist which seemed to hang between them.

'There was an accident?' Tentatively, she broke the brooding quiet.

'Some kind of mechanical failure.' His tone was brusque with remembered pain. 'They were flying down here from Rome for my grandfather's birthday. I had been allowed home from school for the occasion too, and I remember going with Nonno Giovanni to meet them at the airfield, whining because they were so late and I was getting bored.

'And then someone came and called my grandfather away into another room. I could watch him through the glass partition, although I could not hear what was being said. But I saw his face—and I knew.'

'How—how old were you?' Flora asked, her heart twisting.

'I was ten. Usually I flew with them too, and I had been angry because they had gone to Rome without me, to collect Nonno Giovanni's birthday gift.'

He shook his head. 'To this day I do not know what it was they had bought for him. But it could never have been worth the price they paid for it.'

She said quietly, 'Marco—I'm so sorry. I—I had no idea, even though you've always talked about your grandfather rather than your parents. It must have been terrible for you.'

'Yes,' he agreed. 'It was a bad time for us all. And I hardly had time to mourn before Nonno Giovanni began to train me as the next head of the family and the future chairman of Altimazza.'

She gasped. 'But you were just a small child.'

'The circumstances demanded that I grow up quickly,' Marco said drily. 'That I should understand and accept the responsibilities waiting for me.'

She leaned back against him. Her voice was husky. 'And when you became a man, what if you'd decided that kind of life wasn't for you?'

'Ah, *mia cara*, that was never an option.' He was silent for a moment. 'Only once was I offered a choice— and then I chose wrongly.' His voice was suddenly harsh.

She said hesitantly, 'But now you're free—surely?'

His arms tightened around her. She felt his mouth, gentle on the nape of her neck. 'I want to believe that, *mia bella*. *Dio*—how much I want to believe it.' There was a note almost of anguish in his tone.

He said no more, and she did not like to probe further.

Later they anchored in a small bay and swam, then picnicked on board. Afterwards, Marco made love to her with slow, passionate intensity, his eyes fixed almost painfully on her face, as if asking a question he dared not speak aloud.

What is it, my love? her heart cried out to him. *Ask me—please...*

When they arrived back at San Silvestro Alfredo was waiting on the landing stage, grave-faced.

'There has been a telephone call, *signore*—from the laboratories. They need to speak urgently with you.'

Marco cursed softly, then turned to Flora. 'Forgive me, *carissima*. I had better see what they want.' He set off up the path to the house, with Alfredo behind him, leaving Flora to follow more slowly.

She had showered and put on a slip of a dress, sleeveless and scoop-necked in an ivory silky fabric which showed off her growing tan, by the time Marco came into the room, his face serious and preoccupied.

He said without preamble, 'Flora, I have to go to Milan straight away. We have been conducting tests on a new drug to help asthma sufferers, which we believe could be a real breakthrough, but there seem to be problems—something which I must deal with immediately.'

'Oh.' Flora put down her mascara wand. 'Do you want me to come with you?'

'I think you would be too much of a distraction, *mia bella*.' His tone was rueful. 'Stay here and relax, and I will be back in a couple of days.'

'Then shall I pack for you?'

He shook his head. 'Alfredo has already done so. The helicopter is coming for me very soon.'

He came across to her and pulled her to her feet. 'I hate to leave you, *carissima*.' His tone thickened. 'But this is important.'

'Of course. And I'll be fine.' She smiled up at him, resolutely ignoring the ball of ice beginning to form in the pit of her stomach. Because this enforced absence would eat into the diminishing amount of time she had to spend with him. 'Alfredo will look after me.'

'You have won his heart.' He raised her hand to his lips. 'And that of everyone here.'

Apart from Ninetta. She thought it, but did not say it. Then Marco was kissing her, and she stopped thinking, offering herself totally the yearning demand of his mouth. Aware of nothing but the warmth and strength of him against her.

At last he almost tore his lips from hers. 'I must go,' he muttered huskily. 'I have to change my clothes.'

Left alone, Flora could hear the steady beat of the helicopter's approach. Coming, she thought, with a stab of anguish, to take him away. And it was ridiculous to feel so bereft—so scared—when he would be back so soon.

It must be the story about his parents which was weighing so heavily on her, she thought with a shiver.

When he emerged from his dressing room he looked almost alien in the formal dark suit. Flora looked across the room and saw a stranger.

Her smile was so forced it hurt. 'Please—take care.' *Or take me with you.*

'My heart's sweetness.' He looked back at her with passionate understanding. He took half a step towards her, then deliberately checked. 'I shall come back. And then I must talk to you.' He paused. 'Because there are things to be said. Issues, alas, that can no longer be avoided.'

He's going to tell me it's over, Flora thought, with a lurch of the heart. *That all good things must end. That it's time we returned to our separate worlds and got on with our lives.*

With a courage she had not known she possessed, she lifted her chin, went on smiling. 'I'll be here,' she said. 'Waiting.'

She went out on to the balcony and watched the helicopter take off and whirl away over the trees. Stood, a hand shading her eyes, until it vanished, and the throb of the engine could be heard no longer.

Her hands tightened on the balustrade as she fought the tears, harsh and bitter in her throat.

Only a couple of days, she reminded herself as she turned and trailed desolately back into the room. She could surely survive that.

But her real dread was the nights that she would spend alone in that enormous bed, without his arms around her in the darkness, or his voice drowsily murmuring her name as they woke to sunlight dappling through the window shutters.

And all those other endless nights to come, when she returned to England...

She pressed a clenched fist fiercely against her trembling mouth.

She'd known the score from the first, yet she'd allowed herself to be seduced by the atmosphere at the *castello*. To drift into a dream world where she and Marco stayed together always. Which was crazy.

It felt so right for her, she thought, but that did not guarantee that he necessarily shared her view. He was looking for entertainment, not commitment. Besides, he was a wealthy man. When the time came he would be sharing his life with a girl from his own social milieu.

As for herself—well, she was back in the real world now, and she was not going to allow herself to fall to pieces.

And if there was heartbreak ahead, maybe it was no more than she deserved for what she'd done to Chris.

She'd betrayed him totally, and yet, she realised guiltily, this was the first time she'd even spared him a thought. He seemed to belong to some distant, unreal part of her life. But he was flesh and blood, would be hurting because of her, and he deserved to have his pain acknowledged.

I was unfair to him from the start, she thought sadly. And particularly when I said I'd marry him. But we'd been seeing each other regularly for months and it seemed the next, logical progression. And—somehow— I persuaded myself that I loved him enough for marriage.

Because I didn't know what love could be—not then.

I should have known it couldn't work—after that one disastrous night. I should have stopped it there and then.

She'd been trying for weeks to parry Chris's growing insistence on making love to her. Finally she'd simply run out of excuses.

She couldn't even explain her own reluctance. After all, she wasn't a child, and it had been a natural stage in her relationship with the man she planned to marry. A man, moreover, who was good-looking, undeniably virile, and eager for her.

Yet the fact that she'd still been able to resist the increasing ardour of Chris's kisses should have been warning enough that all was not well.

She'd felt paralysed with awkwardness from the moment she'd arrived at Chris's flat and found the scene set with candles, flowers and music playing softly. There had even been a bottle of champagne chilling on ice.

Like something from Chapter Two of *The Seducer's Handbook*, she'd thought, wanting at first to laugh, and then, very badly, to run away.

And that had been the only real desire she'd experienced. She'd felt only numb as Chris had undressed her almost gloatingly. He hadn't been selfish. She knew that now. He had done his best to arouse her, holding his own excitement and need in check.

And she'd held him, eyes closed, and whispered, 'Yes,' when he'd asked if she was all right.

But it hadn't been true. Because everything about it had been wrong. And the pain of his first attempt to enter her had made her cry out as her muscles locked in shocked rejection.

She'd pushed him away almost violently, her frozen body slicked with sweat. 'No—I can't—please...'

He'd been kind at first, understanding. Had even comforted her. But it had soon become evident that he was determined to try again.

And each time her mind had gone into recoil as her body closed against him.

And eventually he'd become impatient, then really angry, and finally sullenly accepting.

'You have a real problem, Flora,' he'd flung at her over his shoulder as he reached for his clothes. 'I suggest you get yourself sorted, and soon. Maybe you should see a doctor—or a therapist.'

And she'd buried her shamed, unhappy face in the pillow and thought that perhaps he was right.

Until Marco had looked at her—touched her hand—kissed her. Made her burn for him. Established his possession of her long before the physical joining of their bodies. Transformed her surrender into glory.

When Chris had come back from his holiday in the Bahamas, she'd expected him to exert increasing pressure on her to go to bed with him, and had steeled herself to agree, telling herself it could never be that bad again.

But their time apart seemed to have engendered a more philosophical attitude in him, and he'd made no more attempts to force the issue.

Perhaps he'd thought that patience would eventually bring him his reward. Or maybe he'd simply been waiting for her to tell him that the medical treatment she hadn't even sought had been successful.

She had been telling herself that once they were married and settled they would have all the time in the world to work out their sexual relationship. That compatibility was not necessarily instant.

That Chris would make a good husband—the best— and sex was not the whole of a marriage.

Every excuse under the sun.

And I—almost—made myself believe them, she thought. I could have gone through with it. Only Hes wasn't fooled for a minute. And, of course, Marco, who looked into my eyes and saw that I was completely unawakened.

Well, no one would think that now, she told herself with a wry smile at the mirror as she walked to the door, on her way downstairs to her first solitary dinner.

As she'd feared, time hung heavy on her hands without him.

He telephoned, of course. Hurried calls during the day between meetings that were not going well. And longer, more personal conversations late into the evening, which sent her to bed burning and restless.

He does it deliberately, she thought, twining her arms round his pillow and pulling it close. He would have to be punished on his return, and she knew exactly how. And she drifted off to sleep at last, smiling like a cat.

He'd been gone for three days when he finally called to say he would be home the following evening.

At last, her heart sang, but aloud she said sedately, 'Has the problem with the tests been sorted?'

He sighed. 'Alas, no. There is a serious flaw in the product, as I have suspected for some time, and we may have to start again from the beginning. I am authorising a new research programme, with a new director,' he added with a touch of grimness. 'Dr Farese believed he could take advantage of my absence and push the new drug through by cutting down the testing process. He knows differently now.'

Flora was silent for a moment. Then she said with slight constraint, 'Has all this happened because you've been spending too much time with me?'

'A little, perhaps.' His tone was rueful. 'But I do not regret one moment of it, Flora *mia*. However, it means that I must devote more time to Altimazza from now on.'

Her hand tightened round the receiver. 'Yes—yes, of course.'

'But enough of that.' He paused. 'Have you missed me?'

She knew that now, of all times, she ought to play it cool—make some flip, teasing remark. Instead she heard herself say yearningly, 'Oh, so much.' She took a deep breath. 'I'm going to tell Marta to have everything you most like for dinner—pasta with truffles, and that veal thing. Unless you'd prefer the chicken...?'

He was laughing. 'Choose what you will, *bellissima mia*. I am hungry only for you.'

She said with sudden shyness, 'And I for you, Marco.'

'Then imagine that I am with you, *cara*.' His voice sank huskily, intimately. 'That I am holding you na-

ked—touching you as you like to be touched. You remember, hmm?'

'Marco!' She felt the fierce charge of desire deep
within her. The swift scalding heat between her thighs.
Her voice pleaded with him unsteadily. 'You're not being fair.'

'No,' he conceded softly. 'Perhaps not. But when I
come back, my sweet one, there will be complete honesty between us—whatever the cost.'

She could hear the note of sadness in his voice and
flinched from it, knowing what it must mean. He was
warning her that their brief, rapturous idyll was drawing
to an end.

She took a deep breath. She said quietly, 'I—I can't
wait to see you.'

'It will not be long now,' he told her. 'But I must go.
They are waiting for me.'

She returned his murmured, *'Arriverderci,'* and put
down the telephone, standing for a moment, staring into
space, realising she was going to need every scrap of
emotional courage she possessed to get her through the
next few days.

She heard a brief sound, and turned to see Ninetta
standing in the doorway, watching her. She gasped.
'Oh—you startled me.'

'Scusi, signorina.'

The apology was meek enough, but Flora was certain
that she'd detected a smirk in the dark eyes before they
were deferentially lowered.

She said coolly, 'Did you want something, Ninetta?'

'I came to see if you needed me, *signorina.*' The girl
came further into the room. 'You look pale. Have you
had bad news?'

'On the contrary.' Flora met the sly glance head-on,

her chin lifted. 'The *signore* is coming back tomorrow. I am going to arrange a special dinner for him and I have to decide what to wear.'

Which wouldn't be easy, she acknowledged with an inward sigh. Travelling light had its disadvantages, and Marco had already seen everything she'd brought with her.

'Maybe it is an occasion for a new dress, *signorina*. Rocello has some good shops.'

It was about the first helpful remark Ninetta had ever made, and Flora sent her a surprised glance.

'Yes,' she agreed slowly. 'Perhaps it is.'

She might as well go out in style, she thought, with all flags flying. And she could use the time, as well, to buy some going-home presents—although apart from Hester and Melanie she couldn't think of many people who would welcome one from her.

She paused. 'Is there a morning bus into the town?'

For a moment Ninetta looked genuinely shocked. 'A car and driver will be provided for you, *signorina*. I shall arrange it at once. The *signore* would wish it,' she added, pre-empting any further objections that Flora might have.

I only wish, Flora thought when she was alone again, that I liked her better.

'I understand that you wish to go into town,' Alfredo said as he served her breakfast next morning. 'If you had consulted me, *signorina*, I would have escorted you myself. As it is, young Roberto will be driving you.'

'I'm sure he'll be fine.' Flora placated him, aware that his normally smooth feathers were ruffled. 'You must have far better things to do than wait while I shop.'

'Nothing I could not have postponed.' He was frowning slightly. 'The *signore* placed you in my charge, after all.'

'Well, Roberto will be a perfectly adequate stand-in.' She smiled at him. 'And I'll only be gone an hour or so.' She paused. 'Have I come across Roberto before?'

'I think not, *signorina*. He usually works in the grounds, but he drives the cars on occasion. He is the brother of Ninetta, who waits on you.'

Then I only hope he's more civil, Flora thought as she finished her meal.

Roberto seemed to be a rather stolid young man, with a limited command of English, so the journey into town was completed mostly in silence. However, the views from the winding coast road were sufficiently spectacular to compensate for any lack of conversation.

Rocello was not a large town, but its central square, overlooked by a fine Gothic church, was an imposing one.

Flora arranged to meet the taciturn Roberto by the church in two hours, which would give her time to make her purchases and, hopefully, do a little sightseeing too.

Ninetta had been right about the shops, she soon discovered. There were some delectable boutiques hidden away among the winding side streets, and she soon found a dress she liked—one of her favourite slip styles, with narrow straps and a fluid drift of a skirt, in white, with a stylised flower in crystal beads on the bodice.

A few doors away she came upon a local silversmith, and bought a pair of pretty earrings for Mel, and an elegant chain with twisted links for Hes.

In a small gallery near the square there was a small framed painting of the *castello*, and, after some heart-searching, she decided to buy it. In the days ahead it might help convince her that this had not been all a fantastic dream, she thought wryly.

It was going to be a very hot day, and Flora was quite glad to seek shelter in the shadowy interior of the church, which was famous for its frescoes painted, it was said, by a pupil of Giotto.

But, even so, she still had some time to while away before her appointment with Roberto. She stationed herself under the striped awning of one of the pavement cafés opposite the church, so that she could spot him as soon as he arrived.

She ordered a *cappuccino* and sat nibbling some of the little almond biscuits that came with it, idly watching the tourists, who were milling around with their cameras.

'Signorina Graham. I thought there could not be two women with that glorious shade of hair.'

Flora looked up in surprise to find Tonio Baressi smiling down at her.

'Oh,' she said slowly. 'Good morning.'

He drew out the chair opposite with a flourish. 'May I join you?'

'You seem to have done so already, *signore*.' Flora stole a surreptitious glance at her watch, hoping that Roberto might be early.

If Tonio noticed the tart note in her voice he gave no sign, merely signalling imperiously to the waiter.

'So Marco has gone to Milan and left you to your own devices,' he said, when his espresso arrived. He clicked his tongue. 'But how unchivalrous.'

'He has work to do,' Flora said shortly. My first time in Rocello, she thought, and I have to run into him.

He laughed. 'Whereas you are strictly for his leisure moments, eh? He is very fortunate to have found a woman so understanding of his—other obligations.'

Flora made a business of collecting together her packages. 'You must excuse me,' she said brightly. 'I'd like to have a look inside the church before my driver comes.'

'But surely I saw you coming out of the church a short while ago? You must find those frescoes particularly fascinating.' He was still smiling, but his eyes had narrowed. 'Or did Marco warn you to shun my company?'

'Of course not. How ridiculous.' She bit her lip in vexation, and a certain unease. How long had he been watching her, she wondered, and why?

'I am relieved to hear it. Please—have another *cappuccino*. I insist.'

She thanked him with a forced smile and sat back, trying to look relaxed, while scanning the passing crowd for Roberto.

'I hope you have enjoyed your stay at San Silvestro,' Tonio went on after a pause. 'It is unfortunate that all good things must end, no?'

She gave him a composed look. 'Actually, I still have some holiday left.'

'Yes, but it is hardly the same for you now that Marco has remembered his responsibilities to Altimazza. He can hardly be expected to commute to Milan on a daily basis. And the *castello* can be a lonely place.'

Her smile was taut. 'Please don't concern yourself about me, Signor Baressi. It really isn't necessary.'

'Call me Tonio, I beg. I assure you that I only wish to be your friend.'

'Thank you.' She reached for her bag and extracted enough money to pay for her own coffee. 'That's kind of you, but now I must be going.'

He said, almost idly, 'If you are expecting Roberto,

he has gone back to San Silvestro. I told him I would bring you back to the *castello* myself.'

Flora's lips parted in a gasp of sheer outrage. 'Then you had no right to do any such thing,' she exclaimed heatedly. 'And I prefer to make my own way back. I'll find a taxi…'

His grin was unrepentant. 'You fear I shall make advances to you?' He shook his head. 'I shall not. I offer friendship only. Something you may welcome before long,' he added softly. 'So let us have no more nonsense about taxis. It will be my pleasure to drive you.'

Flora lifted her chin. She said crisply, 'In that case I'd like to leave straight away. Roberto is going to find himself in real trouble with Alfredo for deserting me like this. He could even be sacked.'

He shrugged. 'He will easily find another job.'

Tonio also drove a sports car, but a considerably flashier example than the one Marco had used in London. He also considered himself a far better driver than he actually was, and Flora found herself cringing more than once.

When the coast road was suddenly abandoned, and they turned inland, she stiffened. 'This isn't the way to San Silvestro.'

'A small detour.' He was totally at ease. 'To the other side of the headland. My aunt, the Contessa Baressi, has expressed a wish to meet you. I know you would not wish to disappoint her.'

She said curtly, 'I would have preferred to be consulted in advance. And if Marco wishes me to know his godmother, then he's quite capable of arranging it.'

'Marco,' he said, 'is in Milan.'

'Yes, but he'll be back this evening. I can mention her invitation then…'

'My aunt wishes to see you now,' he said softly. 'And her requests are invariably granted. Even by Marco.' He paused. 'The two families have always been very close. And he and the Contessa have a very special relationship.'

'All the more reason,' she said, 'for him to be there.'

'Unfortunately, the Contessa intends to return to Rome very shortly. She was anxious to make time for you before her departure.'

He turned the car through a stone gateway, following a wide curving driveway up to the house.

It was a large, formal structure, built of local stone over three storeys.

The grounds were neat and well-kept, and an ornate fountain played before the main entrance, but for Flora it lacked the wilder appeal of the *castello*. Or was that simply because she was there under a kind of duress?

She sat very straight in her seat as Tonio brought the car to a halt.

'Please,' she said. 'Will you make some excuse to your aunt and take me back to San Silvestro?'

'Impossible, *mia cara*. She does not take disappointment well.'

He came round and opened her door. His hand gripped her arm, his smile openly triumphant as he observed her pallor—her startled eyes.

He said softly, '*Avanti*. Let's go.'

And he took her up the steps and into the house.

CHAPTER EIGHT

ENTERING the house was like walking into a cave. The hallway was vast and lofty, but also very dark. Flora was acutely conscious of Tonio's hand on her arm, urging her forward. As the elderly maid who had greeted them reached a large pair of double doors and flung them open she shrugged herself free of his grasp with unconcealed contempt, then walked forward, her head held high.

She found herself in a large room, with tall windows on two sides. Although she could at least see where she was going, the heavy drapes and the plethora of fussy furniture made her surroundings seem no less oppressive.

While the atmosphere of hostility, she thought, drawing a swift startled breath, resembled walking into a force field.

And it had to be generated by the two people who were waiting for them.

The Contessa Baressi was a tall woman, with steel-grey hair drawn into an elaborate chignon and the traces of a classic beauty in her thin face. The hands that gripped the arms of her brocaded armchair blazed with rings, and there was a diamond sunburst brooch pinned to the shoulder of her elegant black dress.

The other occupant of the room was standing by one of the windows, staring out. She was much younger—probably in her early twenties, Flora judged. She had a voluptuous figure, set off by her elegant pink linen sun dress, and a mane of black hair cascaded over her shoulders, framing a face that would have been pretty in a kittenish way except for its expression of blank misery. Her entire body was rigid, except for her hands, which were tearing monotonously at the chiffon scarf she was holding. She did not turn to look at the new arrivals, nor give any sign that she was aware of their presence.

Intuition told Flora that this must be the Ottavia on whom she'd expended so many anxious moments, and that her unease might well have been justified.

'Zia Paolina.' Tonio walked to his aunt and kissed her hand with easy deference. 'Allow me to present to you Marco's latest little friend, the Signorina Flora Graham.'

The Contessa's carefully painted mouth was fixed in a thin smile, but the eyes that looked Flora up and down were lizard-cold.

She said in heavily accented English, 'I am glad you could accept my invitation, *signorina*. *Grazie*.'

'You speak as if I had a choice,' Flora returned, meeting the older woman's gaze defiantly. 'Perhaps you would explain why you've had me brought here like this.'

'You do not think I wish to be acquainted with my *figlioccio's*—companions?'

'Frankly, no,' Flora said steadily. 'I'd have thought myself beneath your notice.'

She heard a sound from the direction of the window like the hissing of a small snake.

The Contessa inclined her head slightly. 'Under normal circumstances you would be right. But you, *signorina*, are quite out of the ordinary. And in so many ways. Which made our meeting quite inevitable, believe me.'

'Then I must be singularly dense,' Flora said. 'Because I still can't imagine what I'm doing here.'

The thin brows rose. 'Not dense, perhaps, but certainly a little stupid, as a woman in thrall to a man so often is. My godson's charm has clearly bewitched you—even to the point where you were prepared to break off your engagement and follow him to another country.' She gave a small metallic laugh. 'Such devotion, and all of it, alas, wasted.'

Flora's heart missed a beat. The Contessa, she thought, seemed to know a lot about recent events, even though her view of them was slanted.

She said, 'I think that's our business—Marco's and mine.'

'Ah, no,' the older woman said softly. 'It was never that exclusive, believe me.' She paused. 'Did you know that Marco had also been engaged to be married?'

'Yes.' It dawned on Flora that she knew where this conversation was leading. 'But I understood that had been broken off too.'

'Tragically, yes,' the Contessa acknowledged. 'It was a perfect match, planned from the time when they were both children.'

Flora glanced at the still figure by the window, with the busy, destructive hands. She said softly, 'Only his *fidanzata* preferred another man.'

The Contessa reared up like a cobra preparing to strike. 'Like you, poor child, she was seduced—betrayed by passion. And because of this she ruined her life. Threw away her chance of true happiness.'

'I'm sorry.' Flora stood her ground. 'But I don't see how this concerns me. I'd really like to go home now.'

'Home?' The plucked brows rose austerely. 'Is that how you regard the *castello*? You are presumptuous, *signorina*.'

Flora bit her lip. 'It was just a figure of speech.'

There was a silence, then the Contessa said, 'Be so good as to tell us how you met my godson.'

'We happened to have lunch in the same restaurant,' Flora admitted reluctantly. 'As I was leaving someone tried to snatch my bag, and Marco—came to my rescue.'

'Ah,' said the Contessa. 'Then that, at least, went as planned.'

Flora stared at her. 'Planned? What are you talking about?'

'Yes.' The Contessa's voice was meditative. 'I am afraid you are quite dense. You see, it was not by chance that you encountered Marco that day. He followed you to the restaurant and staged that little comedy afterwards.' She leaned forward, the cold eyes glinting under their heavy lids. 'Do you know why?'

Flora found suddenly that she couldn't speak. There was a tightness in her chest. She was aware of Tonio's gloating smile. Of the haggard face of the girl by the window, who had turned and was watching her now, the dark eyes burning like live coals.

'Now, tell me, *signorina*, what your *fidanzato* said when he found you with Marco at that hotel? He must have been very angry. Did he try to hit him—make a terrible scene?'

Numbly, Flora shook her head.

'And did that not seem strange—a man you had promised to marry simply allowing a stranger to steal you from him without protest? A stranger who had offered him such a terrible insult?'

'I—I expect he had his reasons.' Flora did not recognise her own voice.

'Yes—he had reasons.' The girl by the window spoke for the first time. Moving stiffly, she walked across the room towards Flora, who forced herself to remain where she was when every instinct was screaming at her to run. 'Shall I tell you what they were?' she went on. 'Shall I explain that as soon as he saw Marco—heard his name— he knew exactly who he was, and why he was there. And he turned away in shame.'

She drew a deep shaking breath. 'Because Cristoforo is a man without truth—without honour.'

Flora had been hanging on to her *sangfroid* by her fingertips, anyway, but now she felt it crumble away completely.

She was stumbling, suddenly, through some bleak wilderness. Her voice seemed to come from a far distance. 'You—know Chris?'

The girl threw back her head. 'He did not tell you about me? I knew he would not—the fool—the coward.' She spat the words, and in spite of herself Flora recoiled a step. 'He did not tell you that we met in the Bahamas, on vacation—that from the moment we saw each other nothing and no one else mattered? That we were lovers—and more than lovers. Because I laid my whole life at his feet.'

Her voice shook with frantic emotion. 'I believed he felt as I did, that we would be together always. He— made me believe that—but he lied. On our last night together—when I offered to return to London with him and confront you with the truth that he no longer cared for you—he pretended surprise. He even laughed. He said that he had no intention of breaking his engagement to you because you suited him, and he did not want a wife who would make too many demands.'

Her shrill laugh was edged with hysteria. 'He said what we had shared was only a diversion—a little holiday romance—and that he regretted it if I—I, Ottavia Baressi—had taken it too seriously.'

She shook her head. 'He was so cruel—cruel beyond belief. He said that the best I could do was forget everything that had passed between us and return to my own *fidanzato*. Get on with my life, as he meant to do—with you.'

She wrapped her arms tightly round her body. 'And when, later, I tried to telephone him in London—to speak to him—to reason with him—he did not want to talk to me.'

Flora said carefully, 'But why should you want to do that? When he'd made his position so clear? Why didn't you put him behind you and try and make your—your engagement work?'

'Because I found I was expecting his child. I thought if he knew that, then he might change—realise that we belonged together.'

Flora felt as if she'd been poleaxed. 'You—were going to have a baby? Then he must have said something.'

All this, she thought, had been going on, and she'd suspected nothing—nothing...

'He was so angry. He shouted at me—called me a liar, and other bad names. Said that I was a *sciattona*— a slut—who slept with any man, and that there was no proof that it was his baby. That he wasn't a fool, and he would fight me in court, if necessary, and make a big scandal. Then he laughed and said, "Or you could always blame Signor Valante and bring the wedding day forward."'

She shuddered. 'He thought I would do that—add to the dishonour I had brought to my family—and to Marco. That was when I knew I would be revenged on him. That I would hurt him and ruin his life, as he had done to me. And, because he had left me to go back to you, I decided you should also know what it is to be betrayed and deserted by a man who has pretended to love you.'

Flora's hands turned into fists, her nails scoring the soft palms as she fought for her last remnants of control.

Her voice was small and cold. 'And—Marco agreed to this? I don't believe you.'

Ottavia's eyes glinted with savage satisfaction. 'No. Just as I did not believe that Cristoforo would ever leave me. We were both wrong, *signorina*. And Mamma is, after all, Marco's *madrina*. In Italy that means a great deal. She made him see that it was his duty to avenge me—and his honour also. And that Cristoforo should know what had been done—and why.' She shrugged almost triumphantly. 'So—he came to find you, Flora Graham. And the rest you know.'

Flora's legs felt so weak she was terrified that they would betray her, and she would end up on the floor at Ottavia's feet. She said, 'You had your revenge, Signorina Baressi, as I'm sure Marco reported to you. Was it really necessary to tell me all this?'

'Yes,' Ottavia threw at her. 'Because Marco was supposed to leave you in London, to count the cost of your lust and stupidity. Instead he brought you here, to his home. And you were not given a guest suite, like any of his other whores. No—you must sleep with him in his own room—in the bed where he was born—and his father and grandfather before him. The place where I, as his wife, should have slept. Ninetta, who used to work for Mamma, has told us everything. No one at San Silvestro can believe he would do such a thing. It has outraged everyone.

'And, now, while he is away, you give orders as if

you were the mistress of the house, instead of just his fancy woman—for whom his fancy seems to be waning. If it ever existed at all,' she added contemptuously.

Flora was shaking so violently inside she thought she would fall to pieces, but she couldn't allow that to happen. Not here. Not yet.

She even managed a note of defiance. 'Why else would I be here?'

The Contessa shrugged. 'Maybe he pities you. Or else is grateful for your unstinting co-operation,' she added with cold mockery. 'Certainly your willingness to share his bed must have amused him, and my godson likes to be entertained. But your usefulness was expended in England. He should never have brought you here.'

'Perhaps you had better tell him so.'

'Oh, we shall have a great deal to say to him,' the Contessa said softly. 'Make no mistake about that, Miss Flora Graham.'

She turned to Tonio. 'Our guest is clearly shocked. Fetch her some brandy.'

Flora shook her head. 'I want nothing. Except to get out of here.'

The Contessa leaned back in her chair, studying Flora from under lowered lids. 'No doubt you are eager to go back to the *castello*—to confront Marco on his return and beg him to tell you that none of this is true. If so, you will be disappointed—and even more humiliated than you are now.'

She paused. 'But there is an alternative.' She snapped her fingers and Tonio hurried to pass her a narrow folder from a nearby table. 'This is a plane ticket to England on a flight that leaves this evening. If you wish to take advantage of it my nephew will drive you to the airport. I shall inform Marco myself that you have learned the truth and returned to London. Once you have gone the whole matter can finally be laid to rest.'

She held out the ticket. 'Take it, *signorina*. Learn sense at last. There is nothing left for you here.'

Flora's instinct was to tear the folder into small pieces and throw them at the Contessa. But she couldn't afford to do that, and she knew it. She'd been offered an escape route and she needed to take it, whatever the cost to her pride.

Except she no longer had any pride. Realising how cruelly and cynically she'd been manipulated had left her self-esteem in tatters. She felt bone-weary, and sick at heart. And too anguished even to cry.

She said tonelessly, 'My clothes—belongings—are still at the *castello*.'

'No, they are here,' the Contessa told her. 'I thought you would see where your best interests lay. I told Ninetta to pack your things and have them brought here. You can leave as soon as you wish.'

Flora lifted her chin. 'The sooner, the better, I think. Don't you?'

'Then—*addio, signorina*.' The thin lips stretched in a chill smile. 'We shall not, I think, meet again. Your involvement in this affair was an unfortunate necessity which is now over.'

'Signorina Flora.' Tonio was at the door, holding it open for her.

As she reached it Flora turned, looking back at Ottavia, studying her frankly voluptuous figure in the pink dress. 'Tell me,' she said. 'What happened to the baby?'

Something fleeting came and went in Ottavia's face, but her voice was haughty. 'I did not choose to have it.

Do you think that a Baressi would give birth to an illegitimate child?'

'After today,' Flora said quietly, 'I would say the
Baressis are capable of anything.'

And, she thought, as the stunned numbness began to
wear off and pain tore at her, so are the Valantes. Oh,
Marco—*Marco*...

She drew a deep, shaky breath, then, without another
word or backward glance, she walked through the dark
hall and out towards the harsh dazzle of sunshine.

The drive to the airport seemed endless. She sat beside
Tonio in a kind of frozen stupor, her hands clasped so
tightly in her lap that her fingers ached, her eyes blind
as she stared through the windscreen ahead of her.

'You are not very amusing, *cara*,' her companion
commented after a few miles.

'I seem to have mislaid my sense of humour.'

He clicked his tongue in reproof. 'You must not
brood, you know, because your little holiday in the sun
has been cut short. We could not allow you to cling to
your illusions any longer, and one day you will be grateful to us.'

'Possibly,' Flora rejoined shortly. 'But forgive me if
I'm not overwhelmed with gratitude at the moment.'

Tonio laughed softly. 'You are not very lucky with
your men, are you, *carissima*? Your *fidanzato* betrays
you and your lover takes you for revenge. It is not a
happy situation for you.'

'It hasn't exactly been a joyous time for your cousin
Ottavia either,' Flora came back at him sharply as she
remembered the fleeting moment of pain and vulnerability that had surfaced among the spite and hysteria.

And she realised with shock that she had barely spared a thought for Chris's behaviour in all this.

'Oh, Ottavia will survive,' he said with insouciance. 'She has the Baressi name and money behind her, after all, and there has been no open scandal. My aunt is a careful woman.'

Flora bit her lip. 'I believe you.'

Tonio lowered his voice confidentially. 'I think she hopes that even now she can persuade Marco to remember the ties between our families and resume his engagement to Ottavia.'

Flora turned her head slowly and stared at him. 'You actually think that—after everything that's happened?'

'Why not?' He shrugged. 'It was not a love match the first time. Marco, you see, does not really care about women. Oh, he likes them as decoration, to be seen with in public, and he enjoys their bodies. But that is all.'

He shrugged again. 'It was time for him to marry, and one woman is very like another to him. That must have been the only reason for his engagement to Ottavia. She is beautiful, certainly, but so demanding.'

She said stonily, 'Then you won't be offering to console her?'

He laughed. 'She has never tempted me. But you, *carissima*, are a different proposition,' he added, giving her a sidelong glance. 'We could always change your air ticket to a later date. Italy has many beauties and I would be happy to be your guide. What do you think?'

'You really don't want to know what I think.' She was suddenly aware that his hand was straying in the direction of her knee, and stiffened. 'And if you lay one finger on me, *signore*, I'll break your jaw.'

He shrugged. 'Well, it is your loss, not mine. But then,

you are a loser all round, Signorina Flora,' he added with a sly smile.

They completed the rest of the journey in silence. When they arrived at the airport Tonio reached into his jacket and produced an envelope which he extended to her.

'What is this?' Flora made no attempt to take it.

'A further gift from my aunt.' He peeled back a corner of the flap, revealing the substantial wad of banknotes inside. 'She is aware that Marco would have been generous with you on parting and does not wish you to suffer financially from her intervention. She offers this as compensation.'

'She's very thoughtful.' Flora opened the passenger door. 'But I'm not for sale.'

Tonio got out as well, and retrieved her bag from the boot. 'Oh, I think you were sold, Flora *mia*,' he said softly. 'And for thirty pieces of silver. *Ciao*, baby.'

As she walked to the glass doors leading to the main concourse she heard him drive away. And then—and only then—she allowed one slow, scalding tear to escape down the curve of her cheek.

'You look terrible,' said Hester, in a tone that mingled brutal candour with concern.

'Thanks for the vote of confidence,' Flora retorted.

'I'm being serious.' Hester poured coffee from the percolator and handed a cup to Flora. 'Ever since you got back from that Italian trip you've looked like death on a stick. You barely ate enough at dinner tonight to keep a fly alive—and not for the first time. If you lose much more weight you'll disappear altogether. And don't think I can't hear you pacing up and down your room every night, when you should be asleep.'

Flora gave her a troubled look. 'Oh, Hes, am I keeping

you awake? I'm so sorry. Maybe it's time I started looking for another place of my own.'

'No, it isn't,' Hester said roundly. 'I prefer to have you here, where I can at least keep a panic-stricken eye on you. But I would like to know what's sent you into this headlong decline.'

Flora stared down at her coffee. She could smell its slightly smoky fragrance and was aware of an odd shiver of distaste.

'It's just frantic at work, that's all,' she evaded. 'Phone ringing non-stop ever since I got back. If it goes on like this I might have to consider hiring someone else.'

'Well, let's hear it for the businesswoman of the year.' Hester gave her a wry look. 'So why aren't you turning cartwheels for joy instead of looking as if ruin and misery were staring you in the face?' She paused, then said gently, 'Be honest, honey. Are you missing Chris—is that it?' She sighed. 'I know I never thought you were the perfect pair, but I wonder now if I didn't push you into doing something you now regret.'

Flora forced a smile. 'I wasn't pushed—I jumped. And I have no regrets at all. I realised that my feelings for Chris were only lukewarm at best, and, anyway, he— wasn't the man I'd believed him to be. End of story.'

'Really?' Hester asked sceptically. 'Somehow I feel I missed out on a few vital episodes, but I won't pry. However, I'd like to know what I can do to help.'

'You've already done it,' Flora said with swift warmth. 'Letting me move in with you while my flat is being sold—and not asking questions,' she added with difficulty.

She wanted to add, 'One day I'll tell you everything,' but she wasn't sure she ever could—not even to Hester, her best friend in the world.

How could she confess to anyone what a monumental, abject fool she'd made of herself? she thought, as she lay awake that night. Let alone admit the even more damaging truth that, try as she might, she was unable to dismiss Marco Valante from her mind and heart?

It was the shame of that knowledge—of the yearning that the mere thought of him could still engender—that pursued her by day and haunted her at night, driving her to walk the floor, fighting the demons of desire that warred within her.

It was nearly six weeks since her headlong flight from Italy, and yet she was no nearer to putting his betrayal in the past, where it belonged, or blocking him from her consciousness.

Each day she'd waited for him to get in touch—to explain the indefensible, or at least apologise. But there had been no contact at all. No letter. No phone call.

Perhaps he'd grown secretly tired of the game he was playing with her, and had been glad of his godmother's intervention.

After the first two weeks of silence she'd taken a cab to his cousin's house in Chelsea, only to find a removals van outside and the new owner's furniture being carried in.

Vittoria, too, had gone. But even if she'd been there, and Flora could have summoned up the courage to introduce herself, what could she have found to say to her? Is Marco well? Is he happy?

And just how pathetic is that? she asked herself with bitter self-derision.

Especially when he seemed to have had no trouble in forgetting her existence altogether.

Her first action on her return had been to put her flat on the market, her next to vacate her rented office space for alternative premises in a different area.

All that trouble to cover her tracks, she thought with irony, when in fact there'd been no need. But she'd had to get out of the flat. She couldn't bear to live with its memories.

She'd found a clutch of increasingly desperate telephone messages from Chris when she returned. Somehow she'd forced herself to dial his number and listen to the impassioned outpourings and demands that they should meet and talk.

At last she'd said, in a voice of quiet steel, 'I think you should be saying this to Ottavia Baressi,' and replaced the receiver, cutting off the ensuing stunned silence.

In spite of Hester's assurances, she knew it was time she started looking for another place to live. Before too long Sally would return and want her room back.

And I have to draw a line under the past and get on with my life, she thought. So I'll take positive action—start flat-hunting tomorrow.

But in the morning she felt so horribly ill that she was more inclined to reserve space in the nearest cemetery.

'It can't be anything I've eaten, because we've had exactly the same and you're fine,' she said as she emerged pale and shivering from the bathroom. 'I must have picked up some virus.'

'Undoubtedly,' Hester agreed cordially. 'I hope you feel better soon.'

And, oddly enough, Flora did. She even recovered sufficiently to go into work, and managed a full day there without further mishap. Although she found herself recoiling from the harmless ham and lettuce sandwich that she'd ordered for her lunch.

'Strange, isn't it?' she commented to Hester that evening.

'Extraordinary.' Hes tossed a bag with a chemist's label into her lap. 'Try this.'

Flora broke the seal and stared down at the slim packet it contained.

She cleared her throat. 'It's a pregnancy testing kit,' she said at last.

'Good,' Hester said affably. 'I was afraid they'd swapped it for a mystery prize. You'll find the instructions inside.'

Flora let the packet fall as if it was red-hot. 'No.'

'As you wish.' Hester shrugged. 'I just thought it was a possibility you might want to eliminate.' She gave her friend a level look. 'Well—don't you?'

'Yes.' Flora bit her lip. 'I suppose so—damn you.'

Even before she checked the result she knew it would be positive. She'd blamed the recent disruption in her monthly cycle on stress, but she knew now she'd simply been burying her head in the sand.

She stared down at the coloured bands on the kit and the bathroom swung round her in a sudden dizzying arc, forcing her to cling to the side of the basin until the moment passed.

She put a hand on her stomach. She thought, Marco's baby. I—I'm going to have Marco's baby... And felt joy and anguish clash inside her with all the force of an electric charge.

Then she opened the door and went slowly back to the living room.

Hester took one look at her white face and trembling mouth, put her into a chair, made her a cup of strong, scalding tea, and stood over her while she drank it.

She said gently, 'I think you'll have to contact Chris, my pet, whether you want to or not.'

'Chris?' Flora looked at her blankly. 'What has Chris got to do with it?' She paused. 'Oh, God, you thought...'

'A reasonable assumption, under the circumstances.' Hester drew up the opposite chair and gave her a searching glance. 'But totally wrong, it seems. I presume you're telling me, instead, that this baby is the result of the torrid affair with your glamorous Italian?' She shook her head. 'I can't believe it. My God, I almost feel sorry for Chris.'

'Then don't,' Flora said with a flash of her old spirit. 'Because I didn't start this. I—I discovered, you see, that Chris had met someone else too, while he was on holiday that time in Bahamas.'

'And you decided what was sauce for the goose?' Hester gave a tuneless whistle. 'Very unwise, my pet.'

'No,' Flora denied tiredly. 'It wasn't like that. I actually only learned about Chris quite a while after—afterwards,' she added, biting her lip.

Hester was silent for a moment. 'Are you going to tell Marco Valante that fatherhood awaits him?'

'There's no point. He doesn't feature in my life any more.' Flora spoke with difficulty, her voice constricted. 'It was a terrible mistake, and—it's over.'

'Not completely,' Hester said bluntly. 'As there are consequences.'

Flora forced a travesty of a smile. 'Only one consequence—I hope. And it's my problem, so I'll deal with it.'

Hester nodded meditatively. 'What are you planning to do? Request a termination?'

Flora had a sudden vision of Ottavia Baressi, struggling to hide a nightmare of pain behind defiant words. Suddenly—defensively—she wrapped her arms round her body, as if protecting the tiny life within her.

How could I possibly do that to Marco's child? she thought with a pang. When it's all I'll ever have of him.

Aloud, she said slowly, 'I know it would be the sensible solution—only I've never been very wise. I can't do it, Hes.'

Her friend frowned. 'Think about it, love,' she urged quietly. 'Yes, you have a career, and a home, so you're better off than a lot of women in your situation. But it still isn't easy trying to bring up a child single-handed. Even with the active support of the father there are all kinds of difficulties.' She hesitated. 'Are you quite sure you won't contact your Italian about all this?'

'No.' Flora shook her head wearily. 'That's quite impossible, and he's not *my* Italian.'

'Whatever, you don't think he has the right to know that you've created a life together?'

'No, he forfeited that—totally.' Flora sent her an appealing look. 'Please don't ask me to explain.'

Hester lifted her hands in a gesture of surrender. 'I'll shut up here and now,' she said. 'But I can think of several people who won't. Starting,' she added gently, 'with your mother.'

'Oh, God,' Flora said wretchedly. 'She's not even speaking to me at the moment as it is.'

'Well, that could be a good thing,' Hester said, straight-faced. 'Keep the fight going and the baby could be in university before she finds out.'

And, in spite of all the fear and misery threatening to crush her, Flora, to her own complete astonishment, found herself giggling weakly.

CHAPTER NINE

FLORA came out of the health centre and stood for a moment, hunting in her bag for her sun glasses. The noise of the city traffic hurtling past was deafening, but she was oblivious to it, locked in her own private world.

Because there was no mistake. It was all true.

Her doctor had just confirmed that her pregnancy test had been totally accurate, and, once Flora's resolve to have the baby had been established, had dealt briskly with the practicalities. Her medical insurance would secure her a bed in a good, private maternity clinic, and she would be contacted in the next few days by the practice midwife who would monitor her well-being in the coming months.

He had also assured her that the sickness that assailed her each morning would probably pass within a month or two.

Tactfully, the doctor had not probed, nor attempted to raise any of the other issues surrounding the coming baby, and Flora was grateful for that.

Her mind was still reeling from the knowledge that Marco's child was growing inside her. She had to come to terms with that before she could cope with anything else, however pressing.

And there were matters to be dealt with. The estate agent had contacted her two days earlier to say that he'd received an offer of the full asking price for her flat, and that the couple concerned were also interested in buying some of the furniture, if she wanted to sell.

'And do you?' Hester asked.

'I think so,' Flora said slowly. 'It might be good to clear my decks—start again from scratch.' She grimaced. 'After all, I'm not looking for a showcase for my career any more, but a family home.'

'Wow,' said Hester. She paused. 'You're really taking this in your stride, honey.'

Perhaps that was because having a baby was small potatoes compared with some of the shocks she'd experienced recently, Flora thought wryly.

She forced a smile. 'It's all front. Underneath, I'm really a quivering mass of insecurity.'

But the sale of the flat was a positive step, and, hopefully, the bed might be included in the furniture that the Morgans wanted to buy. Because there was no way that Flora could have ever spent another night in it, even though it was probably where the baby had been conceived.

After that first incredible, rapturous night, Marco, she remembered, had always been careful to use protection.

As an afterthought, she told herself bitterly, it had been an abject failure.

She glanced at her watch, then walked to the kerb and hailed a passing cab. The agent had suggested it might be simpler if she and Mrs Morgan handled the sale of the furniture between them, and she'd reluctantly agreed, so they were meeting there that morning.

She'd listed the flat's contents, and pencilled in realistic asking prices alongside the main items, making a separate note of the few personal things she intended to keep and which Hester was going to help her remove.

Get it over and done with, she thought as she gave the flat's address to the driver. And then I can move on—make some real plans. Adjust and compromise.

Maybe find somewhere with enough space to enable me to work from home.

She had mixed feelings as she unlocked the door and let herself in. This had been so much her own individual space, yet now it only seemed to speak to her of Marco.

Chris had spent far more time there, but he'd never stamped his personality on the place in the way Marco had done in a few brief hours.

He seemed to be everywhere, sliding his arms round her waist in the kitchen and nuzzling her neck, sharing the narrow bath, sprawling on the sofa with his head in her lap. And, of course, making love to her with heart-stopping skill in the bedroom.

Making himself quite effortlessly part of her environment, she thought with a gasp of sheer pain. And completely essential to her life and happiness.

God, but he'd been clever. Or had she been just a pitiable fool, wanting so hard to believe in the fairy tale?

Whatever, she was older and wiser now, she told herself with determination. And the life and happiness she'd envisaged would have to take a wholly different form.

Her answering machine was blinking, and she frowned as she pressed the 'Play' button. Most people now contacted her through work, but there were bound to be a few who'd slipped through the net.

I'll have to make another list, she thought, sighing, as she retrieved her notebook from her bag. And ask Mrs Morgan if she wants the line to be transferred.

There were only three calls—the first from a girlfriend who'd only just heard about her broken engagement and clearly wanted all the gory details. The second was from her stepsister, furiously demanding to know if she'd come to her senses yet and who was going to pay for the page boy suit.

And the third, inevitably, was from Chris, in a new role as the voice of sweet reason, suggesting that they'd both behaved very badly but that he, at least, was prepared to let bygones be bygones and try again.

Flora listened to it, open-mouthed at his sheer effrontery, then stabbed at the 'Delete' button, nearly breaking a nail in the process.

Somehow, she thought grimly, she was going to have to convince him not to contact her ever again.

She'd assumed her mention of Ottavia would be enough to keep him away, but clearly he was experiencing a sense of decency by-pass.

She was still seething when the doorbell rang, and had to hurriedly arrange her face into more tranquil and pleasant lines as she went to answer its summons. After all, she didn't want to send the unknown Mrs Morgan fleeing in fright down the street, she thought, as she flung open the door.

And stopped, her smile freezing on her lips, her senses screaming into shock, as she saw who was waiting for her.

'*Buongiorno*,' said Marco.

The sound of his voice with its familiar husky note roused her from her sudden stupor. She grabbed at the door, intending to slam it in his face, but he was too fast for her, and too strong. She'd forgotten the deceptive muscularity of the lean body under those elegant suits.

He simply walked past her into the entrance hall. 'Now you may close the door,' he said softly.

'Get out of here. Get out—now.' Her voice cracked in the middle. 'Or I'll call the police—tell them you forced your way in...'

'With no evidence?' he asked crushingly. 'I think not.

And then I shall tell them it is just a lovers' quarrel, and
we will see which of us they believe.'

'You can't stay,' Flora said rapidly. 'I'm expecting a
visitor...' She paused, her eyes flying to his face with
sudden suspicion. 'Or am I?' She drew a deep breath.
'My God, I don't believe this. You've caught me again
in the same trap. The flat isn't sold at all, is it? It's just
another trick, and the Morgans probably don't even exist.'

'They are quite real, and they are genuinely buying
your flat,' Marco returned. 'But not, unfortunately, the
furniture. We stretched the truth about that.'

'"We"?' Flora echoed derisively. 'Surely a practised
liar like you, *signore*, doesn't need an accomplice.'

He said slowly, 'If you are hoping you will goad me
into losing my temper and walking out, you will be disappointed. I came here to talk to you, Flora *mia*, and I
shall not leave until I have done so.' He paused. 'But
not in this hallway. Let us go into your sitting room.'

Flora did not budge. 'You can talk,' she said clearly.
'But I don't have to listen.'

The green eyes glinted at her. 'Do not put me to the
trouble of fetching you, *mia cara*.'

Her hesitation was only momentary. Fetching meant
touching, and an instinct older than the world told her
that, as long as she lived, she would never be ready to
feel his hands on her again.

Skirting round him with minute care, she walked into
the living room and went to stand by the window, her
arms folded defensively across her body.

Marco propped himself in the doorway, his expression
unreadable as he looked her over.

He said, 'You are thinner.'

Flora bit her lip, staring down at the gleaming boards.

'Please don't concern yourself,' she said. 'Because the situation is purely temporary, I assure you.' And could have wept with the terrible irony of it all.

'Have you been ill?'

'No, I've just had a check-up and I'm in excellent health.' She lifted her chin and faced him defiantly. 'I'm sorry if you thought I'd be wasting away—or suicidal. What a blow to your male pride to find me simply—getting on with my life.'

'Why did you decide to sell the flat?'

She shrugged. 'The blank canvas didn't seem appropriate any more.' She paused. 'Is this all you want to ask? Why didn't you get your private detective to submit a questionnaire, and I could have ticked the right boxes?'

'A box would not have told me how angry you are with me.'

'No, but it would have spared me this meeting.' She shook her head. 'Why have you come here? You must have known I would never want to see you again.'

'Yes,' he acknowledged quietly. 'I was afraid it would be so. Which was why I delayed my journey. I hoped, if I gave you time, you might, in turn, allow me the opportunity to explain.'

'That's unnecessary. Your godmother supplied all the explanation I could ever need. I know everything, *signore*, so you may as well go back where you came from.'

'You are determined not to listen to me,' he said slowly. 'Even after all we have been to each other.'

'I know what you once were to me,' Flora said bitingly. 'Thanks to the Contessa, I'm now aware of all I was to you. There's nothing more to be said.'

'There is a great deal more,' he snapped. 'And I was coming back from Milan to say it to you—to tell you everything. To confess and ask your forgiveness. Only to find you had gone and all hell had broken loose.'

'Oh, please.' To her fury, she realised she was trembling. 'Am I really supposed to believe that?' She shook her head. 'Don't tell me any more of your lies, Marco. I won't be made a fool of a second time.'

'No,' he said bitterly. 'I am the one who has been a fool—and worse than a fool. What point is there in pretending otherwise?'

'None at all,' she said. 'But pretending is what you do best, *signore*, and old habits die hard.'

He said slowly, 'While we are on the subject of pretence, *signorina*, do you intend to maintain that you did not expect me to come after you? And that there is nothing left in your heart of that passion—the need that we shared?'

'Your conceit, Signor Valante, is only matched by your arrogance.' Flora's voice sparked with anger.

'That is no answer.'

'It's the only one you're going to get,' she flashed.

His laugh was husky, almost painful. 'Then I will ask another question. Flora—will you be my wife?'

The world suddenly seemed to lurch sideways. There was a strange roaring in her ears and she saw the floor rising to meet her.

When awareness slowly returned, she found she was lying on the sofa and Marco was kneeling beside her, holding a glass of water.

'Drink this,' he directed shortly, and she complied unwillingly. He watched her, his mouth drawn into a grim, straight line.

He said, 'And you say you are not sick.'

'I'm not.' Flora handed back the glass and sat up gingerly. 'I had a shock, that's all.'

'Is it really so shocking to receive a proposal of marriage?'

'From you—yes.' She could taste the sourness of tears in her throat. 'But then why should I really be surprised? It's time you were married, isn't it? And one woman is as good as any other. I'm told that's your philosophy. Be honest, *signore*.'

He was silent for a long moment. 'It may have been— once. God forgive me. But not now.'

'So, what is it this time?' Flora stared at him, her eyes hard. 'A belated attempt to salve your guilty conscience? To offer some recompense for the way you treated me?'

'I want you,' he said quietly. 'And I swore I would move heaven and earth to get you back.'

'Except you don't really believe you'll have to go to those lengths,' she threw at him. 'Not when I was such a push-over the first time around.' She gestured wildly. 'You think you have only to smile, and take my hand— and I'll follow you anywhere. But not this time, *signore*. Because I'm not playing your game any more. I've changed, and I tell you this—I'd rather die than have you touch me—you bastard.'

There was another tingling silence, then Marco said, 'Ah,' and got to his feet. The dark face was cool, composed, and the green eyes steady as they met hers.

He said, 'Then I agree with you, Flora *mia*. There is no more to be said, and I will leave you in peace to enjoy your life.'

As he turned to walk to the door the telephone rang suddenly.

He checked. 'Do you wish me to answer that for you?'

'The machine will pick up the message.' She hardly recognised her own voice. She felt as if she'd been left dying on some battlefield. As perhaps she had.

There was a click, and a woman's voice, clear and pleasant, filled the room. 'This is Barbara Wayne, Miss Graham, the midwife from the health centre. Dr Arthur asked me to contact you and arrange a preliminary appointment. Perhaps you'd call me back and suggest a convenient time—early next week, say? Thank you.'

Flora sat as if she'd been turned to stone, listening to the tape switch off and run back. Her mouth was bone-dry and her heart was beating an alarmed tattoo against her ribcage. She did not dare look at Marco, but the words of the message seemed to hang in the room.

Useless to hope that he had not picked up its exact implication.

If it had just been five minutes later, she thought, fighting back a sob of desperation. Just five minutes... He would have been gone. And she would have been safe. Whereas now...

When he eventually spoke, his tone was almost remote. The polite interest of a stranger. 'Is it true? Are you carrying my child?'

She set her teeth to stop them chattering. 'What— makes you think it's yours?'

'Now who is playing games?' There was a note under the surface of his voice that made her shiver. 'Do not prevaricate—or lie to me. Are you having our baby?'

She closed her eyes. 'Yes.'

'At last, some honesty.' There was another terrible silence, then he sighed. 'Well, even if I am a bastard, as you say, Flora *mia*, I will not allow my child to be born as one. You and I will be married as soon as it can be arranged.'

'No.' She was on her feet. 'I won't do it. You can't make me.'

He smiled grimly. 'I think I can, *mia bella*. You have

made it clear you find me repulsive.' He shrugged. 'I can accept that. But our child will be born within the protection of marriage.' His voice hardened. 'What happens afterwards will be a matter for negotiation, but it will not include the usual demands a husband makes of his wife.'

'To hell with your negotiations.' Flora was shaking. 'I still say no.'

'You wish to give up the baby?' Marco asked coldly. 'Or do you want me to fight you for custody through the courts, with all the attendant lurid publicity that will entail? Because I guarantee you will lose.'

'You can't say that.' The breath caught in her throat. 'Judges favour mothers.'

'Not always. And can you afford the risk—or the cost of a long legal war?' His smile froze her. 'I do not think so.'

He paused. 'But, if you marry me, I promise complete financial support for you and the baby in return for proper visitation rights. I shall not even require you to live under my roof after the birth,' he added drily. 'And in time we can divorce discreetly.'

There was a terrible tightness in her chest, as if someone had grasped her heart and was squeezing out every last drop of blood.

She said thickly, 'You've betrayed me once. Why should I trust you this time?'

His mouth curled. 'Because I don't bed unwilling women, *cara*. As my wife, and the mother of my child, you will receive my respect, but nothing more.' He paused, his gaze faintly mocking. 'Do you want my lawyers to draw up a written assurance?'

'No.' She bit her lip. 'That—won't be necessary.'

'Do I take it, then, that you agree to my terms?'

She said, dully, 'I don't seem to have a great deal of choice.'

'Then you may choose now. Do you wish a large wedding or a small one?'

'A small one,' she said. 'And as quiet as possible.' She lifted her chin. 'I'm not proud of what I'm doing.'

'It is not what I would wish either,' Marco said quietly. 'But we must consider what is best for the child we have made together.'

She walked over to the window and stood, staring unseeingly at the street. 'Have you thought of what your godmother will say about this?'

He said curtly, 'Her views are of no concern to me. In any case, she is giving up the villa and returning to Rome, so you will not be obliged to meet with her again.'

She said with difficulty, 'But you—do expect me to live at the *castello*?'

'It is a tradition for Valante children to be born there—as I am sure you already know.' His tone was brusque.

Yes, she thought, with a stab of anguish. In that big canopied bed in the tower, where we were lovers...

Dear God, I can't bear it—I *can't*...

She didn't look at him. 'I presume you will be spending most of your time in Milan?'

'Naturally,' he said drily. 'I would not be the first husband to use work as an excuse to keep his distance. Although not usually so early in the marriage.'

'No,' she said. 'I—I suppose not.'

She kept her back turned because she dared not—
dared not—face him. Because he might look into her
eyes and see all the confusion of misery and yearning
that was suddenly rising inside her in spite of herself.

And she knew if he came to her, and took her in his
arms, she would be lost for ever. She could not take that
risk.

He said suddenly, 'Your friend Hester. How much
have you told her?'

'Just that I had a stupid, dangerous affair, and am now
pregnant as a result.' She spoke defiantly. How silly, she
thought, to have imagined that there was anywhere she
could go where he wouldn't find her exactly when he
wished. 'I also said that I wanted nothing more to do
with you, so I shall have some explaining to do.'

'I am sure you will make your—change of heart convincing,' he said softly. 'Do you wish her to be a witness
at our wedding?'

She forced a smile. 'I don't think I could keep her
away if I tried.'

'Perhaps you should let me talk to her, so that I can
reassure her that this marriage is in everyone's best interests.' He hesitated. 'Will you both have dinner with
me at my hotel this evening?'

'Thank you,' she said. 'But that—won't be necessary.'
She steadied her voice. 'I've agreed to go through a wedding ceremony with you. Let that be enough.'

He said icily, 'As you wish. I will contact you, then,
only when the arrangements are made.'

'I think it would be better,' she said, then weakened
her position by adding, 'If you don't mind.'

'Why should I mind? As you reminded me, *cara*, I

am a philosopher, and one woman is like any other. I will try not to forget again.'

His tone was sardonic. 'However, I should warn you that my respect for you as my wife will not necessarily guarantee my fidelity. I do not intend to be lonely, although I shall be discreet. I trust you can accept that?'

'Of course.' Her voice was barely audible.

'Good.' He sounded almost brisk. 'Then I will leave you in peace, as you desire. *Arriverderci*, Flora *mia.*'

She heard him leave the room, and, presently, the sound of the front door closing.

She made her way slowly to the sofa and sank down on its cushions. Well, she had managed to keep him at a serious distance, she thought, and, under the circumstances, that was a personal triumph. So why did she feel as if she'd suffered a crushing defeat instead?

I do not intend to be lonely. The words reverberated over and over in her mind, creating images she did not wish to contemplate.

Especially when it seemed she had condemned herself to an agony of loneliness for the rest of her life.

She drew a deep, shuddering breath. Well, she had done what she had to do—if she was to preserve her self-respect—and her sanity.

And now—somehow—she had to live with the consequences.

Hester was hovering, her eyes alive with curiosity, when Flora got home that evening.

'So,' she said. 'Why are we too busy to have dinner with Marco Valante tonight?'

Flora gasped. 'How do you know about that?'

'Because he phoned about half an hour ago to express his regrets and say that the invitation was still open.' She glanced at her watch. 'And, as he doesn't sound like the kind of guy who takes rejection well, that gives us just over an hour to glam up and get there.'

Flora became a living statue. 'No,' she said baldly.

'Is that a real no? Or an ''I could be persuaded in the fullness of time'' job?'

'A real no,' Flora said hotly. 'Oh, how dare he?'

Hester shrugged. 'Presumably because he wants company at dinner?'

Flora shook her head. 'It's really not as simple as that.'

'Then tell me about it,' said Hester. 'You have my undivided attention. And I already know that he's undoubtedly the baby's father, so you can skip that bit.'

Flora took a deep breath. 'We're going to be married.'

'Right,' Hester said evenly, after a minute. 'When was this decision made?'

'Today. He—just turned up. Unexpectedly,' she added with constraint.

'Good choice of word,' Hester approved affably. 'Because I have the feeling I've just stepped into a parallel universe here. Or was it some other man you were swearing you never wanted to see again only twenty-four hours ago?'

'I didn't—and I don't. But he's found out about the baby and he refuses to allow it to be born illegitimate.' She paused. 'So we made a deal—marriage in return for financial support and reasonable access.'

Hester gave her a long look. 'This sounds more like a business arrangement than a relationship.'

'Yes,' said Flora. 'That's exactly what it is—and nothing more.'

There was a loaded silence, then Hester said carefully, 'May I just recap here? I've known you for years, Flo, and you're not the promiscuous kind. You never have been. But this is the man for whom you suddenly and spectacularly dumped Chris, remember? Not only that but you allowed this Marco Valante to sweep you off and have unprotected sex with you. He's made you act completely out of character ever since you met, so "business arrangement" hardly covers it.'

'And I told you that the whole thing was a disastrous mistake.' Flora made herself meet her friend's concerned gaze. 'On both sides,' she added. 'So we're just trying to make the best of a bad job.'

'But all this civilised behaviour doesn't include having dinner with the guy?' Hester shook her head. 'It sounds to me as if you're running scared, Flo.'

There was another taut silence, then Flora sighed defeatedly. 'Very well, then. Call him back and tell him we'll be there. I presume he's staying at the Mayfair Tower?'

'You know he is.' Hester gave her a swift hug. 'Besides, the food there is bound to be better than the ham salad we had planned—especially when you're eating for two now,' she added slyly.

Flora gave her a constrained smile. 'Please don't remind me.'

Marco was waiting for them in the bar, meeting Flora's fulminating look with equanimity and no overt air of triumph.

Hester was wary to begin with, but was soon blinking under the full force of his charm.

He was relaxed, amusing and attentive to Flora, without undue fuss. And, apart from offering her his arm as they went into the dining room, he was scrupulous about avoiding physical contact with her.

He should have been an actor, Flora thought sourly as she sipped her sole glass of vintage champagne.

But she couldn't fault him as a host, and the food and wine were delicious.

The only awkward moment occurred at the end of the evening, when he was seeing them to a waiting taxi. Acutely aware of Hester's expectant gaze, Flora allowed him to take her hand and kiss it.

He said softly, 'I'll call you tomorrow, *carissima*,' and bent to kiss her cheek.

It was the merest brush of his lips, but her whole body surged in a response of such force that she nearly cried out.

She murmured something, then stepped back, avoiding his gaze.

'So,' Hester said, as they drove home. 'You still maintain this marriage is just a business arrangement?'

'Yes,' Flora said defensively. 'What of it?'

Hester shrugged. 'Just that, when questioned, nine out of ten women said that, given the chance, they'd rip his clothes off and drag him into bed. And the tenth was in her nineties and short-sighted.'

She groaned. 'God, Flo, he exudes sex like lesser men do aftershave. I felt it when I first saw him and it wasn't even directed at me. Also, he's seriously rich and definitely powerful. So—why the arm's length treatment? Are you completely mad?'

'I certainly was,' Flora returned shortly. 'Which is why I'm in this appalling mess now. And I'm not going down that path again. Ever.' She hesitated. 'I do have my reasons, Hes.'

'Then I have to admire your will-power, even if I don't understand it.' Hester took her hand and gave it a comforting squeeze. 'And I wish you luck, honey, because something tells me that you're absolutely going to need it.'

And as she lay awake that night, trying unsuccessfully to ignore the demands of her unsatisfied body, Flora was forced to concede unhappily that Hester could well be right.

CHAPTER TEN

THE ring was plain, gold, unflashy and made no overt statement, but each time Flora moved her hand she was acutely aware of its presence—and its significance.

She was now Marco's wife, legally if in no other way.

And she had to admit reluctantly that so far he had kept his word unfalteringly about that.

She had dreaded that on her arrival at the *castello* she would be expected to occupy the tower rooms again, even if she did sleep there alone, but to her relief she had been given another suite on the opposite side of the building, large and airy and decorated in light pastels.

'You may, of course, change anything you wish,' Marco had said courteously as she'd looked over her new surroundings.

'It's totally charming. I wouldn't want to alter a thing,' Flora had returned with equal politeness.

But it had been a tricky moment, because Marco had reacted with surprising heat when Flora had refused point-blank to sell her business.

'I've worked hard to build it up.' She'd faced him defiantly. 'And I can keep in touch on an everyday basis via the internet. I intend to fly home once a month for consultancy purposes.'

He was frowning darkly. 'Is that wise—when you are pregnant?'

'I'm perfectly fit,' she said. 'And anyway, it's not up for negotiation. I'm going to need my job to go back to—later.'

A muscle flickered at the side of his mouth. He said coolly, 'There is no need for you to work again. I have said I will make financial arrangements for you and the child.'

Flora lifted her chin. 'All the same, I love my job, and I prefer to maintain my independence. Also I've managed to find additional help, so I shan't have to knock myself out in the coming months.'

During the inevitable flurry of preparations for the wedding she'd heard on the grapevine that a young designer called Jane Allen was looking for a change of scene. Flora had met her, liked her immediately, established it was mutual, and that she would frankly relish being flung in at the deep end, and signed her up on the spot.

But Marco, she knew, had not been appeased in the slightest.

On a happier note, she had been touched by the warmth of her reception at the *castello*. All the staff from Alfredo downwards seemed genuinely pleased by her return as the Signora.

She'd been agreeably surprised to discover that Ninetta had gone, along with her brother, and presumably was now in Rome with the Contessa, so that particular fly had been removed from the ointment.

And it saved me having to fire her, Flora thought grimly.

When she was subjected to some very obvious cossetting, she realised resignedly that the staff had guessed with the speed of light why their young mistress was sometimes unwell in the mornings.

She also discovered that the Signore's decision to sleep alone was regarded as a sign of his concern for his bride's fragile health so early in her pregnancy. Not all men, it was hinted, were so kind or considerate at such a delicate time.

Saint Marco, thought Flora, concealing her gritted teeth under a dulcet smile.

But she could hardly complain that he was adhering so strictly to the terms of the deal, after she'd made it abundantly clear that she wanted him nowhere near her, she reminded herself unhappily.

Except that she was lonely. She was surrounded by devoted people, but she realised immediately that the *castello* was only really alive when Marco came back from Milan at the weekend.

And it was hard to remain aloof—to mirror his cool courtesy—when she longed to run to him and fling herself into his arms on his return.

He had suggested once that she might wish to invite her family to stay with her, but Flora had not taken up the idea. Her mother had reacted badly to news of the wedding, and had refused point-blank to attend. She was still convinced that Marco was connected with the Mafia, and prophesied nothing but doom and disaster. And Flora knew of old that where she led the rest of the family would follow.

The good news, however, was that Hester had holiday left, and was coming to stay in the autumn.

In the meantime, being pampered in the lap of luxury and discreetly coached in the management of a large household by Alfredo and his wife was hardly the worst fate that could have befallen her.

And if she kept repeating that to herself, she might, eventually, come to believe it, she thought, sighing.

Gradually she was noticing her body changing, adapting lushly to its new role, and the eminent gynaecologist that

Marco had engaged to look after her expressed complete satisfaction with her progress.

He also mentioned discreetly that now the pregnancy was firmly established the Signora could happily resume marital relations with her husband, and went away thinking sentimentally how charming it was that his latest patient should blush so deeply at such an ordinary suggestion.

The truth was that Flora was fighting a bitter war with herself—her emotions locked in mortal combat with her common sense.

Marco had claimed he'd come to find her because he wanted her, but he had never, even in their most passionately intimate moments, said that he loved her.

And desire, however strong, was such a transient thing, she told herself, troubled. It took far more than that to make a marriage, especially when the female half was on the verge of swelling up like a barrage balloon. That needed the kind of love she would sell her soul for.

And, since she'd arrived at the *castello*, Marco had never given the slightest hint by word or sign that he'd been tempted to break his self-imposed rules. On the contrary, she acknowledged with a faint sigh.

Which could indicate that only his weekends with her were celibate. That during his working week in Milan he had already found someone else to share his nights.

And that meant that all Flora had to offer him was the tiny human being growing inside her. Once she'd given birth she would be totally surplus to requirements.

The realisation was preying on her mind—driving her crazy.

She should be relaxed and tranquil, as the consultant had told her, and instead she was being torn apart by misery and the kind of jealousy she had never dreamed could exist.

As a consequence, when he was at the *castello* she heard her voice becoming clipped and cool, knew that her body language was guarded and even hostile.

Because she was already preparing herself for the pain of parting. Armouring herself against a hurt that would be as damaging as it was inevitable.

At the same time she was fighting a real sense of shame that she could feel all this for a man who had taken and used her only to fuel his need for revenge. A man she had tried so hard to hate.

Oh, why couldn't he have just left her and gone once he'd achieved his purpose? she thought in anguish. Why had he brought her to his home—and allowed her to fall deeply and irrevocably in love with him?

And, once the truth was out, why couldn't he have left her alone to recover from the trauma of it in peace? Instead, he had condemned her to this half-life, and she wasn't sure how much she could take.

Her trips back to London were only a passing distraction, too, she'd discovered. Business was good, clients were plentiful, and Jane was running the company with flair. So much so that Flora wasn't sure she was really needed there either, and knew that sooner or later Jane was going to offer to buy her out.

I'm going to be like a stateless person, she thought.

When Hester came to stay she wasn't alone. She was accompanied by Andrew, who was tall, brown-haired and humorous, and who looked at Hester so adoringly that Flora felt a lump in her throat. Her wary wise-cracking friend was suddenly transformed into a woman with a dream in her eyes and a smile of pure fulfilment curving her lips.

And Flora hated herself for feeling envious in the face of their obvious joy.

'The wedding's going to be in the late spring,' Hester confided. 'By which time the baby will be here, and you can wear something glamorous as matron of honour.'

'It's a date.' Flora kept her smile pinned in place, and perhaps Hes noticed, because she gave her a swift hug.

'How are things?' she whispered. 'I must say Marco's the perfect host.'

'Everything's fine,' Flora returned.

It was while she was waving them goodbye that she was conscious for the first time of a faint fluttering like a tiny bird in her abdomen.

'Oh.' She touched herself with a questioning hand.

'Is something wrong?' Marco's tone was sharp.

'No.' She marshalled a smile. 'On the contrary. I think the baby just moved.'

He took a half-step towards her, his hand going out, then stopped, the dark face closing over.

He said quietly, 'That is—wonderful news. But I hope you will not become too uncomfortable.'

'No,' she said, choking back the threatened tears of disappointment. 'I—I gather that can happen.' She gave him a brief, meaningless smile, and went back into the *castello*. By the time she came down to dinner he was already on his way back to Milan.

As her body had swelled she'd been glad to see the end of the intense heat of summer, although she missed her daily gentle swim. Autumn at the *castello* was cool and rainy, and she walked every day instead.

On one of her forays she found a small terrier dog of indeterminate breed crouching miserably under a tree, and coaxed him to follow her home. He wasn't received with unmixed joy by the staff.

'He is a stray, *signora*. He could be diseased,' Alfredo told her, concerned.

'Then ask the vet to come and look him over.' Flora stroked the small shaggy head with a gentle hand. 'I wonder where he came from?'

Alfredo pursed his lips. 'From one of the rented villas, *signora*. People do not always take their animals home after a holiday.'

'How vile,' Flora said with some heat. 'Anyway, he'll be company for me. And he'll be fine once he's had a bath and something to eat.'

Alfredo went off muttering, but by the time the little dog had been vetted and groomed he looked altogether more respectable, and, after only a few days, felt so much at home that an armchair in the *salotto* had become his designated abode.

'And we will see what the Signore has to say about that,' Alfredo said ominously.

But Marco seemed merely amused. 'You should have said you wanted a dog, *cara*,' he remarked, fondling the little animal's pointed ears and receiving an adoring look in return that made Flora silently grind her teeth. 'I would have found you a pedigree litter to choose from.'

'Thank you,' Flora said politely. 'But I think dogs pick their owners, and I prefer my little mutt.'

And Mutt he was, from then on.

But, as an apparent consequence of his introduction into the household, Marco started staying in Milan for the weekends too, confirming Flora's unhappy conviction that he had a mistress there.

But he was at home for Christmas and New Year, which were celebrated quietly, although Alfredo had told her that there had often been large parties in the past.

'But they are a lot of work, *signora*,' he said. 'And

the Signore will be anxious that you do not become overtired.'

Perhaps, thought Flora. Or more likely he did not wish to introduce his temporary wife to his family and friends when he knew it would be the only Christmas she would spend at the *castello*.

Her gift from Marco came in a flat velvet case. One perfect pearl, like a captured tear on its thin gold chain, she thought as he fastened it round her throat, her body shivering in involuntary delight as his fingers brushed briefly against her skin.

In her turn, she'd been careful to avoid anything too overtly personal and gave him a tall, frighteningly expensive crystal decanter that she'd found in an antique shop on her last visit to London.

And he thanked her with a smile that did not reach his eyes.

The weather turned much colder in January, and although Flora still took Mutt for his daily run, she did not go so far afield. She found she tired easily these days, especially as the baby was particularly active at night. Like a drum being beaten from the inside, she thought, remembering a line from a Meryl Streep movie she'd once seen.

Sometimes the movements were clearly visible, and she was aware of Marco watching her one evening, as she lay on the sofa, his attention frowningly absorbed on the tiny kicks and thumps that rippled the cling of her dress.

Do you want to touch? she longed to say. Do you want to feel how it feels?

But then he got up abruptly from his chair and went to his study to work, and the moment passed, unshared.

There was a small shop selling delectable babywear in one of the streets off the town square, and Flora was a regular visit every time new stock came in.

One day, as she emerged with her latest purchases, she realised she was being watched, and, looking round, saw Ninetta standing on the opposite side of the street, staring at her.

She half lifted a hand, but the other woman ducked her head and scuttled away.

She mentioned the encounter casually to Alfredo as he drove her home.

'The Contessa Baressi's villa has been sold, *signora*. I think some members of the family have come down to remove their personal possessions.'

'Oh.' Her tone was subdued.

'But have no fear, *signora*,' he added reassuringly. 'The Signore's orders are clear, and even if they call at the *castello* they will not be admitted.'

Mutt was waiting for her at the door, tail wagging furiously.

'All right, old boy.' Flora bent with difficulty to pat him. 'I'll take you out now. Fetch his leash for me, will you, Alfredo?'

'Do you think that is wise, *signora*?' He peered at the sky. 'It will be dark soon.'

'I won't go far,' she promised.

The wind was cold on the coast road, and she walked as quickly as she could, her head bent, while Mutt pranced eagerly ahead of her in the rapidly fading light.

Traffic was almost non-existent in winter, and she frowned as she heard the sound of a car approaching fast. She whistled to Mutt, who came running, and clipped on his lead. As she straightened she was caught in the beam of headlights, and flung up a hand to shield her eyes. She expected the car to pull over, but it seemed to be coming straight for her, and she cried out, throwing herself desperately to one side, fleetingly aware of a face, framed in a mass of dark hair, in the driving seat.

She fell heavily, and felt the fume-filled draught on her face as the car went past, its tyres screaming on the wet surface of the road. Mutt, barking hysterically, tried to chase after it, but fortunately she had his lead twisted round her wrist, and after a few abortive attempts to free himself he trotted back and licked her face.

Flora lay very still, her cheek pressed against damp freezing turf, all her senses at fever pitch as she tried to assess what damage might have been done.

Kick me, she pleaded silently to the baby. Kick me hard. But nothing happened.

When, eventually, she tried to move, she felt her ankle screaming at her to stop, and lay back again. She knew she needed to stay calm, but as the minutes passed she began to feel chilled and also extremely scared.

The driver of the car must have seen her fall, she thought in shocked bewilderment, but had made no attempt to stop even though it must have been obvious that she was heavily pregnant.

How long would it be before she was missed at the *castello*? And, when she was, how would they know which direction she had taken?

She swallowed convulsively. 'Oh, Mutt,' she whispered. 'I think I could be in real trouble.'

As if in confirmation, Mutt flattened his ears, threw back his head, and began to howl.

Time became a blur of cold, and thin rain, and Mutt's distress. She tried several times to get up, but the pain in her ankle invariably sent her wincing back to the ground. She was sure it wasn't broken, but it could be badly sprained, which was just as inconvenient.

She became aware that she was drifting in and out of consciousness, and knew that this was the biggest danger. Mutt was quiet too, as if he'd decided his efforts were in vain, and she loosened his lead and whispered, 'Home, boy,' praying that the sight of him would speed up the search.

Unless, of course, he got sidetracked by a stray cat, or some other legitimate prey, she thought as she heard him in the distance, bursting into a frenzy of excited barking.

But that wasn't the only noise. There were voices, she realised, and bobbing lights.

Or was she just delirious with the cold and imagining it all?

Because it seemed as if Marco was beside her, his voice saying brokenly, 'Flora—*mia carissima*. Ah, *Dio*, my angel, my sweet love. What has happened to you?'

She knew that was impossible, because Marco was miles away in Milan, and anyway he didn't care about her enough to say things like that.

Only his arms were strong around her, and she was breathing the familiar scent of his skin, listening to him murmuring the endearments in his own language that he had once whispered to her when they were making love. And somehow this surpassed every moment of rapture she had ever known with him.

But as he tried to lift her she cried out, 'My ankle,' and fell back alone into the darkness.

When she opened her eyes again there was light so bright that it was almost painful. And there was a soft mattress under her aching body, a sharp hospital smell in the air, and tight strapping round her throbbing ankle.

There was also Marco, his face haggard, until he turned into a bearded man in a white coat, who smiled kindly and asked how she felt.

'Like one big bruise,' she said, her voice husky. And then, with sudden fear, 'My baby?'

'Still in place, Signora Valante, and waiting for a proper birthday. You are a strong lady, and your child is strong too.'

'Thank God,' she whispered, and lay back against the pillow, tears trickling down her face. When she could speak, she said, 'I thought—my husband...'

'He is here, *signora*. I will let you talk to him, then you must rest, and in the morning, if all is well, he can take you home.'

'Everything will be,' she said.

'But first I must ask what happened to you. How you came to be lying by the road in such weather.'

She frowned, trying to remember. 'There was a car,' she said slowly. 'Going too fast. I tried to get out of the way, and fell.'

'Do you know what kind of car—or did you see the number plate?'

She shook her head. 'It all happened so fast.'

'Then we must thank God it was not worse,' he said gravely, and left her.

When she opened her eyes again, Marco was sitting by the bed.

He said hoarsely, 'I thought I had lost you, my love, my dearest heart. *Santa Madonna*, I was so frightened. When I saw you lying there on the grass...'

'But I'm safe,' she told him softly. 'And your baby is safe too.' She pushed aside the covers and took his hand, placing it under the hospital gown on the bare mound of her abdomen. The baby moved suddenly, forcefully, as if woken from a sound sleep, and Flora looked at her husband and smiled, and saw his face transformed—transfigured.

He bent his head and put his cheek against her belly, and she felt his tears on her skin.

He said, brokenly, 'Flora—oh, Flora *mia*, I love you so much. These last months have been a nightmare. I could not reach you. I thought I never would. That you would never want to be my wife, no matter how I longed for you. That even when our child was born you might not turn to me.'

He took a deep breath. '*Mia cara*, can you ever forgive the wrong I did you and let me be your husband in truth? I swear I will spend the rest of my life trying to make you happy.'

She ran a caressing hand over his dishevelled hair. 'I think I might.' Her voice trembled into a smile. 'If you'll kiss me, and tell me again that you love me.'

He raised his head sharply, his eyes scanning her face. He said her name, then his mouth was on hers, passionately, tenderly, in a kiss that was also a vow.

A long time later, she said, 'Why aren't you in Milan?'

'What a question, *mia bella*,' Marco said lazily. 'Anyone would think you were not pleased to see me.' He'd managed somehow to squeeze himself on to the narrow bed beside her, and was lying with her wrapped in his arms and her head on his chest.

'I am,' she said. 'But I'd still like a straight answer.'

He was silent for a moment. '*Cara*, I have thought about you every day we have been apart, but today it was different. From the moment I awoke this morning I had this strange feeling that you needed me, that I should come to you. And then Alfredo telephoned me, as usual, and told me that Tonio and Ottavia had returned and were staying at the villa. I knew my instinct was right and I should come home at once.'

Ottavia, thought Flora in horror, remembering that briefly glimpsed face at the wheel of the car.

She must have tensed, because he said at once, 'Is something wrong?'

It might have been, she thought. But it wasn't. Because if Ottavia had been tempted to run her down she'd pulled out at the last moment. Perhaps it was enough for her to know that the girl she hated had taken a dive into the mud.

Whatever, she thought, it's because of her that Marco is here with me now. And because of that I can forgive her anything. So I'll keep her secret. Because she has caused enough trouble and I only want to be happy.

Aloud, she said, 'I didn't know Alfredo phoned you each day.'

'I needed to ask about you, *mia cara*. To make sure you were well, and perhaps happy. All the questions I dared not ask you.' He sighed. 'Every time we were together I wanted to fall on my knees in front of you and beg for another chance, but I was afraid I would just make you angry, and that you would use that as an excuse to leave me again.'

She said gently, 'I think I forgave you a long time ago. And, whatever your motivation, it brought us together. I can't forget that.'

'Yet it so nearly did not,' he said slowly. 'When I first came to England I was very angry. Your former *fidanzato* had done great damage to the Baressi family, and to the girl to whom I was reluctantly engaged.'

He shook his head. '*Dio*, Ottavia was hysterical—threatening suicide. And then there was my godmother, telling me with every breath it was my duty to avenge Ottavia's honour, and mine.'

'Were you very fond of her?'

'I was grateful. She could be kind, especially when my parents died. But not fond. She was too cold a woman.'

'So why did you agree to this revenge scheme?'

He said ruefully, 'Because she gave me no peace, and also I felt this Cristoforo deserved to be punished.'

He paused. 'And I felt guilty too, for asking Ottavia to marry me for no better reason than it had always been expected of us. She knew that I did not love her, and I think was hurt by it. This may have driven her to behave as she did. She wanted attention, and sex, and the appearance of love—and she had none of them from me. So she looked for them elsewhere and found Cristoforo, who did not love her either.

'It was Ottavia who insisted that any form of revenge should involve you, because you were the reason Cristoforo had left her. But by the time I reached England I'd had time to think, and I decided that I would pursue your *fidanzato* only. Attack him financially, and ruin him.'

'So why did you change your mind?' Flora asked.

He said slowly, 'Because I was curious. The detective I had engaged had tracked you down, and I went to the restaurant where you were having lunch in order to see the girl who had been preferred to Ottavia.'

He paused. 'And when I saw you, *mia bella*, I wanted you so badly that it scared me, because I had never felt like that for any woman before. And, if I am being honest, I did not want to feel it for you. I told myself that to have you would be the quickest way to cure myself of such a need. So—I reverted to my original plan.'

She sighed. 'And I just—fell into your hand.'

He put his lips remorsefully to the curve of her cheek. 'But I was not cured, *carissima*. And the more I tried to satisfy my appetite for you, the hungrier I got. And it wasn't just your body I wanted, either. I found I was longing to protect you and cherish you for my whole life. I wanted you as my wife, and the mother of my children.'

His voice hardened. 'And I was even more determined to take you away from your *fidanzato* because I knew he would never love you as I did.

'Then, after the plan had worked, it was too late to tell you the truth, because I was scared I would lose you. So I took the coward's way out and said nothing, and lost you anyway.'

'But you came after me,' she reminded him gently. 'That wasn't cowardly.'

He winced. 'But it was the worst day of my life, *cara*. Because I could see how I had hurt you—and that you hated me for it. And I was helpless. There was no excuse I could make for what I had done. Not then—because you would not have listened.'

He cupped her chin in his hand. 'But what I came to tell you, my darling one, and what you have to know and believe, is that I did not take you for revenge alone, but because I could not live without you.'

He bent his head, and his mouth was gentle as it took hers for a long moment.

When her breathing had steadied again, she said, 'If the phone hadn't rung when it did, would you have gone—walked out of my life?'

'I told myself so,' he admitted. 'But in my heart I

knew that I would keep trying to get you back. And then, by a miracle, I was given another chance.'

'But you were so cold,' she said. 'So businesslike with your terms.'

'I was in shock,' Marco told her frankly. 'And I was angry, too, because I knew that if I had not heard that message you would not have told me about our baby. And that hurt.'

'I've thought all this time that you regretted marrying me,' she said. 'You spent so much time away from me in Milan—I thought perhaps you'd found someone else.'

He gave a low laugh. 'Because of that stupid thing I said? I told you, Flora *mia*, I was hurt, and I wanted to hit back. And also to see if I could make you jealous a little, because that would mean that you cared. And I was ready to clutch at any straw.'

She pulled a face. 'I cared as much as you could ever have wanted,' she told him candidly.

'But not as much as I did, I think.' His voice was rueful, self-accusatory. '*Dio*, I was even jealous of your poor Mutt.'

'Marco!' Flora gave a gurgle of laughter. 'You can't be serious.'

'I grudged him every kind word. That was when I decided, for my own sanity, to stay away from the *castello* and stop torturing myself.'

'And I was so lonely,' she said. 'I needed some kind of outlet for all the love I had pent up inside me. You don't still dislike him, do you?'

'On the contrary, I am grateful to him. It was his howling that gave us a clue where to find you, and then he came running out of the darkness and led us back to you.' He paused. 'But I have no plans to allow him to sleep on our bed, *mia cara*, as I am told he does on yours. I am not that magnanimous.'

She gave him a demure look from under her lashes. 'Are you suggesting, *signore*, that you and I should share a bed again?'

'I do not suggest, *signora*. I demand. I need to hold you in my arms at night to convince myself that my other miracle has been granted.' His voice sank to a whisper. 'That you love me, *carissima*, and want to be with me.'

She put up a hand and stroked his face, smoothing away the lines of strain and weariness, her eyes luminous with tenderness.

She said softly, 'For the rest of my life, my dearest love.'

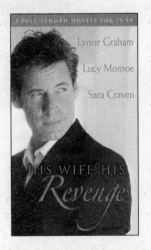

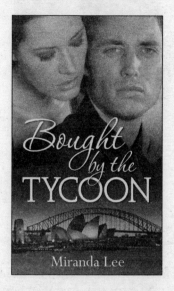

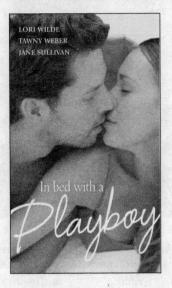

Secrets always find a place to hide...

When DEA agent Rodrigo Ramirez finds undercover work at Gloryanne Barnes's nearby farm, Gloryanne's sweet innocence is too much temptation for him. Confused and bitter about love, Rodrigo's not sure if his reckless offer of marriage is just a means to completing his mission – or something more.

But as Gloryanne's bittersweet miracle and Rodrigo's double life collide, two people must decide if there's a chance for the future they both secretly desire.

Available 6th February 2009

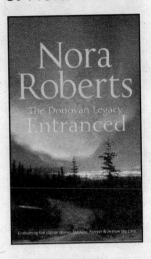